Ride Harder
Ride Book 2

Gordon L. Rottman

HARTWOOD PUBLISHING
PHOENIX, AZ

Published By: The Hartwood Publishing Group, LLC,
Hartwood Publishing, Phoenix, Arizona
www.hartwoodpublishing.com

Ride Harder

Dedication

To my truly wonderful family.

Author Acknowledgement

Mil gracia — many thanks to all those who helped me out with their time and talent to complete *Ride Harder*. I am especially grateful to CEO and Editor-in-Chief Georgia Woods — who also designed the cover — as well as Executive Editor Lisa Dugan and Senior Editor Debbie Gillen of Hartwood Publishing Group. I am also grateful to my great critique group for their honest critiques, advice, ideas, and support: Stan Marshall (author of *Half the Distance*, Hartwood, 2017), Linda Bromley, Heather Walters, Julie Herman, and Linda Griggs. My longtime friend Steve Seale provided excellent plot and action ideas, and Stanley Fisher shared his knowledge of railroading. I am extremely grateful to my cousin, Consuelo "Chely" Garcia, for checking and correcting the book's Spanish. Thanks too to my wife Enriqueta for putting up with my long hours at the computer and researching.

Author Notes

A geographical commentary

The Texas-Mexico border, or *la Frontera,* and the Rio Grande River, or Rio Bravo del Norte — depending on which side of the border one resides — divides two nations and two cultures. The story of *Ride Harder* unfolds in south-central Texas and in the northeast of the Mexican state of Coahuila (co-a-we-la). The Mexican International Railroad (*Ferrocarril Internacional Mexicano*) runs from Piedras Negras/Eagle Pass south to Torreón.

One of Marta's handguns is a Remington .41-caliber two-barrel *derringer.* When spelled with two "r"s and lower case, derringer (derr-in-jur) refers to a type of pocket handgun rather than an authentic Deringer pistol made by Henry Deringer (1786-1868). Unlicensed copies of similar pistols were sometimes marketed as "Derringers" with two "r"s.

Reference: *The Big Book of Gun Trivia: Everything you want to know, don't want to know, and don't know you need to know* by Gordon L. Rottman (an e-book, Osprey Publishing, 2013).

Rebellion on the Rio Grande

While the possibility of an 1887 uprising in northern Mexico and southern Texas instigated by a wealthy *hacendado* and former general may seem improbable, there are historical precedents. In 1840, Jesús de Cárdenas and General Antonio Canales Rosillo did indeed initiate a revolt to establish a Republic of the Rio Grande. Their combined insurgent army, comprised of Mexicans, Texans, and Indians, was defeated by the Mexican Army.

There was another such conflict on the lower Rio Grande. Juan Cortina, a Mexican rancher and military leader, formed an insurgent army to seize part of the Nesesus Strip inside Texas. His forces were defeated by the Texas Rangers, Texas Militia, and the US Army during the First Cortina War—1859 and by Confederate forces during the Second Cortina War—1861.

While there was no such conflict in 1887, the cooperative deployment of Mexican and US Army forces against the Apaches and Tarahumares mentioned in the novel did in fact occur.

CHAPTER ONE

Some mornings just weren't as good as others. Marta was stomping round kicking rocks and shaking her finger at somebody who weren't there. I was expecting her to start chewing prickly pears and spitting thorns. She was justly put out.

I weren't too happy my own self, us being stuck out on the Eagle Pass-Del Rio Road without much of anything. Humiliating too seeing three road agents plain got the drop on us. They were sitting their horses in a mesquite stand pointing pistols at arm's length. They'd taken our horses, saddles, guns, and a couple of thousand in hard-won cash that they didn't know was in my saddlebags. That would wipe the silver lining off your cloud. I figured they'd be doing a happy days jig…bastards.

So I was feeling pretty down, and Marta came tramping over as prickly as a cactus. That was all I needed, all the thunder and lightning of a storm without the wind and the rain. I could of surely used some rain, seeing as we didn't have any water. South Texas in March was pleasing weather, but it was warm enough to bring up a thirst. Them robbers hadn't had the common decency to leave us a canteen. Lower than catfish turds.

Marta was standing over me—I was sitting on a rock—tapping her foot, her arms crossed. I looked up, and she was about as pissed as my mama the day I set the hayrick on fire—didn't mean to, just trying out a cigarette I'd rolled with her makings. First time Mama broke my nose.

"What you looking at me for, *niña*? It ain't my fault. Sumbitches got the drop on us good."

From under the sombrero she'd taken off a dead bandito last December, her big ol' black eyes were glaring a hole right through me. She'd held up her left hand to let me know again they'd taken her silver ring.

Here it comes.

Like a clap of thunder, she slapped her hands, stomped her sandaled foot, and jabbed her middle finger down the side trail.

"*Qué?* You want me to go after them thieving desperadoes? I ain't got no *caballo, pistola, carabina,* or *escopeta,*" the last being her own shotgun the road agents took. "You know they even took your derringer, uh, *poco pistola.*"

She slashed her hand cross her throat, then made a strangling motion and a scary gurgling choking noise. I know a lot of bad Mex words for people you're mad at, and I bet she was thinking all of them and some I'd never heard. I say *thinking*, seeing Marta's as mute as an angel's statue, not that she's exactly an angel.

"All we can do is start on *el camino por Del Rio* and hope some friendly riders or *vaqueros* or a freight wagon comes along. I can borrow some *dinero* from that gun dealer, uh, *vendedor de armas* I know. Besides, I can have Roberto make you another ring."

That didn't cut it. She grabbed hold of my hands and pulled. Being fourteen-three hands high, that's not even five-foot, she'd not be able to get me up, but I stood anyway. I learned some time ago there's no sense fighting her will. She'd really gotten mad at me the time I measured her with my hands like measuring up a horse I was buying.

"Well, all right then. There's no telling how far we gotta walk. Heck, I'm hungry, *tengo hambre*. I need some chuck, uh, *comida*. We might be walking *mañana* and still ain't found them *pendejos*. We need some *agua* too."

Marta knows about as much American as I do Mex, but she knew what I was saying. She'd rolled her eyes and nodded like she'd take care of all that. She pulled a jackknife out of one of her deep skirt pockets, kneeled down, and cut a piece of cloth from the bottom of her black skirt. We walked down the trail the three outlaws had departed on with our traitorous horses galloping with them. It was easy to follow the tracks of the close-herded mob. I'd filed three notches in the horseshoe's toe on Clipper's right fore hoof. Made it easier to find him when I let him free-range.

Marta unraveled some heavy yarn from her shawl as we walked. When she had three long strands, she pleated them into a four-foot cord. Presently she cut the cord in two pieces and knotted one to each end of the rectangle of skirt cloth.

Waving for me to stop, she walked on ahead picking up rocks and then signaled for me to follow behind her. She tied a loop on one of the cords and hooked it with her middle finger, and held the live end of the other in her fist. She put a rock in that cloth patch. About forty feet away sat a big ol' lop-eared jackrabbit. They were all over the place, it being springtime. She spun that rig round twice, then slung it overhand, letting go of the cord she was gripping. The rock missed the jack by only a foot.

"Well, I be twixed. That's pretty damn good."

She shrugged her shoulders, not happy about missing.

About ten throws later, she thumped a jack, ran over to it, snapped its neck, trotted back to me, motioned me to cup my hands, and slit its throat. With my hands full of blood, she'd made a drinking motion after lapping some up her own self to bloody her lips and nose.

"Well, hell. *Salud* to you too," I said and drank up. Pretty salty and sour, and kinda messy. Got blood in my whiskers.

Marta streaked blood on her cheeks like injun war paint. Don't know about that girl sometimes. She might be a horseshoe short of a full gallop. And even in our predicament, she thought it was funny.

She squatted right there, picked up a stick, and nodded her head at the mesquite-covered prairie. All right, I knew to collect sticks for a fire. Picking little lint balls off her wool shawl, she'd rolled them into a wad. She piled tiny bits of wood and bark scraps in a bed. She pulled out her jackknife, and leaving the blade closed, she struck it against a flint rock. By the time I got back, she had an ember burning in the kindling and blew it to life. She had the jack skinned and gutted in three minutes and stuck on a spit I'd whittled.

That roasted rabbit was pretty good. She gave me most of it. Marta's family had lived on the road. She didn't need much of anything to get along.

Soon we were following the trail again. After about three miles, Marta was limping…that old bullet wound. She acted like it was no bother.

It was obvious where the mob had turned into a well-traveled arroyo. Just what in tarnation was I going to do if we found them scalawags?

∞⸘

Marta and I were lying on a little ridge. About fifty yards away was an adobe shack with a smoking stovepipe. A shed, outhouse, chicken coop, and corral sat out back. Six horses and a mule loitered in the corral. The mule was for the Michigan market wagon, and the extra horse might mean there were four bad men instead of three.

The adobe had a door in the front and a little window in the back. We'd scouted the other side. There was a cistern pump that looked mighty inviting.

We'd walked about six miles, and it was getting on to noon. "I don't think we're going to take them with your jackknife and throwing sling. *¿Y ahora qué, Marta?*" — And now what?

She didn't pay me any mind, just upped and darted for the shed. "Heck." I followed.

There was a corncrib made of crisscrossed mesquite limbs beside the shed. Hacked into the end of one of the limbs was a machete knife. She pulled it out and handed it to me. *Dang.* She plucked a double-bit axe from a chopping block. *Double dang!* There were braids of habanero peppers and onions hanging on the crib. Marta stuffed them peppers in her shirt front. Going into the shed, she came out sniffing a bucket of coal-tar creosote she carried, making a face.

Pointing at the adobe's door, she made a cut-throat motion and jerked her war-painted head for me to go and take care of it. Is there a triple dang?

Clipper whinnied at me from the corral.

We quietly snuck over to the adobe. She dropped her big hat on the ground and bent over, gripping her hands together. All right, I got it. I boosted her to the roof and handed up the axe and creosote.

Now I've heard of plugging chimneys and smoking fellas out of a house, but Marta had her own idea. She waved away the smoke puffing out the stovepipe and listened into it. Nodding her head, she pulled out the peppers and dropped them one-by-one down the stovepipe, poured in the creosote, and then plugged it with her shawl. She gave me a wicked grin and took up her axe. This could get ugly.

Didn't take long before I smelled burning peppers and creosote stink, and heard, "What the hellfire's goin' on? Alf, check dat stove-pipe!"

The stove's iron door squeaked open. "Shit fire, it's burnin' my eyes!" That led to a bunch of cursing and hacking coughs. "What'd ya put in there, ya stupid bitch?" I heard a slap, and a woman started bawling, the way some do.

The first outlaw came out holding a bandana over his eyes. I swung the machete knife with a two-handed hold, taking his hands clean off, one still holding the bandana when it hit the ground. That whack didn't help his face none, either. He ran round screaming through his extra wide mouth and waving his stumpy arms. I had to catch and trip him to take his Smith & Wesson. The second fella came out, Colts in hand and blazing away, but he couldn't see through his burning eyeballs, and I chest-shot him twice. I head-shot the first fella to shush his screaming.

There was so much spicy tar smoke coming out the door, I didn't make out the third outlaw until he stumbled out waving a Winchester and bellowing like a bull. Marta, standing over the door, dropped that four pound double-bit axe straight down on his head, knocking him out cold.

"Well, that weren't so hard." I felt it a disagreeable chore, but they reaped what they'd sown.

The woman came busting out, hands to eyes, stumbling round and crying like a windmill needing grease.

Marta sat herself on the roof's edge and jumped into my arms. She was just a little slip of a thing. Gave me a kiss and her scary laugh. I think she liked those shenanigans too much.

The woman, she was a big 'un, and she cussed up a storm when she made out the men lying on the ground. Her huge jugs were bouncing round like two pups in a sack, and her butt must have been a yard wide. Real nasty mouth. Marta conked her on the back of the head with the axe handle to hush her up.

Marta wiped tears from her eyes and held up her burned shawl with a frown. Those habaneros had been stinging my eyes too. She dusted her hands off and arched an eyebrow, silently saying, *And you said we couldn't take them.*

I just shook my head. "I'll buy, uh, *Te voy a comprar uno nuevo.*"

That's when she spotted her ring on the woman's pinky. I thought she was going to tear off the finger taking her ring back.

Marta grinned, about as pleased as she could be. She surely looked pretty when she did that, even with dried rabbit blood and tears on her face. Looking round at those folks on the ground remindered me that Marta may have lived rough on the road all her sixteen years, but she don't tolerate disorderly behavior.

We made Del Rio before dark. Marta rode Rojizo with Clipper and the outlaws' horses strung behind her. Her 16-gauge Parker Brothers was hung in its customary place on her saddle. I drove the market wagon loaded down with everything we could take from the out-laws' farmstead, even that stove. They had a lot of ill-gotten loot. A lot of that stuff we could use setting up the new ranch—tools, furniture, and such. Some we'd sell, mostly the guns. The horses would build our *remuda*. We'd let the chickens loose. Found almost fifty dollars cash, some pesos too. Them fools hadn't even found our money pouch bound for the bank.

I'd been in Del Rio a few times since we come back from Mexico. Marta hadn't. It had taken her this long to get back on her feet to travel.

And we had all four of the outlaws in the wagon too, minus a pair of hands. I'd left his mitts for the coyotes. The outlaws smelled powerful strong of burnt habaneros. So did we. The live fella, all trussed up, cried about the knot on his head, and the woman blub-bered about losing her men. I didn't know which one was the most annoying.

At the town marshal's office, the two deaders, the Drechsler broth-ers, brought twenty-five bucks bounty each. The live one, a cousin, didn't have a bounty, but was dragged into the slammer. The mar-shal was peeved, not for having to pay out the bounties but having to pay to bury them two and the live one who had to be fed on oc-casion.

In spite of that, the marshal said, "I'm plum proud to meet ya, Mr. Eugen. Read all 'bout y'all in that *Del Rio Record* story." The article was tacked up with the wanted posters. He looked Marta over. "So this is your woman?" He'd shaken his head. "Hard to believe she kilt that dastardly bandito *El Xiuhcoatl.*"

"And his little shit brother too," I said proudly.

"She wear war paint often?"

"Only when on the warpath."

The tubby, foul-mouthed woman, Beulah Goodfellow, we set free. She'd rambled down the street smelling like tar and habanero and raving about having nothing left and both her men murdered by a pair of bloody-faced, thieving hellions. "They even broke my little finger stealing my ring."

I gave her ten bucks. She spit on me but took the sawbuck. Marta hadn't approved giving her the money, but she knew I was a sap for down-and-outs. If I hadn't been, well, we'd never have hooked up like we did.

We checked into the San Felipe Hotel and washed up best we could. I could tell the clerk smelled them peppers. He loaned us a bottle of orange flower toilet waters. With Marta in a fresh shirt and skirt, scrubbed up, her full lips smiling and that light in her dark eyes, she surely looked good.

I laid us on a prime beefsteak supper with all the trimmings. We could afford that sort of indulgence, but the hotel manager said it was on the house owing to our contribution to law and order on the Rio Grande frontier. Word had already spread about the Drechsler brothers. They had that newspaper article framed on the wall just because I stayed there when I come to Del Rio. Wish I was smart enough to be able to read it all.

Marta rolled our after-dinner cigs, and we had some really good coffee in fancy cups — lots better than the sewage I boiled up on the trail. She went through a slice of hot peach pie and reached for mine. I'd got it for her anyway; it was too sweet for me.

"Tomorrow we'll see if we can find out what your real *nombre* is and try and find Flaco's sister. What y'all call a sister, *hermana*?

She'd nodded, stubbing out her cig on her supper platter, and squeezed my hand real hard.

I liked seeing that little gal happy. Last year been a tough one for her.

Hell, the winter of 1886 had been tough for a lot of folks. The Great Die-Up had cost millions of head of cattle from Canada, across the States and Territories, and into Mexico. Marta's family had been murdered by damn injuns. We'd seen some good men and women die because of the bandito *El Xiuhcoatl* and the traitor Maxwell. And a lot of bad men died too when we rode into Mexico and fetched back

Clayton DeWitt's daughters and Marta. There *is* a Hell on Earth.

I tried not to think about that hard ride, but there were nights I couldn't think of nothing else.

CHAPTER TWO

I woke with a tickle in my ear. Marta had spooned up to me with a twitchy finger. She was ready for coffee. Me too, but I didn't want to unbed just yet.

She had a good night, only woke up twice from nightmares. She hung onto me like a horseshoe fresh-nailed to a hoof.

I watched her, still wearing long johns, pull on her customary brown shirt and black skirt and spend a way long time brushing all her long black hair. She used to not let me see all that hair, like it was carnal-stirring. Done with that, she put on her rebozo, a waist-long brown cape with a square head hole. It was sewed with fancy red, orange, and tan thread. She still carried a shawl, but only wore it on her shoulders, not over her head since she's taken to wearing a sombrero. Holding up the scorched shawl, she remindered me she needed another.

I crawled out and pulled on my duds, feeling a little out of sorts. What if we did find out her real name today? I've only known her as Marta ever since I found her wandering alone after her family been murdered. Could I still call her Marta?

In the dining room we dug into fried eggs, bacon, beans, biscuits, and grits. And coffee. Marta had gotten good handling a knife and fork. Before, the only thing she customarily ate with was a spoon and rolled up tortillas. I asked the waiter for a jar of lick, seeing Marta puts molasses on just about anything. She was pouring it on her biscuits when I glanced at the door as a clientele came through — that's what Mrs. Moran back in Eagle Pass called her paying customers. I looked back to Marta and caught her with a less than innocent grin.

"What'd you do now?" I noticed a brown smear in her grits. "Did you put lick in your *sémola*?"

Still grinning, she leaned her elbow on the table and commenced to pour lick into her grits without taking her eyes off me.

"Girl, you just plum *loco* ruining *buena sémola* like that."

She pointed at the crock that I'd just dolloped butter from onto my grits, made a face, and shook her head. I laughed. She didn't cotton to me putting butter on mine.

She spooned down her own grits with gusto.

"What if I poured lick, eh, what y'all call it, *melaza*, on my *huevos*?" She nodded and handed me the sticky jar.

"*Olvídelo*" — forget it.

First chore was to put that money in the bank. Two-thousand eight hundred fifty dollars made us as rich as some ranchers hereabouts. The fifty came from the bounty on those two scumbags. I'd not ever dreamed of having that kind of money. Marta had found the leather satchel when she looted the bandito chief El Xiuhcoatl. She'd done that directly after blowing his head apart with her shotgun and while I was trying to bleed to death. She'd also found Clay DeWitt's sixteen hundred ransom dollars he'd paid for his girls, for which he was grateful to get back.

I hated thinking about them girls, Agnes and Doris, fourteen and sixteen, and what they'd gone through. Doris was making it, got some real grit. Agnes...we didn't know. Marta, well, she's Marta. She's dealing with it, some nights better than others.

I'd told Clay he should have a cut of *Xiuhcoatl's* money, but he wasn't having any of that. He reminded me that once they got his girls back, they'd turned back to the ranch. I stayed, to go after Marta. Flaco went with me and died for it. I didn't blame any of them for going back. We'd lost some good men, and it being the worse winter in living memory, everyone was all beat in after hard riding. I don't think many of them had much fight left. I barely did. And they had to get those two girls out of there. I don't have words for what happened to them, and to Marta too. As it was, Clay and the others made it back with empty saddlebags, as food-poor as muskrats in wintering over.

Clay gave every man on that hard ride a hundred dollars over regular wages. Those who rode on into eternity, he gave the hundred to their kin. I had Flaco's hundred, and we were here to find his sister over in Las Vacas. I didn't take my hundred from Clay; the whole deal had cost him enough. But he'd done something else for us. Set us up in secret to buy part of the V-Bar-M Ranch that the traitor Maxwell's wife was selling off before Clay filed a lawsuit.

We rode over to Perry Street and the Roach, McLymont & Company in the old H. J. Ware Building. Roach's was a mercantile selling ranching goods. It was also San Felipe Del Rio's nearest thing to a bank.

Clay had already set me up an account. Took him a lot of explaining to get it through my dumbass head — according to my mama — on how it worked and why I should put my money in the hands of strangers. All that money was going to be given over to the Fairfax Land & Cattle Company up in Dallas. They had to have it in-hand by the end of the month or I lost out on the deal. And a sweet deal it was: 12,000 acres for a dollar and thirty-six cents each. I'd have to pay up on it every August and February. I hoped I could keep track of that.

We tied Clipper and Rojizo to the brick building's hitching rail. I told Marta to stay with the guns. She thumped her chest and pointed at the door, her thick eyebrows frowning.

"You want to go in, *entrar*?"

Nodding her head, she made a motion like counting money, stuffing it into a jar, and held it tight to her.

"You want to see where they put our *dinero*? Well, let me see if it's all right to take our guns in. *Quedate*," motioning for her to stay. You just don't walk into banks with lots of guns.

I went in and asked the jittery clerk at his desk about bringing in our guns while we did business. I never trusted no one with a bow tie.

"Why certainly, Mr. Eugen," said the clerk. "We'd feel safer with you here armed to the teeth."

Sometimes it's good to have a fierce reputation.

I went out and got the girl, and we hauled in the guns. The guns we took from the robbers, they were wrapped up in blankets under the liberated saddles. I don't think they were expecting my Winchester and three revolvers, and Marta's scattergun and Colt Lightning. I snapped my fingers. With a scowl, she set her over-and-under derringer on the side table.

I looked round for any spies or questionable characters before setting the leather pouch on the desk.

The man, peering over his spectacles, counted it twice. "Exactly two-thousand and eight hundred fifty dollars, Mr. Eugen. It is not often that we receive such substantial deposits."

"Clay DeWitt said you'd give me a receipt thing?"

"Indeed, sir. We do appreciate your business."

"And it'll be safe here until it's given over to Fairfax Land & Cattle?"

"Yes, sir. As safe as can be." He seemed a little put out my questioning that.

"My woman here would like to see where you put it, she being of distrusting nature. Me too, 'cause I don't want to have to chase some thieving outlaws down for taking it. Done that once today."

"That's highly irregular. Let me check with Mr. Ro…" He glanced over at a desk.

The man there stood and said, "Most certainly, Mr. Eugen. Bellwood, show the gentleman our Diebold." He called me a gentleman but acted like Marta wasn't there.

The clerk took us into a backroom. It had a wooden door, but behind it was an iron-bar door like a jail. Had a big box lock on it. The room had brick walls, no window. Against a wall was a big, dark green safe with fancy gold letters on its double doors. I couldn't make out what they said. That safe was taller than me and over half that wide.

"Made by the Diebold Safe & Lock Company of New York. The most secure safe anywhere in south Texas. Has a second set of doors inside." He was sure proud of it.

"Being damn Yankee-made, is it any good, then?"

He laughed. "Oh, yes sir, regardless of it being made by damn Yankees."

Marta looked it over suspicious like. Side-glancing at the clerk, she gave it a hard kick, scrunching up her face. She nodded and limped off.

"She's good with it," I said.

"You have a pleasant day, Mr. Eugen."

We ran into Early Thursday. Early really had been born early on a Thursday. His little brother, Noon Thursday, had been born on a Monday night, and his little sister, Dawn, on a Tuesday afternoon. Anyway, Early was running the Thursday spread, his dad being rocking chair-senile. The Dew and Thursday spreads had long helped one another out in hard times.

"When you going to put your brand on that little woman of yours, Bud?" Early looked like he was always squinting and grinning.

"Soon as we figure out her real name, not that she'll tolerate any branding."

"How you going to do that, seeing she don't talk none?"

"Gabi asked her all these yes and no questions. Got it out of her she was borned outside Las Vacas. Probably she's signed up in some big book at the church."

"That'll be plum good, knowing what to call her. But if you don't know her name, how'll you know who's her in that book?"

"Gabi figured out her birthday by asking her questions. Ought to be able to decipher who she is from that."

We watched Marta smack some sense into someone's parked wagon mule that had snapped at Rojizo's flank. I saw her once punch a rude mule in the snout, sending it hee-hawing to a corral corner.

Early laughed, "She just don't put up with no nonsense from anyone. She's only sixteen?" he asked. "Acts older…"

"Kinda young, I know…" I started.

"Well, getting hitched age in Texas is fourteen, fifteen in Mexico."

"Yeah." I looked Early in the eye and admitted something. "She's been good for me. Lets me know all what I can do." I looked away. Kind of embarrassing to say that.

Early slapped me on the shoulder. "Bud, there ain't many women like her. You a lucky cowpoke."

I smiled. "I know. I don't deserve her. My mama would say the same thing, but I don't much give a care on what she thinks. Be seeing you later, pard."

"Luck on finding her name. Let me know." He touched his hat brim to Marta. She gave back a grinning nod.

We rode back to the hotel where the cook fetched one of her boys who talks good American. We saddled him one of our new horses and headed for Congregacion Las Vacas. He'd do any Mex talking we needed. Juan was sixteen and as skinny as a beanpole. I was surprised he wasn't nicknamed Flaco. I gave him two bits for the job.

"Who you look for, *señor*?"

"We're looking for the sister of Héctor Vega Acosta, went by Flaco. Her name's Regina."

"He a *Rural* one time?"

"He was," I said.

"I know his sister. She easy to find." He told that to Marta.

Del Rio means "on the river," but the town's five miles from the Rio Grande. We crossed on the flatbed ferry and stopped at the Las Vacas customs office. Juan went in and got in a long talk with the Mex customs agent.

"He say go to *Tiendita Ramos*. Eh, it is store for foods. They know her."

We rode a couple of blocks through the dusty streets lined with adobes to a corner family-run grocer, a *bodega*. They're always on corners so they can see down all the streets. It's where neighbors come to gossip and hear the latest news.

Juan came out after a few minutes. "She work in bakery one *cuadra*...eh, block over there, *Panadería Del Pueblo*. Work for her aunt."

"Easiest tracking job I ever done."

I told Juan to tell the aunt running the bakery we had some news about Flaco. She was kind of suspicious of us, but took us into the family home behind the bakery and asked us to sit at the kitchen table. The smell of baking rolls and tortillas was making my stomach growl like a bear coming out of its winter sleepover. After giving us cups of *tisanes* — herb tea, she called for Regina.

This was the first time I'd been in a Mex home in a town. Walls were all whitewashed and the floor made of tile. Everything was real clean. Not like the peon *jacalitos* I'd been in. A bashful little girl brought in hot-off-the-stove tortillas. Marta shot out to the horses and came back with the jar of lick she'd snitched from the hotel. Well, she thought she'd snitched it, but I'd paid for it.

A girl stepped in careful like a rabbit, her eyes flashing round. She was expecting no good news. I've never been round Mex girls much, excepting Marta, and she ain't like...well, she's different. I couldn't guess how old this girl was. A couple of hands taller than Marta. Kinda pretty, but for her nose, a little bent. She wore eyeglasses too, something you don't much see on Mex girls or many Mexes.

"Joo have news of Héctor?" she asked in good American. I could tell she was being real strong and expecting the worse, gripping her own hands.

"*Señorita*, I'm Bud Eugen. This here's Marta. Your brother was a friend of mine at the Dew, uh, DeWitt Ranch. You might want to sit down." This wasn't going to be easy.

She said something to her aunt but stayed on her feet.

"I'm sorry to have to tell you this, but Héctor got killed last January, January second, if I remember right."

She sat down, but didn't start crying like I expected. The aunt didn't either when the girl told her what I'd said.

I told them the whole tale, of *El Xiuhcoatl* kidnapping the two DeWitt girls, Marta, and another girl, Inés. Of how we chased after them and had a battle with *Rurales* with Flaco getting us out of that spot. How we'd tracked the gang into the *Sierra Madre*. We bushwhacked them, got them pinned down, and Clay got his girls back, but they kept Marta and Inés. After everyone else turned back to Texas plum worn out, Flaco stayed with me. He died when we got bushwhacked. That was a bad time, making myself go on alone. I found Inés, beat to death. I caught up with them banditos and stole Marta back the hard way. It was a long hard ride back to Texas being chased all the way.

I wanted the girl to know that I'd not have gotten Marta or the DeWitt girls back without Flaco.

In the end, she only said, "I knew he would die in front of a gun."

"He was a good man and good friend, *señorita*." I told her some stories about Flaco, how we'd sit out on the *campo* and talk when we were monitoring the Rio Grande and guarding the herds from banditos. We'd had some good times in Del Rio when we'd come into town before Christmas. That's the last time she'd seen Flaco. I told her I'd buried him in a decent grave marked by a Mexican buckeye. It would be showing its purple flowers now.

"Clay DeWitt gave everyone who went on that ride a bonus." I opened a tobacco bag and laid eight Double Eagles in front of her. The aunt, seeing that many gold twenty-dollar coins about passed out. Clay had added a month's wages, and I'd put in an extra forty over the hundred for Clay's bonus.

Regina's eyes were as wide as saucers. "It take me three or four years to make that much moneys."

"Looks like you're a wealthy lady now."

She got a real serious look. "*Señor*, please do not look to my aunt.

Joo make like joo are surprise and do not understand. Joo understand?"

"Sure thing." *What's going on here?*

"I cannot take dee moneys because my aunt will take it. Joo give me later."

"Sure." I understood now.

She pushed the money back and said loudly, "I cannot take dee moneys. Now joo make a argument to me."

"Well...eh, it's your money, and Flaco woulda wanted you to have it."

"Joo say loud. I no take joo moneys," she said real loud.

The aunt was looking at her all put out.

"You oughta take it, but I'll give it to you later."

"I no take!" She said something to her aunt. The aunt said something back like she wanted her to do the decent thing and take the money. Marta was looking at us like we was barking crazy.

"All right. I'll keep it...for you!" I put the coins back in the tobacco bag and then my pocket.

Marta was glaring at me like I'd changed my mind about giving Regina the money.

The aunt was still trying to convince her, but gave up and stomped out of the room. Regina whispered something to Marta, which set her to nod and smile wicked-like. She knew all about trickery, the little sneak.

We talked some more. She feared the aunt wouldn't let her go back to school, and try and take some of the money, and the aunt had no idea she already had some money saved.

Señorita Regina Pilar Vega Acosta was a smart girl. She did the bookkeeping for her aunt's bakery.

"Can you read?"

Her chin tilted up. "Of course."

"How about reading American?"

"I read English good."

That started me thinking. "We're going to the Santa Maria de Guadalupe Church to find out Marta's real name. She was born here 'bouts and may be signed up in a book they've got. Can you go with us to help out? Marta doesn't know how to read."

"She does not say much, either."

"No, she don't, because she was kicked in the head by a mule when she was little."

"Oh, I am sorry — *Lo siento*." She gave Marta a kind frown.

Marta shrugged.

I told her how no amount of asking Marta Mex girl names ever came up with her real name. A priest I'd tried to give her to in Uvalde had named her Marta after a Bible story about two orphans.

"I'll pay you," I said.

"Joo have give me enough. I be happy to go. I must say Rosary for Héctor and ask priest to bless him."

"Will your aunt let you go?"

"She will because I say Rosary."

I gave Juan another two bits and sent him back to the hotel, and Regina rode behind Marta on Rojizo.

"No one say anything about Marta's guns?" she asked.

"Only if they ain't got no sense."

"That is no surprises," she said with a laugh.

CHAPTER THREE

There wasn't much to the church, just like there wasn't much to Las Vacas. The town wasn't near as big as Piedras Negras 'cross from Eagle Pass. Compared to Eagle Pass, Del Rio couldn't brag about much of anything either, except its ever-running spring and miles of irrigation ditches.

In the stone and adobe church, Regina and Marta went to the altar and kneeled on some steps and crossed themselves. They had these bead strings, and Regina was saying the Rosary, and I guess Marta was saying it in her own way.

The church was cool and dark. Just a few candles going. It was quiet in there. After a long spell, Regina whispered something to Marta, and she upped and left through a side door. I shifted on the hard bench and waited. There was no rushing a woman doing this stuff. I kinda liked the quiet anyway.

Regina soon came back, touched Marta on the shoulder, and waved to me.

I followed them to a side room with a waiting priest, an old fella with a kindly look and salt-and-pepper hair.

"This is Father Bernardo. He can help joo. There is no civil registration office. Dee church is charge to keep dee *Registro Civil.*"

"*Bud Eugen. ¿Cómo está, Padre? Esta es Marta.*"

"*Muy bien, gracias hijo.*" He smiled at Marta, patted her hand. "*Una hija de Dios.*" — A daughter of God.

I wouldn't go so far to say that, but I guess he said it because she can't talk.

On a little table with an oil lamp was a big leather book. This was it.

Maybe we wouldn't find her in there, and I could still call her Marta. But that was no good. I wanted to know who she was.

Marta was looking at it with big eyes, like it promised something.

Padre Bernardo waved his hand, *"Por favor, siéntate."*

We all sat. The padre opened the book after crossing himself. Fancy swirling words and numbers with lines drawn top to bottom covered the page.

The padre and Regina were talking numbers. She adjusted her glasses and said, *"Quince de Octubre de mil ochocientos setenta y uno"* — Fifteen October 1871. I'd told her the date.

He turned pages and said, *"Ahhh,"* and ran a finger down a line. Stopping, he said, *"Décimoquinto dia de Octubre de mil ochocientos setenta y uno,"* and then, *"Chichua Josefa Hinojosa Francisca."*

Marta grew the biggest smile I even seen and slapped the table. She gave me her "there you go" nod.

"That's it, Chichua's *es su nombre?"*

Marta nodded real hard.

"Que así sea." —So be it, said the padre.

That made me happy. Now we knew. It made me sad too. I shuffled round a bit before I could ask, "Chichua." Sounded queer, like it didn't fit her. "Is it all right if I still call you…*nombre*…Marta?"

Marta knocked her chair over when she flung her arms round me.

"She say yes," said Regina.

By asking Marta questions, Regina got out of her that her little brother and sister weren't in the book, being borned in Texas.

Padre Bernardo wrote everything down on a piece of paper, the day she was born, the day they signed her in the book almost a month later, and her parents' names, Jaimenacho and Asalia Hinojosa Francisca. He signed and dated it, and then folded it with a green ribbon and stamped a red wax seal on it. We went back to the chapel. The padre lighted up a candle and said a blessing for Flaco. I gave him some pesos.

Regina didn't say nothing on the way back to the bakery. The tears in her eyes said it all. It got to me too, saying *adiós* to Flaco.

Marta. I could still call her Marta, but it was good to know who she was, 'cause Chichua Josefa Hinojosa Francisca was going on a wedding license.

"Señorita Acosta, is it all right if I call you Regina?"

"Sí, Señor Eugen."

"You can call me Bud, if that's good with you."

She smiled. *"Sí. Mis amigas y amigos* call me Gina."

"You gone to school, Gina?"

"Sí, dee *preparatoria* school in Piedras Negras." She sounded proud.

Well, that was a lot more schooling than me. "That all you do, bookkeeping?" I liked her honest eyes.

"I can kill dee goats and chickens, bake all we sell in bakery, and wash and sew clothes."

I had to laugh, could tell she was funning me. "You go to your school to do all that?"

She got serious. "I study to be teacher."

"So you're still going to school?"

"No more. I saving moneys to go *Universidad Autónoma de Coahuila*. Dee money joo give me. It is enough. This year they let womans go there first time. It is in Saltillo. That is capital of Coahuila State."

"Down south. And you keep the books for your aunt?"

"Sí."

"I won't beat round the cactus...Gina. Would you might like to work for me?"

She straightened up behind Marta and looked at me with squinted eyes. "What work?"

"Clay DeWitt has a lady working for him at his ranch he calls a majordomo."

"Mayordomo, a *gerente,* a manager joo call?"

"I guess so, sorta like a foreman."

"What she do?"

"She bosses the house crew Mexes, keeps the ranch books, does the buying for the kitchen. Gets things done."

"Joo have *rancho?"*

"Clay DeWitt, best man I ever work for...one of the best men I ever known, he set me up to buy a ranch, part of the V-Bar-M. The owner, a bastard...sorry, named Maxwell, he's the one what put *El Xiuhcoatl* up to kidnapping Clay's daughters and Marta and stealing his breeding bull. The kidnapping was just a cover for him stealing the bull. He was going to keep it on a ranch cross the Rio and take his cows over for breeding. Anyway, we strung him up." I hadn't told that part in the story earlier.

She looked at me queer-like. "Strung him ups?"

"Lynched, uh, hanged him with *cuerda*."

"Oh."

Marta nodded and smiled wickedly.

"He had it coming. So did the other two we caught with him."

Gina looked a little green.

"Anyways, Maxwell's wife made a deal to sell off part of the ranch before Clay sued for…I'm trying to remember, for damages, expenses, and despair or something."

"So she sell it to joo?"

"Maxwell's wife don't know it's going to me because it was sold by a middleman land company up in Dallas, twelve thousand acres. Clay set all that up for me."

She arched an eyebrow.

"It's next to Clay's ranch. His being thirty-six thousand acres."

"This *Señor* Clay must like joo."

"Yeah. I tolt him I ain't never done nothing like run a ranch. Never been a foreman. It's hard 'nough just taking care of my own self and Marta."

"Joo need help for dee bookkeeping?"

"I surely do."

"Where is *rancho*?"

"About ten miles south on the Eagle Pass Road. That's about, what, three leagues?"

"I know miles."

"Not far, anyway. I could use you to talk to Marta when I need to, and I want to learn better Mex, uh, Spanish. She wants to learn to read too."

She nodded her head. "So I be teacher too?"

"Yeah, if that's all right."

She asked some more questions about the job. Where she would live—she'd have a room in the adobe ranch house. I'd have a hand go with her on weekends to Del Rio, and they could pick up any goods and groceries we needed.

She started talking to Marta, asking questions with a lot of head shaking and nodding. I had no idea what they were talking about.

"I like Marta. How much joo pay?"

"Fifteen dollars a month, room and board. A horse too. You can ride?"

"*Sí. Listo.* When we go to *rancho*?"

"You want the job?"

She gave a sharp nod, smiled. "Joo honest man, Bud Eugen. Joo no hab to give me dee moneys, joo could hab keep it."

"I ain't that way. I thought now that you come into all that money you'd head back to school."

"I think maybe I learn more on *rancho* for now."

"We're going tomorrow."

We kinda looked at each other, started to move, didn't, and then shook hands, her looking me in the eye. I liked her. Marta grinned.

"One trouble," she frowned. "My aunt, she no let me go."

"Can maybe I talk to her? You could come back here on weekends and still take care of your aunt's books."

"No. She no like."

"Well…"

"No. I just go in morning. No tell her."

"You think that's a good idea?" I knew Mex girls always minded their elders. They was real strict about that. Made me think though that Marta must of been a handful for her mama and papa.

"I go. Joo come to *bodega,* dee grocer, *amaneciendo,* eh, when sun come ups. Joo can do?"

"Surely."

"I go with joo."

"So long as you're good with it."

She did some more talking to Marta as we took her back to the bakery. I think Marta enjoyed the conspiring. I was worrying we might get Gina in trouble.

It wouldn't surprise me if she weren't there at sunrise. I hoped she would be.

We swung by the hotel and picked up the wagon to haul all those outlaws' guns and cartridges. Next stop was Haggler's Gun Shop, the sign saying — *Repair work promptly attended to and well done.* Musty told me that.

"Welcome, Mr. Eugen," Gunther Haggler shouted as the door's trip bell jangled.

That same newspaper story was pasted on the wall. Troubled me that folks made something of it. I ain't no different than anyone else.

I didn't leave no tracks that weren't going to blow away.

"I see you've collected up more guns," said Gunther. "Thought by now you'd had enough of that, ha-ha."

Marta came in with another armload of guns.

"I was hoping to meet that lady of yours who did in *El Xiuhcoatl*."

"You're looking at her."

"She done it? That little gal?" He looked a shade disbelieving.

"She did."

"Well, I'll be," he said, shaking his head and pushing his glasses back up. "How'd you come by all these guns, if you don't mind my asking?"

I told him the story, sort of. I didn't say how they got the drop on us. Just that they took off with our horses, and we went after them. Felt kind of bad fibbing, especially with Marta there, even though she couldn't understand...I don't think.

"Them sumbitch Drechsler brothers surely made a mistake messing with y'all, ha-ha."

One's gotta keep his reputation up.

"My word. Them outlaws been preying on that road for the longest time. Always hearing about them. Good for business seeing folks have to buy replacement guns," he smiled.

Lotta guns as he said: a cheap William Moore double-barrel 12-gauge, a couple of Remington single-barrel shotguns, some old German double-barrel cut-down to a couch gun, and a very fine Charles Daly drilling with double 10-gauge Damascus barrels and a .38-55 Winchester under-barrel — a three-barrel gun — them Krauts. It hurt to sell that one, but he paid a hundred even for it. Didn't need no big ol' 10-gauge anyway. Give it mud wheels and a team of horses, and you got artillery.

Haggler held up one of the Remington shotguns with letters carved in the stock. "By dandy if I didn't sell this'n to Clyde Atkins last year! Maybe he'll buy it back."

Six Winchesters, '73s and '70s, twelve revolvers of all makes, three old single-shot breech-loading big-bore Sharps and Ballard rifles, and some junk guns. Lotta ammunition too, though I kept what we could use, saving it back to give to Musty and Gent when they come in.

"My word. That's a lotta guns."

"You going to be able to pass all these off?"

"For certain. Lots of new folks moving in. Farmers putting in vegetable and fruit farms, cotton too. Goat and sheep-raisers coming in. All that water we get out of San Felipe Spring. They're digging irrigation ditches all over."

"Just what we need, a bunch of woolly shepherds and smelly goat herders running 'round with guns."

"Most of them come here all peaceful-like with a mule, plow, and Bible. Then they find out how it is and come to me for a gun." He tallied up the figures. "Business been good. Course it might drop off iffin you keep killing off banditos and highwaymen, ha-ha."

"I reckon. I was thinking about opening my own gun shop up and giving you a little competition."

He didn't give me a "ha-ha."

Marta counted cartridges and wrote the numbers on a piece of paper with a little picture of what they looked like.

"You can write *números*, Marta?" I asked.

She nodded seriously.

"You're just full of surprises, eh, *Me sorprende usted.*"

She smiled, went back to scribing with the stubby pencil and sticking out her tongue tip.

"You need anything, Mr. Eugen?"

"Bud'll do."

"Surely, Bud."

"For my woman's 16-gauge, a box each of Number 1 buckshot and Number 4 birdshot, and two of Number 6. She'll be back to hunting soon."

He stacked the twenty-five-round cartons on the counter. "Anything else, Bud?"

I looked at Marta. She reached into her deep skirt pockets and pulled out her Colt Lightning double-action and over-and-under derringer.

"Oh, yeah. Need a box of .38 Long Colt, and what does this derringer thing shoot anyways?"

He set down a fifty-round carton of Colt cartridges. "Those Remington derringers shoot this little .41 Short rimfire," he said, setting another carton on the counter.

"We don't need no fifty rounds. Can I buy half a box?"

"Sure thing…"

Marta crossly thumped her chest, pointed the derringer at the wall, and made like she was shooting, even made a little *"chu, chu"* sound.

"Right then. Full box, she wants to practice."

"She get that Lightning and derringer from where I think?"

"Yep, she took them off banditos. The derringer was in *El Xiuh-coatl's* boot."

I didn't much like the Lightning. It's called a "gunsmith's favorite" 'cause it gave them plenty of work fixing them. Its .38 Long Colt didn't have much bite, but for shooting someone coming hard at you up close, it would do. Light enough for Marta to handle.

"Bud, can I ask you a favor?"

"Surely, Gunther." Why not? I had been going to ask him to loan me some money if we hadn't tracked down those highwaymen.

"Could I see your woman's Parker?"

"*Marta, la escopeta, por favor.*"

We'd left our long guns beside the door. She caught up the scattergun, broke it open, making sure it was unloaded, and handed it to me.

I passed it to Gunther.

He admired the flowery and viney engraved Parker Brothers double-barrel, snapped it shut, and aimed at the wall. "This is a fine piece. I can picture her aiming it at that bandito chief."

"Well, she didn't have to aim seeing as she stuck it twixt his eyes 'fore pulling both triggers."

Eyeing Marta, he said, "Oh my."

Clay DeWitt came in with Doris, Musty, and Gent before dark. Roberto and one of his sons were driving the supply wagon to carry home goods.

At the hotel over supper I told the story of our getting dry-gulched by the Drechsler brothers. I didn't hide nothing from Clay. 'Cause I knew Musty and Gent would be telling all the crew back at the Dew. But when you let your private horse in with a ranch's *remuda*, you're throwing in with the crew, and you don't hide nothing.

Clay was laughing and slapping his leg the whole time. "You the damnedest pair of outlaw eradicators I ever seen!"

Eradicators, one of them sawbuck words. I told them about us finding out Marta's name. "Her name's Chichua, means love, but we can still call her Marta."

Clay shook his head. "I'd never figured that for her name."

I told him too about hiring on Regina Acosta as my majordomo.

Clay nodded. "Flaco's sister. Good move that, Bud. You can use the help."

Marta sat back in her chair puffing on a rollie and sipping coffee. She'd taken to putting lick in that too. Marta stayed right beside Doris, a pretty blonde who was whispering in Mex to Marta. They'd been treated wicked hard, had suffered the same outrages. They shared a hotel bed that night. I didn't like bedding down alone, but there were a lot of nights Marta stayed with Doris. They was just good for each other, talking things out. I'd not begrudge them comfort after what they'd been through.

CHAPTER FOUR

Before first light, Marta and I took the wagon to pick up Gina. Had to wait on the ferry because they didn't cross before sun-up. I was afraid we might get there too late. I was expecting to have to be all sneaky. Marta was too, probably hoping for it.

No need. Gina was sitting on the customs officer's steps near the ferry landing. She had two flour sacks and a lard can crate with all her things packed.

"Your *tía* not going to like this, Gina?"

"She old-fashioned. I leave her letter, explain. But we go now. She looking for me."

"I just don't wanna see you get in trouble."

"I tell her I come back on, eh, *Sábado y Domingo*...joo say Satday and Sunday? I come for church and to keep her books."

"Will she let you leave again?"

"I will talk to her, give her, eh, *poco de dinero*. She understand."

I figured Marta and I'd come with her next time.

Back at the hotel, we met Clay, Doris, Musty, and Gent. They were already working on coffee and hot biscuits dripping apple butter.

"This here's Gina Acosta. She's going to be my majordomo." I told her everyone's name.

She was a mite nervous, twisting her hands until Doris welcomed her in Mex.

"Gina," Clay said, "Bud and I were talking last night. We'd like to take you down to the Dew, that's my ranch, for a couple of weeks.

Gabriella, she's my majordomo." He chuckled at the word; he just called her the house crew boss, "She'll show you everything you need to know."

"Very good. I hope to learn," said a still Nervous Nelly Gina.

"You'll like Gabi," said Doris. "She's a first rate lady and will take care of you."

The waiter came up. "We got a passel of prime pork chops. How's that sound to y'all?"

Gina told Marta they had *chuletas de cerdo*.

Marta slapped the tabletop with a big smile, thumped her chest, pointed at the kitchen, and grabbed Gina's arm. They headed for the kitchen, Gina showing a spooked face.

"Now what?" I asked.

"I think Marta's going to burn the chops," said Doris, laughing. "In a good way."

I noticed her jar of lick was missing from the table.

We talked about what all supplies we had to pick up for the ranch. I had a long list and had kept some money out of the bank. I had another three hundred forty-eight to put in from all the guns and cartridges I'd sold. After talking to Clay, I decided to keep it out for expenses to start up the ranch. Going to have to come up with a name and register a brand soon.

"How's your roundup going, Bud?" Clay grew a serious look when he talked ranching.

"Real good. The other day we went across the river. Brought in almost two hundred head."

"Any of 'em *not* got brands?" asked Musty with a smile.

"I ain't touching branded head," I bristled up. "Excepting the four with Dew brands I brought back." I'd hired a couple of 'queros to help, and we were keeping them on the Dew.

"Jus' the others bein' a little branded?" He was talking about the ear notches some of the Mex *rancheros* used instead of a burning iron to mark their stock.

"Well, maybe a few, I ain't close checked *all* their ears, there being too many."

"A lot of cattle died this past winter," Clay said.

"The Thursdays said they lost maybe twenty percent. The Dew lost nearly ten percent," said Gent.

"We came though it pretty good. Lots worse up in the Panhandle. Ruined some ranchers. Going to run up beef prices," Clay said thoughtfully.

"I know an ol' boy in San Angelo, 'bout wiped out herds all round there. No work for punches. He made a living skinning dead beeves, hundreds of 'em. Had to hire a darkie to drive his wagon, takes the hides in to sell."

"Not a job I'd look for," Gent said.

"Yeah, and in a month or two they'll be back picking up the bones for fertilizer meal," said Clay.

"Bone manure. That might be something we should look at, Boss," I said. "Lots of farmers coming in here and planting."

"That's a good idea, Bub. Let me think on that, ask around some."

"Talkin' to some Wormwood boys in the Double Eagle last night, they said stock prices might go up as high a last year's," said Musty.

"They still talking to you boys after y'all dusted up ol' Brownie Jaeger before the Ride?" asked Clay.

That's what everyone called it who came back from Mexico, "the Ride."

"Oh, they's all right with us," said Gent. "But I don't think I'd wanna run into Brownie in a dark alley all by my lonesome. Come to think of it, I ain't seen him for a spell."

"What kind of price you think we can expect?" I was worrying about paying off that five percent per annum semi-annually deal.

"You know it dropped two years before, owing to that Texas fever outbreak and the '85 drought after that, so we're hoping it'll go above that, maybe thirty, forty dollars a head. How many head you collect up so far, Bud?"

"About six hundred. Expecting more. Hoping for close to eight hundred."

"That'll be good," said Clay. "Being on the Rio Grande, we don't have to worry about drought, as far as losing cattle, but the price per hundredweight drops anyway, no matter you got water or not."

"Lots of calves made it through the Die Up, Boss. More than I'd of expected. Been rounding up lots of them."

"That'll give you a good herd next year."

Marta and Gina busted out of the kitchen batwing doors carrying platters, followed by the waiter with more.

"My word, what have we got here?" asked Clay.

The platters were full with big pork chops, fried eggs, and grits with more biscuits.

Gina announced, "Marta cook pork chops in molasses, cider vinegar, and cracked red pepper."

Biting off a forkful, Clay declared, "Gracious. This is almost as good as her frijole beans."

Gina looked at me.

"You'll find out."

We spent the morning picking up all what was needed at Roach-McLymont's, the Perry Mercantile, and the Hansen General Store. Marta grabbed up a gallon can of unsulfured molasses there.

We also swung by the Val Verde Winery and visited with Frank Qualia. Clay bought a case of red wine. Us hands were pondering on just how fancy-dancy that was, and he remarked, "You boys should try it to gain a smack of refinement instead of the crazy-making rot gut y'all swill. Wine takes an evolved palate."

"They say the same thing 'bout mountain oysters," said Gent.

"Hey!" said Musty. "Ain't nothin' wrong with *huevos de toro*. What y'all call 'em, Gina?"

"*Criadillas,*" she said.

Marta smacked her lips, as she did when you named most food-stuffs.

"If booze don't burn when ya set a match to it, then it ain't much of a booze," declared Musty.

"Ain't wine what they drink in church?" asked Gent.

"I'll show y'all the proper way to sip wine when we get home," said Clay.

"Ya don't belt it, ya jus' sip it...?" trailed off Musty.

"A gentleman sips wine to fully enjoy its bouquet," said Clay. "Topped afterward with a fine one dollar Cabañas Cuban cigar."

Marta handed Musty a cig she'd rolled and lit it with her own.

"Too rich for me," said Musty, easing back in his chair. "I'll stick with my personal custom-made rollies."

"What's a bouquet?" Gent asked.

"The wine's smell."

"Then why in tarnation didn't ya say so?"

"This never gets easier," muttered Clay.

Dinner was peppered potato soup, so-so cornbread, and a beer at the Double Eagle before heading home. Marta put lick on the cornbread but not in the soup—I half expected her to. Everybody puts lick on cornbread, but Gina'd never had it. She tried it and much liked it, giving a pretty smile. The girls stuck to coffee.

Dinner was the only time the saloon let ladies in. They weren't too happy about us bringing in two Mex girls, but Marta and I were known, what with that newspaper story nailed to the wall. Somebody had pencil-underlined my name every time it was printed.

A few things were left to pick up. I bought a shawl from a Mex vendor lady on the plaza. Pretty copper-brown thing, made all the more pretty when smiling Marta hung it over her shoulders. We headed out of town with Roberto and his son driving Clay's wagon. Marta took our wagon's reins and sat Gina beside her to show her how. Looked like we were going to make a ranch woman out of her.

On the edge of town, a crowd of six riders came out of a side street and turned right into us. They pulled up just before mixing up with us. They were as surprised as we were. The wind blew away our dust clouds.

They were V-Bar-M boys with their new foreman, Cal Hodges. He didn't waste no time with saying, "Good afternoon." I figured it was about to become a bad one.

Clay saw what was coming. "Everyone stand easy," he shouted.

Even if those V-Bar boys had a bone to pick with us, Clay was much respected by every cowpuncher there 'bouts. Word was they figured us guilty of murdering their boss, Maxwell, along with their late foreman.

Clay stared down Hodges. "Cal, best take your boys on into town and don't say a word one. Now's not the time for this."

Cal squinted, and his hand slid to his gun butt, and that's all it took. I heard a familiar double click behind me. *Oh, dang, here we go.* I glanced back, and just as I expected, Marta had her shotgun leveled directly at Cal's now pale face. Folks tended to pay no attention to her, and she got the drop on them.

"What the hell's the meaning of this…" started Cal, all indignant. His mouth hung open with tobacco juice dribbling.

"If I were you boys, I'd be reaching for the clouds and not make any sudden moves," said Clay in a bored tone. Everyone on both sides had hands on their guns. It could get real messy here.

"This is highly irregular, Clay. I ain't never had no Mex gal pull a scattergun on me, and I sure as hell ain't gonna start allowin' it now. Call her off."

"Hell, Cal, there's no calling her off. This little lady killed *El Xiuh-coatl* and for good measure, his brother. Killed three of his banditos too." Clay smiled hugely. "Besides, allowing it or not, it's done."

Everyone in the V-Bar crowd slid their hands up.

It was Gina who eased things up. *"Marta, deja la escopeta. Nadie hará daño a Bud."*

I think she told Marta to lower her shotgun and that no one was going to hurt me. Marta's gotten kinda protective of me of late. Kind of embarrassing.

"That little gal done all that?" asked Cal.

"Sure as shooting."

Somebody laughed. Marta eased the muzzle down, but not by much.

Cal slowly lowered his hands, looking pretty put out, and wiped at the spittle. "I trust you'll have the decency not to spread it 'round that a Mex girl got the drop on us, Clay."

"Ah hell, Cal. You know there's no way I can keep these boys from telling the best yarn since we come back from Mexico."

Musty and Gent were glaring at the V-Bar boys, and they glared back just as hard, mean. I wasn't too genial my own self.

"We'll just go our own ways, and we'll have no more words," said Clay.

"Tell her that we're leaving." Cal tipped his hat. *"Buenos días, señorita."*

Gina talked to Marta. She nodded and lowered the shotgun. She didn't take her eyes off them boys.

The V-Bar boys edged round us and went on their way without any rush. They all give Marta and her scattergun a nervous look. We didn't start moving until they were well down the street.

CHAPTER FIVE

About a mile down the road, we ran into the Eagle Pass to Del Rio stagecoach. Ol' Debs Freemont was driving. I'd often jawed with him on the road passing through the Dew.

"Howdy, Mr. Clay, Bud, all y'alls."

"Howdy yourself, Deb. How's the road behind you?"

"Road's good," shouted the Jehu, as big round as a dumpling. "Army boy convoy you'll probably pass as they movin' slow. A half-dozen riders with four freight wagons carrying supplies bound for Fort Duncan."

We waved farewell to him and his passengers as he cracked the reins.

Gent was grousing about Cal Hodges making threatening moves back in town.

"There's another reason Cal don't like me," said Musty. 'Bout three year ago, I sold him a gelding. He got all pissy with me when we met up again. Complained 'bout that horse bein' blind in one eye. I tolt him I'd been honest with him over the deal. I'd plainly tolt him that it was a prime horse, but he didn't look good."

"Hell, I'd of shot you," Gent said with a chuckle.

"I'll remember that if I do any horse trading with you," said Clay.

"He tell truth?" asked Gina. Marta had her handling the reins by then.

"Within reason," I said.

I busied myself watching the tracks the army convoy left. I watch tracks by habit to keep in good form. Can't let these eyes get out of the habit of looking for the uncommon things. Things that's always there, but you might not see them if your eyes aren't taught to look. Gave me something to do while bouncing down a road.

I figured there were four mules for each of the four wagons, and there were seven riders. Down the road a piece, a bunch of riders had come in on a side trail through the mesquite from the right, from toward the Rio Grande. I backtracked a little and figured they were six, well mounted, and traveling heavy, but there were two mules with them making light tracks. They weren't pack mules. I could tell since they had come on after the convoy, and they over-stepped the horse and wagon tracks and weren't side-by-side like the teamed mules.

Some will tell you that mule and horse tracks are the same, but they're not. Mules have a more oval track, and the hind hoof steps right in the fore hoof's print. Horse's hoofs don't or might over-step them just a bit.

These horses and mules were moving at a faster pace than the army horses. Their toes were dug in more with longer strides between the fore and hind hoofs. That seemed strange. Most folks keep a steady walk when traveling any distance. Something didn't feel, or look, right.

"Clay, hold on up there."

He turned in his saddle. "What is it?"

"Something smells here, with the tracks." I caught up and told him what.

"Musty," he shouted. "Bud's got suspicions. Best we pay attention. Go on ahead and take an easy look-see over yonder rise."

Musty waved and trotted ahead, slowing down as he went up the crest a hundred yards ahead. Marta laid the shotgun in her lap, knowing something was up.

Gina had big eyes. "Is things wrong?"

Marta nodded. I swear she could see things about to go sour.

Musty ducked down in the saddle as he moved up real slow. He raised up to see over the crest and kept going to see more.

A ways off, rifles crackled like walking on chinaberries. Musty came off the saddle dragging his Whitney Kennedy with him and ran up the rise.

Clay yelled to Roberto to stay back with the girls. Gent and I tore out after Clay, bringing up our Winchesters. Dismounting and ducking low, we ran up the slope. Musty was lying in a creosote ring when we puffed up.

I heard a panting noise, and Marta hit the ground beside me with her shotgun. Already had a pair of shotshells between her teeth for a fast reload. I didn't waste breath telling her to go back. Kinda made me feel better with her watching my back.

The black-painted freight wagons were almost half a mile away, making it hard to figure out who was who. Horses all over the place. Some with men on them. Men were running round shooting.

"Damn," said Musty. "They got 'em good."

Men were running out of the mesquite from the right toward the wagons. One of the wagon mules was down, and so were a couple of horses.

"We going in there, Boss?" asked Musty unstrapping his Colt.

"We're way outnumbered and got the girls. Let's not get mixed up in this one," said Clay. "Too far. They'll see us coming from way off."

"We could circle through the mesquite, Boss."

"Hell, they'll be gone by then."

Men were jumping onto the wagons. Others pulled traces off the dead mule and hitched up one of the spares they'd brought. Now I knew what those two mules were for. Off they went, trailing dust with men on horses following. Maybe sixteen, eighteen riders. They left a bunch of bodies on the road and to the side.

Nobody said anything for a spell. Finally Clay said sadly, "Let's go take a look."

We stopped short of the battleground and dismounted. Clay said to keep the girls back. Of course Marta paid no mind, but Gina and Doris stayed on the wagons.

"Doris," shouted Clay. "You wait there and keep your eyes closed, honey." In a whisper he said, "She don't need to be seeing none of this."

Seven soldiers and four teamsters lay dead, all full of holes. Every one of them been shot in the head too, to make sure. There were two dead bushwhackers too. Mexes.

"They don't look like banditos, Boss," I said. "Outfitted like *vaqueros*. Except for that." Both had an orange sash round their waists. I pulled one off and stuck it in my belt thinking about how Flaco kept his old *Rurales* red necktie, just in case. I handed the other sash to Musty. He liked souvenirs.

"Damnation," said Gent, looking at Clay, who shook his head.

"They took all their guns, belts, pulled their boots off, and even took some of their uniforms," muttered Clay.

"What the hell just happened here?" asked Gent.

"I don't know, partner. Sane folks don't bushwhack soldiers."

"Exceptin' injuns," said Musty.

"No such as a sane injun," declared Gent.

"These weren't injuns," said Clay. "We got to report this. Have to go back to town."

"All right if we pull them off the road, Boss?"

"Yeah, the least we can do." Clay looked about. "Musty, Gent, how about you boys staying here so no one tampers with them?"

"Can do, Boss."

"I'm sure the soldier boys will be out here pronto. We'll pick you up on our way back. Keep your eyes open too."

Marta jerked her head at the dead horses and began uncinching a saddle with the idea in her mind of selling the tack. I had Gina tell her we'd have to give them back to the army. She shrugged and left them alone. That didn't keep her from going through the bushwhackers' pockets. Even after what she'd been through, that didn't stop her none. She showed me eighteen pesos and pocketed the coins.

Camp Del Rio was just east of town on a low plateau above the spring. Like the town, not much to it. Didn't even have a fence round it. There were a few adobe and plank buildings, and wooden stables. The soldiers lived in white tents all lined up neat. Even the outhouses were lined up. Musty said soldier boys shit by the numbers. "Their horses got a better roof over their heads than they do."

At a little shack on the road, the guard called for the sergeant of the guard. Clay told him he needed to talk to the commander 'cause something serious bad happened on the road concerning the army. He sent the guard off, and after a spell, he and another soldier came out and told us to follow them.

One of the white-painted adobes had a flagpole in front with thirteen stripes and thirty-eight stars flying in the breeze. Clay motioned me to come in with him.

Standing behind a desk was this officer. Wore a long mustache and kinda long brown hair. Wore a buttoned up blue wool coat, even though it had warmed up.

"I'm First Lieutenant Runnels, Detachment Commander, Troop A, 8th Cavalry."

"Clay DeWitt, DeWitt Ranch."

"Bud Eugen, chief scout and cattle punch." I figured that fit with him being all military-like. Didn't have a name for my ranch yet.

He didn't move to shake hands or give us a seat. "I understand you have some trouble to report, Mr. DeWitt." He sounded kinda uppity.

"I do. About an hour ago your wagons got bushwhacked by maybe twenty Mexes. All seven of your men and the teamsters are dead, and they rode off with the wagons and all the horses."

The lieutenant went white and plopped down in his chair. "Where did this happen?" he asked, kinda weakly.

"About three mile south on the Eagle Pass Road. I left two boys there to watch over them."

"They're all dead, and the wagons were taken. Are you certain?"

"We saw it happen. They headed off with the wagons and probably crossed into Mexico."

"The Mexes took all the guns, boots, and uniforms off some," I said.

"It looked like they knew what they were doing, Lieutenant. The Mexes took them from one side and from behind. Gunned all your men down in a few minutes. They even had spare wagon mules. They left two dead Mexes."

I showed him the orange sash. "They were all wearing this."

He went paler, if that was possible. "Estevan Guerrero."

"He's still around?" said Clay. "Haven't heard nothing about him for the longest spell. Crooked as a dog's hind legs."

"He's been causing trouble, whipping up his followers down in Las Esperanza."

I asked who the freighters were.

"Schubert and Sons. German outfit. We contract them often." He called over his shoulder, "First Sergeant Muller!"

A big square-head Kraut charged in and saluted. "Sir!"

I was sure he'd been right round corner listening.

"Locate Lieutenant Hampton, and with my compliments, dispatch the lieutenant and Sergeant Dunner immediately with two squads plus two scouts." He told him what had happened. "One squad will remain at the ambush site, and the other under Lieutenant Hampton will track the raiders, probably to where they crossed the Rio

Grande. He is not to cross the river, however. I will directly follow with more men and a wagon for the dead."

Next he penned out what had happened while asking us more questions. He gave it to a dispatch rider to deliver to the Western Union telegraph office and send it to Fort Clark Springs, thirty miles to the east at Brackettville.

"Gentlemen, you will have to excuse me. I must depart to the scene of action. The army most certainly appreciates your responsibility in reporting this. I am certain a senior officer will arrive tomorrow to investigate. Were you heading back to your ranch?"

"Yes, we were," said Clay, all guarded.

As we tromped down the steps, the lieutenant said, "I'm afraid I must insist that you remain here overnight. The officer will wish to interview you when he arrives."

Clay groaned.

"I realize this is an imposition, but this is an extremely serious situation. I cannot say any more at this stage. Where will you be staying?"

"We'll be at the San Felipe Hotel. Tell my boys I left there to meet us at the hotel."

"Very well. I will send a messenger to summon you when needed. I must be off now."

"Well, cow crap," muttered Clay. "Stuck here another night. We got work to do."

Musty and Gent were grinning.

"You boys surely spend a lot of time with them Double Eagle prairie doves," groused Clay.

"Only as long as it takes, Boss," Gent said, looking him in the eye. Gent was pretty much upfront about things.

"Since ya's pay for twenty minutes, what ya doin' the other fifteen?" Musty was pretty upfront too.

About a dozen and a half cavalrymen thundered out of the camp and down the road.

Riding into town, there were a lot of people in the streets jawing. Didn't know how they heard about the ambush so fast. Clay asked Bitter Bill, a punch from the Thursday spread, what all the hoop rah was.

"Roach-McLymont's been robbed by desperados. A whole bunch

of people shot dead."

My face must of gone ghost white for Marta looked at me knowing something bad had scairt me.

"Let's go!" shouted Clay, spurring his horse. I beat him there.

A crowd was collected outside. We only got in because of Clay. Folks gave way for him.

The marshal was talking to Mr. Roach, who didn't look so good. When he saw me he turned kind of sickly.

"What happened here, Fred?" Clay asked the marshal.

"Eight damn crooks robbed the place, Clay. Four busted in, and four stayed outside. They cleaned out the safe."

I got belly sick all of a sudden.

Mr. Roach said, "They were all Mexes except two were white men, Texicans by their voices. One of them sounded peculiar. They came in, and one of the white men told Bellwood to open the safe. He said he couldn't do that. That peculiar sounding white man simply shot Bellwood 'tween the eyes without mercy or a second-chance."

Blood was spattered on Mr. Roach's suit, the wall behind Bellwood's desk, and on the floor, along with brains and bits of skull. Turned out poor Bellwood was the only person shot in spite of what Bitter Bill had claimed.

"Then he told me to open the safe. I didn't want to, but I had no..."

"Quit fretting over it, Henry," said the marshal. "You didn't have any choice."

Roach was looking at the floor. He looked at us. "I can't say how sorry I am, Mr. DeWitt, Mr. Eugen."

"It's all gone?" I was having trouble getting a hold on that.

Clay didn't look any better than I felt. He'd lost a lot more money than me.

But, if I didn't make that down payment on the ranch by the end of the month, the deal was off. Even if I got the money up later, Maxwell's wife would probably find out who was buying it and turn me down. Our one chance to get our own ranch was drying up like a cattle tank in August. Our two thousand and eight hundred fifty dollars, gone.

What am I going to tell Marta?

I looked out the door, and Gina was talking to Marta. Marta's eyes got that look, and she jumped off the wagon.

I didn't want to be there anymore. I needed air.

Clay looked out the door. "Bud, here she comes!"

Marta came through the door with the eyes of a hunting puma, shotgun in hand. Mr. Roach shot into the strong room with the safe, and I heard the iron-bar door slam shut.

"Marta, no fuego!" I grabbed the shotgun's long barrel, and she tried to yank it away. I jerked it out of her hands.

She stumbled back, and the glare she gave me would have scairt a puma. She turned and ran out the door with Gina following after giving me a despairing look.

Damn bankers. But it wasn't their fault. I shoulda held onto the money. I don't know. There were a lot of things I maybe shoulda done. What had I just done to Marta?

Clay looked at me. "You know the difference between a banker and bank robber?"

I just stared at him.

"Bank robber got a getaway plan."

I went after Marta.

The three of us sat on the edge of a water trough drinking something brand new, bottles of sweet, strange tasting soda water made up in Waco called Dr. Pepper. Got it 'cause Marta liked sweet stuff so much.

I told Marta, through Gina, what had happened, after apologizing about taking her shotgun, for her own good, I added. You just didn't shoot somebody with the marshal standing there. He probably wouldn't side with you as a witness. I told her that we'd get through this somehow, that all was not lost. We'd fight our way through, her and me, like we had all those times before. We'd have that ranch.

It wasn't so hard saying this through Gina. I thought it would be.

Marta was hanging on my arm, all teared up. Gina looked at me, "Joo good man, *Señor* Eugen."

I didn't know how I was going to do that, get the ranch one way or the other, but I would.

CHAPTER SIX

We reached the hotel and got our rooms back. Gina would bunk with Marta and Doris. "I watch Marta for joo."

Marta ignored me and went to her room. I figured it best to let her boil it out of her mind. Not much I could say to ease things up. She always did a good job of getting over things troubling herself — one tough woman. She'd let me know when she'd be fit for company, usually by bumping against me. Maybe even a half-smile and arched eyebrow.

Clay had gone back to see the lieutenant. When he came back, us boys had a sit-down with him in the dining room.

"The lieutenant suspects the robbery was likely a diversion for the ambush, plus giving Guerrero more funds for his revolt." Clay said grimily.

"What's a diversion?" asked Musty.

"A distraction."

What's a dis..."

"Makes you look the other way."

"Who's this Guerrero anyway?" I asked. "Seemed the lieutenant was a mite spooked to hear that name."

"Estevan Guerrero," said Clay. "Big rancher. Got a huge spread down around Las Esperanza. About seventy miles southwest of here. Was a general in the Mexican Army. Guerrero means warrior, by the way. He's a self-made revolutionary, wants to break away from Mexico and take northern Coahuila and even Texas, up to the

Nueces, with him. They call his followers *Guerreristas.*"

"Anytime the Mexes get riled up, they want the Nueces Strip back," said Gent.

"That was in the treaty with Mexico, they got the Nueces Strip," remindered Clay. "Just that over the years, we kinda took over the Strip."

"He came all that way from Las Esperanza just to steal some supply wagons?"

"And rob Roach-McLymont's," I grumbled.

"I been pondering on that," said Clay. "I wonder what was in those wagons with seven soldiers out-riding them."

"Guns, ammunition?" asked Musty.

"Most likely."

"Lotta guns and bullets on four freighters," said Gent.

"This Guerrero make trouble before?" I asked.

"Two years ago he kicked up trouble at Zaragoza near Eagle Pass, took over the town, declared it the temporary capital of the Republic of the Rio Bravo. Federales had to run him out."

"They didn't just up and shoot him?" I asked, that being the customary way of solving problems down there.

"He's got connections with the governor of Coahuila, José María Garza Galán, and Guerrero's a *hacendado*. Owns a big part of one of the original Spanish land grants. *Hacendados* are sort of the lords of the land. He owns a big coal mine too, *Minera Carbonifera Las Esperanza*, called MICALE for short."

"But weren't he trying to take away part of Coahuila? I'd of thought the governor wouldn't think kindly of that," said Gent.

"Galán's in on it all. Governors are powerful potent down there."

"His boys did some raidin' up here too, dry-gulchin' stagecoaches and freighters," said Musty. "They didn't bother regular folks, no robbin' and so on."

"Until now," I remindered him.

"They sure had some run ins with the army and Rangers," Gent said.

"They all wear these orange sashes?" I asked, fingering the one I'd picked up.

"Yep. When they do something for their revolution," said Gent. "Don't show them other times."

"Why orange?"

"They have a flag sort of like the Mexican, green and white with orange 'stead of the red."

"I surely hope he's not starting a new ruckus up here. Got enough troubles as is," said Clay.

"Killing a bunch of soldiers, stealing guns or ammunition, and robbing a bank, looks like the ruckus is only beginning," I said, giving my opinion.

∿ℰ

The girls holed up in their room. Marta and Doris were surely down. Gina was with them, and I could hear her telling stories to keep their mind off this wicked day. They'd found a friend in Gina.

Musty talked me into going to the Double Eagle, knowing I was feeling powerful low.

"What ya gonna do? Stew in your room all by your lonesome?"

We left Clay in the hotel lobby with a bottle of wine, a queer looking glass, a cigar, and a big book called *The Pathfinder* wrote by some fella named Cooper. "This has been a civilized establishment ever since they outlawed riding horses into saloons and hotel lobbies."

He bid us farewell, his feet propped up on a coffee table, after giving us a half-assed warning about consorting with painted cats at the Double Eagle.

I had no itch for them, but Gent said, "Hell, I don't attend no whorehouse to gossip with the spittoon washer."

"Besides," said Musty, "I got me a special lady there."

A short walk and we were at the Double Eagle.

"Hi ya, Musty. What'll it be boys?" A brassy redhead bussed Musty and tousled his hair.

"This here's Callie Thurmond, the future Mrs. Musson."

She let loose a deep, hearty laugh. Sounded like lots of fun. Gent and I intro'ed ourselves, coming to our feet.

"A beer and a ball," I shouted.

Musty looked at Gent. "Best make it just the one, Bud. Ya don't need to be chasin' your beer with a shot of rotgut."

I didn't say nothing, but he was right. "You got a fine man there, ma'am," I said.

"That's what every cowpuncher here 'bouts says, if I'm to take the word of the likes of these sort. See ya later, lover," and she was off to fetch our drinks.

"Some gal."

"I'm passionately fond of that woman. Her floor name's Jiggles."

I could see why.

A couple of ol' boys with fiddle and guitar set bar stools on the stage. They busted out with "Old Dan Tucker," then "Sourwood Mountain" and "Sweet Betsey from Pike" to get everyone foot-stomping. When they cut into "Weevily Wheat," the cowboys took to dancing with whores and each other and even the two Kraut hurdy-gurdy girls, who set aside their fly-whisks and brooms.

A tall skinny fella with pants too short, and worn too high, and playing a Jew's harp, came out cracking limericks.

"A bather whose clothing was strewed
By winds that left her quite nude
Saw a man come along
And unless we are wrong
You expected this line to be lewd."

"What's lewd mean?" asked Musty.

"Nasty."

"Well, hell yeah. What's so funny about it since it weren't lewd?"

After plonking on his Jew's harp, the comic began again.

"There was an old man with a beard
Who said, it's just how I feared!
Two owls and a hen
Four larks and a wren
Have all built their nests in my beard."

Musty muttered, "That ain't funny, either."

The fella tried again. The crowd had become unpleasantly quiet after getting riled up dancing.

"There once was a lady from France..."

Faces lit up, seeing anything French is known to be lewd.

"Who bragged of her prowess at dance.
The joke was on her
When her competitor
Sneaked up and dumped ants in her pants."

Musty growled, "That boy better start gettin' funny 'fore I shoot him."

"That would get a bigger laugh," said Gent, looking over the scowling crowd.

The first beer bottle missed the fella. He was smart enough to hightail it offstage before the others found their mark.

The shotgun guard, Jeremiah Daffern, jumped up on the stage. He being so big, it surprised me he could jump up there.

Pointing his scattergun at the first thrower, he shouted, "Tate, ya threw the first one, get your raggedy butt up here and clean up them dead soldiers!"

"Yes, sir."

Everyone was laughing at Tate, so he started throwing bottles at them. That started free-for-all throwing. Jeremiah started throwing bottles too.

"This is gettin' outta hand," grumbled Musty.

That's when the shotgun went off into the ceiling. The throwing of dead and wounded soldiers ceased real fast. "By double-barreled jumping jiminetty, that's 'nough, y'all damn crackbrains!" Jeremiah bellowed.

"Hope there wasn't no one in a whore's crib up there," I said looking at the ceiling.

"Hell," said Gent. "Jeremiah only loads that scattergun with dry pinto beans."

Augustin Lešikar, the Double Eagle's owner, commenced waving his arms and cursing everyone for busting beer bottles he could sell back to the San Antonio brewer, not that everyone could understand his gurgly Czech-Texican.

Things calmed down, and we all had some laughs when a fat girl came out juggling billiard balls and beer bottles. She was juggling around more than just balls and bottles.

They closed the stage curtain after her for six minutes to let everyone quiet down.

Three soldier boys came in and took a corner table. They all had two yellow stripes declaring them corporals. Lew Cassel, the Dew's foreman, had been a corporal. He always said if you wanted to find out what was going on, that's who you talked to.

"Where ya goin'?" asked Musty.

"Going to find out what them soldier boys over yonder know."

Timing it to when the soldiers' first round about reached dregs, I bought four brews from Jiggles, eh, Callie, and walked to their table. "Mind if I join y'all?"

They looked me over leery like. Soldiers don't much rub elbows with cowpokes. Seeing the beers, the oldest one waved his hand. "Have a sit, mister."

"Thank you." I set the beers and myself down. "Bud Eugen, Dew Ranch," I said, holding out my hand to shake all round.

They only gave their last names, Yonkers—sorta the foreman of this crew, Feierabend—a Kraut, and Adamson—who barely spoke.

"If ya're thinkin' 'bout donnin' the blue, I'll tell ya, ya're better off followin' a cow's butt," said Yonkers.

"Nah, just wanted to see what you fellas heard of that bushwhack today."

"That's all everyone talkin' 'bout."

"Ve not to be speaking of dat to zivilians," said Feierabend.

"I saw it."

That perked their ears up. I told them all about it, and even what their lieutenant had told us. They hadn't known half of what I told them.

"Notin' but latrine rumors all we heard," said Yonders. "Bud Eugen. You're that fella what killed all 'em bandits in Mexico."

"I am." Wishing he'd not brought that up. "It wasn't just me, had a lot of help...at first."

I had to tell them all about the ride. The Kraut ordered up another round from the fallen angel, Bessy, leaning over to show off her jugs. Her floor name was Sugartits. Whores kept fluttering round, but Yonkers waved them off. They glared daggers at me for distracting their clientele from their goodly graces.

The most pestering dove was Nasty Nancy, about as low ugly a girl could be and still work in a hook house. She had high ideas of her cleverness in bed, saying men were so copiously satisfied with her talents they had no need to ever come back.

I finally got the soldiers back to the ambush by the third round. We clinked bottles.

After more jawing, I asked, "What was worth stealing to kill seven soldiers and four teamsters for?"

Yonkers squinted his eyes, looked round. "Can ya keep your mouth shut, Bud?"

"No. Tell me."

He leaned toward me. "They took three special guns."

"Three...guns."

"Yep."

"Just three guns?"

"Three Gatling battery guns."

"What's a Gatling gun? Like a cannon?"

"Let's just say, it shoots a lot o' bullets real fast."

I knocked on Clay's door.

"You just now getting in, Bud? Marta's been pacing up and down the hall."

"What's a Gatling gun?" I kinda slurred it after all the beer.

"What about it?"

"Them ambushers took three of them."

"Shit fire."

Lying in bed, losing that money was gnawing on me hard.

The door creaked open, and Marta climbed into bed, spooned up against me, gripped my hand. She cried without making a sound, every shaking sob cutting me like a knife. That money was our future. I wanted to give her a better life.

"*Voy detrás del dinero.*" — I am going after the money.

She nodded into my shoulder. Gave kinda scary growl.

"But you ain't going this time, you little rascal."

She didn't understand that last. I'd deal with that later.

CHAPTER SEVEN

Breakfast and dinner both were quiet. Nobody was much in a talking mood. Marta, Gina, and I passed time cleaning that tar-pepper smelling stove and grooming our new horses and mule. Neither the stove nor the livestock had been much good cared for.

A soldier showed up after dinner. He gave Clay Major Knott's compliments and a note asking to see him posthaste. Clay was fuming that we'd be stuck here another night.

An hour later that soldier came back and gave me Major Knott's compliments too, and I went with him. What did I do now?

Major Vincent Knott wore a white-speckled black U.S. Grant beard and horseshoe mustache. His uniform was travel-dusty, and he had on knee-high riding boots and was still strapped with a Schofield revolver. Lieutenant Runnels sat in a chair at the end of the desk.

After introductions, the major said, "Mr. Eugen, I deeply appreciate you answering my summons and for so expeditiously reporting yesterday's ambuscade. These are grave times."

He asked me to tell everything I'd seen of the ambush and asked questions about details. He even asked me how good—"proficient" he called it—I thought the bandits were.

The major said, "We received reports that Guerrero is preparing to undertake some devious martial endeavor. He is gathering arms, munitions, and *matériel*. He has also been recruiting minions of ill repute. There are reports of American turncoats joining his insurrection movement. There is little doubt that this is true in light of the Americans involved in the bank robbery."

"He's taking in Americans, Texicans?" I asked. A rich Mex. Strange that.

"Indeed he is. He's also recruiting former Mexican Federals. Gentlemen, I see a crisis approaching that causes me to tremble for the safety of our country. Across the international frontier lies a perilous threat coiled and poised to strike at our liberties and rights. It is buttressed by those enthroned in high places with corrupt goals, who despise all we represent. The theft of these weapons will embolden our enemies to strike anywhere or anytime to achieve their malicious objectives."

"Uh, right," said Clay.

I figured it was best for me to stay quiet, seeing I had no idea what he was talking about, but it surely sounded grand and rousing, even if it was making my eyes cross.

"We possess information that within three weeks Guerrero will launch his expedition to seize a stronghold within striking distance of the United States border. The region he has selected as his objective is inadequately garrisoned by the Mexican Army."

"Do you know where that'll be, this objective?" asked Clay.

"The *Cinco Manantiales*."

"The Five Springs," translated Clay. "That's too close to home for me."

I knew where he was talking about. There's five villages there, about thirty miles southwest of Eagle Pass and fifty miles south of the Dew.

"The Dew's inside the Nueces Strip, and these insurrectionists want the Strip back," said Clay. "Is the Mexican Army doing anything about it?"

The major said, "They know about it, but the garrisons in Coahuila and Nuevo Leon States have been stripped and dispatched to Chihuahua and Sonora States in northwest Mexico. The garrisons in Saltillo and Monterrey are mere sergeant's patrols now. Mexico had deployed five thousand troops into the northern Sierras to destroy the Apaches and Tarahumares, in cooperation, I might add, with our own campaign in Arizona."

"So you're saying that part of Mexico, right across the Rio Grande, is sorta wide open?"

"That is true," said the major. "We have dispatched some troops of cavalry to the Department of Arizona ourselves, but we're making efforts to reinforce our frontier garrisons. However, I have to secure this portion of the border with the available troops, which are not many. What I am about to tell you is in strictest confidence, and I beseech you to not reveal this information to anyone."

Clay and I both nodded. "Sure thing." I wondered why he was telling *us* these secrets.

Getting even more serious, he said, "The wagons stolen by the raiders contained a special arms shipment intended to reinforce our border posts."

I started to say I'd heard they were Gatling guns, but it came to me it would be best to play the dummy.

"Have either of you gentlemen heard of a Gatling battery gun?"

"Yes, sir," we both said. *Well, since he's asking.*

"Three of those wagons were each carrying a Gatling gun with its disassembled carriage and limber, tools, and spare parts. The fourth carried ammunition. They were destined for Fort Duncan at Eagle Pass, Fort McIntosh in Laredo, and Fort Ringgold in Rio Grande City."

The major took a little book from his desk, opened it, and handed it to Clay. Nodding his head, he passed it to me. It was a drawing of a Gatling gun. It was on two wheels like a cannon, but instead of one big barrel, it had ten rifle barrels in a circle.

The major sat back in his chair folding his hands.

Clay looked at me and then back to the major. "Are you going to take soldiers and go after them?"

He put on a pained expression. "My sense of duty desires to, but alas, we are prohibited from crossing the international border. Ten years ago, the army did pursue hostile Indians and bandits into Mexico. This is no longer allowed. We're supposed to employ diplomacy now."

"I didn't think so. I'm not sure why you're telling us all this, Major," said Clay.

The major looked at me. "Mr. Eugen, your reputation precedes you." Pulled from a drawer, he laid that dang-blasted newspaper story on the desk.

I felt like running for the door. I squinted at Clay, and he gave me a look telling me to settle down.

"Gentlemen, I propose a small covert expedition into Mexico to Guerrero's stronghold at Las Esperanza, some seventy miles southwest from where we sit, locate the three Gatling guns, and recover or destroy them." He was peering at me like I was supposed to say something.

So I did. "How many men you figuring that would take?"

"That has not yet been decided."

"You know how many men Guerrero's got?" I asked.

"At least three hundred. Very possibly more."

I tried to keep from choking. When the thirteen of us went after *El Xiuhcoatl*, he had nineteen banditos. We'd picked up a couple of more boys on the way. Eight of us made it back to the Dew with three of the four taken girls. The only place the banditos went was to Hell.

"Well then. What do you know about his setup, where the guns might be?"

"We know absolutely nothing of the *Guerreristas'* dispositions or deployment except his lands are situated to the south and west of Las Esperanza."

I nodded toward Lieutenant Runnels, figuring what his part in this was going to be. "So, how's he going to pull this off?"

The major leaned over his desk toward me. "Let me ask you something, Mr. Eugen. If you were tasked for such an undertaking, how many men would you require?"

"Three hundred men, you say? Well hell, I don't know if I'd have the notion to undertake an undertaking like that." My laugh wasn't fooling no one.

"For the sake of argument, Mr. Eugen, if you were convinced to pursue such an enterprise..."

I thought about having gone after those banditos, just Flaco and me after everyone else turned back.

"Three."

The major sat back. "Three! You say you could do it with three men?"

"If one was a good Mex what knowed the country."

"And you say three men with one hundred to one odds could do it?"

"I ain't saying it could be done by *any* number of damn fools, but that would be the best odds. If nothing else, it makes it easier on the *Guerreristas*."

"How so?"

"They only gotta dig three graves."

The major paid that no mind. "Lieutenant, what is your opinion regarding a three-man foray?"

Without looking at me, he said, "Absolutely impossible, sir. Why, that would be a fool's errand."

"How many men would you require, Lieutenant?"

"A troop, full up, fifty to sixty men, sir. Hand-picked."

"That's going to mean a powerful lot of grave digging by the *Guerreristas*. Unless they leave y'all to the buzzards. Most likely, I suspect."

The lieutenant looked at me for the first time, "Obviously you are not versed in the art and science of modern warfare."

"No, he's not," said Clay, "but he can sneak up on a pair of humping coyotes and steal their supper rabbit." He folded his arms and nodded. "I seen him do it."

The major could laugh after all.

The lieutenant glared. "A single bold thrust deep into the enemy's stronghold to locate the guns, liberate them, destroying them only as a last resort, and victoriously withdrawing to the border. Such a strike might well prevent Guerrero from carrying out his foul depredations altogether. Being an agile, light force, we would evade pursuit."

I started to say that Marta and me had been small and agile too, but during those freezing, hungry days running back for Texas, the banditos caught up with us twice. We both got bullet holes to show for it.

Instead, I said, "Victoriously withdrawing. That's what we call runnin' like hell. That many men would never make it there. They'd see you coming two, three days out."

"I would travel only at night."

"And take longer getting there and still most likely get spotted. And you would never make it back. They'd be on your tail *and* cut ahead of you. They do that."

He didn't say nothing, so I went on. "I don't see any way of bringing the guns back. Being chased, wagons would never make it, and there's only a few places you can cross the river with wagons. They'd be waiting for you at those crossings. Dynamite the guns, and let it be. Break up in twos, if you're taking that many, and run for it. Someone might even make it back."

The lieutenant looked like he didn't want to agree with me.

"So what you are saying, Mr. Eugen," said the major, "is that you would somehow infiltrate into the hostile encampment, destroy the guns with dynamite, and make good your escape."

"Humph," said the lieutenant. "That would be impossible in all except ideal circumstances."

Clay plucked a cockle burr off his boot. "Bud, how's 'bout telling these gentlemen how you sneaked into *El Xiuhcoatl's* camp and stole his brother from under his nose."

Clay was sounding like he was setting me up for this job. Sure didn't sound like he was doing me any favors boasting about me.

But, I told them the story anyways, of me finding the banditos' camp where Marta was held after a long chase. The seven still living banditos, we'd killed a dozen, didn't know I was coming after them. I snucked in in the early morning hour of the dead. I couldn't find Marta since it was so dark, but I found and grabbed *El Xiuhcoatl's* brother and snucked him out with a knife at his throat. I traded that bastard's brother for Marta, but we killed the brother 'cause he tried to pull a fast one, and we had to make a hard run for it, three freezing sleet and rain-filled days, really bad days.

"Those details were not in the newspaper article," said the major.

The lieutenant didn't say nothing.

"First Sergeant," the major shouted sudden-like.

"Sir."

"My compliments to Lieutenant Hampton. He is to fall in the battery gun detail for a demonstration."

He told the first sergeant to have coffee brought for his guests. The major asked me more questions about that hard ride while we drank coffee from fancy cups and little plates.

He asked me what it was that helped me the most to get out of that fix.

"When I got to a point where I knew I couldn't quit, ever."

Walking to the rifle range behind the camp, I asked the first sergeant why the stables were right beside the range.

"Helps the horses get used to gunfire."

I saw my first Gatling gun on the rifle range. It was bigger than I'd of thought. It sat on two wheels like a cannon. Behind it was what they called a limber, also with two wheels, and it carried the ammunition and tools and stuff.

The major said, "It's a Model 1878 made by Colt's Patent Firearms

Manufacturing Company."

The gun was mostly brass, polished like only soldiers can make it. Except the ten barrels were steel. I could see it was heavy.

Five soldiers stood round the gun, and a corporal told us what all the parts were. Said it weighed two hundred pounds, just the gun. Some other soldiers, I guess with nothing to do, showed up to watch.

So it fired ten shots all at once, and then you reloaded. I guess it could replace ten riflemen, but you're shooting all ten barrels at the same place. Certain to make one fella real dead.

The major ordered, "Commence the demonstration, Corporal."

The corporal shouted, "Take equipments!" and the soldiers ran about readying the gun.

"Prepare to fire!" The crew all stood at stiff attention.

"Load!" A fella picked up this brass arm and stuck it in the top of the gun. Another fella had two twenty-round cartons, tore the bottoms off, and just as slick as can be, racked them into that arm one atop the other with them pointing forward like the barrels. There were forty .45-70 cartridges in the arm's two grooves with room for more.

"Hostiles, two hundred yards, prepare to engage!"

Way off, three hostile foot-wide planks were stuck in the ground, about five feet tall. Beside them was a fence post about as tall.

A soldier behind the gun bent over and sighted. He turned some little wheels under the gun. "Ready to fire!" He took hold of a crank on the right side.

"On my command," yelled the corporal. "Commence…firing!"

The soldier cranked the handle like on a cistern chain pump and the barrels turned. Nothing happened at first and then a round cracked off, and it was one shot after another faster than I could count. Another soldier racked in two more cartons of cartridges while the shooting was going on. Looked like he was cranking as fast as he could. It was a constant rattle of shots with empty cartridges spewing out the left side like a mule with the shits. The planks and post two hundred yards away turned to splinters with dirt and gravel flying all over. There wasn't any hostiles left standing.

I looked silly with my mouth hanging open.

"Cease firing. Secure piece."

"The crew just fired eighty rounds in ten seconds. One gun can fire up to five hundred rounds per minute," said the major over the shot's echoes. "That's why it's designated a battery gun. One Gatling can generate as much firepower as a four-gun battery of 3-inch artillery firing canister shot or two hundred riflemen. It can easily range from eight hundred to a thousand yards."

Clay whistled. I couldn't say anything.

We walked down to the planks. They were just pieces of wood scattered on the ground peppered with finger-size holes. The fence post was cut down, and pieces of it had holes all the way through—straight through six-inches of blue oak.

"Gentlemen, you can imagine what just one of these guns could do if turned on American soldiers or citizens."

"I see they shoot the .45-70," I said.

"That is correct, the .45-70, the same as used in our Springfield carbines. However, one of the stolen guns is of greater caliber. It is a 1-inch."

"A 1-inch, like a whole inch? That's an awful big bullet."

"Indeed. It has two types of ammunition, a solid lead projectile weighing almost half a pound and a canister round with twenty-one .45-caliber lead balls. One can well imagine the mutilation such a weapon could inflict on infantry or cavalry. The 1-inch solid projectiles will penetrate a two-foot thick adobe wall and could halt an oncoming locomotive."

"And one of those stolen guns was a 1-incher?" asked Clay.

"Correct. It was destined for Fort McIntosh in Laredo, which is already in possession of one of the older .50-caliber Gatling guns."

"So how bad do you want them back?"

"I'll tell you in my office, Mr. Eugen."

I was thinking that the guns were one thing, but they had something else of mine.

CHAPTER EIGHT

Back in the headquarters, I was wondering where this was really going. It sounded plain loco, but I already had it in my head I was going after our money, not just mine and Marta's, but Clay's. I owed him, a lot.

The major looked serious. "Mr. Eugen, Mr. Clay, who I deliberated with last night, attests to your high character and proficiency in shooting and wilderness skills, tracking, and steadiness in dire situations."

Clay winked at me.

I didn't think his bragging on me was doing me any favors.

The major said, "There are many details to discuss further, but would you consider a contract to trek into Mexico, locate the Gatling guns, and endeavor in their recovery or destruction?"

I glanced at Clay. He nodded. I frowned. "I don't know. It would depend on who I..."

"You may select any reasonable number of men of your choosing," nodded the major.

"It's pretty risky. Might be a one-way..."

"I am prepared to compensate you two thousand dollars."

I thought a bit. That could change things for me and Marta, even if I didn't get our money back. "Pretty lean chance of making it..."

"One thousand in advance plus reimbursement of your expenses."

"Re-em — what?"

"He'll pay you back for any money you spend out of pocket, for chuck, bullets, and anything else. Right, major?" said Clay.

"Absolutely, for any justifiable expenses."

"They don't give receipts out down there," said Clay.

"Understood," said the major. "I take it Mr. Eugen is a man good for his word."

"Most certainly."

"Marta will get the other thousand if I don't make it back?"

The major started to ask something, but Clay said, "His wife-to-be." That sounded peculiar to me. Never heard it spoken out before.

"Of course," agreed the major.

"What about pay for anyone going with me?"

"That will have to be individually negotiated and will of course be substantially less."

"In writing," said Clay.

"Certainly. One other item," said the major. "Lieutenant Runnels and his aide would accompany you."

That brought me to a stop like sliding into a cactus. "No offense intended, but has he ever been in Old Mexico?" I said this to the major.

The lieutenant bristled up. "I have reconnoitered the right bank of the Rio Grande from Laredo to the Pecos."

"Well, whatever you reckoned along that river ain't anything like what's on the far side. What's the 'right bank' anyways? There a wrong bank?"

"The right bank in relation to downstream. The left bank would be the Mexican side," said Runnels.

"Do you know what they call the river on the *left bank* or what a *mestizo* is? What are *hacendados, rancheros, vaqueros,* and *peones?* And what's a *don* or a *patrón?*"

"The Rio Grande, I presume, eh, no, and different occupations?"

"It's the *Rio Bravo del Norte* — Rough River of the North. *Mestizos* are part Injun and part Spanish, meaning most Mexes. It ain't jobs, it's where they stand in showing them proper respect. I don't know about this, Major. We need a Mex that knows the land and the ways down there."

"I'm not keen on including a Mexican in such an expedition, sir," chirped the lieutenant.

"He's a tomfool then," I said matter-of-fact like.

"He's a commissioned officer and gentleman by act of Congress," the major said, without getting too crabby.

"Makes him an official fool then," I said.

The lieutenant shot to his feet, and so did I.

"Now, now gentlemen. Let us keep this civil. You *are* going to have to work together in harmony, if you should accept this contact, Mr. Eugen. Lieutenant Runnels will have to be present to make the decision on whether to recover the guns or destroy them. That is without question his responsibility."

"The only way I'd do it is that I got the say on how to get there and get back, what to do and not to do on the way."

Looking at Runnels, the major said, "The lieutenant agrees, do you not?"

"Yes, sir." With a big frown.

"Then we have much to discuss," said the major.

"First off," I said, "who's this aide?"

"I have in mind Trooper Gunton, sir," Runnels said to the major.

"He speak Mex?" I asked.

"He's an exemplary soldier, an excellent horse wrangler, and an expert marksman."

"Can he speak Mex and knows the country?" I asked again.

"No, he does not in both instances."

"Need a soldier that speaks Mex at least," I said. "There any here? Any good ones?"

The major lit himself a cigar after offering us all one from a can. Clay took one, seeing he knew how to fancy light one up.

"Is the lieutenant familiar with Scout Sanchez?" asked the major.

"I'm familiar with the name and...reputation, but I've not had him detailed to me on patrol."

"First Sergeant!" shouted the major.

"Sir."

"Summon Scout Samson Long Shadow Sanchez."

The first sergeant went to attention, clearing his throat. "Sir, begging the Major's pardon, sir."

The major turned with a frown. "You have something to say First Sergeant?" Like he knew that he did.

"With all due respect, sir, Trooper Sanchez resides more in the guardhouse than the barracks. He's a thieving pickpocket, larcenist, pilferer, and would steal the coins off a dead man's eyes."

I asked, "He a good horseman, can he shoot?"

"Topnotch."

"He *habla* Mex and been down there?"

"That he does, born in Mexico me thinks, or maybe Oklahoma Injun Territory."

"Pickpocket?"

"Absconded with a circuit-riding sutler's purse, he did. That was never proved, though."

"Sounds like the kind of hand we'll need."

The first sergeant looked at me sideways. "Keep your hand on your wallet."

"No matter. Them bank-robbing *Guerreristas* took just about all my money anyways."

"Sanchez is the best Black Seminole scout assigned to the regiment," said the major. "Don't you agree, First Sergeant?"

He made a sour face like he hated admitting it. "Sir, he can track a sidewinder in a sandstorm."

Clay nodded and looked at me. "I think I know who you got in mind for your man."

"Musty," I said.

"Think he'll sign on?"

"He's looking to get hitched. Needs more money than his bride makes hooking in the Double Eagle."

Clay nodded understanding. The first sergeant winked. The lieutenant got all sourpuss-looking. The major laughed.

"I'll fetch up Sanchez as soon as I get him presentable, sir. He's in the guardhouse again...excessive drinking and wenching...I mean consorting with promiscuous women."

The lieutenant slowly shook his head.

"Will he stay sober?" asked Clay.

"Oh yes, sir. Once you set him in a saddle and send him a tracking or shooting hostiles, he's as fine-tuned as an Appalachian fiddle."

Clay said something I'd not thought on. "Major, your lieutenant here and the scout, they need to outfit like civilians. Can't have a single army thing on them. That's from head to toe, tack and gear, and guns too."

"I'll make funding available. Lieutenant, you need to purchase the necessary items in town. Ensure you retain receipts."

We talked about what all they needed until Sanchez was marched in.

The scout had a face of dusky brown leather and black eyes that peered right through you. He wasn't too tall, but built as solid as an adobe. Saluting the major, "Sir, Private Sanchez reportin' as ordered." Sounded like a Texican.

Except for his brown hair down to his shoulders, silver earrings, and red and white checked bandana, he looked like any other soldier boy turned out in a midnight blue jacket and sky blue pants plus a black vest with red and white beads. On his cap he had crossed arrows instead of crossed swords. He wore knee-high buckskin leggings with lots of straps and buckles, vaquero boots, no high cavalry boots.

"Private Sanchez," began the major, "you come highly recommended, regardless of your periodic guardhouse incarcerations. Would you be interested in some field work for a change?"

"When do we leave, sir?"

Sounded like he was a lot more willing than me for this...expedition, but we needed that money back.

"You're not interested in the nature of the mission?"

"Jus' followin' orders, sir."

The major looked Sanchez in the eye. "This is a voluntary mission, detached duty. The aim is to accompany two special-contract civilians and Lieutenant Runnels into Mexico to recover or destroy essential government property that has fallen into the hands of nefarious brigands."

Sanchez put on half a smile. "We're goin' after them Gatling guns."

The major looked surprised.

The first sergeant smiled. "Barracks talk floats 'round, sir."

"Indeed, more like it takes flight on its own wings," muttered the major. "Yes, Trooper, we are. It will be a dangerous mission requiring a covert approach to Las Esperanza. Have you ever frequented that area?"

"I been there, sir, maybe three, four year ago."

The major looked at me, and I nodded. He'd have to do.

"Sir, do y'all know who took those guns?" Sanchez asked.

The major narrowed his eyes. "Guerrero."

"That do make it risky, sir."

"Having second thoughts, *Corporal*?"

Sanchez grew a tight grin over the sudden promotion. "Trooper Davis was my buddy, sir. I'd like to pay thems bushwhackin' murderers back, beggin' the Major's pardon. When would we be leavin', sir?"

"You and Lieutenant Runnels must first equip and provision

yourselves, to include acquiring civilian clothes. You will be able to do so in town on the morrow. The lieutenant will provide the necessary funding."

"Besides what all we talked about," I said, "no army horses, either."

"I have my own," said Runnels. "It's not marred with army brands. Regardless, that will cause a delay. It will take considerable time to inspect the available livestock and make the purchases."

"I can help you out with that and save time," said Clay. "Got some fine horses to lease. Tack too. And pack mules."

"You'll each need a spare." I knew soldiers didn't take no spares. They might be needed, I thought. Marta and I'd of never made it out of Mexico if it weren't for our spares.

"Does that mean we must first journey to your ranch?" asked Runnels.

"Bud's going to have to drop his woman and supplies off there before he goes anywhere. And he and Musty need to provision up too, get their own spares."

"That will cost us valuable time."

"Those *Guerreristas* would be expecting hot pursuit straight off," Clay said. "A couple of days' wait might be a good thing. Those heavy wagon tracks will still be there."

"That'll be the best place to cross into Mexico," I said. "I've been 'cross there and know a little about the lay of the land. We don't want to be crossing here at Las Vacas anyways. Wrong folks might take notice."

"Excellent points," said the major. "Considering Mr. Eugen's experience, it would be wise for him to select the route."

I asked Sanchez about the way he'd follow to Las Esperanza. On the wall was a map of both sides of the border.

Sanchez pointed at Del Rio. "We're here. Where's your ranch where we're crossin' the *rio*?"

"Right here just across the Kinney County line," said Clay pointing at the Dew fifteen miles southeast of Del Rio.

"That's good. After crossin', we strike southwest 'bout fifteen miles and hit Santa Carlos. Not much there. Might be best to pass it. Then it's another twenty, twenty-five miles south to Zaragoza and the other villages of *los Cinco Manantiales*."

"There's five villages there," said Clay. "Any danger going through them, it being closer to Las Esperanza?"

"Sure," said Sanchez. "That's the way they work down there. They got folks paid off as lookouts in towns miles out." Sanchez looked thoughtful. "Best way is for y'all to pass by *los Cinco Manantiales* at night. I'll go through durin' the day, makin' like I'm lookin' for work. See what I can find out."

"However," said Runnels, "we do need to pass through the towns in order to reconnoiter them and render a sketch map of each. It may be necessary for US troops to operate there since that area may be Guerrero's objective."

The major looked at me. I said, "We can do that, just have to be careful."

Sanchez shrugged, knowing it would do no good to argue with officers. "From *Cinco Manantiales*, it's about sixty miles to Las Esperanza by road. Ain't no direc' road." He put his finger on the town. "Lots of other towns and villages round about there."

"What's the ground like?" I asked.

"Pretty much flat, but it gets a little higher the deeper into Mexico ya go. The flats got a lot of gravel. Makes for hard trackin'. Now on the other side of Las Esperanza, it's in the foothills of the *Sierra Madre Oriental*. Lots of narrow valleys, ridges, and canyons. Good water, lots of streams and rivers. Trees too, not like further north."

We talked more about it. Sure a lot of planning. Not like when we hound-dogged into Mexico after the girls.

Runnels and Sanchez would meet us for breakfast at the hotel. We'd outfit them before heading to the Dew.

Riding back to the hotel, I was thinking about our robbed money. Chances of getting it back were slim to nothing. Where would it be, was it already spent? Even if Guerrero had it in a safe or something, it would be hard to get at. They said two Texicans were in on the robbery. One of them sounded peculiar, Mr. Roach had said. To be in on that, they had to be trusted. I would've sure liked to know who they were.

"Clay, I'll meet you at the hotel. Gotta visit Roach-McLymont's."

"Don't do nothing rash, son."

"Just got some questions for them."

CHAPTER NINE

Mr. Roach was a mite nervous when I came through the door. He had on a fresh coat, his morning coat having been splattered with Mr. Bellwood. "Your woman's not with you, is she, Mr. Eugen?"

"Nope, she's out practicing with her shotgun. You said there were two Texicans with the robbers. What can you tell me about them?"

Mr. Roach looked thankful Marta wasn't with me, but ruffled at what her shooting practice might lead to. "They were all wearing bandanas over their faces. The one who appeared in charge, he was a big brawny man, dark hair. He spoke peculiar, like he didn't have all his teeth. He also had a well-healed cut...let's see, under his left eye directly above the bandana." Roach put on a sad face. "He's the one who shot down Mr. Bellwood in cold blood, God rest his soul."

"How about the other Texican?"

"Nothing remarkable about him, maybe smallish." He squinted his eyes remembering. "Oh, yes. He had a fancy holster with a large 'K' worked on it."

"Brown or black?" I asked.

"Brown it was, like most."

"Anything about his voice, anything else?"

"Nothing notable. He spoke few words," replied the banker.

"Thanks much."

"Is there anything else I can do for you, Mr..."

He finished talking to a swinging door. *Gotta talk to Musty.* I headed to the Double Eagle.

∽✦

Musty and Bitter Bill, the Thursday spread hand who had first told us of the bank robbery, were sipping beer and smacking on pretzels. Fortunately there weren't no entertainers trying to entertain. Alley Ann—I guess that's where she got her start—was smooching on Bill and feeding him pretzels.

"Howdy, Bill, Alley." I shook Bill's hand. Alley gave me a pat on my butt and a cat's smile. Made me think she oughta be called Alley Cat. She used to go by Alley Alice, but someone told her maybe it wasn't a keen idea for a prairie nymph to use a floor name with "lice" in it.

Earlene set a beer mug in front of me.

"Thanks, hon. Put it on Musty's tab." I looked at Musty. "Remember them Wormwood spread cowpokes what mugged Slick, took his wages and his pa's watch right before Christmas?"

"Sure 'nough," Musty said after swallowing a gulp of beer.

"Who was the big asshole that took the watch, the one Slick pistol-walloped up the side of his thick head?"

"Oh, that were Brownie Jaeger, dumb sombitch from Wichita Falls."

"Yep, had some missing front teeth, talked funny like," I said.

"He's the one."

"I'm thinking he was the bank robbery honcho. Shot Mr. Bellwood and took my money."

"You shittin' me!"

"Nope, not even a little. Any his buddies have a name starting with 'K'?"

Musty looked real thoughtful, something he didn't much like doing. "Sure 'nough. Charlie Kern, he was there wit' Brownie that night. 'Nother dumb sumbitch, him from Nacogdoches."

"They still working on the Wormwood?"

"Don't rightly know," he said. "We can find out."

"I heard they quit or somethin'," mumbled Bitter Bill through a mouthful of pretzels.

"Alley," said Musty. "Do me a favor."

"Sure thing, Mus." She was licking pretzel salt off her fingers.

"Wiggle on down to the Horseshoe Saloon and ask 'round where Brownie Jaeger and Charlie Kern be nowadays. Don't let no one know it's us askin'."

"I know how to sneaky ask the whereabouts of fellas," Alley pouted. "I ain't seen them myself for a spell. That's a good thing," she pondered aloud.

"Hey, who gonna feed me pretzels?" complained Bill.

"They fit in your paws." I tossed Alley a quarter.

"You a real Texican gentleman, Bud. Not like some pikers round here." Her catty smile would scare a stockyard dog. Alley's black hair came down in a forehead devil's peak framing her small dark eyes and making her look even more like a cat.

Bill stood, brushed crumbs off his vest front, and wandered off to the privy. "Gotta drain the Gila monster."

"You mean let the worm spit," muttered Alley as she swayed off.

Musty looked at me hard. "What's goin' on, Bud?"

Real quick I told him about the visit with the army, about our "expedition" to Mexico to blow up the Gatling guns—had to tell him what they were—or steal them back. I told him about Guerrero's big plans. And that a lieutenant and a scout were going with us. I told him about Sanchez. "You got any problems doing this with a Black Seminole injun?"

"Ya say Sanchez' a good man, an army scout, and speaks Mex?"

"He is, and he does."

"I ain't got no squabble, then. And the army's gonna pay us?"

"You'll get five hundred, half up front." I let him mull on that, then, "And half of whatever we can take from Guerrero's bunch... after I get my money back," I added.

"What's the loot cut for them army boys?"

"Half for you, half for me. They don't get none. They're paid by the army to do valorous things for glory. Whatever we take for ourselves in Mexico, well, it's what we bring back from Mexico." I looked into his gray eyes. "It's risky. Crazy loco risky."

Musty was looking thoughtful again, painfully so. "Bud, I still feel powerful guilty not goin' wit ya when ya went after Marta."

"Don't let that gnaw on—"

"No, it does. I'll go wit ya, no matter how hard the ride."

I leaned forward in my chair. Over the beer-wet table, we shook hands eye-to-eye. A sealed deal.

Alley came back and took a seat, fluffing up her ruffles. I'd ordered her a Cactus Wine—tequila and peyote tea. Made my eyes water when I passed it to her.

"Why, Bud, a lady'd think you're courtin' her."

"Find out anything?"

"Them snakes got themselves fired from the Wormwood last month. They was rustlin' up unbranded Wormwood calves and sellin' them for pennies to the dollar to those V-Bar outhouse good-for-nothin's and burnt on their V-Bar brand."

"Take a low kinda rustler to steal innocent calves," grumbled Musty.

"No one ain't seen them since," went on Alley. "I asked some of the girls too. Lucky those two weren't lynched by that Wormwood mob. You know, on the road through Wormwood they got a pecan tree they string up rustlers and thieves from. Leave a pick and shovel for anybody passin' to bury them if they fancy to." She shook her head. "Some people."

"You done good, Alley. Thanks."

"My pleasure, Bud."

"How old are you, Alley?"

"Nineteen, I think."

"You been hooking how long?"

"Four years, I guess."

"Surprised you ain't hitched yet."

"Look at what I gotta pick from…and you're took." She shrugged. "Been thinkin' 'bout headin' up San Antone way. Better pickin's accordin' to Julie Jugs, she been up there."

"How come *she* didn't get hitched up there?"

Alley shrugged, shot down the Cactus Wine in one slug, and went looking for Bitter Bill.

"She a real cockholster, but she a good woman," Musty muttered.

I nodded. "She is."

Musty looked real uncomfortable. "Now I gotta tell Callie I'll be outta pocket for a spell. Makin' us some money. She'll like that part. She longtime tired of keepin' dusty cowboys happy. Wants to settle down with a regular."

He was upstairs a long time breaking it to Jiggles, I mean Callie. He was leaving for a spell and couldn't say what or where or how long.

I still had to tell Marta I was going and she weren't. That was going to go over like a fart in a bunkhouse — guaranteed there'd be some calamitous comment.

CHAPTER TEN

Marta's midnight-black eyes slammed through me like a hammer hitting a cartridge.

"She not glad happy," said Gina. She opened the hotel room's window to the cool sundown air.

That was like being told a branding iron slapped on the butt was going to hurt. *No kiddin'?*

"Marta, it's too dangerous for you to go down there. I'm surprised you're even thinking about going back into that hell."

Marta glared, shook her head. Her tight lips told me, "No matter."

"You can't go. *No vayas.*"

Marta pounded her closed hand on her chest, pointed toward Mexico, and then grabbed my vest front with both hands gripping hard. She'd gotten strong mittens after learning to horseshoe from Alberto.

My eyes were stinging. "I don't want to leave you. That's the last thing I want. But I swore to protect you. I can't, won't take you."

She let go.

"Marta..." I took her hand.

She yanked it away. The hurt in her eyes tore at me. She gave me a desperate look, unable to say the words she wanted to change my mule-stubborn mind.

"Lordy, darling, this is the last thing I want to do, to leave you and go back there. It'll hurt me too. It's hurting me now just talking about it!"

Marta slapped my chest, jabbed her finger toward Mexico, and slapped her own chest.

"No! I will not take you! — ¡Usted no va!"

Marta turned away, crossing her arms, her foot a tapping. Her foot tapping was like a dynamite fuse burning. Count the seconds before it blew up.

Gina stayed in a corner, embarrassed with the feud boiling up, and not knowing Marta's ways, she had no idea what was brewing or festering or about to blow up.

Marta turned back real fast, stepped up glaring into my face. She slapped her chest, jabbed a finger at me, slapped her chest again and then again, and shook her head hard.

"You do not want me," was what Marta's eyes said.

"Marta, you know that's not true." That hurt me bad. "How can you say that?" I was trying to hang onto my temper.

More hand slapping and pointing and boot stamping.

"You're saying you don't need me to protect you? I can leave, and you'll protect yourself. Marta, I…" I looked at Gina. "I need a little help here. I don't rightly understand girls."

"I can tell."

"You're no help."

"How joo know what she say?" asked Gina, arching her eyebrows, "How she know what joo say?"

"Dang if I know."

"How long joo go?" Gina asked.

"Two weeks, maybe three, most likely."

"Where she stay when joo go?"

"Usted y Gina se alojarán en el rancho," I said.

Marta shook her head. She didn't want to wait at the ranch with Gina. She surprised me by taking up a piece of paper and pencil and drew on it. Marta held it up, and there was an adobe house and two stick people — me and her. I didn't figure she could do that.

She pointed at the stick people, then to me and her, then at the drawing of the adobe.

"She, joo, stays together in this house?"

"That's the adobe on our ranch to be."

Gina nodded.

"I'm going to Mexico to get our dinero back. Or we ain't going to get that ranch."

Gina told Marta. It didn't bother me none with Gina in on this.

"And for doing that the Army's going to pay me, almost as much as we lost from the bank."

Marta shook her head, pointed at mine and her drawing, slapped the adobe. She pointed toward Mexico, shaking her head more. All of a sudden, she ripped the paper in two and threw the wadded up piece with her stick figure out the window.

"Joo go Mexico and joo leave her, she not be here when joo come back."

My heart was just stomped on. Before I could say anything, before I could even think straight, Marta grabbed her shawl and darted out the room.

I started after her, but Gina stopped me with a hand. "I go. Joo no go. Joo make more worse."

That didn't make me feel better, but I wouldn't know what to say or do anyhow.

I sat in the rocker and tried to wait it out. Gina would round her up and talk sense into her. She could do that. Ol' Bill Tuckworthy at the Triple-Bar, that was the spread I worked before coming to the Dew, once said, "You can talk your face off tryin' to convince your woman of a good sense thing, and she won't hear a word. Get her woman friend to tell her the same thing, and she'll bitch at ya for not comin' up with the idea."

I thought about those hard days in Mexico and what all I'd done, what we'd done. A lot of good men and women had died. I thought about that soul-freezing hard ride back. Sometimes I couldn't take another step, but Marta kept us going. Other times, I had to keep her in the saddle and moving forward.

I dozed off seeing faces I'll never forget, and blood-spattered rocks and frozen ground. Footsteps woke me. Gina's boots.

Gina stood in the door, just a dark shape in her black dress and jacket.

Marta wasn't with her.

"Where's..."

"She go."

I jumped to my feet. "Where'd she go, what'd she say?"

"She no say much. I no see. Her horse gone. I see this." She handed me a piece of paper. In big letters it said, *voy DeW.*

"That's the DeWitt Ranch's brand," I told Gina.

"*Voy* means I go. '*Voy al Rancho la DeWitt*', she say."

"She wrote that?"

Gina nodded.

"I never knowed she could do that." I strapped on my gun belt.

"Where joo go?"

"Going after her. She done this before."

"I go too."

"No, you stay here in case she... Well, all right. Might be good having you 'long."

"Maybe no good joo go."

I paid that no mind.

We saddled horses and went down Pecan Street past the unfinished Val Verde County Courthouse. I was asking Texans, and Gina asked Mexes, if they'd seen Marta. Most everyone knew who she was.

But no one had seen her heading south out of town on her sorrel. It made no sense for her to go north or east. Nothing there for her. West was Mexico. Didn't expect her to head there. Maybe she just didn't take the road, but took to the brush straight off to lose me. She's not afraid of doing something like that.

Gabi was at the Dew. That was our home for now. That's where she'd go. I knew what she was up to; making a point. If I wasn't taking her with me, then she'd show me that she didn't need me.

I was deciding whether to go after her or not. I didn't want her out alone. I didn't care how good she could take care of herself with her Colt and derringer. She left her shotgun in the room with all her other stuff. "Dang that girl putting me in this predicament!"

Trying to decide what to do was troubling me. I had to make that ride into Mexico, or we'd not have our own home, ever. Trying to catch up with her was a waste of time. I knew she'd ride like thunder and take to the brush. If she didn't wanna be found, she'd not be found. She'd make the Dew in three hours, even in the dark. I couldn't just ride off not telling Clay and Musty. Had to go back and work this out.

"What you got there, Eugen?" gasped a voice behind me. "Another Mex whore? One ain't enough?"

Matthew Atwood was Maxwell's grandson. Well, he was more than that, he was Maxwell's worthless shithead grandson who thought he was inheriting the V-Bar-M.

"Mind your mouth, Atwood. This here's a lady and speaks better American than you."

"English," muttered Gina.

"So what, just another Mex bitch."

I knew he was trying to bait me. I didn't say nothing. Glanced at Gina, and she was turned red.

Atwood leaned over his saddle horn on crossed arms. "Got nothing to say?" He always wore a sneer on his straggly bearded face.

"Nothing to waste saying to you." I turned back to the hotel.

"You running away, Eugen? You shoulda run away the day y'all murder-lynched my grandpa. That wouldn't have happened if I'd been there."

"Ahhh hell, Atwood. If you'd been there, you woulda swung right alongside him." I didn't feel no need to be civil over the passing of his thieving grandpa kicking at the end of a rope. It was because of that sumbitch that Marta and the girls lived through hell and so many died.

"Maybe we'll meet on the road someday."

I yanked my lariat's thong loose, threw a loop, swung it twice, and lassoed Atwood before he got his arms up. I spurred Clipper and yanked the sumbitch onto the ground, hitting like a wet hay bale. Scared the crap outta his horse, for real.

"I ain't in no mood for this, Atwood." I noticed he had full saddlebags and a big bedroll.

I let up slack and worried the lariat off the squirming dirt bag. He went for his pistol, but fumbled it to the ground as clumsy as a broke-leg double-jointed drunk.

"Don't, Atwood. I got other things to do besides explaining to the marshal why I shot your kneecap off." Crossed my mind he was real lucky Marta wasn't here with her shotgun. A missing kneecap would be the lesser of his worries.

He scrambled to his feet looking round for anyone watching. A few folks were.

"Just ride on home, Atwood." I sawed Clipper round. *"Vamos, Gina."*

"I'll be looking for you, Eugen. You best be checking your back all the time!"

"I'd expect nothing less, Atwood. You ain't got the balls to face a man."

"You a gutless sumbitch, Eugen!"

That didn't bother me none. Mama had called me one all the time. I wondered if she only said that out of habit, it being what she called most men, or if she was being honest with me for once. We rode off, and I didn't look back.

"He come for joo? I worry."

"Nahhh. He's all mouth. No gooder than a hardtack weevil." I thought about how pissed he was going to be when he found out I was buying part of his grandpa's ranch.

"Damn your blood, Eugen!" was the last I heard of him.

After all that trouble looking for that girl, there stood Rojizo half asleep at the hotel's hitching rail.

I musta bristled up, for Gina said, "Joo no hit her."

That stopped me, and I turned to her. "I ain't never hit no woman."

"Some mans do."

"I ain't one of them." There were times I'd wanted to give Marta a good spanking, but I'd not do that, either. I'd gotten enough spankings from Mama, using a one-by-four or the fire poker, a soup ladle once—her idea of whipping sticks.

I'll fess up. Mama taught me one good thing. Ain't never smart to hit a woman. One of her saloon louts beat her up one night...not that she didn't have it coming, seeing she'd sold his saddle he'd worked hard to steal. She paid him back in his sleep with the fire poker...*in his sleep.* Yep, same poker she'd used on me.

Doris opened the room door. "Uncle Bud, don't do..."

"I ain't doing nothing to her."

Marta was sitting on the floor in a corner, her arms wrapped round her legs. She was looking at me with tears on her cheeks. She turned round, looking like a kid told to sit in the corner. I used to have to sit in a corner when I was bad, the corner of the pigpen. I thought of her as one tough woman, but she was still a little girl too.

Standing over her was getting nowhere, so I sat cross-legged on the floor. She glanced at me real fast, then back to staring a hole through the wall. I held out a peppermint stick. She snatched it and shoved it into a skirt pocket.

"Marta, I ain't going to tell you again why you can't go. You know why."

Gina told her what I'd said without my asking.

"I'm going, and I'm coming back. I got every reason to comeback no matter what man, critter, or nature throws at me."

She gritted her teeth. Remembering.

"I need a safe place to come back to, Marta. A place where I know you're waiting for me, to cover me with your shotgun, with a fire going, a place to bed down, and your frijole beans."

Marta kinda smiled when I mentioned them frijole beans.

"You're my reason for coming back. You know I'd go through the fires of hell and the ice-rain we rode through before, just to come back to you."

Marta, all serious, stared at me, her eyes tearing up more. She glanced at Gina, nodded.

"She stay," said Gina, her voice shaking. "We, eh…she wait for joo. Joo have safe place come back to."

I looked at Gina and Doris. "What you two crying for?"

Marta climbed into my bed that night, spooned up to me. She didn't cry, didn't have no nightmares.

CHAPTER ELEVEN

We ate another quiet breakfast. Lieutenant Runnels, in uniform, looked out of sorts eating with us all, especially with Mex girls. He sure wasn't uncomfortable with Doris. Called her Miss Doris Ann. Doris didn't seem to mind the attention. Sanchez ate out back since his kind weren't allowed in the establishment. I was going to say something to the hotel foreman, but Sanchez said to let it ride.

Clay had told Musty the money deal from the army, and he went for it like a chicken after a bug.

I talked to the lieutenant about what they'd need and where we'd go to get it.

Guns were important. "We'd go to Haggler's Gun Shop," I said. "He's gotten a new selection of guns in." Gunther would appreciate me throwing business his way.

Runnels kept eyeing Marta putting lick on her biscuits and in her coffee. "She does like her molasses, doesn't she?"

"I ain't ever seen her put it on stewed tomatoes, but that don't mean she won't give it a go sometime."

Runnels asked Musty and me what hardware we carried.

Musty, all proud, announced he had a Whitney Kennedy .45-60 lever-action. Runnels had heard of them but never seen one. Musty also had a Colt .45. He didn't mention it, but he had a Merwin-Herbert .44-30 Mex as his backup in a rear-assed holster. Just about everyone on the ride had picked up one or two from all the *Rurales* we'd gunned down.

"I got a Winchester '73 rifle, not a carbine. I like the longer reach. My pistol's a Remington '76. Both of them .44-40. That's something you and Sanchez need to do, get rifles and pistols in .44-40. We can use each another's ammunition."

"Excellent suggestion," said Runnels, nodding. "I will do that with our rifles and Sanchez' revolver, but I have a personal Smith & Wesson .44 Russian I intend to carry."

"That's a fine piece," said Musty.

I'd also be carrying a Merwin-Herbert and a .45 Smith & Wesson Schofield for backup. The Schofield had been Flaco's. Like Musty, I didn't mention my Texas reloads. Different bullets, but I liked those pistols.

Marta was pretty down. She weren't tucking away her chuck with her usual gusto.

Gina and Doris were making small talk in Spanish with Marta. Kinda one-sided with Marta picking at her eggs and bacon, sopping up the bacon drippings with a biscuit, the staff of life.

"I'll be missin' Marta's frijole beans," said Musty.

Me too.

"What is this of *frijoles* all the times," asked Gina.

"*Ya lo verá*" — You'll see, said Doris with a smile.

We got Runnels and Sanchez outfitted pretty fast. Got their duds at the Hansen General Store with a lot of canned goods and other chuck. Runnels called civilian clothes "mufti," whatever that means. He wanted to buy fancy quality clothes including a five dollar hat. I had to tell him he'd look too fancy-pants and would draw eyes. He needed to look rough-side out. I swayed him to buy shirts of bleached domestic and denim waist overalls.

"He got a five dollar hat on a nickel head," muttered Musty. Sanchez laughed.

We picked up canteens, water bags, cooking gear, bedroll makings, and so on at the Perry Mercantile. We coulda got stuff from Roach-McLymont's, but I wasn't in no mood to throw any business their way. They did poorly hanging onto their money.

At Hagglers they both got a Winchester '73 carbine in .44-40. The lever-actions were no stranger to them even if they had used those government single-shots.

Sanchez was pleased, saying, "Lots better than them single-shot trapdoor Springfields the army makes us use."

Runnels briskly said, "The government selected the best available firearm design Springfield Armory could develop."

"Yes, sir," said Sanchez. "Shooting three shots from a Springfield while a Winchester puts out fourteen helps save ammunition." He winked at me, and I smiled back. Runnels frowned.

Sanchez also got a .44-40 Colt single-action. It was just about like his issue .45 Colt. It was more than enough, but he got six fifty-round cartons of .44-40, Runnels four, and he got another two cartons of .44 Russian. He said he already had a couple of cartons.

All three of the guns they bought were from that Drechsler brothers' lot I'd brung in before. I had plenty ammunition and gave Musty some we'd taken from the Drechslers.

Marta stayed outside all impatient. She took up a wad of straw and busily brushed Rojizo shiny.

The lieutenant had a handsome black Morgan with brownish underside shading. He said the Army Remount Service provided officers with horses, but they had to pay for them. Lots of officers bought their own instead. Sanchez rode a condemned army mount he'd leave at the Dew for a good range mustang.

Clay had gotten me and Musty's checks from the major and was holding them for us.

Runnels and Sanchez looked too new. I took their coats, tied them in a wad, knotted my lariat to it, and Sanchez dragged them down the road a spell. "That'll wear off the new." Runnels declared his self "flabbergasted." I figured he'd be flabbergasted about a lot things before this ride was over.

On the way to the Dew, Marta and Gina and myself broke off. Marta wanted to show Gina what was to be our ranch house, if things ever looked up.

Gina had taken to a blue roan, a light and fast little horse we'd gotten from the Drechslers'. She named it *Azul*—Blue. I told her it was hers. The saddle too.

We turned right off the Del Rio-Eagle Pass Road and rode three-quarters of a mile toward the Rio Grande. It was about two miles to the Rio to the southwest and six miles southeast to the Dew. Close neighbors in cattle country. We could hear Runnels and Sanchez sighting in their new guns down the road. They'd catch up with us.

The house was on an island of mesquite and oaks and facing east. Behind the house were a windmill — still working — and a stone water tank. Out back were mesquite and plank sheds for stables, feed, hay, and a workshop, all needing work. North of the house was a two-room adobe. It'll be the bunkhouse. Marta had picked a place near the big thirty-foot across tank for her vegetable garden. A two-holer was off to the side. Four round corrals — *potreros* — were nearby. I planned to build a bathhouse for Marta. I'd put in running water pipes to it and the kitchen like they had at the Dew.

The adobe house was in good shape for a place that hadn't been lived in for no telling how long, excepting overnight drifters. When Maxwell had bought the land to add to his Vermejo-Maxwell Ranch, he'd had no need for the house here, excepting for line riders, so it sat empty. It needed new doors and window shutters; they was all gone to firewood, and a few easy-to-fix leaks. Nothing inside expecting dust, cobwebs, and dry sheep crap — lots of all three.

Walls were a foot and a half thick. There was a lone room on the north end, separated by a wide breezeway from the other four rooms set end-to-end. Off the backside of the last room was a sixth room. The backside was covered by a big tin roof over the summer kitchen with a tiled floor. There was a really good stone oven, and the iron stove we took from the Drechsler brothers' would set in the inside kitchen.

Marta was laughing for once. She pulled Gina through the house, pointing out the end room off the breezeway was ours, then the big room with a fireplace, inside kitchen, and two bedrooms for little kids — rocking her arms like holding a baby — that kind of embarrassed me. Made me think about what was coming...kids. I didn't know about that. She was just a kid her own self, sorta.

The room off the back end would be Gina's. She stood at the window running her hand on the dusty window ledge. I don't know why she got teary-eyed.

"I'll be putting up a tin roof across the whole front, a veranda it's called, to shade-cool the house in the summer."

"I like."

"It's going to be hard here at first, well, probably for a long time. Lots to do starting from scratch. I ain't come up with a name yet."

"*Vamos a hacer un buen hogar aquí.* I help you make good home here," she said to Marta.

Marta grinned and gave her a hug.

Coming into the Dew — the DeWitt Ranch — was like coming home.

Cresting the ridge and looking down on the ranch made my mind wander, thinking back when Marta and me saw it the first time November last. We'd rode two days and a morning up from Eagle Pass. Made me think too when we were carried back across the Rio lying in a wagon and us both smote with bullet holes.

The day before we'd stood together facing *El Xiuhcoatl* and his last two banditos as they charged us on the bank of the Rio Grande. I thought we was goners for sure as I got bullet bit. We shot two banditos out of their saddles. Marta went down. Thought I'd lost her, so I didn't care to live another minute. I took *El Xiuhcoatl* down spending my last bullets, but like the Devil, he came back up going for Marta who, to my disbelief, was trying to get up. She knew she couldn't lay there playing possum. She had to fight back or die. In the end, it was her that finished off that demon. Her being too weak to heft up her shotgun, *El Xiuhcoatl*, torn and shot through and through, held the barrels for her. He'd chosen her to end his nightmare as a show of respect; it was really her who had defeated him. She helped him on his way by planting the muzzles against his forehead and letting go both.

I thought I'd died, but came to in the dark with no Marta about. But I was in my bloody bedroll, and she'd left cold food. I came to again in the morning light to find Clay, Musty, Gent, Gabi, and a new hire, Laris Bean, patching me up and hoisting me into a wagon. And there was Marta, horrible battered, but smiling.

She'd shucked her boots and swum that freezing river. Carrying bullets, she'd walked barefoot and crawled five miles cross rocks and cactus all night in the freezing rain to the Dew. As terrible a shape she was in, she had to guide them back to where she'd hid me.

Gabi took charge of us, like she did most things, being Clay's majordomo.

They had given me a slug of bitter laudanum, so things were fuzzy. They laid me on the kitchen table and cut all my rags off and kinda cleaned me up with a horse sponge. I pitched a fit being unclothed in front of those women, but Gabi said it weren't no big deal...don't know what she meant by that. A bullet had gouged down to the bone in my right forearm, another cut into my right calf, and one went through the shoulder muscle on the left side of my neck. That was the worst hit. There were three bullet pieces in my right leg and two in my left shoulder. And I had a head cold and a something awful runny nose.

The other Mex ladies gave Marta a bath after they cut her filthy long johns off, all she'd had to wear for her whole freezing time in hell, that and a blanket. Her bath water was so foul with blood, sweat, and dirt, they dumped and scrubbed the galvanized tub and heated up more for my turn. I'd never felt anything like that, easing into that hot water after almost two weeks of freezing cold and living like an animal.

Doc Griever, summoned from town, showed up in the afternoon. According to the smell of honey, he'd been partaking of Rousseau's Laudanum himself. Marta and me took our turns on the kitchen table doubling as a surgeon's table. Marta had taken a bullet graze on the left wrist and a bullet fragment below her elbow. Two more bullet fragments were in her left calf and one in her thigh. A .36-caliber bullet had broken a right rib, and two were in her right thigh. I heard her cries as he dug them out. 'Bout tore me up. Skull fragments were in her left forearm—from *El Xiuhcoatl* when he'd lost his crown. All that after almost two weeks of the banditos' hard riding, sleet and rain, little food and sleep, beatings, and worse.

All bandaged and dabbed with mercurochrome, at nightfall we were more of less coherent. We tucked away all the bean soup and hot bread and butter we could with piping hot chocolate and corn *champurrado*. It was the first time Marta had eaten in two days. She'd turned down food until I was brought home and fed. Clay's girls, they'd gone through the same hell as Marta, but they'd been taken home before I went after Marta. They put me in the spare bedroom and Marta in Doris's room. Agnes wasn't coming out of it good, and she stayed in her room so big sister Doris could look after her. Agnes wouldn't step out of the room. She didn't want to see no one who knew what happened to her, excepting her ma and pa, Doris, Gabi of course, and Marta. She'd sit with Agnes holding her hand, just being calm. I'd hear Agnes screaming at night, daytime too when she dozed off.

Doped on laudanum, I was unconscious all night. When I came out of it late in the morning, Marta was spooned up to me as customary.

We were alive, and we had a future.

I was able to un-bedridden myself after a week. One of Marta's thigh bullet wounds festered. Gabi lanced it and cleaned it out with tequila, after Marta took a belt of it. It was three weeks before she started hobbling round on a crutch. She didn't put up with that for long. She was back to cooking, but couldn't stay on her feet too long. She didn't do any rabbit hunting or horseshoeing.

Everyone was happy she was cooking up her frijole beans again. Fore long, she was back to giving the boys shaves and haircuts. When not working, she'd limp round the ranch grounds getting stronger. I started thinking of her as tough, not something I'd usually call a girl.

Clay had us move into our own room in the back house right alongside Lew, the foreman, and Gabi's rooms. Marta got a pay raise, her now being the head cook.

In the meantime, I paid Roberto to hammer out a finger ring from a silver eight-reales coin. I'd made a promise to Marta. I'd just never got up the nerve to tell her. We'd been through a lot, and she was always there when I needed her, and I tried to be there for her. Not that I could always figure out when that would be. Even before she got taken by *El Xiuhcoatl*, I'd made up my mind I wanted her to stay with me, always. She could have whatever I had. I didn't expect that would ever be much, but we could make it. Well, we'd come into a lot of money, *El Xiuhcoatl's*. I wanted to tell her she'd not have to worry about ever having a place to live. I felt the fool for having tried to give her away to churches or anyone else.

Gabi told me I needed a real wedding band. She made sure all the coupon books were saved from the Arbuckle's Ariosa coffee bags. Seeing the ranch bought cases holding a hundred of the one-pound bags, it wouldn't take long to save up enough coupons to get a wedding band by mail all the way from Pittsburgh. Once I had enough, they'd start saving them up for Musty.

It was a sunny, but chilly, February morning. Marta, Gabi, and I saddled up. Clipper had gravel stuck in his frog's cleft. I straddled and lifted his right foreleg and cleaned it out with my jackknife. Marta struck a Lucifer to light her fresh-rolled cig. Spooked, Clipper took a step back. I lost my footing and fell ass-backward.

Marta laughed so hard she fell off Rojizo, but jumped back to her feet with the cig still in her lips, but half dangling broken, and still holding the match, which burned her fingers before she tossed it. It being my turn to laugh, she stuck her tongue out at me.

Marta, Gabi, and I rode to the ridge top overlooking the DeWitt Ranch; the ridge from which we'd first seen it in November. Chimney smoke streamed low to the ground to the southeast. We'd had no idea then how our lives were going to change.

El Nortada gusted into our faces. The smells of dust, damp leaves, and wood smoke drifted over us. But there was another smell, one you couldn't exactly fix. It smelled of bright sun, mesquite, sagebrush, cactus, and cattle ranges. It was blown cross hundreds of miles from beyond New Mexico, across Texas, and over this ridge. A *vaquero* once told me it was the sweetest scent of all, the smell of this land.

Gabi had told me what to say and do, but I was surely nervous. We dismounted, and I stepped in front of Marta, giving her a smile, and took a knee. She put on a surprised look and glanced at Gabi. Marta's lips went tight, and she looked at me funny.

"Marta, I been wanting to tell you this," I said, and Gabi said it again in Mex. My voice was quivering like an excited horse's flanks.

"We only been together for shy of four months, but I never met no girl like you." I took her hand and pulled the sock off of it. "There ain't nobody I could ever trust like you."

Marta's eyes were going back and forth between me and Gabi. Like she couldn't figure what's going on. Gabi patted her shoulder as she said it in Mex.

Then I stuttered out, *"Yo te amo no solo, eh, por lo que tu...eres sino por lo que soy, eh, cuando estoy contigo"* —I love you, not only for what you are but for what I am when I am with you.

My Gabi-taught Mex fell apart. *"Sería un honor sí...*dang. I'd be honored if you were to take my hand and stay with me for the rest of our lives, no matter what troubles come our way. I want you with me always." Gabi said it for me. I managed to brute out, *"¿Marta, te casas conmigo?"* – Will you marry me?

Marta stood there sorta like a doe looking at a puma, glanced sideways at Gabi, who nodded with a big smile. I slipped the silver ring onto her finger. Marta threw herself at me, about taking me off my knee. I've never felt a kiss that long, that soft, and that warm.

"Les deseo felicidad" —I wish you happiness, Gabi said with a smile.

Shucks, that wasn't so hard.

CHAPTER TWELVE

And now, when I got our stolen money back and the money from the army — if I didn't get myself made dead — and turned in that first payment to the Fairfax Land & Cattle Company, we were getting married. We had Marta's real name to put on the marriage license. I'd have to get that from the Maverick County Courthouse for two-bits. This all looked like it was going to happen.

Course, getting killed would spoil all that and was making me take pause about how smart this deal was. I surely didn't want to leave Marta all alone, even if I knew she'd be taken care of for life at the Dew. I set my mind to getting that money.

Gent was with Runnels and Sanchez picking their horses from the remuda. We'd had an argument about the spares. Runnels didn't want to take any, army practice. I believed in them. He argued that for the four of us, ten horses and pack mules were too much to handle. Thinking about it, he was right. But I said we were taking one spare no matter what in case one went lame.

Musty already had our two pack mules cut out. We took mules instead of horses cause they could go longer than horses without water. They were trained good too. Knew how to work their way round trees and brush without pulling off their packs, and wouldn't try and buck themselves to death when a dangling rope touched them snake-like. Musty picked a known reliable spare.

Sanchez knew his horseflesh. He'd pick a likely horse for himself after watching it for a spell. He'd saddle it watching how it behaved. He eared one to get him to cooperate. I thought he was going to chew its ear off.

He let it loose. "Horse'll kick the lid off soon as I mount."

He'd lead each horse forward to test their mood before mounting. The scout picked a *grula,* a charcoal gray dun known to be a good range mount. "Good color for hiding in mesquite."

We checked all the horses' shoes, replacing some, making sure they were shod tight. Sanchez was good at shoeing. Paid a lot of attention using the hoof nippers to trim flaky soles and rasped the soles proper to level them.

"We take better care of horses than ourselves in the army," he said.

The lieutenant was looking at lariats hanging in the tack room. "Should not Sanchez and I have one of these?"

"You know how to lasso?"

"I do not."

"Then it's best you don't try looking like a cowpoke." Sanchez rook a lariat, though. We also took a long rope to make a one-rope corral.

"Let's gear up, get our chuck packed." I knew Marta, in charge of the kitchen, would be generous with provisions.

Runnels had a leather notebook he wrote down every penny he paid out to lease the horses, pack mules, tack, chuck, and other stuff. Clay was going to do all right on this deal even without the spares.

Marta had dinner going. She had to oversee another cook, Carmina, doing up the hands' supper in the outside kitchen.

She was making her frijole beans. She knew I liked them above all things. In spite of her feelings in regards to me leaving, she was seeing me off with a good meal.

Felicia had the makings going for cornbread, putting in yellow cornmeal, baking powder and soda, salt and sugar, some eggs, and buttermilk. Marta held her up. She was looking at an airtight of creamed corn. What was she thinking up now?

She cut open three of those airtights and dumped the creamed corn into the big mixing bowl of cornbread batter. She chopped up a handful of jalapeños and tossed them in. Felicia rolled her eyes, but she helped pour the thick batter into six deep Dutch kettles, five for the hands. She had an adobe oven going outside full of coals. They set the covered kettles on the glowing coals. With a sharpshooter shovel, Marta gently banked the coals against the kettles' sides and laid a layer atop the lids, tamped just so. When baking cornbread, she trusted no one to oversee the job. The bottoms, edges, and tops were always evenly done.

All would argue her cornbread was the best ever, big steaming chunks dripping butter, cut as soon as the lid was flipped off. I'd no idea what creamed corn would do to it. I mean, it's cornbread, but soupy corn? I don't know about that girl sometimes.

We'd finished packing best we could. Sanchez was at the corral talking with Musty, Gent, and some of the other boys. Runnels looked outta place, like he'd never been on a ranch before.

I asked if he had everything he needed. He said he was good and asked me to show him around. I was right. He'd only passed through ranches before. He was surprised that we did most everything for ourselves when I showed him the smokehouse, dairy cow shed, workshop, and smithy. Self-contained, Clay called it.

Doris called us to come into the big house to sup with Clay. Sanchez weren't invited. I told Musty to make sure he got fed and not to let any of the boys give him a bad time.

"I don't think he'd put up with no nonsense," said Musty.

I saw Sanchez later sitting alone by the stone cattle tank eating his frijole beans and cornbread. I'd make sure he got put up in the feed shed where Marta and I used to bed down.

Runnels was "absolutely astounded" by Marta's frijole beans and cornbread. Her adding that creamed corn made it something special, sweet tasting.

Gina, an experienced baker, said, "I understand now," and congratulated Marta.

Over supper, First Lieutenant Zachariah Runnels told us about his life wearing the blue. Didn't much sound like something I'd cotton to. Course he was an officer and looked at things a lots different than someone like Sanchez or those corporals at the Double Eagle. Runnels was from West Virginia, said it broke away from Virginia during the War for Southern Independence — what he called the War of the Rebellion — and sided with the Yankees.

"I wouldn't brag on that too much," I said.

He'd gone to a big school for four years called West Point where they taught officers to be officers. They also taught him to be an engineer, and he could build bridges, roads, and buildings if need be. At the "Point," as he called it, he did boxing and fencing. Called them sports. Strange to me. I never thought of fighting as a sport, but for settling scores and arguments. Oh, and there was Mama's kind of fighting, just because she didn't have nothing else to do.

After commissioning, whatever that was, Runnels was at the School of Application for Infantry and Cavalry at Fort Leavenworth up in Kansas. That sounded fancy. Then he was at Fort Concho in the middle of Texas before going to Fort Clark and then Camp Davis at Del Rio. I got the idea he'd like to be back at Clark, or better yet, somewhere back East not so hot and dry.

"It must be a difficult life for a soldier's wife. Are you married, Mr. Runnels?" asked Mrs. DeWitt.

I noticed Doris blush. Marta grinned and elbowed me. She figures things out real fast.

Runnels answered, smiling, "Regretfully, ma'am, I am not. Marriage is a delicate topic in the army."

"How so, Mr. Runnels?"

"One must ask one's commanding officer permission to marry. Within the Service it's governed by unwritten rules." He cleared his throat and deepened his voice. "Lieutenants shall not marry, captains may marry, majors should marry, and colonels must marry."

"Sounds like you don't have to think much for your own self," I said.

Runnels gave a frown, shook his head, and said, "You are so right, Mr. Eugen."

"What are your prospects of being promoted to captain?" asked Doris quietly.

Clay winked at me.

Mrs. DeWitt, it was her turn to blush, said, "I apologize, Mr. Runnels. My daughter can be overly inquisitive." She gave her tall, yellow-haired daughter a stern frown.

Doris whispered something to Gina, and they both giggled the way girls do.

"That is quite all right, madam." Runnels gave a kind of little bow to Doris. "Perhaps this year, or the next. Of course, the success of this expedition may have a bearing on my future prospects."

Iffin you don't get yourself and me shot to pieces or worse. I kept that to myself, having been reared by my mama to keep my mouth shut. Reflecting back, I guess I'd done tolerably good in that regard. Besides her ready use of boards, crockpots, fists, or anything else heavy, I still had all my chompers, excepting that septic back tooth a barber yanked out at the Burnet County Fair a few year back.

Doris excused herself and took a plate to feed Agnes.

Clay poured us wine in those queer glasses. He toasted our success. "May God speed your rapid and safe return to this home."

Wine. Too sweet. I'd rather have a beer. I guess Marta liked it, cause she poured herself another glass, smacking her lips.

It was sometime past midnight, probably lots past. I couldn't sleep and climbed out of the bed so's not to bother Marta. I checked the tack room. Our saddles, bedrolls, chuck, feed, water bags, and gear were stacked there. Everything but our guns. Even had a pick and shovel packed. Always seemed somebody needed burying. Beside, you can cook bannock on a shovel blade, even use it like a frying pan. A pick-mattock's good too. Stuck in the ground, it was a good tarp tie-down when there weren't no bush in the right place.

When we was packing, Runnels had a good idea, said to split the loads between the two pack mules. I would of loaded all the grain on one. This way, if we lost a mule, we'd still have some of everything. He even split the dynamite between the mules, and he and Sanchez both carried blasting caps and Bickford time fuses.

I walked over to the *potrero*. The five horses and two pack mules were all standing there looking at me like they was asking if it was already time to go.

It was silent excepting for a steady wind blowing from the southeast. It felt good. The stars sparkled like silver dust and bits of glass.

Gravel crunched, and Marta was standing beside me wearing long johns and sandals, wrapped in a *sarape*. She clucked her tongue, and a few of the horses walked over to the gate, their heads bobbing. They munched green hay out of her hand. Clipper ducked his head through the gate poles and nuzzled me, then Marta.

She wrapped her arms round me and held on real tight.

"I'll be coming back for you, darling. *Voy a volver mi amor.*"

She nodded. Looking up at me, the moon glow made her eyes look like black crystals on a fancy lamp.

We tucked ourselves back into bed. She just wanted to be warm and safe one more night. Maybe I could still catch a little sleep.

We sat our horses atop the low bluff in the bend of the Rio Grande we called the Sheep's Head. The sun was crawling up to turn the ragged clouds pink. The wind blew in gusts like it was running from the light.

I pointed out to Runnels, Sanchez, and Musty where we'd cross a half-mile from where we stood. Told them what the land was like on the far side, in Mexico. Marta and Gina were with us. Roberto's boy come along too, to stay with the girls. I'd told Clay I didn't want nobody else tagging along just to wish us *adiós.* That makes it harder. Hard enough with Marta there, but I'd not even think of telling her to stay behind. That was a sure way for her to come on horseback anyway.

A horse nickered, and Doris rode up. Runnels had a real surprised look. Looked pleased too.

"We wanna cover as many miles as we can today. We'll be passing through *Rancho Mariposa,* and the sooner we clear that piece of land, the better."

Didn't need no *Mariposa* 'queros running 'cross us. Word was they still wanted *venganza* for us hanging old man Garza's thieving son.

I turned Clipper and sidled up to Marta. She and Gina had *serapes* wrapped round themselves. I'd made sure they'd not brung bedrolls and her shotgun. I knew she could get a mind of her own.

"Two, three weeks we be back," I said looking into Marta's frowning dark eyes.

"*Estaremos de vuelta en dos o tres semanas,*" said Gina.

Marta, with a tight glare, held up two fingers and thrust her arm at me.

"Two week if joo..." Gina started.

"I know. *Voy a volver a usted.*"

Marta nodded, one sharp jerk of her head. "See to it," is what she meant.

She threw her hand round the back on my neck pulling me to her. Gave me a hard, long kiss. There was a moment that I told myself I couldn't leave her. Couldn't bear to be away from her again.

The others all turned away, excepting Gina. She had tears in her eyes.

"You take good care of her," I said.

"I think she take good care of me." Gina smiled, reached over, and gripped my hand in both hers. "*Vaya con Dios, Güero.*"

Runnels rode over to Doris. "Miss Doris, thank you for coming to send us off."

"The least I can do, Mr. Runnels. I wish you well and a fast and safe return."

Doris surely looked pretty, her cheeks made red by the chill air and the rising sun making her hair golden fire. Close together, they spoke a little more.

I gave Marta another squeeze and sawed Clipper round. "Let's go to Mexico."

"Honor and glory," said Runnels with feeling.

"*La sangre y la muerte,*" said Sanchez with less feeling.

I think that means "blood and death."

I made myself not look back. Felt like I was carrying a heavy weight. Told myself to keep my eyes on the chore at hand, going into Mexico.

Coming down the bluff, we followed a cow trail through the carrizo cane to the riverbank. "We need to spread out," I told Runnels. "Twenty yards apart."

We crossed the crap-brown river all at once, going saddle-deep, and then clattered up the stony bank. The horses shook themselves. Eyeballing round, I was having powerful second feelings on this. Been here before with no fond memories. Just over the low ridge to the left was where Marta and I made our last stand. I didn't ever want to go back there. I guess all the man and horse bones were well scattered by coyotes and javelina.

Mexico, it ain't like no other place. A man could get swallowed up there never to be seen again.

I looked back to the Sheep's Head bluff. Marta, Gina, Doris, and the boy were way tiny, but I waved. Marta waved her sombrero back. Felt like there was a hole in my chest.

"We need to cover some ground and get off *Mariposa* land," I told Runnels.

Musty nodded. I knew what he was thinking.

We followed the now barely-seen old trail where the banditos had herded our stolen cattle...and Marta and Clay's girls. I saw the arroyo that led off to the hacienda where we'd strung up them traitors what started that hell we lived through. I had expected to find the girls there. I remembered the bad things that happened in that house, things I tried not to think about on quiet nights.

On higher ground, I looked back toward the Sheep's Head. No one was to be seen. I felt bad leaving her, but I had no choice. I wondered what she'd think of me and how much she'd really miss me.

I'm already missing her more than I ever had.

I dug my spurs into Clipper's sides. "Let's get this done with."

CHAPTER THIRTEEN

We struck south for fifteen miles to hit the Zaragoza Road below Santa Carlos. It was another twenty, twenty-five miles south to Zaragoza and the other villages of *los Cinco Manantiales* — the Five Springs.

The land was as level as a board, but we crossed lots of streams and arroyos, wet and dry. Lots of scrub and mesquite. Trees lined most of the streams.

While we were cutting cross-country, Runnels used a Singer's Patent Compass to keep us heading south-southwest.

Sanchez had one too, showed me how to use it. "This arrow always point north."

"Who wants to go north all the time?"

He laughed. He told me all about it and had me keep us on the "line of march" as Runnels called it, since we were riding cross-country. It helped us stick to a straighter path and make better time. Made good sense. I'd have to get one in Del Rio.

"Mr. Eugen..." started Runnels.

"Best you be calling me something else, and not Bud, either. We get all formal sounding, it'll attract attention. I'll be calling you Runnels if you don't mind. It's for the best."

He rode for a piece, quiet. "You are correct...Bud. We must use discretion. Feel free to call me Zach for my *nom de guerre*."

"'Zach?' Your nam da what?"

"*Nom de guerre.* A name assumed by a commander in wartime to protect his family. Zachariah is my given name after the Holy Prophet Zachariah, the father of John the Baptist."

I didn't see what that had to do with anything. Sure a long time ago. "Your alias is Zach then."

"And you can call me Musty," a voice piped in from behind us.

Zach nodded. "What shall I call you then, Bud?"

I thought about that newspaper story with my name all over it and Brownie Jaeger too. I was pretty sure he'd not remember my face from that night. Especially since I was standing in the shadows and he was occupied with Slick's attentions. Least the paper didn't say my given name...Athel. I don't tell anybody that. Marta don't even know.

"How about..."

"Spud," said Musty. "Sounds like Bud, iffin one of us says Bud accidental like."

"That'll do, I guess. Spud Watkins." Miss Watkins was a neighbor. Liked that lady cause she'd fed me when Mama threw me out.

Zach laughed. "Spud Watkins it is."

Sanchez turned in his saddle, "All right if I call you Zach...sir?"

"When necessary, corporal, as the mission requires."

Ol' Zach looked real uncomfortable. *The army's sure got its ways*, I thought. I laughed.

"What I was going to ask you is in regards to Miss Doris." Zach gave a shy grin. "Do you know her well?"

"Only since November last. She's a fine young lady."

"I agree with you. Very well read."

"That she is, I guess. She sure talks about things I don't know nothing about. Her mama and Gabi teaches her and Miss Agnes. They teach the Mex girls on the ranch too. Marta sits in when she's got time. They got about twenty books, Encylo—something British."

"*Encyclopædia Britannica*," he said. "The fount of knowledge."

"That's it," I said. "Mrs. DeWitt got them from New Orleans."

"It is a shame, what happened to that tender young lady, Miss Agnes."

"It is. Agnes ain't come out of it like Marta and Doris, not saying they ain't had it hard. Miss Doris expects to run the Dew someday."

Runnel's eyes widened at that.

That idea, a woman running a ranch, was hard for me to bite on, but what the heck. "Doris's plenty smart and tough 'nough, a real Texican woman. She can ride real good, knows almost as much about horses and cattle as any punch." I added, "Doris speaks good Mex."

"So I noticed."

"She's a grand singer too."

"Is she?"

"Like church chimes."

It was near dark when we reached the Santa Carlos-Zaragoza Road. Barking dogs told us where the village was so we could pass it by. The road was just a rutted track through the mesquite with lots of horse and burro tracks. It didn't look like it was too lively used. I figured some of those tracks were the army wagons and ambushers. There were heavy wagon ruts through, and they were fresh even if there were a lot of other tracks over them.

We backed off from the road a good ways for supper and built a little fire down in a deep arroyo away from trees. A fire under a tree makes it glow to be seen from way off. Smoke would glow too, but there wasn't anything to be done for that seeing we had only smoky mesquite.

We all picked up firewood, excepting Zach. I was starting to understand this army officer thing. They did a lot of thinking and didn't do much back-work.

They're sorta like a foreman, but while the foreman weren't expected to gather up firewood, he'd collect a chunk of wood to donate to the fire. Zach didn't even do that.

A good crew worked out because everyone pitched in and took on the chores they liked best. Any punch can do about any job, and there's plenty to go round, but you can mostly take on the ones you're best fit for.

I could see that Runnels weren't going to take on much. Well, cowpokes got ways of nudging a man into what needs doing.

We didn't bother with a lookout. We'd not run 'cross anyone, heard nothing, and we'd moved our campsite after eating and putting out the fire.

In my bedroll, looking up at that big ol' sky, all I could think of was Marta back there alone. I best be taking care of business and getting back home. Home, I liked that idea.

A gunshot kicked me awake.

"What?" said Musty all slurry.

"Was that a shot?" asked Zach.

"I think it two," said Sanchez. "Can't tell direction."

There was not a sound excepting the breeze and the horses' usual noises.

"I knowed it was a shot…" started Musty.

"Shhh," hissed Zach.

We heard three or four horses at a run on the road. They didn't slow and were gone. No other troublesome noises. We laid there a long time, pistols ready, not making a sound.

After a spell, Zach said, "We can stand down. Whatever happened must have passed by."

"Maybe some drunked up 'queros," whispered Musty.

Zach's flint lighter flared for a moment. "At half after two a.m.?"

"Well maybe not. They gots more sense than to be gallivanting round this time of morning," agreed Musty.

"We'll stand one-hour watches until dawn. I'll take the first and will pass my pocket watch and lighter on. Be so good as not to twist the stem on top. We'll maintain absolute silence."

Zach didn't need to tell us that.

When the sunrise made a yellow line across the tree tops, I sent Sanchez down to the road to watch it. When it got lighter, I made a big circle round the camp looking for sign. This left Musty and Zach to do up breakfast. As I rode out, Musty was showing the lieutenant how to cut up jerky and stir it into beans with an airtight of stewed tomatoes and how to warm tortillas. I had a suspicion Zach would be doing that for tomorrow's breakfast as everyone else would find more important chores. Zach admitted tortillas was better than army hardtack.

I circled a good hundred yards out. Didn't see a sign one of anyone snooping round. Course I couldn't be dead sure. The ground was hard and rocky and the light still dim. Mesquite shadows cast by the rising sun were long and darkened the ground.

We set off hoping to make it most of the way to Zaragoza at day's end. Sanchez rode ahead. We'd change that job every hour there 'bouts. With seven horses and mules, we crowded the narrow road. More fresh horse tracks on the road. Couldn't say how many.

When it was my turn to bring up the rear and take look-sees behind us, I started thinking. We didn't know much about where we was going, or its layout, and next to nothing about this army that Estevan Guerrero was putting together. A rancher, a *hacendado,* putting together a three-hundred man army to take over part of Mexico and Texas. I ain't figured that one out yet. Man had to be barking dog loco. Or maybe he was real smart. Nah, gotta be as crazy as a drunk raccoon. We did that once at the Triple-Bar. Soaked some bread in cheap rum and left it out for the 'coons. Well, in the morning, oh… never mind.

I don't know if Zach had something in mind, one of those army plans, but I hoped it was something better than the four of us charging in there shooting up the place, blowing those Gatling guns to little pieces, if we got to them, and riding hard as hell for Texas. Course I didn't have any better of a plan than that when I went after Marta. Just track those scoundrels down, grab her, ride hard…and ride some more.

We'd have to sneak into that stronghold or whatever it was. Just like I'd had to sneak into the banditos' camp to find Marta. I'd done what ol' Pancho had taught me back at the Triple-Bar. "Eef joo walk een dee camp of dee enemy, walk like joo belong there, not sneaking round." That's what I'd done. Walked right in there, but easy like. I hadn't found Marta, but I came out with the bandito jefe's sorry-ass brother. I aimed to trade him for Marta, and it worked out, excepting the brother got real dead because he was as stupid as a damn Yankee store clerk come to Texas aiming to be a cattle baron, and Marta's deadeye shooting. Maybe we could do something like that. Or maybe not.

An army in a stronghold. That's a lot different than me tip-toeing round a bandito camp with only seven of them and them all sawing logs.

That stayed in my head, ol' Pancho's, "Walk like joo belong there, not sneaking round." Guerrero was taking gringos into his army, the major said.

"Hell," I said. "We'll just throw in with them."

Zach glanced back at me.

"Just thinking aloud."

I pondered that a spell. The biggest problem I saw was the dynamite. We couldn't just ride in there with it. I thought I'd worked it out and sidled up to Zach. "Got an idea how to do this."

"I would like to hear your proposal."

Proposal? Hell, I ain't asking to marry him. "We don't know squat about the deal there in Las Esperanza. We sure as hell can't go charging in there, and even sneaking in would be a hard chore."

"Agreed."

"So they're taking on gringos. What if we were to sign up as hands, join up with them?"

Zach didn't say nothing. Looked like he was thinking, nodded to himself a couple of times.

"Your proposal has merit, but what about the dynamite? It would be ill-advised to ride in with it. There would be a high probability of it being discovered and if we said we'd brought it for the cause, then we'd have to give it over to them."

"I thought about that. We'd stash it nearby, where all four of us know where it is and can get to it when we need it."

He nodded. "If we have the freedom of movement to come and go as we please or their sentinels are so lax to allow us to freely slip in and out with little risk of detection."

"Yeah, there's that."

"I offer an amendment to your proposal. I admittedly might have difficulty in maintaining a convincing façade to conceal my identity."

"You might be right." His talking is pretty high-toned.

"If you and Sanchez were to join the *Guerreristas*, Mr. Musty and I would establish a covert bivouac in a secluded area. We would maintain contact with you through written messages hidden at some convenient point, a letter cache."

"Cache?"

"It is a French term for a hiding place."

"Can Sanchez read and write?" I asked.

Zach looked at me sideways, I guess figuring I couldn't. "Yes, he can. You would report information, locate the Gatling guns, and devise a plan to recover or destroy them. I would relay any information I acquire to you." He quickly added, "I would of course retain authority to make the final decision on the guns. However, your estimate that it would be more practical to dynamite them is in all likelihood correct."

"Sounds like a good idea. Specially since Sanchez speaks Mex."

"We would also provide support."

"Support?"

"Yes. How to put this? Ah, yes. When, for example, a battalion is deployed in battle, two or three companies will be in the firing line, facing the enemy. Do you follow?"

"Yep."

"One other company is positioned to the rear, allowing it to be moved forward to reinforce the firing line, counterattack an enemy breakthrough, or to move to one flank or the other to protect it if the enemy should advance from that direction."

"Where they could infiladdle the enemy from the flank," I said proudly. I'd learned them army words from Lew, our foreman. He used to be a horse soldier.

Zach just smiled. "Enfilade, I believe it's called."

"So, you would be like this support, come and help us out if need be?"

"Absolutely."

"So we'll be in the middle of an army of *Guerreristas*, and the two of you would be on the outside and come charging in there to pull our butts out of the fire?"

"Yes." He squinted his eyes.

"So how are we supposed to whistle you up?"

Runnels didn't say nothing for a spell. "I understand your concerns. We would retain the dynamite and prepare the charges. We would secret them in a place that you might be able to reach surreptitiously when the time is ripe to destroy the guns. We would also be in a position to cover your withdrawal."

I nodded. Big words, but I knew what he meant—hightailing it like a scalded dog. It would have been good to have someone covering us when Marta and I lit out after exchanging her for the bandito chief's dead brother. That could of gone better.

It sounded like he was thinking like I was, that blowing the guns up straight off was the best deal. No trying to snatch them and run because the guns would have to be in wagons. They'd catch us easy.

"What's it take to blow up one of them things, anyway?"

"Actually, a single half-pound stick inserted between the barrels or in the ejection port will effectively destroy a gun. We will endeavor to use two or three sticks, just to be certain. That would require nine sticks, so we have more than enough to destroy something else, possibly the Gatlings' limbers, *Guerreristas'* magazine, armory, wagons, or some such. It's a possibility to be kept in mind when you are surveilling his facilities."

"We'll see."

We chewed on corndodgers and jerky for dinner. Only a short stop to let the horses graze at a stream crossing, which offered them pretty poor pickings.

Sanchez was pulling cartridges out of his belt loops and doing something with a knife.

"Whatcha got going there?"

"Cutting an X into my bullets."

"You mean like a man that can't write making his mark?"

"Like that. You cut an X in the nose of a bullet, and when it hits a man, it spreads the lead open, making a big mean hole. Puts 'em down real good."

I started cutting an X in my bullets and so did Musty.

We didn't meet a person one on the road. Nothing much out there. No farms, nothing. Poor land. Spied a few head of scrawny free-ranging cattle.

Zach asked if the mangy, skinny cattle were mavericks.

"Yep, they're called *orejanos* here, ain't got no owners, no brands. Folks here 'bouts butcher them as need be."

"So *vaqueros* lasso them for butchering?"

"Nope, peons. They just shoot them with a shotgun."

"Not very sporting."

"They don't have much fun down here and don't fool round none. There's nothing round here to be sportful of."

Zach pulled a blue package out of his saddlebag and started eating...well, what looked like rabbit turds. Seeing I was looking at him queer-like, he said, "Sun-dried table fruit, called raisins. They come from California."

"Raisins?"

"Dried grapes."

"All right. We eat dried apples, pears, and peaches all the time. Boil them up real syrupy-like and put them on hot biscuits or tortillas. Real good. Never heard of dried grapes. Why they get their own special name, raisins?"

"It's from the French name, *raisin sec* for dry grape."

"But they from California?"

"Indeed."

"They speak French in California?"

"No, they do not."

"Then why...never mind."

"I don't know, either," Zach muttered.

Musty come lickety-splitting down the road and pulled up. "Buncha Mexes up the road. Looks like some kinda trouble."

Sanchez had his Winchester out and was standing in his stirrups peering up the road. He levered in a round.

CHAPTER FOURTEEN

We headed up the road with rifles out. Ahead of us two dozen peons wore their white and tan and brown tattered clothes, sombreros, and sandals. Three sat boney, poor-looking horses, and a couple were on burros. Some had worn and battered muzzle-loaders or olden army long rifles. A couple had ancient shotguns, most had nothing but machetes or ironwood clubs. That'll ding your noggin.

Facedown on the road lay a naked man, dead still, so covered with dust and dirt, he looked like the clay dolls kids make. A lariat was under his arms and stringed to a sorry looking saddle. Another rope was over a big mesquite tree limb. Must be the local gallows. Stringed to a burro was a scrawny goat. This Pedro in the dirt was about to become a *piñata*. Maybe that's what all the clubs were for.

The strangest thing was the gringo sitting a big dirty white horse. His hat, coat, and trousers were brown. He was tall, lanky, and as brown as his duds. A brace of well-used Colt Peacemakers hung butts-out on his belt. In a saddle scabbard was a Winchester. He held no guns, but looked to have things well in-hand.

He stared hard at the Mexes, not taking his eyes off one, who looked to be the *jefe*. The tall gringo wore a long, drooping mustache and big lamb chops, all brown too.

"Are you in need of any assistance, sir?" asked Zach.

"No sir. Everything's just peachy," in a gravelly voice.

"May I inquire of the situation here?"

The stranger turned and gave us a once over. "Seems these ol' boys, they're the vigilante here 'bouts, are determined to hang this fella for rustlin' this here sad lookin' goat."

"String him up for goat?" asked Musty. "That ain't right."

"That's what I been tryin' to tell 'em. Stealin' a horse, that's a hangin' offense, but a mangy goat, decidedly irregular. I think he's gotten adequate punishment in the eyes of the law, if there were any law with eyes here 'bouts."

"He still breathing, or are they going to hang him to make their point?" I asked.

"I don't rightly know. He ain't moved none exceptin' some little twitches. They dragged him hell knows how far."

Musty nudged his horse over to the Pedro on the ground and poured some water on him from his water bag. He groaned. One of the Mexes rolled him over, and Musty splashed more on his face, causing him to cough and moan.

"Damn, he been dragged good." I could see a kneecap bone, and gravel was ground into him all over his scraped hide.

The vigilantes were muttering among themselves and seemed displeased at being interrupted in their dispersal of justice by a gringo and now backed — "supported" Zach would say — by more gringos and a darkie.

"Do they not have a town marshal here?" asked Zach.

"Only so-called law out here is *Rurales,* who come round on occasion and hassle them," I said. "Even they wouldn't hang this *vato* just for stealing a goat."

"That's good to hear."

"They'd just shoot him after he dug his own grave."

"Any you gents speak Mex?" the stranger asked. "Mine ain't much beyond askin' for a bottle, a woman, or tradin' horses."

Sanchez brought his horse forward. He was unhappy-like looking at the stranger.

"How 'bout you tellin' this here peon posse we don't mean to interfere, but goat-stealing just ain't a hangin' offense, not even in Mexico."

Sanchez passed that on. The *jefe* got his tail up and rattled something back about not needing no gringo help, especially in Mexico.

"I think it good idea we go," said Sanchez.

I saw what he meant. The peons were grumbling and spreading out. We didn't have no rooster in this cockfight.

"Maybe we outta let 'em take care of their business and mind our own," said Musty.

"That good idea," said Sanchez. "No matter to us. I ain't likely to lose sleep over this."

"That would be the wisest decision," said Zach. "We have other business to attend to."

I wished he'd not said that, because the stranger glanced at him curious-like.

"Here come the real say round these parts," said Musty, peering up the road.

Coming down the road were a batch of women in their black and white dresses. They didn't look none too happy. The oldest one in the lead tore right into the *jefe*. We real fast saw the ladies didn't go for these horse-dragging, lynching shenanigans. The other men were backing off, and some of their wives were giving them a what-for. Some of the younger Pedros wandered off, remembering they had chores.

A couple of young boys led up a burro cart, and the women hollered and badgered until the Pedros loaded that torn up, dragged *vato* into it, none too gentle.

The older woman looked at the stranger and said something. Her face told of a hard life. Hell, all them women had hard faces from living rough.

The stranger looked at Sanchez.

"She say they sorry they bother you with this, but she thank y'all for keeping these fools from doing something stupid."

The stranger swept his hat off and bowed to the lady. *"No hay de qué, señora."*

"Muchas gracias, señor," she said, bowing herself. Remindered me of Gabi at the Dew, a strong-willed, sure-of-herself woman.

According to Sanchez, she went on to say her son was feeble-minded, but knows better than to steal another man's goat. "He only confused. She thankful we save his life and called us honorable men, not like these heroes here, she said."

The stranger told Sanchez, "Tell them I will come this way again and trust I will find this young man in good health." He had his hand on a pistol when he said that, sort of a way to put meaning in his words.

The women left with the cart. Two girls in the back were trying to clean up the poor Pedro. The men followed the cart, keeping their distance from the women.

The goat they let go. Sanchez eyed it.

"We don't need no goat for supper, and we sure don't need no trouble from them vigilantes for goat rustlin'," Musty warned.

We all laughed, including the stranger.

Zach said, "They bore the most ancient of arms. A British Brown Bess musket .69-caliber, and a Harper Ferry .54-caliber Model of 1841 Mississippi rifle. That was used by some American units during the Mexican-American War."

I nudged his shin for sounding so high-brow. "I heard of that fight," I said. "We come out on top, right?"

Zach looked at me surprised. "Most certainly, December 29th, 1845. That's when Texas was admitted to the Union as a state."

"I know that. Just pulling your leg."

"A dark day that was, being made a part of the Damn Yankee United States," grumbled Musty. "How come it's called the Mexican-American War iffin' we won?"

"I don't know that, either," Zach muttered. "You gentlemen have a different perspective of viewing things."

Whatever he meant by that.

I noticed the stranger giving us all a close look over. He was curious about two cowpokes, a dandified dude, and a Black Seminole riding together. No matter the scruffy outfit Zach was wearing, he still looked a dude. I needed to tell him to lose the brilliantine hair oil. He shouldn't be trimming his mustache every morning with a little scissors and mirror, either.

I moved toward the stranger, and passing Zach, whispered, "I'll do the talking."

"Any trouble behind you if you're heading north?" I asked.

"Goin' south as you," he said.

I figured he'd only been a short ways ahead of us, and I wondered if he knew anything or had anything to do with the shots and horses we'd heard. I'd not ask. You don't ask too many questions on the road. It was best to let the other man talk. "We're coming down to look into horse-buying prospects."

"I don't know if you'll find much joy. Some *rancheros* down Las Esperanza way are buyin' up all the horse flesh they can find."

"We ain't heard nothing about that. They lose a lot of horses in the Die-Up?" I asked.

"Not so much," he said. "Don't know what they want them all

for. You'd be better off doin' like me. I'm buyin' yearlin's to run back north and sell to ranchers to restock their herds. Lot of them hard hit."

"True that. You taking them back up by your lonesome?"

"Oh no. Plannin' on hirin' some *vaqueros*. They work cheap, do the best job, and I don't have to pay their way back home."

"Sounds like a good idea." I leaned toward him and stuck out my hand. "Spud Watkins," I said.

"Ormsby Mitchel, from Brackettville," he returned.

Musty introduced himself as Frank Musson. I didn't even know Frank was his real name.

Runnels said his name was Zach Kemble. He told me later Kemble was his mother's maiden name.

Sanchez didn't say nothing. Zach just poked his thumb over his shoulder and said, "Samson Long Shadow."

"Where you all aimin' to head?" he asked.

"Zaragoza's the first stop. Then we'll make the rounds to the rest of *los Cinco Manantiales.* Further south if we have to."

"They got some good horses round the Five Springs," he said, "but most of what they got is goats, more goats than people. Mind if I tag along with you boys as far as Zaragoza?"

I glanced at Zach. He gave a nod. Sanchez winked and tilted his head. As if saying, "Keep an eye on him." I nodded.

"Sure. We expect to make it tomorrow early."

Musty took the lead, and Samson and I fell back. Zach and Mitchel rode side-by-side, doing a lot of talking. I didn't worry too much of Zach letting anything slip. Figured he was feeling out Mitchel.

"You gave me a look," I said to Samson. "Something wrong with Mitchel?"

"I don't know. He look like a cattleman to you?"

"No, he don't. Got a new lariat and no rope-rub marks on his saddle horn. What did you see?"

"No brand on horse. Did not come from ranch. Maybe he buy from horse trader, but that do not sound right."

"You got a good eye," I told him.

There wasn't much going on along the road. We passed or met a few burro and ox carts, some peons on foot. One ol' Pedro and a boy led four burros with huge bundles of yucca leaves. Sanchez said, "They dry the leaves for fire starters, then pile mesquite on it."

We only ran into a couple of *vaqueros*. They said there were no more than the usual dangers, it might be quiet, but anything could happen. They were as talkative as any *vaqueros*. We asked about horses to keep up our story with Mitchel.

We passed a mob of peons, all ages from babes-in-arms to old white-hairs, carrying a litter with a *sarape*-wrapped body.

Came upon a boy with six goat heads lined up on a big rock and shooing away flies. He wanted a peso apiece for them. That had to be the asking price for gringos. Nobody was interested.

We crossed the Rio San Rodrigo, a pretty little clear-water river lined by trees. A couple of girls sat slapping rags on rocks, doing their laundry. I saw they was washing upstream from the ford. Smart, cause if they'd been downstream, anyone crossing would send muddy water down. I'd learned that from Marta. Didn't see no *jacalitos*. Their poor shacks had to be close. The girls didn't bolt when we splashed through the ford, but kept an eye on us. An old man was on the other side of the road propped against a tree fishing... well, sleeping. Didn't look like he minded to catch anything or not.

It was a long day of leaving behind hoof prints and seeing nothing of notice, other than just being in Mexico and expecting about anything.

Coming up on a stream toward dusk, we found two men and three boys confounded with a problem. A dead burro was laying in the stream with water washing over it. They had an old rope round its haunches with the men tugging at it and the boys trying to lever the critter with poles. The rotten rope broke, and the poles weren't getting any purchase on the slippery rock bottom.

One of them Pedros told Samson they lived downstream, and the dead burro was spoiling their water.

Zach paid no mind, but without a word spoken, I readied my lariat and Sampson told the boys to lift the burro's head from the water. Tossing the loop, they caught and cinched it round its neck. Clipper gave his best to drag the expired critter from the water. Them Pedros got all excited, shouting, "*¡Arriba! ¡Ándale!*"

With true peon hospitality, they offered us the mule's hindquarter of our choice. Smelling soggy and more than a few days expired, we *muchas gracias*'ed them and respectively declined.

"As you said, it is different here, Mr. Eug...Spud," Zach said.

Mitchel had ridden ahead a piece, so Sanchez asked the boys if any wagons had gone through anytime recent. "They say four wagons come with about twenty men. Two gringos too. Two day ago."

That had to be the guns, and Jaeger and Kern too. We were closing in on the money-thieving murderers.

"Ask them what color the wagons were," said Zach.

Sanchez said, "Black with red wheels and little white lines."

"Yeah, Kraut freighters," I said. "They like to paint their wagons the Kraut flag colors."

Sanchez paid the boys some centavos to catch him a couple of dozen crawfishes they fetched up. They were big ones. *Langostinos*, the Mexes called them.

Our night was about the same as the night before with the supper fire well off the road. Sanchez leveled some of the glowing coals and tossed them crawfishes on. They baked in a minute, and he passed them round. We plucked off the heads, legs, and little nippers and pulled the meat out of the shells. They was surely good with warm tortillas and apricot preserves. We each got a couple of more to treat on because Zach shook his head. Didn't know what he was missing by eating an airtight of corned beef and potato hash.

We moved to a no-fire campsite. Zach gave Mitchel the first watch, knowing most of us would still be awake. We weren't taking no chances with the stranger. He knew that.

It was a quiet night.

Chapter Fifteen

I always woke up early when in a bedroll on the trail. Sleeping in a room, it wasn't the same. Didn't know why, except I felt that open sky and nothing was closing me in.

I liked to see the sun come up. All I had to do was roll over and look east. There was a yellow line cross the horizon, the sky pink and milky blue. I liked it too with Marta spooned up to me and smelling of spices and fire. When on the trail, I knew she'd been up already making breakfast at the Dew. I would have surely liked to be drinking a cup of her coffee and watching her cook. I could almost smell it. Made me miss my woman all the more.

Clipper snorted, and Zach and Musty were making wake-up noises. Mitchel was up watering a bush. Sanchez already had a fire going with the coffee pot on. He knew how to do it right. Bring it to a boil and let it sit until the boil died down. Then he put in the coffee and slowly stirred it into the water. He let it sit for a couple of more minutes before stirring it again. He put in a shot of salt and stirred more. I ain't ever figure out how, but that salt takes the bitter taste out.

Saddling Clipper, I made a couple of circles round the camp and then looked over the road. Nothing out of the ordinary.

Musty had brought a tin of bacon grease, and Sanchez was frying jerky in a skillet. Then he fried up corndodgers in the sizzling grease. I opened an airtight of peaches with one of those new lever can openers and passed the can round.

Mitchel contributed some board-stiff tortillas. I sprinkled water on mine and held it over the fire on a green stick for a short spell, and that made them softer and gooder. Learned that from Marta.

I know one thing. Mitchel hadn't said nothing, but he didn't have no use for Sanchez. I guess I used to be that way too, the customary Texican way, but I sure learned lots about people from Marta and Flaco the past few months.

Zaragoza wasn't too far. We were looking to rid ourselves of Mitchel. Zach said he'd gotten nothing meaningful out of him when they talked. The longer he herded with us, the more nervous-making he was. When we first talked about this, we were going to go round those towns with just Sanchez passing through to get news, but with Mitchel along, we had to look like we were really in the market for horses and had to go through town.

We rode into Zaragoza before noon. Not many folks round, mostly kids and goats. Lots of goats. We headed to the *Presidencia Municipal*, like the city hall, to get names of horse breeders.

With that, Mitchel said he'd part with us and was going on to Las Esperanza. He seemed as glad to be rid of us as we were of him.

We watched him ride down the street, and he disappeared with a wave. With him traveling alone, riding his fine looking horse, most likely he wouldn't never be seen again.

Sanchez shook his head. "His name's Nathaniel Bunt. He's a Texas Ranger. I seen him at Fort Duncan a couple of times."

"You shittin' me!" said Musty.

He made that hissing noise injuns make to be quiet.

We rode quiet for a spell. Zach looked rattled.

"He said he's going to Las Esperanza. You think he's going down to spy, maybe even join up himself? I asked.

"Most likely," said Sanchez.

After a spell, Zach said, "I didn't recognize him, but he has a reputation for undertaking special assignments. He took care of that election dispute down in Webb County without it turning into a war, and no one was killed this time. The governor always has Bunt with him when he's visiting border towns."

"He don't know you?" asked Sanchez.

"No. He does not."

Sanchez spit on the ground. "I ain't got no damn use for Rangers."

"We'll have to keep an eye out for him in Las Esperanza," I said.

"Indeed," said Zach. "He could complicate our mission."

The adobe houses sat square on the narrow streets. No boardwalks.

"Streets sure skinny," Musty said.

"They have law that say so," said Sanchez.

That perked up Zach. "How so?"

"They called Laws of the Indies. Tells how towns and villages are built. Laws the Spanish bring. Where it mostly hot, streets are narrow, and mostly cold, they are wide."

"What difference does that make?" asked Zach.

"Narrow streets be in the shade more. Wide streets get more sunlight."

"That makes good sense from an engineering and human habitation standpoint," said Zach.

What the heck is he talking about?

"Mexes not as dumb as you think," Sanchez said. "Wide streets too for town that are *presidios,* eh, army forts. Wide streets for horses to move through."

Zach nodded. "And military defensive principals considered too."

The streets were pretty straight, but not as true as in most towns. The plaza was only two blocks from the river. We pulled up to the *Presidencia Municipal* on the plaza's south side.

"Y'all best stays out here." Sanchez went into the big adobe building to find out the names of breeders and any news.

Sanchez came out after a spell with some breeder names. Course we weren't really buying no horses, but it was best to have a supposed reason for being there.

"There's big talk about Guerrero and strange goings on down there. They say Las Esperanza not a good place to go. Ex-soldiers, bandits, troublemakers all go down there."

"Shucks, sounds like the Double Eagle," said Musty, winking at me. "We'll fit in as snug as a cartridge in a gun chamber."

"They also say we not find many horses round here."

"Good thing we ain't really aimin' to buy," muttered Musty.

"They say somethin' else," said Sanchez. "I ask about wagons coming through. They say four with maybe ten, twelve men."

"Only a dozen men?" said Zach. "The last report was twenty."

"And I ask, they say no gringos."

That got my attention. Where were Jaeger and Kern?

"They must have split off, but for what purpose?" Zach asked.

No one had any ideas. "We'll have to be all the more alert," said Zach.

Musty was hoping we'd find a cantina to stay at overnight.

"We have some things to talk about," said Zach. "I don't think we should stay in town. There's too many prying eyes. However, I wish to reconnoiter this town."

We rode through Zaragoza taking it easy. No one seemed to pay much attention, but I knew they were looking us over and words were flying about.

I saw Zach was making a map of the village in his notebook. "If the towns of the Five Springs are Guerrero's objective, then American forces may have to engage here. I'm making a map and noting key features such as the town hall, church, water wells, the cemetery, and so on. I'll map Morelos and Allende too."

Two of the towns, Nava and Villa Unión, were too far out of the way.

Sanchez found a shop with a sign hung, *CARNICERIA*. A butcher. He bought a butchered kid goat along with some onions and a dollop of lard wrapped in greasy paper. He also got fresh tortillas at a *panadería*. Zach wrote the expenses in his notebook.

Morelos was only a few miles south, and Zach mapped the smaller village with its straight streets. I guess Zach was right to do the mapmaking, but we were sure attracting attention, even if it didn't look like it. Sanchez kept remindering us to smile and nod at people on the streets. "Makes big difference on what they think 'bout ya."

"There's three places called Morelos in Mexico," said Sanchez. "This village, and way south near Mexico City is a bigger city and state called Morelos."

We stopped at the *Presidencia Municipal* and got horse breeders' names there too.

"Not many horses round here the man say," reported Sanchez. "He say they have all the goats we ever need."

We took special care picking camp that night. Went way into the mesquite in a direction away from Nava, but toward Allende. Sanchez had let drop we'd be heading to Nava, which we weren't. I worried about Allende tomorrow, though. It was certain that word had spread of us strangers. Mexes are usually hospitable, but we could tell things were uneven here. The Pedros here abouts looked uneasy, like they was expecting a lightning storm.

We stopped early, and Sanchez dressed the goat while Musty got the fire up. I stayed horsed and scouted out all round. I didn't want no surprises while we were supping in case someone was looking for us.

We raised a lot of smoke, so when it was done, we doused the fire and moved aways off to eat. The goat was juicy and dang good. Musty had done up refried beans with lard cooked in it. He'd also cooked up dried pears in sugar and water syrup with a dash of bourbon for desert.

After eating, we moved again as the sun set. It was a quiet night, but I didn't much sleep thinking about Marta, that we were drawing too much attention, and what was waiting for us in Las Esperanza. I also thought about Brownie Jaeger. He'd coldblooded murdered Mr. Bellwood at the bank, took me and Marta's money, and a lot of other poor hardworking folks' money. I swore there was no way he was coming outta of this breathing.

It was still two days to Las Esperanza. We needed to get down there and find them guns…and my money.

We got an early start after a quick cold breakfast. We were only a mile from Allende, and the road to Las Esperanza ran through the town, the largest of the Five Springs' villages.

Usually there were lots of folks on the roads between towns in the morning before it gets hot, but there was no one to be seen. Then we come upon a buckboard with two old men in it. It was pulled to the roadside, and they watched us pass. They didn't say anything back when we *buenos días*'ed them. Sanchez give me a sharp look.

I said, "Mus, ease on up ahead a piece. Rifles out, everyone. Y'all keep your eyes peeled. We're about to get dry-gulched."

Zach's eyes got big. Sanchez went deadly slit-eyed. Musty grinned.

"Zach, you cover the left. Sanchez, right. I'm dropping back." I could cover them, being good for long shots, and watch our backside.

Coming round barely a curve, there was a supposed-to-be-hurt boy lying in the road. *Here we go.* I swung to check our behind.

"*¡Dispara el muchacho!*" shouted Sanchez, spurring his horse and cracking a shot into the air.

That "hurt" kid upped and ran like a birdshot-stung coyote.

A man jumped out of the mesquite behind us. My rifle was up. "*¡Alto! ¡Yo disparo!*" He dropped his long shotgun and stuck his hands up. I heard men busting through the mesquite up ahead, high-tailing it outta there. They knew the jig was up and most likely didn't have no heart in the dastardly scheme. Musty fired a couple of shots into the sky to hurry them.

Sanchez sawed round and trotted up to the Pedro I had in my sights. He ripped loose with some strong words. I picked up he was asking if this is how they treat visitors in Allende, and that he had dishonored his town, his family, and himself. He told him to unload his Greener Facile Princeps shotgun—he plucked out two 12-gauge shells—threw it into the mesquite, and sent him shamefaced up the road. Told him he was lucky to still be among the living.

"They no bother us no more."

"What'd ya say to set that kid a runnin'?" asked Musty.

"Shoot the boy."

"That'll do it," said Musty with a laugh.

Shortly Zach sidled up by me. "I have to admit, I didn't see anything out of the ordinary. How did you..."

"Got no idea. Just learned to stay alive out here. It's *la Frontera*."

"Is there still any danger?"

"We in Mexico, ain't we?"

Those dummies back there weren't no real banditos, just down and outs probably suspecting we had some *dinero*. I was still nervous, but nothing more happened. Zach wanted to spend as little time as we could in Allende. He set to making his map, but it wasn't so detailed as the others. We didn't take time to find out who any horse breeders were.

The railroad station was on the southeast side of town. Zach said that was important and also marked where the water tank and coal yard were.

Musty said something to Sanchez, and they went up to the stationmaster's office—*jefe de estación*. They came back, and Musty said it was two days ride to Las Esperanza and no telling if we'd have to deal with more bushwhackers. He also said there was a couple of shifty-eyed characters hanging out at the station. They both had pistols. Not something you saw in the open down there, excepting for banditos on the job.

"The morning southbound from Piedras Negras is comin' soon," said Musty.

"What of it?" asked Zach.

"It stops at San Juan de Sabinas."

"Where is that?"

"The nearest stop to Las Esperanza. For fourteen bucks, the four of us and the horses, we'll be in Sabinas in a few hours."

We had a quick talk. Since Zach and Musty were to stay hidden when we got to Las Esperanza, they would get off the train with our spares and the mules at Peyotes, the stop about ten miles before Sabinas. They didn't need to be seen with us.

Sanchez said, "There's a big *almacén*, eh, a warehouse, opposite the station in Sabinas. Bud and I wait for you there. We meet you there tonight. That good, sir?"

Zach nodded. "Then we'll make our way twelve miles to Las Esperanza and find a covert bivouac for us and a place near Guerrero's ranch for the letter cache."

We worked out the plan. If the warehouse wasn't a good place to meet, we'd meet under the Rio Sabinas railroad bridge just southwest of the station.

A half-hour later, *Ferrocarril Internacional Mexicano* locomotive No. 103 chugged into the station with two passenger cars, six boxcars, two flatcars, and a gondola stacked with feedbags.

While Sanchez and Musty hazed the horses and pack mules into a boxcar, Zach said, "That Musty was thinking. Good idea this." Zach put the receipt he got from the stationmaster in his notebook.

I nodded. "He's a good man to have your back."

"Fourteen bucks," muttered Musty, walking up to me. "Almost half what I make a month."

It came to me that I hadn't never been on a railroad train.

I never rode a horse that could lope as fast as that train. We rode in the boxcar with the horses. Too many curious people in the passenger cars that might ask questions. The smell got so bad, we shoveled horseshit out the door. Sanchez sat in the door swinging his legs. I was nervous about being too close to the door. After a spell and seeing Sanchez hadn't fallen out, I took a floor seat, but kept my legs inside. He said in the army they rode a lot of trains. Zach sat against a wall and wrote in his notebook. Musty stayed way back from the door. "I'll keep the horses settled down."

Black smoke poured past, and the flat land stretched out forever, mesquite, yucca, cactus, and rocks. Flat land would make it good if we had to ride back hard, but anyone chasing us could ride fast too.

We made a stop at Leons where bundles of cowhides were loaded and old feed sacks with cattle bones and horns sticking out. The station was just a shed. Saw a few poor cane and mesquite stick *jacalitos* and weather-beat adobes nearby. A family got off with a batch of kids and a half-dozen goats. No one got on. Like at Allende, there were two hombres with pistols and a shotgun. They were looking over the train good, including the family that got off. Sanchez whispered, "Don't pay 'em no mind." We stayed in the dark back of the boxcar.

The next stop was Peyotes. Nearby was a ranch giving its name to the stop. There weren't no watchers there for some reason. That was good because it was where we parted ways with Zach and Musty until that night.

We helped them get the three horses and two mules off, them being hesitant to jump the three feet to the ground. There was no platform, just a heavy wooden ramp, but there weren't anyone to help lift it up. Sanchez told us to act like we didn't know Zach and Musty. No goodbyes.

Me and Sanchez leaned out the door, with me hanging on tight, and watched them get smaller as the train picked up speed. I surely didn't like leaving them back there. Just too many things could go wrong. It's Mexico.

CHAPTER SIXTEEN

The locomotive's whistle blew when we passed a sign: SABI-NAS.

"We don't hang round here," said Sanchez. "We get off and leave, pronto."

I nodded. We shut the door on the right side where the station would be and opened the other door.

The train slowed to a stop with a lot of banging and squealing and hissing steam. The horses spooked every time that happened. We jumped to the ground and tugged on the reins to trick the horses out. They took little dancing steps and finally came out, their forelegs reaching for the ground. Clipper gave me a snort, telling me he didn't like this. Sanchez' horse even nipped at him he was so offended.

"You give him a name yet?" I asked.

"Ocala, it mean Spring in Seminole. That's when I got him, it's springtime."

Sanchez was antsy to get a move on. Down the track a couple of *pistoleros* were watching folks getting off the passenger cars. The warehouse he'd told us about was across a siding track with a long train of ore cars full of coal.

Coal dust was on everything and blown by the wind. Kids with baskets, feed sacks, and woven straw tote bags picked up coal lumps that had fallen off the train. The runny nosed kids were coal dust-covered too. Some of them kids were littler than the sacks they dragged.

They'd fight over choice chunks of coal with the bigger kids, even girls, beating up each other and on the little ones too. Gotta hand it to the little ones. They was tough and sometimes won out cause they stuck together. Sanchez said they sold the coal on the street for money, food, clothes, or whatnot.

There was one girl, maybe eleven, twelve reached for a big chunk, and an older boy kicked it away and grabbed it. That girl lit out after him, jumped on his back, knocked his face into the dirt, yanked his bag from him, dumped it out, got her chunk, gave him a good kick in the ribs, and went back to hunting coal. The boy was smart enough to stay to the other side of the tracks. She walked by, and I winked at her. She gave me a grin back from her soot-dusty face, wiping at a bloody nose. Got me to missing Marta.

I waved her over. She come, but kept an eye on me and stayed a safe distance. That *niña* wanted the outrageous price of one peso for her whole sack of coal. She surely knew how to dupe a gringo, but I was a crafty barterer. I held out for *two* pesos. And dang if I didn't walk off after paying her and plum forget that ol' sack of coal and couple of twists of jerky wrapped in grease paper. Guess we were just going to have to cook with mesquite sticks and cow chips that night.

We walked the horses to the end of the coal train and rounded it to the warehouse. It was a big adobe building maybe a hundred feet long, thirty feet wide, double doors on both ends, and little windows way up high. All closed up and no one around. We walked round behind it, leading the horses. There was thick mesquite back there.

"We wait in brush for Zach and Musty."

"Going to be a long night waiting up for them. No telling what time they'll show."

Sanchez wanted to look at the doors. I think he was wondering if there might be something of value inside. Big heavy padlocks on the strap iron-reinforced doors.

Clipper nickered and two *pistoleros* come round the end of the warehouse and another round the other side, revolvers drawn, excepting one with a leveled scattergun. Those 12-gauge barrels looked like railroad tunnels.

"¡*Manos Arriba!*"

We already had our hands up. They plumb got the drop on us.

The shotgun man looked to be the *jefe*. They marched us to a man-door set in the big double doors. The *jefe* unlocked the small door and said, *"Ve adentro."* We went in, got told to drop our gun belts.

It was dark at first, but enough light come through the windows way up high to make things out. There were some freight wagons, lots of empty crates, piles of empty sacks, a big stack of railroad ties, kegs of spikes, and a bunch of tools like spike hammers, picks, shovels, and pry bars. Even a little pump-handle handcar.

The *jefe* told Sanchez a bunch of stuff, and he picked up two shovels and two picks. This weren't looking good.

"What's up? They ain't even asking us who we are or what we're doing here."

"They no care. They say we have money, and they're takin' our horses and guns. They just robbers."

"¡Cállate!" the *jefe* kept yelling.

"You still gotta gun tucked away?" Sanchez asked.

"Yeah."

"I gotta blade. Be ready when I make move."

I nodded. Sanchez weren't saying any American words that sounded like Mex words, like pistol.

They pushed us back outside and into the brush where we started digging holes. One asshole with a big mustache kept chucking rocks at me and not Sanchez. Must have not liked gringos. *You're going the hard way.* The other real skinny *pistolero* kept telling him to stop, to have respect for the dead, I think.

I was worried about my gun showing tucked into the back of my pants and covered by my vest. I could tell Sanchez was eyeballing the *pistoleros*, watching where they was standing. One was always behind me, no matter which way I turned to work on my grave.

Sanchez, all of a sudden like, plopped down on the edge of his hole and said, *"Está demasiado caliente. Agua, por favor."*

Skinny kicked at Sanchez, who twisted round, threw his right arm over Skinny's left leg, yanked him into the hole, and as he scooted past Sanchez, his flick knife slashed the fella's throat. I threw the shovel over my shoulder hoping at least to make Mustache duck. I yanked my pistol out and fired at Shotgun as he raised it. The bullet hit him square on the chin, took off most of his jaw, and come out under his left ear. That X cut in the bullet made a mess. Sanchez slung his pick at Mustache. I turned and fired twice at Mustache, and the slugs hit him in the belly and chest as he lifted his pistol. None of them got one shot off. Skinny was clutching his throat, kicking, but that eased off as his spraying blood played out. Mustache laid there coughing up blood. Tough luck. Shotgun didn't even twitch he was so dead.

"You good?" Sanchez said.

"I'm good. You?"

"No."

That scared me. "You hit?" I stepped toward him.

He was looking at me real sad like. "We gotta dig another hole."

"Ha! Least we got picks and shovels."

First we went over to the siding to see if the three shots had attracted attention. The coal scroungers acted like they hadn't heard a thing. I reloaded my Schofield using .45 Colt cartridges from Mustache's gun belt. He was still coughing up stuff and gagging and gurgling.

I started digging the third hole. Sanchez unsaddled the *pistoleros'* horses, hid their tack and gun rigs in the warehouse, and locked it, keeping the keys. He ran off the horses, and we finished up the burying chore. Mustache had finished his gurgling by the time I rolled him into his hole for his forever dirt nap. I hated leaving those guns behind: five revolvers, three of them Colt '73s, a Smith Russian, and a Richards-Mason Colt Army conversion; two Winchester carbines, and a Remington 12-gauge coach gun, 20-inch barrels. They'd of brought in good money. No way to sell them round there without drawing attention. I did find a nice little walnut handled penknife, and we split the forty-two pesos we found on them. Not much food, just some tortillas and *carne seca* — Mex jerky.

I thought they might have been *Guerreristas*, but since men were riding in to join up, including gringos, I couldn't figure why they were going to squabash us. No orange sashes in their saddlebags.

"I think they jus' banditos looking for an easy mark," said Sanchez.

"Fooled them, didn't we?" I said, wiping my hands off.

"You bet, pard," he said with a grin. He glanced at me, then away knowing he was out of line.

That gave me a start, a darkie injun calling me "pard." But thinking on it, it didn't bother me none. I think if Marta had taught me anything, and she'd taught me a lot, it was to judge a person for what they were their own-self, not what they looked like.

I looked Sanchez in the eye. "We done good, real good working together on that dust up. You can call me pard all you want."

He nodded.

We went way into the brush in case someone came looking for those *pistoleros*. We ate a cold supper before it got dark. Way after dark we moved up near the warehouse real cautious-like to wait for Musty and Zach.

Good thing we were careful. Soon two men come riding round the warehouse, and they weren't Musty and Zach. They rounded the place and left. Nothing special about them, excepting they wore orange sashes we made out in the station light. Sashes or not, we couldn't join up with them now. Still had things to do.

Seeing the warehouse wasn't safe, we headed down to the Rio Sabinas Bridge and waited there. Seemed the warehouse was a popular place for undesirables. The bridge was only about six hundred yards southwest. There was an embankment, maybe twenty feet deep. We found a good place where we could see anyone at the top of the embankment. The river down there was maybe a hundred and fifty yards cross. The bridge was about twice as long to reach from bank to bank. The iron bridge was perched on nine stone pillars. It was the biggest-most bridge I'd ever seen, excepting the one over the Rio Grande at Eagle Pass.

There was plenty of moon and starlight to see by. We tied up the horses back in the mesquite, unsaddled them, and sat ourselves for a long wait. No telling when they'd come riding in. Hoping they didn't run into no trouble. After our own dust up, I was even more nervy for Musty and Zach.

Mex towns were quiet at night. Dogs barking sometimes, someone laughing, a shout, or a baby crying. We munched on our found *carne seca*, lying against the saddles and taking turns dozing. Probably after midnight Sanchez said, "We oughta saddle up in case we have reason to skedaddle when Zach and Musty come in."

Sanchez nudged me awake. "They here," he whispered.

Sure enough, I could make out a mob of horses by the bridge.

Sanchez real quiet took off on foot. In a few minutes he was back. "They good, no problems."

And I'd been worried about *them*. We walked the horses to the bridge.

"Howdy, pard," whispered Musty. "Why here? The warehouse no good?"

"I'll tell you later," I said, shaking his hand.

Zach shook my hand. Glad to be back with us. "No commander likes to divide his forces," he said.

We still had to get through the town and find an out of the way campsite. We followed the road atop the riverbank and headed through the town as quiet as seven horses and mules could manage. They all cooperated for once, like they knew things were dicey.

Outside of town, the road branched into several trails. We had no idea which to take, but they all fanned out more or less north.

"I think we should follow the leftmost trail as it parallels the river," said Zach. "That will supply us water, and the abundant vegetation along the bank is good for a concealed bivouac."

"It's also probably the most traveled of the trails. Not a good idea," I said. I'd gotten off Clipper and was looking at the ground best I could in the moonlight. "Best we take this one. Less horse tracks and cart tracks."

"We'd have no idea where we're going if we randomly follow a trail." Zach wasn't one for giving up on his ideas easy like. "At least we can keep our bearings following the river."

"No matter," I said. He was forgetting I had say on how we got to where we're going. "We'll sort it out at daylight. Nothing else, Sanchez can find somebody to ask."

I climbed back on and headed up the trail I thought best.

After about a mile we came across a stream and took time to water all the horses and fill canteens and water bags. Upstream maybe a hundred yards was a big patch of mesquite and scrub trees good for a hidden camp. We set a picket line for the horses and spread bedrolls. Zach said, "It's going on four o'clock. Not much over three hours till drawn."

"Long day," I said.

"It was," said Musty.

"Yep," said Sanchez.

CHAPTER SEVENTEEN

The sun was up good when we woke up. Zach said we had a lot to do. We choked down a cold breakfast, loaded the horses, and headed out. The ground rose to the left in stepped ridge-lines. More trees. It came to me that today is when we're going in to join up to whatever this all is.

We come cross an old man toting a pack basket with ears of corn. Sanchez asked him the way to Las Esperanza.

"He says two or three leagues. That's maybe eight miles give or take. Up yonder there's a fork. We take the right one. Best to follow the railroad, he says. There's a spur line to the coal mine."

"We don't want to follow that," said Zach. "It will no doubt be watched."

Sure 'nough, not far up the road was a fork. It got hillier, more trees and bush. Little streams too. Over the low trees we spied gray dust clouds drifting cross the sky.

"Sabinas coal mines," said Zach. "Let us halt and consider our movements."

We dismounted for a leg stretch and piss. Zach said, "They will have patrols out, or at least an *avant-poste* on the roads. We must reconnoiter with caution, and we do not want to be seen together."

"Me and Sanchez are going to have to ride in there sometime. The sooner the better," I said.

"Indeed. First we must locate our hidden bivouac and the site for the letter cache. We all need to know where both sites are located be-

fore we split up. We'll move cross country to determine where Guerrero's ranch or base is. We'll select a letter cache at a site that can be
conveniently and covertly reached at night from the base. Then we'll
select the hidden bivouac."

"Covertly?" I asked.

"Secretly, not letting anyone see you."

"Bivouac?"

"A camp," he said.

"Why not just say camp?"

"It's French. Civilians camp, soldiers bivouac."

"Then why you call it Camp Del Rio?"

Zach looked like he was going to say something, but gave it up.

"For your secret camp," I said, "we need to set it near a landmark
we can find at night, and it better be near a stream for the horses."

"Absolutely."

We turned left off the road through scattered trees and brush. Figured it would be best to go into the bush because of road lookouts.
We wanted to get the lay of the land, see where this ranch was first.
We rode upslope over good traveling ground. A clear sky. Quiet too
except for a steam whistle blowing in the distance sometimes.

We injun-filed through the trees with a good break between us,
Sanchez up front, then Musty with the mules, Zach, and then myself
keeping an eye on our back-trail. Through the trees I could see the
mine's chimney, black smoke pouring out. Must have been two hundred feet tall. Never seen nothing like that.

We crossed a branch of the Rio Sabinas. The ground got hillier and
the trees and brush thicker. We were south of the mine.

A flock of big turkeys flapped out of the brush making for the sky.
Scared the livin' daylights out of us and the horses. We crossed a lot
of small arroyos, mostly dry, some not.

We were cresting a low ridge thick with trees. Sanchez held up a
hand without looking back. We stopped. He waved us to dismount.
Tying our horses off, we went up to him. He didn't signal for rifles.

"This look like what we're looking for."

There was a big adobe-walled hacienda almost a mile away with a
two-floor *casa* and smaller buildings, workshops and storage. There
were a couple of big barns with high tin roofs nearby and a warehouse. A little farther off were a dozen adobe houses. Outside the
walls were big *potreros* with more saddle horses than you ever see
on a ranch. Other round corrals penned mules and oxen. Nearby

were lines of wagons and carts. No mules or oxen were hitched to them. Across a cornfield from the hacienda were rows of white tents, square ones and round ones. There were sheds and smoking cook-houses. It was a busy place with men walking and running all over the place, a few women too, and men on horses riding to and fro. There were windmills with water tanks, one in the walled hacienda, one by the corrals, and another behind the houses.

It was a way bigger-looking army camp than was in Del Rio or Eagle Pass.

We were laying in a thicket. Zach, lowering his field glasses, muttered, "There's no flags."

He had his notebook open and was drawing a map of the hacienda and camp across two pages. Took him a spell. We watched all the goings on. There were some groups of men marching round like soldiers—I guess they were. Other groups were on horses. The more I watched, the less I liked the idea of going down amongst them.

After a lot of working his pencil, Zach said, "There's about eighty tents. With four men per tent, that's three hundred and twenty."

"That's a lot of men," said Musty.

"Only an estimate," said Zach. "Some tents might not be full. Additionally, there are other places to quarter troops, the barns, houses, and so on." After giving the place another sweep with his field glasses, "Could be substantially fewer than three hundred, could be far more than four hundred." Looking at me, "I hope you and Sanchez can make a better estimate once you infiltrate the insurgents."

"I guess."

"Use caution when asking for strengths, organization, and what their plans are. If you're too inquisitive, they may become suspicious."

"Got it," I said. *Let's get this roundup going.*

Zach said, "That wraps it up. I was able to note a great amount of detail." Besides the map, he'd wrote a lot of stuff about what he saw.

Sanchez had been looking through the field glasses and said, "See that long arroyo lined by trees? The one running to the southwest, sir?"

"Yes, I do."

"That might be a good way to sneak out to a letter cache, maybe inside the woods it runs into."

"Then let us reconnoiter that area," said Zach.

We mounted and worked our way through the woods about a

quarter-mile. The arroyo ran into the woods and proved to be running with water. Inside the woods we scairt up a couple of deer.

Musty said. "Lots of game here. We won't want for fresh meat."

"That means shooting, which we should avoid," said Zach.

"Sure, we move away to hunt and only take one shot. No one can guess the direction and how far by one shot."

"Can you bag a deer with a single shot?"

Sanchez grinned. Musty rolled his eyes at Zach. Zach said no more about it.

We followed the arroyo deeper into the woods. It was about four to six feet wide, a foot or two deep. Good, clear water. There was a rock outcropping maybe ten-foot high, lots of rocks all sizes scattered round. We dismounted when Zach asked if I thought this would be easy to find in the dark.

"Sure 'nough." There was a flat slab of rock beside the outcropping. I picked up a flagstone about a foot square and set it on the slab. "This good 'nough to put a letter under?"

"It certainly is." Zach picked up two fist-sized rocks and set one then the other on the flagstone. "When you insert a letter, place one of these rocks atop the stone. That way we'll know there's a letter awaiting us."

Musty and I nodded. Sanchez said, "Yes, sir."

"If you come here and the one rock's still there, then we've not picked up the letter. If you see two rocks," setting the second rock on the flat one, "that means we've left a letter."

"Got you," I said.

"We need a danger sign as well," said Zach. He studied the rocks and said, "A third rock. If you see three rocks, then we are in trouble and avoid the cache. Then using caution, check the bivouac to detect any foul play."

"Sounds good," I said.

"Now we must attend to locating our covert bivouac."

"How's bout we jus' follow this arroyo on further, maybe find a good place upstream?" said Musty.

"Let us make it so," said Zach, mounting his Morgan.

We came across a fresh javelina wallow and spooked a three-point buck, its white flag running through the trees.

Zach pointed out a couple of good campsites — bivouacs — but Musty said they needed something set back from the arroyo. The water running over rocks could cover the sound of anyone coming through. We took turns looping out from the arroyo looking for such a place. Presently Sanchez came in. "Found good place. Less than a hundred yards."

He was right. It was a good camp. Lots of brush round it for cover, but with a few small clearings nearby. We'd put up a one-rope corral round a clearing to keep the horses and mules pinned and let them graze. The rope would be moved to another clearing when they'd munched down the grass. The stream was close enough to water them. Musty picked a patch of brush that they could set up a tarp and camp there. Plenty of firewood and cow chips laying about. It was less than half a mile from the letter cache. They'd check it at first light every day.

We helped set up camp. Near the arroyo's bank was a big fallen juniper. It was a good landmark, easy to see at night. Zach told us to bang two sticks together just loud enough to be heard if we came here day or night. They'd answer back with the same.

Sanchez said, "Don't take the same path every day, following the arroyo. That'll leave a trail 'fore long. Swing through the woods and use the other side some days."

We all worked on the camp. No telling how long they'd be here, which meant no telling how long we'd be down below with the *Guerreristas*.

The closer it got to the time to make our move, the less good I felt about it. I kept having to think about that money — was there even any way I could get near my money? Was there any way we could even get near those Gatlings? Would we be able to get out of the base to leave secret letters? But there was Marta. She wanted that ranch, and so did I.

Late in the afternoon Zach called me and Sanchez over. We had a sit-down in the lean-to we'd been working on. He was all serious like.

"Gentlemen, I admire you both for volunteering for this mission. I admire your bravery, and I know in my heart that you have the skills and expertise to carry this off. Your country is counting on you."

I said, "I'll give it my best," but didn't put a lot of feeling into it.

Sanchez only said, "Yes, sir."

Zach looked all raring to go, excepting I was the one going. "The more difficulty, the more glory."

Right.

He talked for a long spell about what kind of information he needed from us, about the Gatlings and where they were, their guards, if we could find out anything about Guerrero's plans, number of men, what we thought about the leadership and morale. That means the state of mind his men were in.

"Don't make any direct inquiries about the Gatlings," he warned. "Someone's bound to eventually mention them."

"Got it."

"You all need to be familiar with the dynamite," Zach told us with a serious look. He waved Musty over.

He was holding a paraffin-covered tan paper stick of dynamite between two fingers like a delicate tea cup at the Fitch Hotel. "Gentlemen, we have twenty-five, half-pound cartridges of Nobel's Extra ammonium nitrate dynamite. Each cartridge is an inch and an eighth in diameter and eight inches long. They're rated as eighty-five percent. That means they're eighty-five percent as powerful as the same amount of nitroglycerin blasting oil. Dynamite is made from three parts nitroglycerin and one part chalk powder as a stabilizer."

I didn't ask what that was, but it sounded like it was a good thing.

Zach told us dynamite had to be kept out of the sun and kept dry. If it got too hot, it would sweat nitroglycerin. It was very dangerous in that condition, and we weren't to handle it and to get rid of it. "Don't' throw it away literally. Rather, carefully bury it in an out of the way place." It could be lit by a match and burn, but probably not blow up.

Probably not? Well, I surely wasn't sticking round to find out if that happened.

He said, "A gunshot striking a dynamite cartridge will detonate it."

He showed us the Bickford fuse, sort of a tar-covered cord smaller than a tie cord. He said it had a core of gunpowder. It had to be kept dry too, and before using it, to cut off four to six inches off the end because it had soaked up humidity. It burned thirty seconds to the foot. With about six inches of fuse on a cartridge we could throw it to go off in fifteen seconds. He said to be careful because the gunpowder inside the fuse was burning a little ahead of the flame on the outside.

Next was blasting caps, copper tubes smaller than a cig. Zach stuck the fuse in one end of the cap and said, "It has a very touchy explosive in it." He had a thing like a pliers he called a fuse cutter. It could cut the Bickford fuse, crimp the cap onto the fuse, and one handle had a pointed end. He pushed it into the end of a dynamite stick and stuck in a blasting cap with a length of fuse.

"When we destroy the Gatling guns, one cartridge will suffice, but three inserted between the barrels, the ejection port too, would ensure complete destruction. Use at least a one-foot fuse. One fused stick will set off the other two."

The blasting stuff would stay with Zach. We wouldn't take a single stick with us.

"Let's do this," I said. "I don't wanna put this off no more."

We saddled up, and Zach and I checked Sanchez, making sure he didn't have anything army-looking. Zach told me to hand my orange sash over to Musty. It didn't need to be found on me.

Musty shook my hand. "Bud, if things get dicey in there, ya get your butt out pronto. Don't let trying to get that money back or anything else keep ya there beyond good sense."

I started to say something.

"I know what ya're going to say, but ya gotta think of that little gal. What it'll do to her if ya don't come back."

I couldn't say nothing now.

"We will be here to support you in any way we can," said Zach. No matter all his talk of honor and glory, I knew he meant it.

"We'll try and get a letter back here tomorrow night."

"Do not take any unnecessary risks to come back here. They may keep you under scrutiny for a time until they trust you. And a last thing. Keep a lookout for that Nathaniel Bunt. If he's there, consider every word you speak to him. If he's suspicious, he'll try and trip you up. Remember too, he's going by Ormsby Mitchel, but he may have changed to another name."

We mounted. I was having some powerful queer feelings.

Zach said, "We'll keep you under observation with my field glasses for as long as we can from the edge of the woods."

"If they stop us and things don't look good, I'll drop my hat on the ground."

"Good idea," said Zach. "If you have to run for it, don't..."

"I know better than to head straight back here."

"Very well. If that occurs, aim for the arroyo where it enters the woods. We'll be there to cover you."

Not if there's two hundred Guerreroistas chasing us, I thought.

Me and Sanchez looked at one another, nodded. I liked the look in his eyes. I could count on him. I didn't feel so low now.

Chapter Eighteen

Staying in the woods, we rode downslope until we reached the arroyo we'd use to reach the letter-hiding place. The arroyo had a thin stream and trees and brush on both sides. That'd give us good cover. Zach and Musty came up behind us.

"Be bold, but be cautious," said Zach, giving a salute.

Sanchez gave a proper salute, I guess. I sorta saluted back. *How can we do both?*

Not much farther was the road coming out of the woods. Less than a mile cross open ground with grazing cattle was the walled hacienda and the white of the tents. Dust and smoke hung over it.

Lots of horse, oxen, wagon, and cart tracks on the road. No surprise.

We weren't halfway cross the open ground when four riders come down the road. Two fanned out right and left, and one dropped back covering the rider coming at us. Except for the man coming at us, they all had their rifles out.

With a hand up, the honcho said, "*¡Alto! Me muestran manos.*"

We raised our hands.

Seeing I was a gringo, the honcho did all his talking to Sanchez, all the time the others keeping rifles on us. They wore brown-gray short jackets and tan, brown, or gray pants, different color and size sombreros. The honcho had a green strip of cloth tied round his right arm. They all had Winchester '73s and pistols. I noticed most of them looked hard used. Zach might want to know that.

He asked Sanchez a batch of questions, and I heard *"gringo"* a lot. At least I didn't hear *"matar."* That means kill.

Finally he said, *"Ven con nosotros"* — Come with us.

They boxed us in, one on both sides, one following, one up front leading us. They didn't take our guns. So far so good.

We came to a guard post about like at the army camp in Del Rio, but with two guards with saddled horses standing. The honcho said something to them, and we went on with our four watchers. Still nothing said about our guns. Saw another pair of riders a short piece away, like they were monitoring like I used to do at the Dew.

We rode on to the hacienda. On the wall was painted *¡VIVA GUR-RERO!* More guards at the gate, three. One with a green armband. They had saddled horses too. If we decided to make a run for it, there were plenty who could ride after us. Maybe it would be hard to sneak outta of here to the letter-hiding place.

Then riders and the guards crowded round us, and the honcho at the gate said, "We will hab joo guns. Put on table."

Sanchez and I looked at one another. There sure weren't much choice. We laid our rifles and all our pistols down.

"Cuchillos también" — Knives too. "Joo get them back."

The guards stayed at the gate, but our riders walked us to the side of the hacienda compound to an adobe house with the mottos *¡LIB-ERAR EL NORTE!* and *¡POR LA CAUSA!* painted by the door. The honcho went in ahead of us saying something to a man standing at a table.

We doffed our hats. My eyes got used to the dim light quick enough.

The man said, "Gentlemen, have a seat." He was American.

He sat behind the table. Tall fella, short salt and pepper beard, big lamb chop sideburns, thin hair atop his head. He looked serious enough, but friendly too. Kinda carried himself like one of the army sergeants I'd talked to.

"You speak good English?" he asked, looking at Sanchez.

"I do, sir."

"Oh, no sirs with me. I'm Sergeant Major Cutter. I look after the American Troop in the Rio Bravo Army of Liberation. You were a scout, were you not?" he said looking at Sanchez.

That sure scared me. Was he already on to us?

"Being a Seminole, your bearing, and calling me 'sir' told me that." Then he looked at me. "You weren't a soldier, what line are you in?"

"Just a cattle punch outta work. Hard times since the Die-Up."

"Indeed, hard times for everyone."

After that he asked a lot of questions. Our names, where we were from, what we'd done for work, schooling—not much—married or not, been in trouble with the law, how much time we'd spent in Mexico—I didn't say nothing about that hard ride—and more stuff.

I told him about my nine years punching cattle, about doing just about any job on a ranch, and that I was a good tracker. He asked me how I'd learned that, and I told him about Ol' Poncho. Told him I was good with guns too.

Sanchez surprised me when he talked about rustling cattle from Texans over Laredo way. He'd worked for some Mex ranchers who wanted to increase their herds. Of course Texicans were rustling cattle on the Mex side too. A lotta underhanded cattle trading went on. He almost got lynched once. Decided after that he'd take his brother's advice and wear the blue and scout for the army. In spite of injuns and banditos, it was a safer job. It looked like whole families of Black Seminoles made their living scouting. Cutter said they had a top notch reputation. When Cutter asked him how long he'd scouted, Sanchez said he'd done three six-month contacts and a few two-month. I knew he'd been scouting longer than that.

"I'd only been in drunk tanks a few times, never no real trouble with the law," I admitted.

"Well hell, that's any cowpoke worth his salt," said Cutter with a laugh.

He seemed to be satisfied with everything we'd said. Then, his eyes suddenly hardened. "Why are you two here?"

I was ready for this. Zach had told me what to say, but said to tell it in my own words. "Well, being out of luck, no work, and no self-respecting punch likes to run the chuck line, I need to make a living. But what's tiring me is them fat cat ranchers lording over us punches, firing us with no notice, turning us out after busting ass for them and their cattle." I put on an angry look. "Bastards, every one of them." Of course I didn't feel that way, but Zach said I'd have to show I was carrying a grudge to turn on my country.

Cutter asked me some questions about that, and I told him a couple of stories about unfairness and plain ol' mistreatment—real stories I'd heard. It was true, not all ranchers were fair.

"This one sumbitch up round San Angelo charged the hands for room and board so they only got half their pay."

Sanchez said he didn't think much of ranchers on both sides of the Rio Grande, and whatever was coming to them, he wanted to be a part of.

"I will admit," said Cutter, "most of the men who come in here applying for the Army of Liberation just want to raise hell, steal all the loot they can. You boys thinking that way?"

Sanchez shook his head real solemn like.

I took that as maybe what Cutter wanted to hear. "Maybe just what I can carry."

Cutter nodded. "A lot of these boys are plum greedy and aim to take anything and everything. I don't know how they think they're going to cart it."

We talked about that some, and he said it's just something they'd have to deal with, but discipline is strict. He said, "You boys might not like the rules."

"I need work. I ain't one to shirk," I said.

He got all solemn looking again. "You need to understand what General Guerrero is attempting to accomplish. Have you heard anything about him, are you familiar with him?"

We both shook our head.

"Have you heard of his goal of establishing a new country with a government that looks out for the welfare of citizens?"

We shook our head.

"El Halcón, the General, is a visionary. He has a grand plan to establish the Republic of the Rio Bravo carved from part of Texas and Coahuila."

I was thinking I didn't know about the Mexes, but I'd wager the Texicans would kick up a fuss worse than they did over that Alamo dustup. Texas, America, and Mexico might have something to say about that, and they have lots bigger armies than however many Guerrero had here. I didn't say nothing though.

Zach had told us not to speak our minds, not to question or show any doubt about Guerrero's scheme.

Musty had said, "Put on your poker face like you're holdin' a lousy two and seven offsuit in your opening hand, but you're really holding two aces. And don't say nothin' agin' his plan."

"I think maybe Guerrero's plan is good idea," Sanchez had said.

Musty and me had laughed. Zach hadn't.

Cutter went on, face all tense and wide-eyed. "It may sound like an ambitious plan, but we feel there will be a general uprising of the peons and small farmers."

Maybe so, on the Mex side of the Rio, I figured. Not likely on the Texas side. Most Mexes worked for somebody and were over there because they didn't like being in Mexico anymore. Some of them even owned land in Texas.

Cutter said, "There's a lot of people want to farm, making an honest living from the soil. They're tired of the big ranchers holding all the land. They'll flock to us to take up arms and hold onto the land."

Maybe, I thought. I kept a poker face. "What about the men that fight for Guerrero. What's in it for us?"

CHAPTER NINETEEN

Cutter leaned back in his chair. His face lost the tense look. He looked more like one of them army sergeants again. "They're paid a modest stipend, and when the land is taken for the Republic, they'll receive a grant of at least six hectares. Larger grants will be given to those with the strongest commitment, demonstrations of valor, and special contributions, and to leaders according to their level."

"Hectares?" I asked.

"Six hectares about fifteen acres," said Sanchez.

I knew one thing, the idea of going after my money so I'd have that 12,000 acres sounded like a better deal than fifteen acres.

"We get a say where that parcel of land is?" Better sound like I was liking what I was hearing.

"Within reason and also according to your standing."

"Sounds good to me," said Sanchez. "I ain't got no chance ever getting any land."

"That's what Guerrero's starting this revolution for, to give deserving men the benefits of owning land."

Sure, I thought. If Guerrero's so troubled about bettering the lives of peons and drifters, how come he ain't divvied up at least some of his own thousands of acres? I knew what the going pay was for his Mex miners. The boy cleaning spittoons in the Double Eagle drew better pay...and benefits for doing chores for the housecats.

Cutter made it clear that the pay was ten dollars a month, a stipend he'd called it. "We have a select group who's been robbing banks in Texas to improve our finances."

No shit, I thought.

"I know it's not much," said Cutter, "but you're fed and bedded here, and your horse too, at no charge. It's the loot when we make our move. There'll be plenty to go around."

Sanchez and I looked at one another. "So how we do this, how do we sign on?"

Cutter asked more questions of us both like if we were willing to follow orders, not get into fights, no gambling or stealing, care for the equipment, undertake work details without complaint, never fall asleep on guard or mistreat horses, and report infractions and troubles to officers.

He made it clear if we signed on and violated the rules or failed in our duties, we would face punishment. He read off all the rules and what the punishments were. It didn't bother me because we were here to break about every rule there was, and I weren't aiming to stick around for any kind of punishment, no matter how deserving.

Cutter called for Sergeant Kraig. He came out of the next room with a green book. Wore a blue armband. Setting the book on the desk with a pen and ink bottle, he told us what to write, name, where from, age — twenty-two and Sanchez twenty-five — that we had horses, and gave us a number that we had to remember. I was 1324 and Sanchez 1325. Kraig gave us orange sashes. We'd wear them on guard duty, evening formation, and other times when told.

"You'll write that number on anything you sign your name. Sergeant Kraig will take you to the troop quarters and stable your horses. You're assigned to the *Tropa Americana* — the American Troop. Welcome aboard, troopers." He shook our hands.

Going back to the compound gate, we followed Kraig leading our horses. They'd given our guns back, but in the camp, we had to keep them unloaded.

"Had a couple accidental like shootin's and a spat between two dumbasses that shot each other to death. Any fightin' will get you in a peck of trouble." Kraig nodded to a sad looking fella standing at attention on top of a big barrel. A board hung round his neck said, "*Ladrón.*" A bored looking guard slouched nearby with a shotgun.

"How long they keep that thief up there?" I asked.

"Twenty-four hours. Looks like he'll topple off 'fore long."

"What happens if he can't stand any longer?"

"Tie him to a tree."

Best keep my nose clean, I thought. I wondered how they tied him to a tree. There's different ways.

"There's another rule. No botherin' or havin' relations with the *seguidores*."

"What's a *seguidore*?"

"That's a follower, a *seguidore*. Means girl soldier, but they don't carry no guns. They the womens what work here for pay. Don't be messin' with them atall. Get ya in more trouble than killin' a man."

"What happens if you kill someone?" I asked, thinking of Jaeger being here.

"They tie you to the corpse and bury the two of you," muttered Kraig.

"They ever done that…never mind. I don't need to know."

We took the horses to a corral and put them in with others. They went through their introduction and biting routine. Horses in other corrals nickered and squealed their greetings. Saddles went in a tack shed, just a big lean-to.

A sign on a stake said TROPA D. AM. Kraig pointed us to a tent among nine. The floor was thick with straw, and a couple of bedrolls sat there. "No smoking in the tents at any time. All the hay. You have to keep it and the area round the tent clean and orderly. Your tent mates'll tell you the rules. Capitan Martinez is the troop commander."

A Mexican?

"Where they at now?" asked Sanchez.

"Building scalin' ladders. Be back soon."

I shrugged. Sanchez nodded.

"What's the colored strips mean?"

"Green's corporal, blue's second sergeant, and first sergeant is yellow. Officers wear silver braid. Your corporal, he'll teach it to you. Bower's his name."

"Sergeant Major Cutter, he wasn't wearing no stripe."

"He don't need to, he says, but if he did, it would be red. I'll scare up Bower. You troopers stay here."

After he left, Sanchez and I looked at each other. I said, "So far so good. What's scaling ladders?"

"Long ladders for climbing walls," said Sanchez. "I got an idea. Let's hide your spare gun here for backup."

"Good idea." I loaded the Schofield — already breaking a rule —

and wrapped it up in a bandana with a dozen spare .45 cartridges.

Sanchez moved a patch of hay and scraped a hole, lined it with hay, and set in the pistol. He covered it over, and I set my bedroll on it.

We heard voices outside and stood. A grisly red face, red-brown hair, and mustache of the same color ducked in. "Howdy, gents. Grover Bower."

We introduced ourselves, shook hands. He seemed not to care about Sanchez being a darkie injun. He asked what we'd done and so on. "Glad you boys are here. A squad's supposed to have eight men. I've got four now counting you two. We've got three full up and building this one. There are six squads in a troop."

"How'd you come to honcho a squad?" I asked.

"Oh, I was foreman," he chuckled, "on a little spread outside San Antone. Had all of four hands to watch over. Sergeant Major Cutter said that made me leadership material. That's what he called it."

"Can you tell us about the troop commander?" asked Sanchez.

"Shore. Capitan Martinez. He a Mex from Corpus Christi. Good man, speaks better 'merican than Mex. The new lieutenant, he jus' joined up, Ormsby Mitchel from Brackettville."

Oh crap! I kept my poker face. Sanchez didn't even blink.

"Used to be a lawman. A city deputy marshal a couple of years ago. Said he got into some kind of trouble and was looking for another line of work. They figured he could keep us all in line." He chuckled.

"Anyone in the troop have army time?" asked Sanchez.

"Not a one," said Bower. "Well, exceptin' one fella who decided he didn't like the blue a couple of months after he gone to soldier."

"A deserter?"

Bower nodded.

"Worse kinda man," muttered Sanchez.

I could think of some who were worse. They're buzzard-picked bones now.

"Coran's in 2nd Squad. I don't much cotton to 'im my own self."

He asked us more questions about ourselves and was impressed Sanchez had been an army scout.

"Let me see where the rest of my squad is, all two of 'em. Dinner, what there is of it, be comin' up soon. Supper's better, but not by much."

We heard Bower outside saying, "Got two new men in. One of

'em a Seminole scout."

The tent flap flew open. "Eugen, you sumbitch!" Matthew Atwood barged in, that hanged traitor Maxwell's shithead grandson.
We went for our guns.

CHAPTER TWENTY

Both our revolvers dry-snapped. I guess we looked kinda stupid pointing empty guns at each other aiming to kill.

My heart was going lickity-split even without a shot fired.

Sanchez pulled his Bowie, kicked Atwood's knee, grabbed his right arm, and yanked it behind his back, sending the revolver flying. The knife blade was hard against his throat.

"Get this bastard nigger off me, you dumb sumbitch!"

I dropped my pistol in its holster and picked up Atwood's Colt, trying to get my breath back. "Atwood, I don't know who you're calling a dumb sumbitch cause it ain't too smart to be name-calling at the bastard nigger holding a knife to your throat."

"I'll cut daylight into you," Sanchez whispered. A trickle of blood ran down Atwood's unshaved throat. The sneer left Atwood's face now that he considered his fix.

And I didn't know what to say.

If Mama taught me one thing, it was how to lie. Now that's not a good thing, and she didn't teach me intentional like. It's just that I heard her lie so much to her saloon louts and other riff-raff she'd brung home, I'd picked up the finer points. She thought she was good at it, but she wasn't. I could tell that by all the bruises she got for trying to outsmart them no-goods. Hell, they was topnotch liars their own selves. So, I guess I learned to tell a working lie, when I had to, by hearing a lot of second-rate lying. Yep, Mama was good for something, kinda, sorta…well, maybe not.

I quick looked out the tent flap. Didn't need no one blundering in.

"Atwood, what the hell you playing at?"

"I'll ask you the same."

"I don't think you're in a good place to be asking questions. What the hell are you doing here?"

"I come down and joined up."

"Well do tell. You gotta do better than that, Atwood. You ain't doing it for money. You're family's got money and land." I knew he didn't know his grandmother was selling part of the V-Bar-M off.

"Well, I am kinda doing it for money. When them bastards robbed Roach-McLymont, they took over five thousand dollars belonging to my family."

"So you come down here with the idea of trying to get that money back. That's a silly thing to do." Maybe just about as silly as me trying to do the same thing.

"And what I found out is that Guerrero's planning on dividing up the big border ranches, including the V-Bar-M and the DeWitt."

How was I going to handle this? I had to think up a lie real fast.

"Atwood, we're on the same side, like it or not. That's why we come down here. I had money in that bank too."

"You had money in Roach-McLymont? What, your cowpoke pay you didn't piss off on Mex whores?"

"I don't consort with no whores..." That newspaper story didn't say anything about me finding *Xiuhcoatl's* money.

"And who's this sumbitch? Ouch, ya sumbitch!" he said as Sanchez let the knife slip.

"I'd damn sure be more politer if I was you, Atwood."

"I seen him before. He's an army scout."

I didn't know what to say, and looked at Sanchez.

"My contract's up, and I got hired on at the Dew," Sanchez said.

"My ass! That's just a story."

"Why would the army send somebody like him down here with me? And Sanchez can hand you your ass if you like. That Bowie's sharp."

"Maybe so," Atwood muttered.

"Look, like it or not, we're on the same side, and we after the same thing."

"You shitting me!"

"I am not."

"Us on the same side after you murdered my grandpa?"

"Can I just cut his throat?" asked Sanchez.

Atwood squirmed.

"Not yet. I'm giving you one chance to throw in with us, or you're going to have another mouth to scream through."

Sanchez moved the blade a hair to start another blood trickle.

"How ya goin' to explain cutting my throat?"

"That'll be no matter to you when you're passing through the gates of hell. How's it going to be, Atwood?"

The dumbass nodded his head, cutting his neck more. "Ouch! Ya mother... Sorry. Yeah, I'll go along with ya. Ain't got no choice, do I?"

Atwood's been nothing but an asshole from what I seen and heard. Yeah, killing him was the other way, but he was right. We'd have to explain that. I didn't like that idea of being buried with the corpse I killed, 'specially the likes of him. Poor company for eternity.

Atwood was like a cocklebur under a saddle keeping me from getting my money, getting to those guns, getting out of here alive, and getting home. I had to think. I wanted to ask him about the Gatling guns, but it'll be best if I don't say nothing.

"You going to shake on it and swear on your grandpa's soul?"

"Fuck you, Eugen! I ain't swearing on his soul to you, you murdering bastard."

"Kill him," I said to Sanchez.

"Whoa, whoa! Just a damn minute now!"

I held up my hand. "What?"

"I'll swear, dammit. Damn your blood, Eugen."

"Some oath. You're going to have to do better than that, you dumbass."

"All right. I swear on Aunt Ruby's grave."

"And go along with me and whatever I say."

"All right. I do." He didn't sound happy.

"On your dear departed grandpa's soul."

"Yeah, that too."

"Say it all!"

"I swear on my Aunt Ruby's grave and my dear departed grandpa's soul, cross my heart and hope to die, to keep my mouth shut and go along with you."

I nodded at Sanchez. He eased off the blade, let Atwood go, but stayed right behind him, the Bowie aimed at his kidneys.

"Sit down. Here's how it's going to be. You're going to keep your mouth shut and not say nothing to no one."

"I'm throwing in with you. Don't mean I gotta like you."

"Don't worry, I ain't liking you none, either. You can't say nothing to no one, and you can't do anything without telling me. You understand?"

His look said he didn't like hearing that. "Yeah, I understand."

"I don't know where the money is, but I bet it's in a guarded safe or lockbox in the hacienda. It's going to be real hard, if not impossible, to get to it. We can try if we get a chance, but the main thing we gotta do is scramble this thing up so they can't pull it off, at least keeping them from going into Texas."

"How are we going to do that?"

"I got no idea. Just keep our eyes and ears open and play our cards as their dealt."

"Not much of a plan, Eugen," said Atwood.

"No, it's not. Remember, my name's Spud Watkins. Say it."

"Ha, that's a good one."

"Say it!"

"All right! Spud, Spud Watkins."

"Don't forget it. It's my *nom de guerre*."

Bower stuck his head in the tent. "See you boys met. Time to eat."

I handed Atwood back his Colt.

We walked toward the two cookhouses, and Bower said we'd have a formation and a nose count before eating. "The troop commander be seeing you boys after chow."

"One of us stay close to Atwood," I said.

"You trust him?" asked Sanchez.

"Nope."

"Can't I accidental-like shoot him?"

"Nope. Not yet anyways. Say, you've never seen Atwood before?"

"Nope."

"How'd you know he needed a knife pulled on him?"

"Just suspecting since you both tried to gun each other down without a hello."

"Yeah, there was that."

"Who's Aunt Ruby?"

I shrugged. "Maybe the only relative that liked him. He's as much use as a melted candle."

Groups of men were coming out of the tents and from the barns and sheds. Sure a lot of Mexes. Sanchez said they were forming up for the noon formation. "Just do like I do. We can get an idea of how many men they got."

We followed Bower, and he showed us where to stand. There were eight groups of men. I guess each was a troop. We were the smallest one, mostly 'mericans and a few Mexes. Bower said they had a couple of Mex's in each squad to translate. They talked good American. I could see that Sanchez was counting the troops. It was an open field, and there were four troops on both sides.

There wasn't much army fanfare, just the troop first sergeants shouting names and everyone answering, "*Presente.*" I kept my eyes open for Jaeger and Kern, and I didn't see Mitchel. Saw only one officer. Sanchez said he was the duty officer "taking the report," whatever that was. The squad leaders walked down the ranks checking to make sure our guns weren't loaded. Bower said only officers keep theirs loaded.

They fell us out, and four troops each went to one of the two cookhouses. Bower was right—the grub wasn't anything special. A gob of beans, gummy rice, and burnt tortillas.

"This'll plug up ya asshole tighter 'an a corncob," said one of the fellas.

The American Troop, what there was of it, sat under some mesquite trees eating the sorry fare. No one much complained. Supper would be better, First Sergeant Harris Malone claimed.

He was from Brownsville in the tip of Texas, spoke some Mex, and had worked on the King Ranch. That being the biggest spread in the world stretching out on six countries kinda made Malone more than just any ol' punch. He'd been a crew boss. "That spread's so big that in four years there was big hunks I ain't never saw."

While we ate, he talked to us, asking the same questions as everybody else.

After chow, we walked down a road with a troop of Mexes. We finished making twelve-foot long scaling ladders, nailing on rungs and wrapping them with wire. We loaded them on long flatbed lumber wagons. We rode those back to the camp and parked the wagons beside the hacienda wall. I thought we'd have to unload them, but they were left on the wagons.

"What do you think the ladders are for?" I asked Sanchez. "Not many high walls in Texas."

"Lots of high walls in Mexico, haciendas, presidios, some churches. Leaving them on the wagons, maybe they'll use 'em soon."

We'd loaded the cut limbs on burros and carried armloads of more. "For tonight's camp fires," said Corporal Bower.

I was hungry, but not looking forward to a poor supper. We first spent an hour grooming horses. Clipper let me know he wasn't happy being boarded with a mob of strange horses.

Another formation before supper. The troop commander, Captain Martinez, was standing in front. A tall fella, a slick head of hair and mustache. Looked like he knew what he was about. Gray vaquero outfit, two holstered Smith Russians. Three silver stripes were above his heart on his jacket.

Ormsby Mitchel stood behind the troop. I guess that was the place for the second-in-command. He didn't take notice of me and Sanchez.

Names were called off. A Mex officer across the field shouted some words. A bugle tooted, and a flag on a pole was brought down on a rope. It looked like the Mex flag, green, white, and orange bars instead of a red one. No eagle, but two yellow stars.

Captain Martinez said in good American, "The adjutant says too many troopers pissing on the ground, not in the latrines. It's not sanitary. Says to stop. Mind that you do."

"Hell, where we going to piss?" I whispered to Sanchez.

"In the latrine out back."

"What's that?" I'd pissed on bushes all my life.

"Like an outhouse hole without the outhouse."

"Oh."

First Sergeant Malone fell us out, and we headed for the cookhouse.

From behind I heard, "You gents couldn't find any horses to buy?"

We turned to face Mitchel.

"Not a one worth having. You were right about a rancher buying them up. Here they all are," I said. "Didn't expect to see you here."

"Likewise," he said as he eyeballed us. "Your partners here too?"

"They headed back north. We heard about this shindig and came in to give it a look see."

His eyes slitted. "You boys didn't strike me as the kind to take to somethin' like this."

"No job prospects makes a man do whatever he's got to."

"Includin' shootin' 'merican soldiers and Texicans?"

"I hope it don't come to that. You think Guerrero can pull this off?"

"I hope it don't come to that myself. But if he does, there may be someone waitin' for him up there. But regardin' his 'bility to do it, he was a general in the Mex army and ain't no slouch when it come to soldierin'. He went to the Mex War College, the Cavalry Academy at Valladolid, and the University of Madrid. Those are in Old Spain."

"Sounds like he knows what he's up to then."

"That's true. He's a heartless sumbitch. He played the broker 'tween the Mex army and sugarcane plantation owners in Oaxaca for sellin' all them Yaqui injuns they rounded up in Sonora. Men, womens, chillins, half of them dyin', railroadin' them slaves all that way and workin' them to death."

He'd looked like he was trying to tell me something more. "I can use some good men, when the right time comes."

I saw something in his hard eyes. What he just said, I could take either way.

He added, "I'd say a man's gotta know when to get outta town after things go bad."

"Uhhh, you can count on us." Yeah, he was telling me something.

Mitchel shook our hands. "You gents have a good evenin'." He walked away, heading for the big tent where the officers ate.

I looked at Sanchez.

He said, "Damn Rangers. What was going on there?"

"I don't think he believes we're here cause we're outta work. He suspects something more about us. We can bet on he's here for the State of Texas. Sounds to me like he's counting on us to help him out when things get to popping."

"Be careful, don't take it for sure that's the way it is. Don't tell him nothing about what we're up to or about Zach and Musty."

"Don't worry. He may be thinking you're scouting contract ain't expired yet."

Sanchez nodded, rubbing his stubble. "Could be."

"Let's eat and hope it's better like they're saying."

Supper was the same as dinner, excepting the tortillas weren't as burnt and there was spicy goat sausage, which wasn't too bad. More talking to the hands in the squad. Nothing said about fast-shooting guns.

Back at the tents, Mateo Aguilar lit up a fire. Bower wrote down what guns we had and their caliber, asked how much ammunition we packed. Turned out we had plenty, and they didn't need to give us any.

"You both got Winchester '73s. Guerrero's passin' 'em out to those ain't got one. You know, you give a rifle to a Mex, and that means something to him. You got a loyal follower."

Since we were the new hands, it was our turn to fill in the old latrine pit and dig a new one. We were laughing when we started, thinking about them graves we'd dug just a couple of days ago. Sanchez told me to never talk inside a tent about anything we didn't want heard, even if it was just us two. "You can never tell when someone's outside. The same goes when you're outside by a tent."

It was growing dark, and we walked over to the corral.

"Not a good idea to try and sneak out tonight to the letter-hiding place," Sanchez said.

"True-that. Give it a try tomorrow?"

"Yep. Got some good information. Eight troops of six squads. That's about four hundred, but it looks like most troops don't have that many."

We found Atwood at the corral. "You still with us?"

Leaning on the mesquite railing, he said, "I been thinking it over. You're probably right. They'll do whatever they damn well want with border ranches."

"Damn straight they will. Hell, a lot of Mexes still say the Nueces Strip belongs to Mexico and the Rio Grande is just another river, ain't no border. No matter what he says, for Guerrero, it's about grabbing land and making money."

"If you take your leave, let me know. I ain't likin' this army life anyways."

"We'll do that." I didn't say nothing to him about my talking to Mitchel. But I did say, "Don't let on that we knowed each other before."

"Don't worry."

It was quiet for a spell, hanging on the railing watching the horses nibble hay. Sanchez walked off. I think he was thinking Atwood might say more with him outta sight.

"I ain't forgetting you killed my grandpa."

What's a man to say to that?

I turned toward Atwood. "I don't know how you feel. I ain't ever had no grandpa. I'll have you know that your grandpa allowed them banditos to take Clay's bull for him to use as a breeder. Them banditos caused ten Dew people, including women and kids, to die. You know what happened to Clay DeWitt's girls and my woman."

When he opened his mouth, I said, "Don't say nothing." I was getting heated up, but backed off some. "This needs to be put behind you for now because we're in some bad shit here. We can take it up later."

He didn't say nothing, just hung on the rail.

"You good with that, put it in the holding corral?" I said.

"Yeah, I am."

"Shake then."

We shook. "We'll put it on hold…for now," he said in a whisper.

"Good 'nough."

He was surely going to be pissed when he found out I was buying a big piece of that ranch without his grandma knowing.

CHAPTER TWENTY-ONE

I opened my eyes to a horn tooting real annoying like. It was dark. "Five-thirty, boys. Up and at 'em," said Bower with a cracked voice.

"They call this reveille," said Sanchez.

I decided then that reveille was a bad thing. Made no matter if that was the same time we got up at the Dew, I didn't like it or that damn horn.

Morning formation was pretty quiet, just hacking and coughing, still dark. A Mex officer shouted something again, and the bugle tooted as the flag ran up the pole. Breakfast weren't half bad, two fired eggs on a tortilla with some kind of hacked meat and tomato sauce and refried beans left over from last night.

Mitchel called the troop together and said to saddle up our horses. "No gear or saddlebags. Bring your rifles. We're doin' an exercise. Goin' to play army."

This exercise thing was like a practice. We'd lineup single file and trot down a trail. Sergeant Malone would be up ahead, and he'd crack a shot into the sky. We'd dismount as fast as we could, and everyone ran up to get on line and pretended to shoot back at the enemy we couldn't see. Everyone was shouting, "Bang, bang!" with gusto. After doing it about a dozen times, we got where everyone was facing and "shooting" in the same direction and stayed on line without getting too scattered. The "bang, bang" shouting wasn't so loud. Then we did it at a gallop. Only took an hour to get it right that way.

I never figured myself a soldier boy, but here I was. Sanchez gave some of the boys pointers. Some listened, some didn't.

We were supposed to dismount real fast and shoot back. Mateo Aguilar caught his left boot in the stirrup trying to dismount when he spiked his horse to a butt-sliding halt.

"He's as dumb as homemade sin," muttered Bower.

The trooper climbed to his feet all sham-faced and his carbine in two parts, the busted off butt and the rest of it. Malone started chewing on him for bringing to ruination a good shooting piece. Two days tortillas and water in the guard house.

After we came back in, I took a look at it. About six inches of split wood stuck out from the receiver like a spike. "I can fix this."

"You got a spare butt stock on ya, Spud?" asked Bower.

I ignored Ollie and headed for the carpenter's shed. Using hide glue, I glued the stock together, and Benito the carpenter clamped it. His callused hands and clean oiled tools told me he was a good chippy.

"Glue ain't goin' to holt that," declared Bower.

"Let it set overnight." I put two feet of rawhide lace in water to soak.

After supper a couple of the boys said they were going to Nueva Rosita to visit the whores at the cantina, *putear* they called it — means whoring, I guess. Sanchez found out real fast that it was no problem to visit the town. Instead, he was going to the letter hiding place.

He already had a letter written up. He said he gave a guess at how many men there are, how they're organized, and that they're getting good training. No word on the guns or coming plans. Told about Mitchel and that we thought he was here on state business and might side with us. He said too that we were in good and safe and the food was pitiable.

He rode out alone after dark rather than go with a bunch of Mexes. This was working good with Sanchez being a darkie. Nobody wanted to ride in with him, and he could make the side trip easy.

Ollie asked me if I wanted to go. "Later sometime," I'd said. Malone warned everyone not to get wicked drunk, or they could look forward to the guard house and tortillas and water.

I sat at the fire talking with Malone and some of the other boys.

Careful about my questions, I didn't learn anything of worth. It was clear they were here for the loot.

Turning in, I worried all this lying ain't going to work. I fretted about tripping up, mixing up stories. I finally fell asleep after long worrying about Sanchez ghosting round in the dark.

At sunrise Sanchez was sound asleep under his sarape. Some of the boys teased him about chasing *las puchas*. That was a more polite name than *putas*. "Wild oats make a mighty poor breakfast." He just winked with a smile and gave me a nod. I knew he'd made it to the letter-hide.

Heading to formation, he said, "No problem getting to the place. Left the letter. Zach had left a note saying all was good with them. I said I can make it about every two or three nights using the whoring excuse."

"That's about three or four times a week. Can you keep that up, pard?"

"Don't worry," he said with a smile. "I can keep it up."

In the carpenter's shed, I took the clamp off the carbine's stock. With Benito turning the carbine, I wrapped thin copper wire as tight as I could round the cracked small of the stock for a hand's length. We tacked the wire ends with cigar box nails and soaked the wire with hide glue. Then we wrapped the wet rawhide lace to cover the wire stretching it tight. I told Agalar to leave it to dry, and in the morning the rawhide would have shrunk tight.

Malone turned the carbine in his hands. "Where'd you learn how to do this, Trooper?"

"From ol' Pancho Salazar at the Triple Bar. Teached me lots about guns. Leaned from some other hands I cross trails with."

He nodded and said, "You did good, Trooper," and tossed the carbine to Agalar. "Don't break it again, *pendejo*."

That afternoon we were going to do some shooting. Lots of them boys had never shot a Winchester '73. Found that out when half of them couldn't fire a shot because they didn't know how the lever latch and trigger stop worked, keeping them from firing. Some didn't even know they could set the hammer on half-cock as a safety. Most didn't know to slide the dust cover atop the receiver forward to keep the action clean, and that when they levered in a round, the cover would slide back.

Malone had me get everyone together and talk them through loading and shooting and how the carbine worked. I never figured myself a teacher, but there I was.

We started them off shooting airtights from the cookhouses, but just about no one could hole them at a hundred feet. Some were close.

"Some them boys couldn't hit a whole flock of barns," muttered Sanchez.

"Some of them'll do better throwing them guns. Maybe better off using it as a club."

So we stuck newspaper sheets on sticks, and some were able to hit them. More a man-sized target anyways.

All this time and we'd not heard a word about Gatling guns, any plans for the Army of Liberation, and nothing about when this shindig was going to bust loose.

Every day was living a lie, and I was getting down on keeping things straight in my head. Trying to keep from slipping up. Just not hearing anything was bothering me.

∿

Breakfast was more sad frijoles, more stale tortillas, and a big wooden spoon of sticky rice was slapped on my and Sanchez's tin plates I was holding.

A ringing voice said, "¡Oye! Joo want *más arroz, señor?*"

I was looking at Gina's wary face.

"What are... How'd you get here?"

Then Marta leaned out from behind Gina with a kinda scared smile.

"What the hell..."

Gina glanced round and shook her head. "We talk later. Go. Go!"

I gave Marta the hardest look I could, like my mama'd give me when I did something unforgivable, like still breathing after walloping on me with a board. "Damn straight we will!"

I didn't give Marta another look. My brain was pitching like a loco bronc. How'd the damn hell and all that's holy did they get here? The reason I suspected I knowed. Damn, damn that rock-headed girl. *Well, hell, settle down.* I shoulda expected it. I realized that I was just as pissed at Gina as Marta for not holding her back. But then, that's like trying to lasso a mustang and stopping it with boot leather.

I need to think on this. It surely changed things. Now I had them to worry about. It was one thing getting my own self back home and the three fellas with me, but now those girls. Another thing, when it all broke loose round here, however we were going to do this, no one could figure that those girls knew me. I had to pass that on to Gina fast like. Thinking about how she told me to go away so fast, she already worked that out.

"What's wrong?" said Sanchez, taking his plate from me.

"Things just got more complicated. The girls showed up."

"Girls, what girls?"

"My woman and Gina."

"What! How'd they get here?"

"By horse, I suspect."

"What are they doing? I mean, how are they…"

"They're cooking."

"Maybe the food'll get better."

"We can hope. I gotta talk to Gina. Meet her tonight. You want more frijoles?"

"Not no more like these."

"I'll be right back." I made my way back to the kitchen shed. This surely put things in a different light, the girls showing up. Like I don't have enough to worry about. I didn't have to wait in line.

Gina poured more beans on my plate. "More if joo want. Nobody like much."

"Y'all act like you don't know me, ever. See that big oak over yonder? Meet me there one hour after dark."

"We in troubles?"

I didn't say nothing but gave her a hard look, gave a harder one to Marta.

Marta rolled her eyes. Smart aleck. I didn't want to admit to myself she was a pleasing sight to see. Made me see how much I was missing her. I was scared for both of them.

It was dark. I'd watched the oak tree and the thick brush round it for a half hour. I sneaked into the brush, took a sorta comfortable rock, and leaned against the big tree. I was pulling hard to keep my anger reined in.

Watching the moon up through the limbs, I settled myself down. In a way I was proud of Marta coming after me. She truly must like me. But I'd never thought she'd come down here after all what she'd been through. And she wasn't good healed yet. I was surely worried about her.

There was a rustle in the brush and crackling twigs, and Marta was in my arms, kissing me hard. Any mad I had in me run away. She laid her head against my chest and locked me in a never-let-go hug.

"*Buena noches,*" whispered Gina.

"You got some explaining to do, girl." I tried to keep it level. No good would come of spooking her.

"It no my fault! Joo tell me look after her," she snapped.

"That meant keeping her at home."

"Joo try stop her!"

"Yeah, got it. So what happened? When y'all come here?"

"Soon as joo go out of sight."

"Straight off? Y'all didn't have no gear, no chuck, no nothing."

"Three bad mans ride after joo. Marta see. She go."

"They was probably only Rancho Mariposa vaqueros. Nothing to it. They jus' seeing what we were up to."

"Marta think not. We follow. Bad mans."

"Of course. And y'all with no guns. What did y'all think you'd do?"

"Marta hab *pistolitas.*"

"Figures. You don't have one."

"Marta give me little one, show me how. We go after bad mans."

"With no gear, no chuck?"

"Shuck?" she asked.

"Food, *comida.*"

"*Sí.* Marta find."

"Y'all didn't steal it, did you?"

"Not all. Marta got monies. I barter for her. She buy *cabeza de cabra,* eh, head of goat for two centavos. Cook good stew."

"I bet."

"We get *camas,* joo call…"

"Yeah, bedrolls. I ain't asking where you got them…"

"We find…"

"Never mind. What about Doris and Roberto's boy?"

"I tell go home, tell *Señor* Clay. Where is other mans, *el Teniente y Mustio?*"

"Mustio? You mean Musty?"

"*Sí.* Why you call him that? *Mustio* means sad. He not sad."

"In American Musty means, sorta smelly like, I guess."

"*Rancio?*" She added, "Is English."

"He can be rancid sometimes. Anyways, they hid out. You don't need to know any more." Clay back at the Dew had to be pitching a fit and worried to death.

"Gina, let me ask you. What were those vaqueros up too? We heard two shots and running horses that first night."

"Not vaqueros, bad mans. We follow all day. No eat. We go close to those bad mans. We watch. They go to sneak up on joos. Marta, she let dee horses go. Shoot her *pistola* two times, makes them run. Those bad mans go after horses. We stay, follow joos to *los Cinco Manantiales.* Joo go on *ferrocarril,* iron train."

So coyotes and 'coons ain't the only things that prowl round in the night, I thought. "So y'all were following us all that time. How'd y'all find your way here after we took the train?"

"I hear joo talk about where joo go here. Woman tells us to go Nueva Rosita. She say this *ranchero,* Guerrero, pay womans to cook, wash, eh, *reparar ropa,* to make clothes good. We go Nueva Rosita."

"So you got hired on as cooks?"

"We come two day ago. Work first in other *cocina,* kitchen. We good cooks. *Oye.* Marta buy, eh, *escopeta* in Allende from boy. He say he find in mesquite outside Allende. Why joos laugh?"

"I seen that shotgun before."

She looked at me queer like. "Marta had, eh, *el herrero...*"

"Blacksmith."

"*Sí.* He cut off barrels and wood thing. Make short," she said making a sawing motion.

"She's got herself a sawn-off shotgun?" I shook my head and groaned over sawing off those pretty Damascus barrels.

"*Sí. Escopeta corta.*" She held her hand up about two-foot apart.

"She got any shells for it, *cartuchos?*"

"She hab two."

Dang, I thought. I'd left a couple of dozen 12-gauge shells in that Sabinas warehouse. Maybe I could round up some. Not that I was hoping she'd need them.

"She still got it, *la escopeta?*"

"*Sí, la ocultó,* she hide it."

"Gina, I feel bad cause Marta dragged you down here." Marta gave me a squeeze, knowing I was talking about her.

"I no can let her go, eh, *solo,* alone."

"I thank you for staying with her, I really do."

Her shadow shrugged. "*Gracias.* Joo no hab troubles on way here?"

"Nope, not a thing," I lied. "Anybody here give you any trouble, like saying anything unpolite, rude to y'all?"

"No troubles with mans here. *Jefe* over kitchen tell us to say if anyone give us troubles."

"Yeah, they tell us the not to mess with the women. Y'all just be careful."

"Marta big worry about joo."

"Yeah, and now she's a big worry for me."

Gina said it in Mex. Marta snapped up and grabbed my shirt, her face right in mine. She slapped her hand on her chest twice, then on mine, and clutched the beads she'd given me. The white and brown beads being me and her.

"Yeah, I know, you worry about me too and you're not ever letting me alone again."

She nodded. Tears were in her eyes, and I chocked down a throat lump. Musta been them clumpy frijoles.

"Gina, look, you come here every night if you can, and I will too. Maybe sometimes I won't be able to get away, so don't worry. We'll stay in touch that way, and maybe you can find out things you can tell me." Marta had wrapped her arms round me again.

"We do."

"I need to know how many men are here…"

"Two hundred and three-eight."

"What?"

"Mans, that many mans are here."

"How'd you know that?"

"We cook for. That not count all, some in hacienda and other places."

"Good. I need to know where them Gatling guns are and anything you hear about what they plan to do. Anyone say anything about them guns?"

"I find out. They call *arma de fuego rápida.* They say big guns on wheels."

"A fast-shooting gun. There's three of them, so keep your eyes open."

"They say four guns," said Gina.

"Just three. Somebody's mixed up. Anyway, don't be asking questions about them, or someone might take notice, Just keep your eyes and ears open."

"How I keep ears opens?"

"*Escucha*. Listen," I said.

"No, *escucha* is hear. *Oír* is to listen."

"Whatever." She was confusing me.

"Now you two skedaddle."

Gina looked at me queer like.

"*Vete*. Get outta here."

Marta didn't want to let go. Neither did I.

That night I was thinking about Marta. Anything was liable to set me thinking about her. If she can't talk, how could she lie? I guess she could deceive someone like pointing in the wrong direction, but that weren't the same. Marta always let me know what she was thinking. Didn't hide nothing. I mean, she'd pull these stunts like following me into trouble in Mexico, but heck, I shoulda seen that coming. I guessed she was about as honest as one could be. She was just going to do what she was going to do. *You can maybe turn a stampede, but no way you're going to stop one straight off by waving arms.*

CHAPTER TWENTY-TWO

Marta and Gina were dishing out breakfast, and you know what? The dang frijoles were better, the rice not so sticky, and the tortillas only a little burnt. Never saw an egg, missed them. It was hard ignoring the girls. Marta tried to ignore me, but kept cutting her sad dark eyes to me.

I had to eat outta of sight of her. Just too hard to see her there and no telling what was coming at us.

We spent the day on picket duty. That was patrolling all round the base. Not bad duty. Just like when I monitored at the Dew. Sanchez and I rode round the south side of the place. That let us get a look at the spread's layout. Sanchez did some notes and sketching he'd take to the letter-hide. We did it from sunup to sunset. I sneaked over to the oak tree when I was relieved.

"I know where guns are," said Gina, near out of breath under the oak tree.

"Good! Where?"

"In the *almacén*. Joo call…"

"A warehouse."

"*Sí*. Dee big warehouse near dee stables. There four guns," she added.

"Four, I don't see how that can be."

"They say."

"Well, I'll figure it out." Marta was hanging on me as tight as a tick.

We talked a bit. They were having no troubles from anyone. They knew that we couldn't stay here long. I hated to see Marta sneak off like a doe slipping through the brush, looking back at me until she disappeared in the dark.

When I got back to the troop tents, Mitchel was waiting for me. "Sergeant Malone, he tells me you're quite a hand with guns."

"Tolerably."

"El Halcón del Norte wants to see ya tomorrow."

"El how con whodie?"

"General Guerrero his own self. Likes to call his self the Falcon of the North."

"I'm in trouble?"

"I suspect not. He'd put the word out he's lookin' for men what know guns, not jus' shootin', but their workin's." He looked at me with a squint, and then his eyes glanced to both sides. "I put your name in. I don't know where this is goin', but this may be an openin', if you follow me."

"I...sure thing."

"Keep your ears and peepers open. Just sayin'. And the general likes to be called sir by gringos."

Did Mitchel know about the Gatlings? Hard to say. *I ain't asking.*

I didn't say nothing to Gina about going to see Guerrero that morning. We got *atole,* kinda like porridge made from corn hominy. Gina gave us an extra full ladle-load.

I was a smit nervous standing in front of Falcon's desk, hat in hand, told to leave my pistols and knifes with the adjutant—*Ayudante* he called himself. Breakfast felt like a big lump in my belly. Or maybe it was something else bringing that on.

The adobe block floor was mostly covered by a dark green rug. Big open windows made the room bright.

The general sat behind a big fancy desk scratching on some papers like I wasn't there. On the wall hung a big map of north Mexico and south Texas. The wiggly blue line of the Rio Grande ran cross it. I worked out the words, *República del Río Bravo.* I was surely a long way from home.

"Lieutenant Mitchel tells me that you are knowledgeable of firearms, Trooper Watkins." He paid no mind to my jumping a mile high.

"Yes, sir, I'm pretty handy with rifles and revolvers." No sense in being shy about it.

"Are you familiar with the mechanical workings of firearms, how they operate?"

"Pretty much I guess, sir. I ain't no gunsmith, but I can fix things."

"So I have heard. Have you any experience with any kind of military arms?"

"Just shot that Springfield single-shot carbine they use. It's not good for much."

"That is a true statement," he said. "No doubt you have heard rumors, but have you ever heard of a Gatling gun, Trooper Watkins?" He looked up from his papers.

I may not be the smartest cattle punch round, but I saw where this was going. "Yes, sir, I have."

"What do you know about it, besides any rumors you may have heard?"

He spoke real good American. That surprised me. Chin beard with sideburns reaching down to the beard and mustache. His dark eyes could look right through you or right into you.

"It's got, I think, eight, ten barrels and sits on two wheels like a cannon. Got a crank on the side and shoots real fast."

"Anything else you can tell me?"

"Yes, sir. It uses the same cartridges as the Springfield, .45-70. I saw one shoot once, sir."

"Really? Where was this?"

I'd better ponder about what I'm going to say, or I can get tripped up. Can't say I saw it at Del Rio less than two weeks past.

"Oh, up at Fort Sam Houston, there at San Antone. They put on a show on Independence Day. They shot up some fence posts. Never seen nothing like it."

"Interesting. Did you see how they operated it?"

"Yes, sir. Saw how they put cartridges in this metal thing sticking out the top and how they cranked it."

He cleared his throat and took a sip from a glass. "Can you read Trooper?"

"No sir, I cannot, mostly."

There was a long quiet. He took another sip and put his eyes on me for a long stare.

"I am going to confide in you something you must swear not to repeat to anyone. Is that clear, Trooper?" All serious like.

"Yes, sir. I swear to keep my mouth shut."

"The rumors you may have heard are true. We have acquired some Gatling guns." He was watching me close.

"That's real prime for our side, sir."

He seemed to like hearing me say it that way. "We have the manuals that go with the Gatling guns. If I were to provide you with a man who can read and has experience with other types of guns, do you think you could help train the gun crews?"

My noggin was going lickety split. This would put me right in the middle of things. Not only being with the Gatlings, but I might be let in on what all's happening here, when they might pull this off.

"Well, sir." I made myself look reluctant like. "I ain't never done nothing like that, don't know about how soldier boys do things by the numbers, but with the book and somebody that can make sense of it, hell...begging your pardon, sir, I'll give it my best for you."

He was leaning on an elbow, chin in hand. He smiled. "Excellent. Tell the adjutant that as of today you are Corporal Watkins." He scribbled on a piece a paper, handed it to me, and shook my hand with a firm grip.

"Congratulations, Corporal. Report to Sergeant Major Cutter here after reveille. You'll meet the gunner I spoke of and will work up a training program with the sergeant major."

"Yes, sir. Thank you much, sir." *Gunner, what kind of gunner?* "Do I get one of those green armbands?"

He kinda waved at me. "Of course."

"Sir, I got a request."

"Yes?" Looking at me wary like. He set his glass down.

"The man that come in with me, Sanchez, he was scout for the army. He might be able to help me out, him knowing the army's ways. He's a good man. Speaks Mex...eh, Spanish and can read," I added.

He leaned back in his chair. "I need good scouts. That is what I planned for him, and you too." He nodded. "The Gatling guns, though, are of the utmost importance, and I do wish for Mexican gun crews. Yes, you may keep your boy then."

"He ain't my boy, sir, begging your pardon. He's just a good man to have round."

He nodded again. "Very well then." He scribbled on another piece of paper. Handed it to me. "Give to the adjutant."

"Thank you much, sir. Eh, just so I know what's going on, can

I ask how many guns there are, so I got an idea of how many men that's gotta be trained?"

"Certainly," he smiled. "There are four guns with a crew of four men each. In the morning then. Dismissed, Corporal."

I saluted. Still felt queer doing that. I had some good news to tell Zach.

Damn, if that weren't something. I got made a corporal just like Sanchez did, being swayed to do a job. Lew, the Dew foreman, took him four years in the army to make corporal. Took me a week. Hoped I'd still be kicking to brag on it to him.

I walked back to the tents thinking about what I'd just seen.

I told Sanchez what happened with my visit to Guerrero. Not only did we know where the guns were, there were four, and we were going to train the crews. Where that fourth gun come from, we had no idea. We had to get that news to Zach tonight.

"Guess I'm going whoring," moaned Sanchez.

I laughed. "I bet you wish you were getting as much as everyone thinks."

I didn't say nothing about all of it to Gina at supper. Just said we couldn't meet that night. I didn't want to do anything chancy with this coming up.

Sitting in the corner of the general's office was a dark green box on little wheels. It was about four feet high and over half that wide. It said Barnes Safe & Lock Company. I wasn't wondering no more where that old goat was keeping my two-thousand and eight hundred and fifty American dollars.

CHAPTER TWENTY-THREE

Things didn't go the way I expected in the morning. Me and Sanchez showed up at the hacienda, but there wasn't any talk about Gatling guns.

Cutter met us at the door. "We've had a problem come up and have to put off your introduction to Gatling guns. The general needs you two as scouts, trackers really. We have a runaway that took something belonging to the general."

Something darted through my head. I hope it wasn't Marta up to her tricks.

In the general's office, he was pacing round the floor wearing out that big green rug. He stopped his marching and faced us, slapping a *cuatra* against his leg. All red-faced, I'd say he was truly pissed off.

"Gentlemen"—first time he'd called us that. He really wanted something. "I have had something valuable stolen from me. I wish to employ your tracking skills to return it. It is of the utmost importance. You will be rewarded and have my undying gratitude."

The best gratitude he could give me was five minutes in his safe. It was setting in the corner looking just as inviting.

"Are you willing?" He asked us that without telling us what the deal was. That told me he was expecting us to say yes.

"Whatever we can do to help," I said.

The general said, "One of my trusted guards stole a rare emerald."

I looked at him waiting for him to say more. He didn't. "What's an emerald?"

He looked back at me like I'd asked him what the sun was.

Cutter said, "It's like a green diamond," and glanced at the general.

"Indeed. Sergeant Amado Montero has stolen a priceless jewel, two horses, and my trust. He has fled I believe to Obayos, a small village. It is over twenty miles to the south. You must depart immediately. I want him found and brought back with the emerald."

"I gotta ask, sir, you know for sure he's going to this village?"

"One of the men told us that he said he had relatives there. There is little else in that region. If he leaves there, it may be difficult to trail him further."

Depends, I thought.

"You want him dead, alive, or no matter, sir?" asked Sanchez.

The general looked at him like that grim reaper fella. "As alive as possible so he can face my retribution fully cognizant."

I didn't know what that meant, but I don't think it foretold anything good for this Montero fella.

They couldn't tell me anything about this Obayos place. Montero was about five-foot four, said to be a good-looking fella. He was a vaquero, same age as me, twenty-two. Could be any number of Mexes. He had a revolver and '73 Winchester. His horse was a gray with black mane and tail. Not many of them around. The spare they didn't know since it had been taken from a corral full of horses. They didn't know when he left. Could of have been anytime during the night, giving him two to eight hours head start. All I got outta them about the land was that it was pretty rough, lots of arroyos of all sizes, scattered trees and brush, and some wide open parts, and poor roads. They didn't call them roads—*caminos*, but *rastros* meaning paths.

We didn't have much to go on. The general was rushing us off, and with good reason if he was right about where Montero was heading. Where he'd go after Obayos was anybody's guess.

I didn't much like this, but he was asking us to, not that we didn't have much say. Going along with it, we could get in gooder with the general.

The general picked up a letter envelope and took out a paper. "This will aid you should you have any dealings with government officials and authorities." He unfolded the paper and read in American,

"Be it known to all concerned patriots and officials of the Republic in

these unsettled times, that the bearer of this letter, Mister Spud Watkins, a trusted and valued agent in my service, is acting on my behalf and with my fullest protection. Your courtesy and assistance provided to Mister Watkins will neither be forgotten nor go unrewarded.

Affirmed this day of the 12th April the year of the Lord 1887.
General Estevan Francisco Guerrero Marín
Brigade General, Advisor to the Governor
Las Esperanza, Coahuila"

Sure fancy words.

He handed me the envelope. "Take good care of this as it not only solicits you aid, but helps you escape difficulties. Do remember the names of those assisting you so that I may reward them. It is important in Mexico to honor such promises."

He said that like he was telling this here Texican that we weren't so honorable.

We were leaving when the general said, "I am sending Sergeant Porras with you. He knows Montero and has previously been in the area to the south. He'll meet you at the corral. I wish for you to depart promptly."

There sure weren't any way to argue about it. I was pretty sure this fella Porras was going along to make sure we came back.

Cutter went with us to our tent to get our gear, hurrying us along. "You didn't know an emerald is an expensive jewel?"

"No I didn't. Not something I needed to know to punch cattle."

We walked on. I thought on what kind of chance we had picking up a trail in this rangeland or if it would be better to dash straight on to this Obayos. We might catch him there or pick his trail up when he left there. Had a better chance of doing that there than here with all the horse tracks everywhere but on tree trunks.

"The general mentioned a reward for bringing him in. He didn't say what," I said.

"No, but I'm certain it'll be generous," Cutter muttered.

A notion came to me. "What if this Montero hides that emerald along the way? We'd never find it."

"If we grab him, bring him in," said Sanchez, "they'll beat it out of him short of killing him."

Cutter looked straight at me. "You know what the emerald is, right?"

Sanchez pitched his eyes to the sky. "*¡Caray!* I knew it."

"Knew what?"

"It is a woman."

I stopped. "You shittin' me."

Cutter shook his head. "Sorry, boys. I tried to get the general to let it go, seeing what's coming up. He's put his brand on that gal, with her being his mistress."

I'd never heard "mistress" before, but I had an idea what it meant, polite way of saying "kept-whore."

"Montero left a ransom note," said Cutter. "Two thousand pesos."

"Well dammit to hell. I already done that once, going after a ransomed girl in Mexico."

Cutter looked at me, and I realized I'd slipped up bad. Sanchez didn't blink.

"How's that?" Cutter asked, kinda specious like.

I needed to get this right. "Awww, just a lovesick cowpuncher run off with a rancher's daughter over in Eagle Pass. He left a ransom note too, but it was them just running off to get hitched. I caught up with them in Negras. I talked him into giving her up and moving on to keep him from getting shot-gunned by the old man."

"You get paid for that chore?"

"Half what that dumb cowpunch was asking for ransom." Yep, I did learn to lie good from Mama. Anyway, it was a story I'd heard in Eagle Pass. "So what's this emerald gal like?"

"Oh, she's about as good a looker as you can ask for. Smart too. Can read, write, and figure cyphers. Name's Esmeralda. That's Spanish for emerald. It's said no one can pronounce her family name. She's half Mexican, half gringo."

"What's she look like?"

"You'll know her when you see her, believe me. Like the general said, she's priceless, and priceless don't mean free."

That started me thinking about when *Xiubcoatl* made off with Marta, Inés, and Clay's girls and wanted a ransom. They took off into Mexico leaving no idea how they wanted to swap the girls for money. They suckered us into Mexico using the girls for bait to take the money and keep the girls, yeah, and to kill all of us. This deal looked sorta the same. Clay said kidnapping's the third oldest profession.

That led me to whisper to Cutter, "That ransom note say how the money's going to be passed to him, or where the swap would be made?"

"It did not."

"So if she's so dang good looking and smart, being kept by a rich *hacendado* in comfort, why'd she run off with a vaquero, a sergeant?"

We walked on without Cutter saying anything for a spell. "Keep this under your hat, Watkins, and your pard too."

"Sure."

"She's all that, but she's twenty-one years old. Montero's a good looking stud with a silver tongue. The general's fifty-four," he said with a wink.

"You don't need to say no more."

"The uniform gets them every time," said Sanchez.

"If you catch up to them, Watkins, be careful, she can talk a priest out of his crucifix."

I nodded. Sanchez just shook his head.

Both Sanchez and me knew there wasn't no way to let Zach know we'd be off on a chase.

We had enough dry chow for a few days. We met Sergeant Porras at the corral. He didn't speak American and didn't say much in Mex, either. Had a face like a wolf and hard eyes.

We saddled the spares. At first I'd thought about leaving the spares so we could move faster. That was taking a chance. Instead, we'd start off on spares and save our horses for later.

I told Sanchez, "Tell Porras we're not looking for a trail round here. We're getting on to Obayos as fast as we can. If they're not there, we'll try and pick up their trail, which I bet we can. They're probably not traveling real fast, the girl being well kept and pampered. Tell Porras to keep up."

I wanted to get this done and get back to business. On the other hand, the general said we'd be rewarded. I'd settle for two-thousand and eight hundred fifty dollars.

It was truly rough ground. We crossed so many arroyos, big and little, shallow and deep, that by the time we got to Minas de Barroteán, we gave the spares a break and switched horses before reaching that village. They hadn't been doing a lot of riding, so this was hard on them. Minas de Barroteán was near a big open pit coal mine, everything black dust-covered. The ground got harder, more rocks, more ridges. We were getting into the foothills of the *Sierra Madre Oriental*. Been there and don't wantta see it again. After passing through a flea-sized village called San José de Aura, we changed back to the spares to keep ours from getting all dumfungled. Pushed them as hard as we could. They were bad lathered before long. We'd asked a few people in both villages if they'd seen a vaquero and a young lady. No one had. They probably skirted both places. Same with anyone we met on the road, but I think they were just saying they hadn't. Sanchez was holding up of course, but Porras weren't happy.

We passed a little rancho off the road. I sent Porras in to see if they'd seen anyone. He came back to say one of the vaqueros seen a man and a woman on the road a few hours earlier. They were riding a gray with a black tail and a sorrel. That kicked up our spirits being the first sign of them.

The sun was dropping toward the big ridge ahead of us. Porras said that Obayos wasn't far ahead. It was on a stream, *Arroyo Obayos*, that cut through the big ridge, a pass called *Puerto Obayos*. It was a deep, narrow gouge with the trail sidling the stream. If we didn't find this emerald in Obayos, I was sure we could pick up their trail through the *puerto*. They'd have to stay on the trial through the *puerto*. I was wondering how much trouble this Montero would be. He'd probably put up a fight.

It was barely still light when we came into Obayos. For the first time, I dismounted and looked at tracks. There were lots of ox and burro tracks and some mule and horse. Hard to tell those two apart in the poor light. The few horse prints were unshod, except for one certain pair.

I mounted. "They been through here, or at least somebody on two shod horses. Not many ironclad hooves in a place like this."

Obayos was about as sad a place I'd ever seen. Not much better than that San Miguel the banditos had their stronghold in during the hard ride. The more I saw of Obayos, San Miguel looked right homey. Most villages have adobes side by side strung along a cobbled or hardpan dirt street. Here adobes were scattered like they didn't wanna be close to neighbors. Lotta yucca, acacia, and mesquite growing between the adobes. Lotta goat pens. The bigger herds had a burro watching over them to chase coyotes away. Goats must be their commerce here.

"Ride on through, eyes open," I said. "Don't pay attention to no one."

Sanchez told that to Porras, and he said something back.

"He say why don't we ask about the two we're chasing?"

"We will. Just not now. Make no noise."

We rode through. Didn't see a soul. All we heard were sorry goat noises. A couple of goat dogs barked. So many tracks, there wasn't any sense looking for shod prints.

On the far side of the village, what there was of it, the road made a turn crossing *Arroyo Obayos* and then slanted up the big ridge to the pass.

"Hang back a little," I told them as I rode ahead. I found a place where enough light fell to make out tracks. I dismounted and walked round stooped over. Yep. No shod prints.

"They're still here." I said, remounted, and turned back to the village. "You see anything what looks like a cantina?"

"Over there," said Sanchez.

We rode over and hitched to a couple of posts. Beside the adobe's door it said CANTINA OBAYOS marked in charcoal-blackened axle grease.

"Don't y'all ask no questions until I tell you to. Act friendly like." Sanchez told that to Porras.

I had Porras go in first, and he gave a friendly, "*¡Hola, mis amigos!*"

"*¡Bienvenido!*" shouted an old man sitting at a mesquite limb table with two other men playing *pitarilla*—kinda cross between checkers and tic-tac-toe. I ain't ever figured it out.

Then he didn't look so welcoming when he saw Sanchez and me. But real quick he went back to a smile. The other two just looked at us with straight faces. All wore everyday peasant garb, shaggy hair, unshaved. I didn't see any guns, machetes, or farmer's tools. A coal oil lantern sorta lit the room smelling of coal smoke, tobacco, sweat, goat, and despair.

"We eatin' here or jus' askin' questions?" said Sanchez.

"We are both."

The old man, his name being Mateo, had us sit on upended canned goods crates at the only other table. He said he could make coffee unless we wanted something with kick. Porras looked like he wanted to be kicked after riding hard all day, but I said, "*Café, por favor.*" Sanchez laughed at Porras's woe down look.

"Look here," I said. "I'm going to the shithouse. Give me a few minutes and then ask ol' Mateo there if a young vaquero and a good-looking woman passed through today. Just say they're friends we're trying to catch up with."

Sanchez nodded. "What ya having?"

"Whatever you're having's good." I stood, "*Señor. ¿Dónde está el baño, por favor?*"

"Afuera y al izquierda."

I walked out and took a knee behind a spiky yucca in back of the cantina. It was dusk now and everything was in shadows.

Shore 'nough, a kid come running out of the cantina's backdoor, bee-lining through the mesquite. I went after her, keeping quiet. She banged on an adobe's plank door and was let in. I could hear voices inside as I ran round to the back. There was a mesquite loafing shed with four horses. Two were saddled, but no saddlebags and bedrolls. One was a gray with black mane and tail, the other a sorrel.

It wasn't two minutes before the backdoor opened, throwing candlelight through the crack. A head poked out, and then two people lugging saddlebags and bedrolls headed for the horses.

I stepped out of the shed's shadow clicking back my Remington's hammer. *"Buenas noches,* y'all."

CHAPTER TWENTY-FOUR

The two stopped dead. It was too dark to see their faces. Someone stuck their head out the adobe's door.

"*¡Vete!*" —Go away! I yelled. The head ducked back in.

"*¡Manos Arriba! ¡Suelte el arma! Lento.*"

They let go their gear and ran their hands up. Montero dropped his Merwin-Hulbert after taking it out slow like I'd said. His carbine was with the gear.

"*Tú también,*" I said to the girl.

She reached in her tan riding skirt and set a little pistol on the ground.

I picked up the guns, keeping mine on them. Her revolver was a little S&W .32 top-break five-shot. Not much of a gun, but it'll bite. "*Anda. Cantina.*" I marched them through the cantina's sagging door. Sanchez and Porras were standing.

"What took ya so long, pard?" Sanchez said with a laugh.

"Tell them fellas to keep their seats and nobody leaves. Send Porras outside to keep anyone away. We'll save his grub."

"*Sientate,*" I told my two prisoners.

Montero and the girl sat, hands still up.

She dropped her small flat-brimmed sombrero, letting it fall behind her held by a neck cord. The lantern light hit her full and about took away my breath. She was surely more than just a "good looker" like Cutter said. She had long blonde and copper hair down the back of her brown tight-waisted jacket. A narrow straight nose, high cheeks, and a strong chin. Her glowing copper eyes were wide open, staring straight into me. Brown hair hung down to her thick black eyebrows, making her eyes look bigger.

I couldn't say anything. Just like Marta, I was stunned quiet.

"Can we put our hands down, cowboy?" she said in American.

"Eh, yeah. Just keep them on the table." I doffed my hat.

She mostly looked American, but just moving her head a little, I could see some Mex in her. Her full lips and eyes with long dark lashes.

She said something to Montero in Mex, and they laid down their hands.

"Who's his relations here you was seeing?"

"Who *are* his relations you *were* seeing..." she corrected. "His step-father's half-sister."

"Close kin, sounds like."

"Very." She sounded serious. "I trust you brought the ransom money."

I just looked at her. She figured out what that meant real fast. "What's your name, anyway?" I asked.

"Esmerelda von Grimmelshausen." Seeing my look, she said, "Papa's a Kraut."

"Got it. Where's you from?"

"Where *are* you from... Schulenburg."

"Of course."

"Your mama's from?"

"Mama's from Monterrey," she said. "You too must have a name."

"Bu...eh, Spud Watkins, Del Rio."

Sanchez was grinning like a cat caught a rat.

I looked at him. "Just shut up."

"I ain't said nothing, pard."

"Well Spud Watkins Del Rio, you're going to take me back."

"Taking both of you back."

"I'd thought the general would have told you to finish off Amado." She'd said that like a foreman ordering a hand to muck out the stables.

"He said to bring you both in."

Amado Montero knew we were talking about him. He'd have been scareder if he knew what we were saying.

"You know what he's going to do to Amado," she said.

"No matter to me."

"You're only following orders like a good little soldier."

"I am."

"You don't strike me as a callous man condoning dreadful acts of retribution, Spud Watkins Del Rio."

She had a way of saying things that, I don't know, gets to my head, staring right into my eyes when she speaks and when I said something. She said things like she knew what would happen. Didn't ask them as questions.

"Amado could simply walk out of here and go on his way."

"I can't let him do that, ma'am."

"You would shoot him if he did."

"If he didn't stop."

She looked at me real hard like. "Yes, you would. I could walk out too, and you would shoot me."

"No, I wouldn't."

"You would stop me."

"I'd stop you. Tie you up if I had to. I don't wantta do…"

"You would in all probability beat me or spank me," she said with a smile at the corner of her mouth.

"What? Why would I do that? I ain't never heard of no such…"

"Some men like that, Mr. Watkins, Spud Watkins." She sounded like a little girl.

"I…"

She smiled even though things were real serious for her. She was having one on me.

"Shut up!" I shouted at Sanchez when he horse-laughed and slapped his leg. Thought he'd fall off his crate.

A shy skinny girl set three wooden plates beside the clay coffee cups and scurried out.

"What're we eating?" I asked.

"*Tacos y frijoles,*" said Sanchez.

"What's in them?"

"Goat, I think."

Forgetting my manners, I said, "You two ate?"

"Have you two *eaten*? Thank you for your consideration, Mr. Watkins. We have."

"All right, that's enough correcting my American! That's just the way I talk."

"English, not 'merican."

I glared at her as hard as I could, scaring her into shutting up.

She rolled her eyes.

Sanchez and I ate one at a time, keeping the prisoners covered. I wasn't trusting them for a second. The girl never took her eyes off me.

"Spud Watkins is not your real name," she suddenly said.

You couldn't put blinders on this gal. "It's my *nom de guerre*."

"Oh, spoken like a truly intrepid soldier." I could almost hear her laugh.

Sanchez spelled Porras so he could eat, and I covered our guests. I was glad Sanchez was gone cause he was enjoying this too much. I left more money than the meal was worth. They really weren't bad tacos, had worse. "We're leaving now. Don't be saying anything to these fellas."

She stood, showing a figure like a fiddle violin. I didn't know they made women like this. Her hair she twisted and wound into a bun sticking in a comb. She was a bit taller than me and moved like she owned the place. I could tell she was used to getting her way or anything she wanted.

We led our horses and the prisoners back to the adobe they'd been in. I had Porras watch the adobe. After searching the saddlebags and bedrolls for guns and knives, I told Montero to *latigo* them on the horses.

The girl said, "I'm perfectly capable of slapping leather on my own horse." It wasn't like she was in a hurry, why would she be? She just wanted to show she could take care of her own self.

I had them mount, and Sanchez pulled a ball of sisal out. He tied their hands in front and looped their reins round the twining. Porras kept their guns.

The girl said, "If I fall, I'll be dragged to death by the reins."

"Don't fall off," I said. We weren't going fast or far tonight, and if one of them fell, the horse would most likely stop. Most likely.

I had her stay right beside me, and Montero and Porras were ahead. Sanchez followed with the spares, checking our back trail and ready to go after anyone trying something stupid.

Once we got going back north, she said, "You are making a mistake, Mr. Watkins. I can offer you other options that will be of benefit to you and your...pards."

I looked at her shape in the dark. "I ain't interested. I've got something back there I have to get, anyway. I'm not leaving it behind."

"Oh, you have a girl waiting for you. I understand."

"What! How…never mind. No more talking."

"So Spud Watkins is in love. Then you know how I feel."

"I said no more talking." Hell, I was afraid to say anything, 'cause every time I did, she figured out more about me or corrected me.

"No more talking," she muttered. "Very well. I swear upon my honor that I will not say another word for as long as you wish," holding up her arm like swearing an oath. "I will remain absolutely silent. I promise. And I shall never speak again if that is what you desire." She ended that with a hurt sound, almost like she'd miss my company.

"So when you going to start this forever lasting spell of silence?"

"I can begin anytime you wish…"

"Then just shut up!"

This weren't going to be no easy ride with this sweet thing that I couldn't begin to figure out and leaving me afraid to open my mouth. Heck, she spoke a fancy American…I mean English.

Three hours later I turned us off the trail into a rocky arroyo with a trickle of water. Following it a couple hundred yards, we found an oak thicket and nearby a grassy patch. We'd hobble the horses there and hobble our prisoners.

With their hands still tied, they unsaddled and spread their bedrolls where I told them.

"One of us'll stay awake so nobody wanders off."

"I'll take the first watch then, Mr. Watkins," the girl offered.

"Right. I'll keep your horse saddled for you."

"Oh, would you? That would be so kind," she said.

"I'll see to it."

"I have to make water," she said.

"You what?"

"That means piss in the Texican dialect," she said flatly.

I led her over to a bush. "Here's good."

"Then stand on the other side and turn your back."

"Nope, I ain't doing that," I said.

"No, I'm *not* doing that…sorry," she started to correct.

"Don't say a thing more."

She shrugged and managed to pull her split skirt down and squatted. Now I was used to Marta doing that, but this was different. I turned away.

"I am finished, Mr. Watkins. I cannot pull up my skirt with my hands tied. You can help me or…"

I cut the twine on her hands. "Pull them up and get to your bedroll, ma'am."

"Mera."

"What?"

"Mera is what my friends call me."

"You mean you have friends?"

"Some," she said.

"Well, I ain't one of them."

"No, I don't suppose so…" That's when she grabbed my collars, double-kneed me in the nuts and belly, and took off like a bobcat after a ground squirrel.

CHAPTER TWENTY-FIVE

Sanchez heard the scuffle and yelled at Porras to tie up Montero. I was on my hands and knees trying to suck in some air and pointed the way she took off. He crashed into the bush just about blind in the dark. I had to get up and help him. Felt like I'd been branded twixt the...never mind. If we didn't bring back that emerald, even if we dragged in the thief, the general would probably go harder on us than on Montero, who was just about doomed, though it hadn't dawned on him yet.

Damn that girl. Suckering me, taking off into nowhere with no place to go. Crap, I was hurting. No one had pulled that on me since the first spread I worked on nine year past. I started after Sanchez, trying to listen for him in the brush.

I stopped. Just a minute. That gal was no fool. She might be pampered, but she weren't stupid. She was not going to run until she couldn't and then walk on out by her lonesome. She could probably do it, but only if she had to. She did not have a thing on her, no money, no weapon, no gear or chuck. I limped back to the horses. She was bound to try and grab one I'd wager.

Porras was leaning back on a rock, his pistol steady on Montero.

"¿Qué pasó?" Porras asked.

"Guarda el hombre y los caballos."

He moved so he could see Montero and the horses.

I saddled Clipper — hurt like hell slinging on the saddle and climbing up. There was only a thin smile of a moon. I figured even in the dark I could see better up on a horse. I circled round, moving real slow. If she was there, she'd hear me, and that'll scare her off. Sooner or later she'd give up and head out on foot. I knew I'd pick up her trail at daylight. No sleep tonight, dammit.

I sat still and listened, heard only our horses, small critters scampering, and disturbed birds. I heard Sanchez come back in. I finally gave it up and took Clipper in and hobbled him, left him saddled. Sanchez didn't say a word when I told him how she got the drop on me. Danged embarrassing.

I took the first watch, still expecting her to try for a horse, but it never happened. She'd go back to the village. We'd go back there. No hurry. We could find her there. Only a couple dozen adobes and *jacalitos*. If she took off south through the pass, we'd follow. Porras said it was a long ways to any good sized towns to the southeast. Nothing but a few little ranchos and villages smaller than Obayos.

Couple hours later I woke up. "I know where she's going," I said. Sanchez on watch said, "*¿Qué?*"

"I know where she's going. That rancho. Remember it? She passed it yesterday coming this way. She could get a horse there, I bet."

Clipper only argued a little when I mounted. It still hurt. "I'm heading there. She's on foot. I can catch her." I was figuring it wasn't that long before dawn. "You fellas eat and all and head that way at dawn. I'll meet you at the rancho cutoff. If I don't show, take Montero on back. I'm getting her one way or the other."

"Careful if you catch her," Sanchez said. "She's slippery as a mud cat."

"No kiddin'."

Striking the road, I kept Clipper at a good trot first, heading back toward the village. A yellow line stretched across the eastern horizon. It brightened, and clouds glowed pink and blue. When light enough, I checked out the road and didn't find her boot prints. I turned back north.

I found the girl's boot tracks about a half mile past the arroyo we'd gone up. Her tracks were narrow and with a smaller heel than a man's boots, not that there were any other boot prints out here. Women's prints weren't as deep as a man's, and if that's not enough, women's toes mostly point out more than a man's, just a little.

I could see a light up ahead and to the right. The rancho. I picked up the trot. Something caught my eye. I'd be damned. It had to be her, bent low in the saddle on a black horse and going full gallop. If she'd been on a light-colored horse, I might not have seen her. She curved out from the rancho through the scattered mesquite. She hit the road, and I lost sight of her as it wound through the mesquite and acacia trees, remindered me of umbrellas. They were a good place to wait out a rain.

I didn't think she'd seen me. If she hadn't seen me, why was she at a gallop? I guess she figured we'd be directly behind her. Or, she didn't buy, beg, borrow, or trade for that horse. I'd keep on at a good trot and let her run out her "loaner" mount.

Reaching her tracks, I slowed and took a good look. Small and really round shoes. They'd be easy to spot. We picked up the trot. Then I remembered San José de Aura up ahead. It was bigger than Obayos. If she saw me after her, somebody like her could get inside that village and get herself hidden after sending the horse on its way. I'd never find her.

The road headed mostly north, but soon it was curving to the north-northwest away from a wide, broken up arroyo. I remembered crossing it this side of the village. We went through a place with a lot of washout arroyos crossing the road. She'd had to slow down. Me too. As the sun crawled higher, I made her out again. She was closer and no longer at a gallop, but keeping a good lope. I saw what I could do. I jogged off the road to the right; it wasn't very good any-way. She was curving left on the road, and I'd be outside that curve, making it a longer distance to cut her off. Yeah, I could cut across inside her curve, but that'd let her make for the village. This way, if I got in close before she spotted me, she'd have to turn farther left away from me and the village. If this went right, I could cut her off from the village and run her horse into the ground. I wasn't taking any bets on what'll happen after that.

I dug heels into Clipper and off we went. It was a painful pound-ing. It done me good though, because it truly pissed me off, and I swore I'd catch that girl. We bounded through arroyos and leaped the small ones. I lost sight of her as the mesquite got higher. Then it cleared. Better ground. We kept a steady run. There she was, at a trot now, her black tiring. Her running hard had tired the horse. She turned and looked straight at me. She lashed with her reins, kicked her heels. I used my *cuarta* for the first time, being mean to Clipper.

"Let's get her!"

Clipper's ears laid back. I aimed between them at the girl. She bent low, her legs stiff in the stirrups. She was making dust and gravel fly.

I had a strong horse, a good horse, but I'd been pushing him hard since we'd left. I didn't know nothing about her horse except it was fresh and she was a light load, but she'd been running it harder than I was Clipper. I was pissed, and she wasn't scared…or maybe not.

I put my head down and lashed the *cuarta*.

I heard nothing, I saw nothing, I only felt, and what I felt I can't describe. We were flying like there was no ground beneath us. I bent low over Clipper's neck with his mane flagging, and I felt the wind rushing. The gray-green mesquite was speeding past. We tore across the rocky ground, ripping through thorny mesquite, jogging and leaning into the sharp turns as she did. I was aware of the hoof beats only when they stopped as Clipper jumped narrow arroyos with gravel spraying. We cleared a felled tree with a spray of leaves, tore up a mound's side, and leaped off its steep end to hit the ground with a jarring jolt, about bringing me to tears. Then a dead run to the next arroyo and over it without breaking stride. Clipper gave it his all only because I asked.

We were right on her. Clipper's strength narrowed the gap. She twisted her path like a sidewinder, but we closed on her. She wasn't looking back. I got beside her stirrup-to-stirrup. She took notice and struck with her reins like a bullwhip. The third lash caught the side of my cheek, stinging like bull nettle.

All right. I slung my *cuarta*, catching her on the left shoulder. And again. She veered away as we dodged round opposite sides of a big mesquite she'd tried to run me into. I tugged on my lariat's thong, slung it into a small loop, and tossed it at her. She ducked and dodged to the right. I spun another loop, bigger, and tossed it, catching her horse's neck, dallied it round my saddle horn, and quick-reined Clipper to a sliding halt with his haunches on the ground scattering gravel, twigs, and dust. Fallen back directly behind her horse, the taut trope caught her at the waist and peeled her off to take a butt over teakettle tumble. The horse came to a stumbling halt with Clipper dragging back on the rope like he does a steer.

The girl was on her back, arms spread out, not moving. I slid off and stumbled over to her. She was breathing hard, eyes closed. I hoped she weren't broke something. Not that I cared, but it was hard to get a broked-bone soul on a horse and lead them home. She'd already been enough trouble.

I dropped to a knee. "You all right?"

I barely dodged the knife slash. I stumbled back, kicked at her and missed, rolled to the side as she came at me fast in a crouch with the knife pointing at me. Made it to my feet, sidestepped, and kicked her in the ribs as she stumbled past. She landed with a woof of air, and I flopped right onto her with all my weight. There wasn't any more air to woof out.

Clipper and her horse, still roped together, were stamping round sizing one another up. Horses are so damn funny. They act like whatever their present state, it's what it's going to be from now on.

I stood and picked up her knife, a little hoof-trimmer she probably stole at the rancho. I noticed her saddle didn't have a blanket she'd thrown on leather so fast. Yeah, she'd stoled the animal for sure.

I sat beside her, out of arm's reach, pistol in hand, and gasping for my own breath.

"Are you going to spank me now, Mr. Watkins, Spud Watkins?" That little girl voice.

"Damn, girl..."

"Mera."

"Yeah, with a two-by-four if I had one."

"That would be more than I bargained for," she said.

"Hell, you're more than I bargained for."

"That's what they all say."

I threw the trimming knife as far as I could.

"That's a waste of a perfectly good knife," she said.

"Better that than having it stuck twixt my ribs."

"Why, Mr. Watkins, I wouldn't really hurt you."

Like I believed that after what she done. "Sure, if making me dead don't count as hurting."

"No, you should say, 'Certainly, if causing my death doesn't...'"

"Just shut up! Stay put."

I settled her horse down—well, it weren't really hers—coiled my lariat, and hung it on Clipper. I started to ask her if she was okay to ride. To hell with it. I cut a couple of latigos off her borrowed saddle. "Get your butt over here!"

She walked up brushing at her skirt. She was still breathing hard, but she had an unruffled look like nothing out of the ordinary had happened. She held up her hands, wrists crossed, and I tied them tight, real tight.

"I need your assistance to mount, Mr. Watkins," she said with a pout.

"Put your boot in that stirrup, hook your wrists round the saddle horn, and pull your own self up like always. See. That weren't so hard."

"Now what, Mr. Watkins?"

"Ride on ahead, and I'll be right behind you. If you even look like you going to dash, I'll shoot the horse and rope-drag you back to your general. But first we're going back to that rancho you stole the horse from. They lynch horse thieves here."

She rolled her eyes again. She hadn't ever had to answer for herself much.

"And don't say a damn word unless I ask you something."

"Yes, sir."

I thumped her on the leg with my *cuarta*. "I mean it!"

She sneered at me.

CHAPTER TWENTY-SIX

We got back to the road and the rancho cutoff. I didn't see no one. I whistled, and Sanchez, Porras, and a sad looking Montero came out of the mesquite behind us. The girl's saddled sorrel was with them.

"Any trouble catching her, pard?" asked Sanchez.

"Not a bit," I fibbed, "excepting making me miss breakfast." I said that to put the girl down, that she weren't no trouble. I doubt she paid it any mind.

Sanchez rubbed his cheek, letting me know he'd noticed the rein's mark on mine. "She got herself a horse quick enough."

"Get off the stolen horse and get on your own," I said. She started to open her mouth.

"Not a damn word, you!" I turned to the others. "She ain't to say a single word unless you ask her something. Keep it shut!" I snapped at her as she mounted her sorrel.

I swatted the black horse's rump, and it took off down the road to the rancho. The ranchero would be trying to figure out why one of his best horses is standing outside the corral saddled and heavy lathered.

"Let's get. We ain't stopping until we turn this emerald over to the general. I don't care if we ride all night."

We passed through San José de Aura and neared Minas de Barroterán marked by a gray cloud of coal dust. Esmeralda had been quiet the whole time and sudden like said, "Minas de Barroterán is such a disgusting scar on the land. I hate seeing Mexico's beauty blemished by such awful places."

No one said nothing back. It was just a coal mine and gave Mexes out here jobs. "No talking," I said.

We passed a few peons on foot, mostly women carrying coal in baskets. I wanted to bypass Barroterán, since it's a bigger town. Bigger means more trouble. The best way to sidestep trouble is to go round it. I was looking for an arroyo crossing the road. We'd leave less sign heading up a rocky arroyo. No one was after us, it was just my habit.

Another peon walked down the road, followed by his wife toting a bushel of picked beans. I knew it was his wife cause he turned to look back when we passed her, making sure she was safe from a gringo and a darkie, I guess.

"How come Mexes always walk ahead of their womens?" I asked Sanchez.

"They don't walk with them cause they're showing they don't have to do women's work. Injuns do the same. But they do let the woman walk in front sometimes."

"How's that?"

"She go first when crossing old log bridge."

An old skinny peon with a fat face rode past on a mule smiling and *buenos días*'ing us. Sanchez asked him something about horse-shoeing, I think to get him talking, find out any news.

Sanchez stopped, and his hands went up.

A shot cracked from the side and another to the front, making our horses jump. Two men were sudden like right in the road, and one came out of the mesquite from the left. They were mule-mounted peons along with a horsed *Rurale* in his gray outfit, red necktie, big sombrero, and pointing a Sharps big-bore carbine. He sent a shiver up my back. Had a couple of run-ins with *Rurales*. The two peons had shotguns. Must be like deputies, but more like his gang. The old man with a fat face behind us was pointing an ancient Colt.

The *Rurale* didn't waste no time starting to talk. I made out something about money and the girl. She all of a sudden looked belly sick.

Sanchez turned and said, "He say we have to pay fifty dollar transit tax…"

"Tell him we ain't got that kind of money." I guess they thought all gringos were rich.

"…or he's going to keep the girl and do…"

"We ain't got no fifty dollars. But maybe this'll help." I lowered my hands and passed the general's letter to Sanchez. He moved his horse forward and handed it to the *Rurale*. He read it, smirked, said something, and dropped it on the ground.

"He don't like the general," Sanchez said.

The *Rurale* told Esmeralda to come over to him, and as about as sickly looking as could be, she rode over, stopping beside him. He rattled off more.

"He wants to see if his carbine bullet will go through all four of us lined up," Sanchez said.

Heck, there's more ways to dies out here than to kill a rat.

The *Rurale* said, "*Bajense de su caballo,*" and we all dismounted, except Esmeralda.

I wasn't worried right now. We were in a good position, the four of us on the ground mingled with seven horses, and he didn't tell us to drop our pieces on the ground. And these sorry looking Pedros weren't no gun throwers. It's move now or never.

Sanchez was closest to the *Rurale*, and I was counting on him to take the Mex lawman and his sidekick out. Montero was hand-tied and still climbing off. I didn't know what Porras would do. I'd have to take the shotgun-man to the left and the fat-face *pistolero* behind us.

Pop pop! Crack and *boom!*

I had both guns out trying to decide which Pedro to shoot first. The one to the left and fat-face behind us turned and muled out of there as fast as they could get the animals moving. I let them go. I looked round. The *Rurale's* saddle was empty, and his sidekick was holding his shotgun high, its single barrel smoking. The girl was pointing a revolver at him. Sanchez was looking round for someone to shoot. Porras and Montero weren't to be seen.

"What the hell! No body move!" *Now what?*

Sanchez yelled for Shotgun to drop the old scattergun and dismount. The girl tuned her pistol on me.

"Don't you even think 'bout it!" I said, pointing both my guns at her. She lowered it.

"Take that away from her," I shouted at Sanchez. She had the good sense to flip it round and hand it to him grip first.

I pushed through the horses. Tied up Montero was flat in the dust hoping he'd not get shot. Porras was sitting with his pistol on the ground and holding his bloody left arm. "Damn!"

I took a look at it. He was winged with birdshot, which had also chewed up the left side of his saddle. A few pellets had hit the horse, but nothing serious. His arm wasn't real bad, but it'd slow him down.

Sanchez and I collected the horses that were starting to wander around. Porras's left stirrup fell off cut by birdshot. I led the girl over to Porras. Her eyes were bigger than saucers now that she realized what had happened. "I...I never shot anyone before."

"I'm sure obliged to you for taking up the habit." I helped her off none too easy. "Where in hell did you get that gun?"

"It's mine."

"Not anymore. Where'd you get it?"

"I removed it from Porras's saddlebag a couple of breaks past."

A pickpocket too. I shook my head, secretly glad she'd pinched it. I'd kick Porras's butt for not watching her better if he weren't already shot. Cutting her wrist twine, I said, "Bandage up Porras. Can you do that, or is it too nasty for you?"

"I am perfectly capable of bandaging his wounds," she replied, rubbing her wrists.

"Make it quick. We need to get outta here."

Sanchez and I dragged the dead *Rurale* into the brush. One bullet had hit him square in the side of the head and other in his jaw. It may have been only an ass-bite .32, but he was sure enough dead. I took his Sharps and its bandolier. It was a .50-90. Damn cartridge was longer than my middle finger. I picked up the general's letter. Hadn't done much good. Maybe someone else would cotton to him better.

"You 'bout ready over that?" I shouted at the girl.

"Almost. If you leave me in peace."

"How bad off is he?"

"They aren't deep, maybe a dozen tiny shot struck him," she said. "The saddle's in worse condition."

She'd torn off his riddled shirt sleeve and wrapped the upper arm after giving him a gulp of Sanchez' tequila and splashed some on the peppered arm. That actually brought tears to his eyes. She took a squig herself.

"Look, we can't hang round here. Get Montero and Porras on their horses," I told Sanchez. He threw me the sisal ball. "Get on," I told the girl.

"You're not going to tie me up after saving your life, are you?"

"Much obliged, ma'am, but yep, I am."

"Do you not trust anyone?"

"Not many and least of all you."

"Thank you, Mr. Watkins."

"Welcome." I stuck the Sharps in my bedroll's latigos and hung on the heavy bandolier. Made me feel like a bandito my own self. "We're going straight through town. The sooner we're away from here the better."

Besides companies of *Rurales* working in Mex states, they had some loners living in towns. They named a few *diputados*—deputies. Mostly they were thugs helping the *Rurale* collect "taxes," which they pocketed. Most likely this fella wouldn't be missed. I weren't taking no chances.

I shooed off the Shotgun peon's horse and told him to get. "*Vamos!*" I chucked his muzzle-loading shotgun into the brush. I gave the *Rurale's* Merwin-Hulbert to Porras.

We rode through on a side street instead of the main. A gringo, couple of Mexes, a black Seminole, and of course Esmeralda turned more than a few heads. We stopped at a stream well out of town and cleaned up Porras and his horse. Esmeralda picked out the shot with my penknife. I know it hurt, having had Marta done the same on me once. Funny, he toughed it out showing no pain. Took three men to hold a man down or one girl to keep him steady without laying a finger on him. She splashed more tequila on and used his other sleeve for a bandage.

Sanchez made a temporary stirrup out of rope for Porras. Called it an injun stirrup.

I tied the girl's wrists again. Almost didn't, but you can't let good looks and well-meaning actions addle you. Maybe the closer we got to her general, the more desperate she'd get. Had to keep an eye on Montero too. He was likely to be facing something a lot more worser than Esmeralda would.

CHAPTER TWENTY-SEVEN

I pushed us. Everyone was worn out and had been riding since two nights before, or at least early morning yesterday. We chewed jerky and tortillas in the saddle. The horses were wearing thin too. They'd had only a little feed and not much good grazing round there.

As long as I didn't say nothing about myself, it was safe, I figured, to talk to the girl. I had an urge too. Didn't know why. I was riding beside her ready for anything.

"You all right after shooting that *Rurale?*"

She looked at me blank-faced. "After announcing what he proposed for me, I had no reservations."

"Yeah, I didn't catch all that. What did he say anyway?"

"A lady doesn't repeat such language."

"Sorry, ma'am. Didn't mean to…"

"No concerns."

"Sounds like you had a good share of schooling," I said, changing the subject.

She looked at me sideways. "I went to the Ursuline Academy in San Antonio operated by French nuns of the Ursuline Order. I boarded there from when I was eight to eighteen."

"You lived there you mean?"

"Indeed. I only saw my parents during the summer and at Thanksgiving, Christmas, and New Year's. I only saw them that often because San Antonio is only a hundred miles from home."

She didn't seem too happy living like that. I wanted to ask her other things, how she got hitched up with the general, what got her into that kinda life, if she knew what he was up to. I figured I had no business asking a lady that stuff, and she'd not say nothing anyways.

"You speak good Mex. Leant that in school?"

"Spanish. Yes, and at home along with German, and French in school."

Dang, she is smart.

"What does your papa do?"

"He's a cotton planter. The fifth largest in Fayette County."

After a spell of silence, she said, "And what of yourself, Mr. Watkins? What do you do so you have two nickels to rub together?"

"Just a cowpoke, ma'am."

"A cowpoke who excels in tracking and finding runaway lovelorn."

"Just doing a job asked of me." *Lovelorn? Must mean horny.*

"The general must exceedingly trust the two of you, a gringo and a *chango,* to fetch his runaway mistress."

Calling herself a mistress kinda embarrassed me. "What's *chango* mean anyway?"

"Monkey," she whispered.

"That's not, well, that's nothing a body should call anyone."

"Do you prefer nigger?"

"I don't call him that, but that's just what darkies are called mostly. Don't mean nothing."

"The same as greaser does not mean anything?"

"I don't call Mexes that."

"You are a rare man, Spud Watkins."

"I get called *gringo* all the time," I said.

"That means little, and you know it," she said, real thorny. "It is hardly derogatory."

"It's more like how they say it. It can be just a word like *Americano* or be, what'd you call it?"

She looked at me, smiling. "Derogatory. It means showing a critical or disrespectful…"

"Yeah, that, and I can figure out what it means."

"How about *galleta*? That's a cracker. Crackers are white." She laughed.

"I had a horse named Cracker once. Best horse I'd ever had." I patted Clipper on the neck so he wouldn't feel bad.

I threw that back to her. "You ever get called a *cholo*?"

She looked at me. "Never in my hearing. Do I look half Mexican?"

"Nope."

"So there." Returning to what started this, she said, "So, how did you come to be set after a runaway courtesan?"

"A what?"

"A harlot, a whore if you will."

"You shouldn't be calling yourself nothing like that." She was surely puzzling me.

"One should accept reality. It is what I am."

I could only shake my head. "The general knew we was trackers, so he sent us. We sure didn't ask for the job."

"I assume the generous general offered recompense?"

"Recom what?"

"Reward."

"He said we'd be rewarded. Didn't say how much."

"He must indeed trust you."

"He sent Porras along as our minder, I guess."

"No doubt. He's done other delicate errands for the general."

"He told me I was going after an emerald that Montero had stole."

That got a good laugh from her. "Indeed, you are bringing back an emerald."

Another quiet spell. Sure a smart girl, with words anyways. Maybe not so smart trifling with the general or getting mixed up with him in the first place. Men with power didn't have friends and loves. They only had possessions.

"So, Mr. Watkins, I understand you performing your soldierly duty and returning the general's precious emerald, but you have no reservations in regards to taking Amado to a dreadful doom?"

"He said as plain as day he wanted you both back, and I'll deliver."

"The general desires me back for, well, a variety of selfish perverse reasons. He wishes Amado returned only for retribution."

"Your Amado knew what he was biting off when he…got tangled up with you."

"Yes, he did."

"You left too soon," I said.

"I beg your pardon?"

"You took off too soon. You shoulda waited until he kicked off his grand plan of conquest. He wouldn't have time to chase after you or even send someone else."

"So, Mr. Watkins, would you pursue me if I were to flee again?"

"Probably not."

"Because you sympathize with my plight."

"You just ain't worth the trouble, ma'am."

We rode a spell. I tried to figure saying it different ways, but finally, "You ain't said a word to Amado since we rounded y'all up."

She looked at me with narrow slit eyes. It was like there was frost on her words. "I've no further need of him since he failed to make good my escape."

That just about made me shiver with cold. "So you used him to get away. There wasn't really nothing going on twixt you two?"

"Only what he imagined."

"So you were just using him for your own ends and don't give a care about him?"

"He knew the risks, and he shaped in his own mind what our relationship was."

"So if you had escaped my first-rate tracking skills, what would have happened to him?"

"He'd awaken one morning in a lonely campsite."

"And you're scolding me for heartlessly taking him back to the general?"

She looked at me again. There wasn't a thing I could read on her face.

It got as dark as the girl's heart, with clouds hiding the last bit of the moon. I stayed closer to her. I wasn't in no mood for her trying to hightail it again.

She sudden whispered, "You have been in the general's inner sanctum."

"His what?"

"Office."

"Yeah, a couple of times. Why?" I was specious of just about anything she said, especially since she was whispering.

"You saw the safe, in the corner."

"Yeah. What of it?" She perked me up with that. But I watched her.

"Of course you know what is kept in a safe."

I made a point of shrugging. "Money, I suspect."

"And other valuables such as gold and silver, even jewels. There's one he didn't keep in it." She laughed quiet.

What was so funny about that? Oh, I got it, jewels. She was an emerald, so to speak. What was she getting at? I didn't say a thing.

"A king's ransom of treasure," she said.

"What king?" Did Mexico have a king? Never heard of him.

"That's a figure of speech. It means a great deal of money."

"And I suppose you know how much."

"No, I don't. The general trusts me no more than anyone else in regards to his…treasure."

She was playing a game here. I didn't know what. "I'm sure he don't trust no one. Makes sense. He's got guards and it's big, would take a lot of dynamite, I bet."

"Or the combination."

"Sure."

"I know it."

I didn't say nothing.

"I primed your interest."

"There's more to it than just opening it. A body would have to get in there and out through all those guards and get away from there."

"A cunning individual could overcome those obstacles, especially once the general launches his campaign of liberation." She said that kinda smart-alecky.

"If he had the combination," I said.

"It's my birthday."

"It is? Today?"

"No, my birthday date is the combination."

I managed to hide my just about gagging. Damn! There it is right beside me, and probably no way to find it out without her spitting it out on her own, not that I'd trust her. She would too, because she wants something. No guessing what that is.

"What would that cost me?" I asked her.

"Take me with you."

It'd cost me a lot more than that I thought. "I'll think on it." Clay always said to leave your options open.

"Don't take too long." She touched her leg to mine and then moved outta arm's reach.

With the wind was picking up and lightning flashing in way off clouds, we rode into the hacienda. A parcel of guards followed when they realized the general's lady was with us. They didn't know she'd gone missing. A guard at the gate said it was just before ten o'clock as he gawked at the girl who acted like this was nothing out of the ordinary.

We tied the horses at the big house's rail.

Montero wasn't looking so good. I didn't feel sorry for him even a little. He was real stupid getting himself tangled up with that girl. Yeah, how could a fella rein back from something like her if she gave him the come-on? Still, dangerous ground. He hadn't stood a chance.

"Take him in," I told Sanchez. One of the guards took Porras to the infirmary.

The girl stood in front of me, her wrists tied. She was sure putting on a brave show. I expected her to say something. She knew it woulda done no good. Not now. I had a guilty feeling, but I'd made up my mind. I was doing this to get in gooder with the general. I still had to get Marta and Gina outta here, get our money, and maybe put a stop to this business or put a hitch in it.

I pulled my jackknife open, took hold of her arm, and looking her in the eye, cut the twine. "I don't want you going in there looking like a prisoner."

"I thank you, Mr. Watkins."

"You might not think this, but I'm hoping the best for you."

"He's not going to maltreat me, physically." She turned and then faced me again. "And I wish the best for you."

The general's adjutant, Major Ignacio, came out. Shaking his head, he led Esmerelda inside. Candles lit the hallway. "Wait here, Corporal. The general will want to see you."

I plopped into a chair. Wished Esmerelda hadn't used all the tequila on Porras's arm.

When Sanchez had come out, he said he'd left Montero standing in front of the general's desk, and there were a couple of guards and the adjutant. He'd been told to wait outside.

Half an hour later I walked into the general's office. There wasn't any blood on the floor, so I guessed Montero was still breathing. Or maybe not. Esmeralda wasn't there, either. I saw another door to the right. Not that I expected a change, but the safe was still in the corner.

"Corporal Watkins! It is so good to see you!" Smiling, he came round the big desk and shook my hand. "I congratulate your success. A glass of scotch?" He poured a glass without me saying one way or the other.

"Please, be seated." He pulled over a chair for himself and sat facing me. "This is very awkward, but I am certain Esmeralda told you a great deal, some of which may be factual and most not so true. There is little doubt she attempted to sway you into aiding her. It's her way. I wish for you to tell me everything that occurred. You need not soften anything."

"Well, sir, we didn't have much trouble picking up their trail when we got to Obayos…"

A half-hour later he stood and thanked me, shaking my hand again. He really was happy with it all. He didn't say nothing about Esmeralda or Montero.

He opened his desk drawer and handed me a leather poke. "Corporal Watkins, in appreciation for your efforts and those of your helpers, you will find approximately two hundred dollars in pesos. I suggest fifty to each of your helpers and the remainder for yourself."

He came round the desk again, slapping me on the back. "I trust you and your helpers will keep this episode to yourselves."

"You can count on that, sir. We just found her when she got lost out on a ride." I finished off a second scotch. Burned real good.

"That is most excellent, Corporal. It is so. I sincerely thank you again. Of course tomorrow it is back to work training crews for the guns, a job of the utmost importance."

"We're looking forward to that, sir."

"Very well. We will speak again soon. *Buenas noches.*"

Outside I gave a rundown to Sanchez and counted out sixty-odd bucks in pesos. We looked in on Porras in the infirmary. They were keeping him there for a day. I thanked him and gave him his third of the pesos. He said he'd never had even close to that much *dinero.*

Sanchez stretched a yawn.

"Let's hit the sack, pard. We gotta get back to soldiering tomorrow."

He gave a sour look.

"Yeah, I didn't like doing that at all my own self."

"What ya think happen to that girl?" he asked.

"Ain't no matter to me."

There were things I didn't like about her, but I was hoping she'd get away sometime, somehow.

CHAPTER TWENTY-EIGHT

The morning meeting with the general had been short. He had a lot going on. He just told us to train the crews good and do it as fast as we could. The Gatlings were going to give us a big advantage. He thanked us again for the errand we'd done for him and for our discretion.

Breakfast had been about the same. Gina wanted to know where we'd been, that Marta was all worried. Marta looked terrible. I told her all was well and that I might not make it that night again, but I'd try.

Gina knew something was up and whispered, "Carefuls."

Me and Sanchez with Sergeant Major Cutter were walking to the tents when he said, "You and Sanchez are on special duty now. The gun crews too, once they get picked."

"Special duty?"

"Means you don't have to do any work details or guard duty. All you'll be doing is training on the guns." He stopped. Sanchez ran into me. "I can't say it strongly enough that no one, any of the crewmen, can say anything about the guns to anyone else. They're not ever to say the word 'Gatling' outside the *almacén*. Is that understood?"

"Yes, sir," we both said. Felt like I was getting the hang of this army business. Least we didn't have to do no saluting.

"Good. Make sure the crewmen understand that. You need to remind them constantly. The guns will be devastating, but even more so if they come as a complete surprise to the enemy."

"Yes, sir."

That set me wondering how much of a surprise they'd be since they were stolen from the enemy. No matter, our real job was to make sure they didn't surprise the enemy by making the guns go away one way or the other.

"Bring your gear. We'll be living in the warehouse."

I remembered to get that revolver I'd hid.

The adobe *almacén* looked like that one in Sabinas, just not as big. *¡VIVA LA REPUBLICA DEL RIO BRAVO!* was splashed on the wall. There was a shotgun guard at the door and another walking the flat roof. Four freight wagons sat outside, black wagon boxes, red wheels, skinny white stripes, and red gears. I had seen them before, the day the guns got bushwhacked. One had some bullet holes in it.

Sanchez and me followed Sergeant Major Cutter through a small door. It said, *¡PROHIBIDA LA ENTRADA! KEEP OUT!* A skull was painted beside the words for anyone who couldn't read.

"The big end doors aren't to be opened. No one comes in unless they are cleared by me and their name's on the list." He talked to the guard for a minute, and mine and Sanchez' names were added to a book.

Light came through the high windows. There were coal oil lanterns. Crates and kegs were stacked along the walls. Lots of it was ammunition. That remindered me to find some shotshells for Marta. There were three limbers and another being built from scratch.

Lined up on the packed dirt floor were sure 'nough four Gatling's covered by tarps.

First thought I had was the major hadn't told us something, but that made no sense. Maybe they'd stolen another, maybe even after we left Del Rio. I remembered the major saying they already had one over in Laredo. Maybe they stole it too. I couldn't see them managing to pinch one out of an army fort. Did the Mex army have Gatlings?

"Guns!" Cutter shouted. "Front and center!"

Two men came out of the *almacén's* back end's shadows. One was limping some.

"The old fart with the gimpy leg is Corporal Dollenberg, and Trooper Swink's the sickly looking cuss," said Cutter. "These are the instructors who are helping train the gun crews."

"Bernheardt Dollenberg," said the older limper. "This here's Ollie Swink," nodding to the pale looking skinny-as-a-fencepost fella. Just a kid. "You must be Corporal Watkins," said the old corporal.

"I am." I gave him my hand. He looked like an honest cuss. His ginger and gray bearded face seen a lot of sun. Swink hadn't seen much daylight, it looked.

"You can call me 'Guns'," said Dollenberg. "That was my handle in the 4th Artillery."

"Him and every other gosh dern cannon shooter," muttered Ollie Swink.

"This here's Sanchez. He's been in the army and can help out."

They glanced at him but didn't say nothing. No hands offered.

I turned to Cutter. "How's about giving us a look at them? I wanta see what we gotta deal with."

Cutter nodded, and they each pulled the tarps off two guns. And there they were at last, what we'd been waiting to find all this time.

The first two in line were the ten-barrel .45-caliber Gatlings, spotless clean and shiny. The third was the 1-incher with six barrels. *Damn, it's big.* The fourth gun wasn't a Gatling at all. *I be dipped!*

"What kind of cannon is that?" I asked Dollenberg standing next to it.

"It's a Hotchkiss 2.65-inch mountain gun."

"Mountain gun? It shoots mountains?"

"They told me you knew something 'bout guns," he frowned, spitting tobacco on the dirt floor.

I was trying to be funny, but he was all serious. "He's just funning," said Cutter, making up for me. He gave me a hard look, telling me to get more serious.

"It's so small it looks like it's only good for shooting hills," I said.

Dollenberg spit again.

"Two-point-sixty-five-inch. I ain't used to numbers like that," I said.

"A little over two and a half inches."

"Got it."

The gun was on two wheels like the Gatlings, but smaller, maybe three feet across. The barrel was less than four feet long.

"It's got more sting than it looks," he said, seeing my doubting eyes. "It shoots a two-pounder shell." He hefted up something like a rifle cartridge but a heck of a lot bigger, about a foot long with a pointed red bullet. "It's got two kinds of shells. This one blows up when it hits the ground. What they call a common round. It's uncommonly fatal. Throws steel splinters all about 'cause it's filled with like a quarter of a stick of dynamite." He set the shell down and picked up another with a flat nose and painted black. "This here's a canister round. The tin casing holds thirty one-ounce lead balls. Like a big-ass shotgun."

I whistled. "Damn big shotgun." I wondered what Marta would think of a shotgun on wheels. She'd probably want one.

"Them balls is.66-caliber, big around as shooter marble or a 16-gauge scattergun slug. It can throw that exploding shell two miles," he said proudly.

"Double damn!"

"Yep, but the truth is you can only hit something at 'bout a thousand yards sometimes...maybe."

"That's still pretty damn good," I said.

"It is."

"Sound like you knows all about it."

"I crewed one back in my army days, up in Montana, the Bear Paw Mountain Battle when we put down Chief Joseph and his Nez Perce. That was back in seventy-seven."

"Long time ago," I said.

"Yep, well, I can still handle this little Hotchkiss. Shoots real fast too, it being a breech-loader, not a muzzle-loader like them big ol' cannon in the War of the Secession."

"Heck, they oughta have put you in charge of the Gatlings 'stead of me."

"Well they would have," he said, standing up and taking a few limping steps. "Excepting I can't get round too good seeing I lost all my toes off my right foot and a couple on the left to Montana frostbite."

"That's gotta be tough." And I'd thought I'd been cold riding out of Mexico in the worse winter memorized by the oldsters. I remembered not being able to feel my toes, nose, fingers, lips, or eyeballs. Hell, couldn't feel my head with both hands.

"I can get round, just can't keep up with you young bucks. I'm supposed to help you out best I can. When we go to war, I'll be in charge of the battery train."

"A train, like a railroad train?"

"You don't know a lot. Like a wagon train carrying all the equipment and spare ammunition. Course, I'd like to run this Hotchkiss," he said, glancing at Cutter.

I walked round the guns while he talked. Everything looked right and proper.

"We're building a limber for the Hotchkiss. That's Ollie Swink's and Benito's job. 'Bout the gun, rumor says it belonged to the Mex army, but the governor of Coahuila, Garza, gave it to Guerrero."

"Mighty neighborly of him," I said. "I can use all the help I can get. I knows about rifles and pistols, seen a Gatling fired, but never done it my own self. We gotta teach some other boys how to."

He picked up a Gatling gun book like the one the major in Del Rio showed us.

"I ain't never seen one fire my own self. Been anxious to." He gave me a friendly look. "Let's get to getting to know these guns then."

We spent the day going through the manuals. The big 1-inch gun operated like the smaller ones, but there were a few differences, mainly how it was loaded, and it didn't fire as fast. It was lots heavier, even with six instead of ten barrels. The damn 1-inch cartridge was six inches long. We learned all about how they worked, how to make them shoot, and took one apart and put it together again. Lots more to it than a Winchester. Once I figured it out how the barrels turned and each was loaded one at a time, fired, and then the empty cases ejected, it was pretty neat. I don't know how Doctor Gatling managed to figure it all out and make it work together.

Ollie Swink and Benito finished up the cannon's limber. They didn't have any green paint like the others were painted, so he poured some black into white to make gray.

At day's end we cleaned them up good, even though they weren't fired. Guns made a big deal out of that. "We'll get the men sorted out for the crews tomorrow. I'm going to put an American in each crew so they understand our commands. We'll do the same thing with them we done today."

Something came to me. With me leaving the American Troop, Matt Atwood would be outta my sight. Couldn't have that. Gotta keep an eye on him.

"Sergeant Major, got a request here. How about making one of them Americans Atwood. He's got some smarts." *Not really.*

"Very well, I'll consider him."

Sanchez was trying to come up with Mex words for the gun parts and writing them on the edge of pagers in a manual. Some he just made up a name according to what the part looked like, a cat's tail— *la cola del gato*—or a chicken's leg—*pierna de pollo.*

"That's pretty smart thinking for a darky injun," cackled Guns.

"What brought you to hire on here, Guns?"

"Well, my pension don't bring in much, and there's only so much I can do for odd jobs. My sacroiliac pains me awful too. But a man's gotta eat." He glanced to the side. "But I gotta tell you, son, I still got a hankering for a little adventure. Call me loco, can't help it. And I likes the senoritas." He winked.

"Nothing wrong with that, I guess." I'd had about all the adventure I'd like down here and had more coming I wasn't looking forward to. And there was that senorita I liked too.

We had a lot to pass onto Zach. Sanchez rode out to visit his supposed lady. He even had a name for her, Gerónima.

"Who's Gerónima?" I asked.

"She my teacher at Seminole Nation Reservation up in Indian Territory. She teach me English."

"She musta been a good teacher for you to remember her."

"She was the most beautiful lady I ever seen."

"More pretty than the emerald?"

"Not that pretty."

I met Marta and Gina at the oak tree and told them not to ask about the guns or mention them to anyone. We'd found them. Marta hung on me hard, crying a little. She was scared, having not seen me for two nights. I only told them that we'd gone after some runaways.

Gina said, "She miss you, no like it here. She want to go home."

"*Yo también*" — Me too.

It took me a long time to go to sleep that night.

CHAPTER TWENTY-NINE

At the morning formation, the report taker seemed all anxious when the troops fell in. Then the troop commanders showed by and took up positions in front of their troops. We'd been told to wear the orange sashes.

"What's goin' on?" men in the American Troop were asking.

The staff came marching in wearing gray uniforms. With them was the general. A lot of the men had never seen him. Something serious was going on. It wasn't that we were going; we hadn't done any training on the Gatlings.

The flag was run up the pole and the report taken all as usual.

The unusual started when an ox cart was driven out. Besides the farrier, there were two men standing in the back. It stopped near the staff, and the men got out and dragged a man out the back and dropped him on the ground.

Major Ignacio, the adjutant, marched out from the gaggle of officers, stood at attention, and unfolded a sheet of paper. He began to read in Spanish, all formal like.

Captain Martinez gave us the gist of what he saw saying.

"This man, Mario Montero, has been found guilty of theft and fleeing with stolen property belonging to Brigade General Guerrero by special court martial. He is sentenced to flogging with two hundred lashes awarded. Punishment is to be carried out immediately."

Kind of a low groan went through the men. Two hundred lashes? I can't even think of what that would be like. Can a man even live through that? Then something almost as bad came to me. We're going to have to stand here and watch this fella get flogged to death. Two hundred! *I ain't watching,* I decided. I glanced at Sanchez. He didn't look good at all and gave me a, "I don't like this" shake of the head. Then something worse came to me. I'd brought Montero back for this. Me. Just like Esmeralda said. Sometimes you're dealt a bad hand. I'd been the dealer this time.

The two guards pulled Montero to his feet. From what I could see, it looked like his face had already taken a beating. The guards seized him up against the cart wheel, must be five feet across. The farrier tied his wrists to the cart's side bars, leaving his feet inches off the ground. The guards dropped two rocks at his feet. The farrier tied his ankles to ropes round the rocks. He was spreadeagled, his back to us. A guard ripped off his shirt. The other guard took off his jacket and shirt and laid them in the cart. He picked up a lariat.

"They going to hang him?" Guns whispered. "There ain't no tree."

"That ain't no lariat," said Ollie Swink.

The guard was a big brawny fella. He shook out the rope. It was an eight-foot bullwhip. A grumble of noise was heard.

The whip stretched across the ground behind the flogger. He suddenly threw his arm in a circle over his head, and the whip cracked like a gunshot. Montero jerked, but the whip ain't even touch him. Another swing of the arm, the crack, and Montero jerked hard.

"*Uno.*" Shouted the adjutant and made a mark in his notebook.

Bending his body to lay on full force, he swung the whip over his head and brought it down across his back.

"*Dos.*"

I jerked like it was being laid on my back.

"*Tres.*"

This was going to be hard on everyone.

"*Cuatro.*"

The whip cracks were making echoes off the hacienda and other building walls.

"*Cinco.*"

Montero jerked with each lay of the whip.

He didn't make a sound until *ocho*—eight. And then each lash brought a kind of groan. Until shy of thirty, when he kinda went limp.

I knew I'd never forget this and never quit blaming myself, and the girl too. No, she may have used him, but I coulda let him go. Or maybe not. Getting on the general's good side, had to do that no matter what it might cost. Maybe I'd be the one tied to that wheel if I hadn't brung him back.

"*Noventa y nueve.*"

Blood and bits of hide splattered. Blood was soaking the back side of Montero's pants. He hadn't moved a bit. Blood was spattered on the sweaty flogger. *Damn, we're only halfway through this.*

"*Cien.*" Even the adjutant sounded worn out just counting. He made another mark.

"*Alto.*"

Kinda of a sigh went through the men. The flogger even looked grateful.

The major walked over to Montero hanging on the cart wheel like a wet, well, bloody rag. He lifted his head up by the hair and then let him droop. He looked toward the general and marched over to him and said a few words.

Is he dead?

The general walked over quickly. The flogger saluted, but the general paid him no mind. He lifted Montero's head up.

I guess he had to see for his self.

Dropping the head, the general stepped back, pulled out his revolver, and shot Montero in the back of the head. Bits of wood flew off the cart's side.

The general walked back to his staff and off the field to the hacienda.

It was like a big relief rolled over the field.

The adjutant ordered for the troops to fallout and attend breakfast.

"Best nobody say nothin'," muttered First Sergeant Malone.

At breakfast I told Gina we were all good and that we'll be busy for a spell.

"What happen up there? We hear the whip many times."

"Somebody got punished for stealing from the general."

"He dead?"

I nodded.

"He really do it?"

"No."

Marta gave me a sad smile. Made me wish we could blow up the damn guns and skedaddle. I slipped Gina eight 12-gauge shells I'd scrounged in the warehouse. They were only No. 3 buckshot, about a quarter-inch. They'd do at close range.

I only ate a little of the oatmeal. Some didn't eat no breakfast.

Sanchez and me met Guns at the warehouse. Ollie Swink and a couple of Mexes were already inside painting patches of gray on the green limbers.

"The gray'll help hide 'em in the brush. We'll do the wagons too. Them being black with red wheels, silly Krauts, they stand out like a donkey in the goat herd."

I could see that. "Good idea."

We heard voices outside, shouted marching commands, so I thought it a good idea to stay inside.

Sergeant Major Cutter came in. "Gentlemen, the command is present for duty."

Outside were twenty men, four of them Americans and one was Matt Atwood. Cutter had had each troop give up two men, and he picked the four Americans himself. He and Sanchez spent the morning talking to each man. Me and Cutter talked to the Americans, all from Texas and mostly with a grudge about something. I'd not have ridden on a cattle drive with any of them.

Cutter said, "Not all of them are mechanically inclined, some less so than others, which aren't exactly much on it themselves. A rifle or a hoe is about as mechanical as they get."

He'd divvied them up in crews of four with one American on each. One Mex who spoke a little American and a Texican he left back along with Ollie Swink for the battery train. A grinning Guns Dollenberg was the gunner in charge of the Hotchkiss crew. Before dinner, Cutter put the fear of God into the men, me too, about never ever saying anything to anyone about the guns.

Over dinner Cutter told us the plan for the *Batería de Artillería*. He'd been appointed to command the battery. Sanchez and me were to help him out. Ollie Swink was the carpenter. Four Mexes and a Texican were going to drive three wagons and help take care of all the mules—farriers—four to a gun and a wagon. Ammunition and gear would be carried in the wagons, what Cutter called battery wagons. The Texican Cutter held back, someone he knew, name of Hobbs. An experienced wrangler and wagoner. Looked to be in his thirties.

I sidled up to Atwood. "I asked for you be put in this outfit. Whatever happens, just follow my lead."

"What's going to happen?" he asked.

"I ain't got no idea. Just be ready for about anything. I'll tell you if I find out anything. Can I count on you?"

"If I can count on you."

"You can," I said. *Unless you get in my way.*

We spent the rest of the day teaching the crews what we'd learned yesterday, how they were fired, and taking them apart. A few of the Mexes couldn't get the hang of disassembly as Cutter called it, so they were taught how to load, and they were good for gun cleaning. Guns had his Hotchkiss crew at the other end of the warehouse going through their shooting routine time after time.

Matt Atwood ended up on the 1-incher crew and ran it pretty good. He'd worked vaqueros, so knew a little Mex and didn't too much mind working with them.

I didn't want to get to know any of these fellas, 'specially the Texicans, well, excepting Atwood. When we made our move, whatever that might be, we might have to take out some of them, including Atwood.

After supper we went to a big corral where a Mex wrangler told us these were our twenty-four mules. We had to take care of them, so that's what we did for the next three hours. Then Cutter told everyone to go to their tents and take their gear to the warehouse — and for the hundredth time, not to say nothing about the guns or what we were up to. We were spending the night in the warehouse.

In the morning we were drawing rations, hitching up the mules, getting our own horses, and heading to the hills for some shooting practice for a couple of days. We weren't to tell anybody we were leaving. Once back in the warehouse, Cutter ordered that no one leave.

Sanchez couldn't get away to tell Zach. I couldn't get away to tell Marta and Gina, and we might not see them in the morning. We were going to just up and disappear. Marta and Gina might hear rumors. This move was sure to be noticed and start rumors. Zach, though, would be in the dark.

Something was troubling me. Couldn't sleep, and it wasn't just all the snoring going on. Why did I like Marta? Might as well say it.

Why did I love her? Didn't know what that was. Something people talk about. When they love, something it was like they're jus' saying they like it more than a lot, like a smooth-working true-shooting rifle, or their favorite-most personal horse, or a really cold beer on a really hot day. Loving a woman though, that was something different, even different from liking your working pard. Ol' Bill Tuckworthy at the Triple-Bar said, "I ain't never did no whore I didn't love, at the minute anyways."

Well, it weren't like that 'tween us. So why did I like, or love, I guess, Marta?

She looked out for me, just like I looked out for her. That was a good thing. I could always count on her. Strange for me to think of a girl that way, but there it was. Couldn't figure why she went out on a limb watching my back, though.

She put up with me. Mama sure didn't, not even a little bit. I weren't the most cleverest and shrewdest punch round, but Marta had been pretty good about tolerating my shenanigans. Course I been pretty tolerable with her stunts. I surely wouldn't slap her round like some assholes do their women.

When Marta got grabbed by them banditos, she held a lot of trust that I'd be coming for her, when I didn't know if I could make it. That's what Gabi told me. Marta never gave up on me even when the banditos said no one was after them no more. I surely didn't know why she was so sure 'bout that, but she was, cause there I was. About the mostest rash thing I ever done. And glad for it. Not so glad for it at the time.

I liked watching her. Pretty as a filly in a parlor when she cleaned up. Her eyes, she looked at me, and I couldn't drag my peepers away from her. Even when giving me her stern look, which I saw a lot. But it was somethin' else. What did Clay call her, one of those sawbuck words? "Determined." Clay said that meant to never give up and to concentrate. Whatever she was doing, she was concentrating up to her chin. And there was that other thing. I jus' never knew what she was going to do. Kept me with my boots in the stirrups, you know? I mean, with most cattle you jus' know what they're going to do, the same old thing they all do. But there's always a few in the herd, there's no telling. Hell, all the cattle could be fighting to get away from a puma, but there's one who'll decide to go after the killer critter her own self. That would be Marta.

Guess I answered my own question. I can do that if I think about something hard enough.

Yeah, I needed to think on getting her home and how to do this job without getting ourselves killed dead.

Did I say she's a prime cook?

In the early morning dark hours we were harnessing up all them mules, a real chore. And we were trying to keep things quiet. A lotta kicking and quarreling going on from man and beast. After the first team was harnessed up, Guns had the idea of bringing a team into the warehouse one at a time and harnessing them. That was quieter, and they didn't fight it as much as in the corral with the other mules getting excited. Had to light up all the coal oil lanterns we could find.

Sanchez tried to find an excuse to slip away too so he could tell Zach. Cutter wanted us there with him, and we didn't push it 'cause it might have caused suspicions.

The guns were hitched up and covered with tarps, and the battery wagons were already loaded with rations, feed, ammunition, tools, and gear. Cutter sent one gun at a time up the northwest trail. I took the first one up, then Sanchez was followed by Hobbs with the battery wagons. Guns took the Hotchkiss up his own self, and Cutter brought up the last. We were holding them up at the northwest gate until all reached it. The two guards were expecting us, didn't ask no questions.

We went on up the road a ways and held up again until it was light enough to head out on a strange winding trail. Waiting for the sun to climb up, Hobbs's crew passed out *carne seca* and tortillas. There was some grousing when Cutter passed word that that was all we were eatin' on this trip along with frijoles. They pissed and moaned about no coffee this morning, and the *carne seca* jerky was made from venison and kinda gamey.

"*Es por la Causa,*" said Cutter.

He really believed in that line of crap.

Everyone was having troubles with the mules 'cause they'd never worked together as teams, made worse by four-mule teams. The leader mules felt obligated to kick the wheeler mules behind them. They all wanted to go their own way at their own speed. The farriers had an airtight full of rocks to throw at offending mules. When we finally headed north for the Rio, I knew it would take some time to get them working right.

With any luck, maybe we'd not have to make that trip north with this army. Maybe we could blow up the damn guns.

CHAPTER THIRTY

By the middle of the morning, we turned up a wide canyon. The mules were still quarreling and working hard at being belligerent. Everyone was pretty much fed up with them and weren't treating them too kindly.

Unhitching the mules 'bout started a rodeo, with them running all hither and thither, as Guns called the ruckus. We got them picketed and fed and then set up our camp. Cutter had brought an old Mex on a burro, who got coffee brewing in a three and a half gallon graniteware boiler to shut up the whiners, and he put beans to hot soak for dinner and supper.

After dinner we set up the shooting range with Ollie Swink and the farriers painting rocks white every hundred yards out to six hundred. The book said the Gatling could reach out to eight hundred to a thousand yards, but Cutter said he didn't see much need to shoot that far and waste ammunition trying to learn how.

Guns, though, convinced Cutter to paint a target rock at a thousand for his Hotchkiss crew's sureness, and they might have a need for it. I was all for it, if nothing else jus' to see them do it. They'd have to use field glasses to even see the thousand-yard rock. Remindered me of the long shot that scout Billy Dixon took at Adobe Walls up in the Panhandle with a .45 Sharps twelve, maybe thirteen years ago. Dixon took three shots at fifteen hundred yards and knocked an injun chief dead off his horse. Injuns didn't pester the buffalo hunters no more.

Everyone was ready to shoot these guns. I don't think some knew what they could really do. Instead, we practiced some more doing what Cutter called "manual of the piece." Each man had a number and certain jobs he was to do. We went over it and over it all afternoon. Me and Sanchez went from gun to gun helping them get it right. Cutter wanted everything to be perfect.

Cutter would call us all together and teach us something, like how to adjust the sight or set the headspace for each bolt. Found out something that surprised me. The Gatling fired the .45-70 cartridge as long as your trigger finger, but it also shot the .45 Schofield, a lot shorter cartridge. Anyway, we had a lot of ammunition, over twelve thousand rounds per gun.

We did that "manual of the piece" drill until it was almost too dark to see. Instead of putting the guns up, we left them be while we ate our sorry supper. Then we were back on the guns doing the drills in the dark. After hauling the guns back to the camp and covering them, we got to take care of the mules and horses for a couple of hours.

I didn't have no trouble sleeping that night. Didn't even take any time worrying about Marta and Zach.

After first light breakfast, we lined up the guns and ran through the "manual of the piece" again and again, changing jobs this time. Some men were grousing about the food, the long hours, and doing everything over and over.

Cutter said, "Soldiers aren't happy unless they're bitching."

After a break, Cutter got all the crews together and had a race of sorts, a "competition" he called it. Each crew had to disassemble and assemble their gun as Cutter timed them. Even the Hotchkiss crew, even if they didn't have much to take apart.

Cutter said, "The fastest crew each gets a bottle of beer."

That made it more interesting, but there was grousing because the guns were different. The 1-inch Gatling, they only had six bolts to take apart instead of ten.

One crew at a time ran through it with everyone watching. Cutter wrote down the times but didn't say what they were. He got everyone round a battery wagon, and standing in the bed, shouted, "¡Odos han ganado!" — All have won!

That set everyone to cheering with the Mexes shouting, "¡Rah rah

rah!"

He passed out the beer for dinner, and all the hands were at peace.

After dinner, Cutter told us we were finally going to do some shooting, and everyone on the crews would fire some shots, not only the gunners. This perked everyone up too.

Each man had to show he could sight in on the two hundred-yard targets, and then Cutter let each fire off ten rounds real slow, popping off one or two shots at a time and showing they could keep the gun on target.

Everyone was impressed with the .45-caliber guns but was waiting to see what the 1-inch would do. It was like a cannon going off when Atwood cranked off the first shot. One of those big old bullets hitting the ground kicked up dirt, gravel, and rocks as high as a standing man. The rest of the crew fired a few of rounds. One man was scared to fire it, but they shamed him into it. Then Atwood cranked five shots into a rock the size of a beer keg and broke it up. Then he tore apart an eight-inch tree, leaving a stump.

The Hotchkiss was last, and everyone was really waiting to see it. Guns loaded it, stuck a primer in the breech, and hooked on a pull cord, the lanyard. He took his time sighting it at five hundred yards and shouted, *"¡Apunten! ¡Listos!"* The crew knew to stand back. He stood back too, gripping the lanyard. *"¡Fuego!"*

The gun went off with a crack and jumped back two feet. It hit right at the bottom of the five hundred-yard rock, and gravel and rocks flew, and a cloud of gray dust and smoke spread.

"¡Aaaayyyyeeee!" everyone shouted, along with some rebel yells.

They fired two more rounds, raising the same shouts. Guns had two men hang an old saddle blanket on a big guajillo bush at about a hundred yards.

They loaded a canister round. Other than his crew, no one knew what it was. He sighted and yanked the lanyard and *Blam!* The old blanket jumped, twigs and limbs were torn off, and clouds of dust kicked up all round the shredded bush.

Guns had a man run down and drag the blanket back. Holding it up, it was full of holes like a big shotgun had hit it. Well, I guess a big shotgun had hit it.

We took a break, and that's when four riders came in. It was General Guerrero his own self. Everybody was on their feet shouting, *"¡Viva la Generale! ¡Viva la República del Río Bravo!"*

He sure looked the part with a gray uniform, silver braid, high cavalry boots, crossed bandoliers, a white Mex cavalry kepi with an orange band, of course an orange sash, and two Merwin-Herbert revolvers. Brought back to my mind him cold-blooded shooting that helpless Montero.

The general went round *abrazo*ing everyone. Kinda strange getting hugged by a Mex. I was used to it, but the other Texicans weren't too keen on it. The general watched while each crew went through the manual of the piece. Each gun fired about twenty rounds. Atwood also fired five 1-incher canister rounds, ripping apart bushes and stumps with over a hundred .45-caliber balls in about three seconds. It was like a storm of lead. I could see what it could do to cavalry.

Guns showed off the Hotchkiss, firing a round apiece of common explosive and canister. The general touched off a round himself, laughing heartily with the explosion. Guns then fiddled with the sight and aimed careful like. He fired a shot and hit directly beside the thousand-yard rock.

"Need a touch more Kentucky windage," Guns grumbled.

The general congratulated him with a back slap and said, "*¡Cañonero supremo!*"

Then came the speech, with talking about in Mex—Sanchez saying his words for us gringos—how important the Artillery Battery was to the Cause and how it would give the Army of the Republic of the Rio Bravo an advantage over our enemies.

Not if I can help it. All this shooting showed me we really had to knock these guns out one way or the other.

The general passed out green corporal arm ribbons to each crew's gunner. I got a blue sergeant's band, and Cutter was made a *teniente*, a lieutenant.

Me a sergeant. If that didn't beat all. I couldn't even spell it.

Before leaving, the general talked to me and Guns and Cutter. "It will not be long before the expedition to the north is launched. You must not speak of this to anyone. I can see that the battery will be ready. Besides these Gatling guns and the cannon, we have other surprises for our enemies."

I took a chance, hoping the general might slip me something. "The American army knows we got these Gatlings. How they going to be a surprise, sir?"

He looked at me with squinty eyes, kinda nervous-making. Cutter started to say something, probably to tell me not to be asking questions about secrets. The general held up his hand, stopping him. "It is good you have questions and concerns regarding our campaign to the north." He looked at each of us. "Let us say for now that it is not the fact that they know we have the guns, and of course they do not know about the cannon, but they do not know how we will employ the Gatlings."

I didn't know what that would be, and figured it best not to ask more, but we had to get that to Zach.

Before leaving he *abrazo*ed everyone and told them to, "Work hard, aim true, and be bold." He had one of his men pass out bottles of beer. Truly a great leader!

We shot the guns for the rest of day, and they were getting good firing ten- to twenty-round bursts. Me and Sanchez took our turns on the Gatlings, including the 1-incher. I wanted to make sure we knew how to work them if we had to. It was surely fun. Guns let us both fire a shot from the Hotchkiss too. I watched real close on how he primed it and attached the lanyard.

It took us until after dark to clean the guns and gear to Cutter's satisfaction, break camp, and load up. Took our time to head back to the base. At the northwest gate we did like before, sent one gun at a time to the warehouse all quiet like. It was well after midnight before everything was unloaded and all the horses and mules were groomed. Damn animals were farting up a storm after all the green grass in the valley. We stayed in the warehouse anyways. Cutter said that was our quarters now, but we'd eat with the other troops. "Don't say nothing about the guns to anyone," he remindered all the hands.

Sanchez thought about sneaking out to get a message to Zach, but we decided it wasn't worth the chance of being stopped by guards. They'd not let anyone out this late. Tomorrow night maybe.

CHAPTER THIRTY-ONE

Morning formation was done, and I lit out for the kitchen, and it wasn't because I was hungry. Gina was there, worry on her face.

"Joo come back! They take Marta. Go to *la hacienda*. She good cook, so they take."

"When, how long?"

"Two day."

"Have you seen her?"

"I no see when she gone. Where joo bean?"

"Working. She's kept at the *hacienda*? Where's she stay?" This was worrying. Not knowing where she was to get her out when the time came and what might be happening to her.

"Other girls say womens to work in *la hacienda* live in little house in courtyard."

"Damn, inside the walled compound."

"There more mans here now."

"More men? Now many?"

"Twenty-two *soldados*, and now we give food to one hundred *zapadores*."

"What's a zapa-whatie?"

"*Za-pa-dor-es*. They peons. Not like *soldados*. They do work. I don't know."

"Can you see Marta? Let me know."

"I try. Now go! We talk too much."

∾⫯

"What's a *zapallos* or something like that?"

"*Zapallos* is squash," Sanchez said. "*Zapadores*, you mean. They're sappers, like engineers in the US Army. They build fieldworks, trenches, breach walls, and stuff."

"Well, the general's got a hundred of them now."

"Yep, I hear. I been talking to soldiers. They say he hired a bunch to do work so the soldiers can do more training. Some, maybe all, will go north. They don't have no guns."

"That's good, no guns."

"Maybe. Found out they got a lotta old .50-70 Remington rolling-blocks in the armory."

"Single-shots, not much good, but they can kill you deader than a Sunday dinner chicken. We got a lot to report to Zach. Where is the armory anyways?"

"It's in northwest corner of the hacienda compound. Small building. Iron door with a guard."

While Sanchez wrote the secret letter reporting all what we did with the guns, I told him about Marta being taken to the *hacienda* and how worrying it was.

We spent the day doing more "manual of the piece" with everyone swapping out duties. We even did it in the dark with the lanterns snuffed out and the windows shuttered. We loaded the limbers with ammunition, replacing what we'd shot up, and cross-loaded ammunition in the battery wagons so there was cannon, 1-inch, and .45-caliber in all three wagons. More spare parts, tools, and other gear were loaded.

After the morning formation, Mitchel caught up with me. He was still careful about asking stuff, but I knew he was digging.

"Congratulations on makin' *sargento*."

"Thanks. Big surprise to me."

"So how did it go? I suspected the Gatlin' guns were in that warehouse all 'long."

He'd just told me he'd known about those guns being here. I'd see how much he really knew. "There's three Gatlings, you hear what caliber they are?"

"Two .45s and a 1-inch. Is that for real? Big sumbitch."

That told me he had someone inside telling him, but he asked if the 1-incher was genuine, so he didn't maybe really trust whoever it was.

"It's for real. Big thing, and it'll damn anyone to Hell that it's pointed at. You know about the fourth gun?"

"Fourth gun?"

He *was* surprised.

"Yep, it's a 1.65-inch mountain gun, a little cannon. Shoots two-pound exploding shells and canister."

"Canister?"

"Fires thirty.66-caliber balls like a shotgun. Shredded limbs off trees."

"Hell-fire. Can the crews handle them? They any good?"

"They good." I couldn't help adding. "I helped train them."

"Ha!" Slapped me on the back. "Well, Lootenant Cutter looted seven men from the American Troop includin' ya and Sanchez. I got two more in from this last crowd and expectin' a couple more any day now what been on detached duty."

Detached duty, that was like what Zach and Sanchez are on. I wondered what the deal was there. I'd ask Sanchez. "What they going to do with the Troop then, being so few men?"

"Escort."

"Escort? Escort what?"

"I suspect him."

I just nodded and gave him a sly smile. He gave me a creepy one back.

I was pretty sure we were on the same side. We weren't saying it forthright, just to be safe. I filled him in on the artillery battery and what it could do.

After cleaning the guns...again, and caring for the mules and horses...again, we finally had the night off.

Sanchez hightailed it out to "visit" Gerónima with a long secret letter filled with secrets. I fretted around trying to think of a way to see Marta and maybe get her out of the *hacienda*. I had no good idea how to do that. I didn't think Cutter could help, and I couldn't go in there asking the general about her. No one could know that we even knew each other. When Gina told me about it, I was so surprised I couldn't think straight and didn't ask her if maybe she could go see her. I'd go to the oak tree and hope Gina was there. It would be dark soon.

Waiting under the oak tree, I was worry-stoning myself to death like injuns do, excepting I didn't have no worry stone to rub. There was noise in the brush, and Marta jumped in my lap, scaring me outta my hide. Throwing her arms round me, she was kissing up a storm.

"She miss you," Gina said.

"I miss you too, girl. Are you all right? — *¿Estás bien?*"

"Te echo de menos," said Gina for me.

I touched Marta's cheek. I felt something not right, and she pulled back sudden like.

"What's wrong? — *¿Qué tienes?*"

"She…" Gina didn't go no further.

I pulled out my Erie cap-lighter. Marta tried to turn away from the flaring fuse, but I saw her black eye. "What happened? — *¿Qué pasa?*" I was boiling already.

"I ask questions, and she tell me man hit her because…she no go with him."

"Dammit to hell! I was afraid something like this would happen. You shouldna come down here, girl!" I tried to keep my voice and rage down.

"Is the man still bothering you?"

Gina asked it for me. "I think she tell someone. But the man still bother her."

Damn, I knew I couldn't say anything.

Gina and I talked it out. Told Marta to tell somebody if he tried something else. It was against the rules. I wanted to know his name in case there was a way I could do something.

"Juan Zanatta. He kitchen *jefe*."

"I'll remember that. She still have the *escopeta*?"

"Yes," nodded Gina. "She leave shotgun me."

I told Gina that things might be happening soon and to be ready for anything, but specially to be ready to head out. Marta drew in the dirt where the house in the compound was that she stayed and the kitchen too.

It killed me to let Marta go. No telling what was going to happen.

Sanchez came back in. Two letters had been waiting for him asking where we were, if we were all right. Zach wanted to know how many more men there were now. They had seen more show up.

I told him what had happened to Marta and that I couldn't myself ask for her to be let out of there.

"Not right for something like that happen to that girl," Sanchez said.

In my bedroll, I laid a long time worrying about Marta. I kept telling myself how tough she is, that she could pretty much take care of herself. She'd made it through that long hard ride. It wasn't just that. She'd had a tough life. Marta was no innocent girl when I'd found her, living rough on the road, her family working whatever jobs they could lasso, having to beg sometimes, and I suspect partaking in a little permanent "borrowing" when passing through towns, farm vegetable patches, and orchards. *Nómadas* they're called, wanders. That life had to be hard on a girl. She was proud, had no shame about her life. And she saw her family murdered horrible like. She'd been dealt bad hands more than not. She'd never known a place she could call home, ever. Spent more nights under the sky than a roof. She got taken by those banditos and saw the worse part of life. I knew she could deal with whatever came at her. But I had to get her out of there, no matter those guns or our money. Yeah, I didn't see much of a future without that money, but for sure, I didn't see any future without Marta.

I woke up hearing some rustling. Sanchez was crawling into his bedroll.

"Where you been, pard?"

"That *pendejo de mierda* what hurt Marta, he'll be a gentleman now."

"What'd you do?"

"Jus' talked to him."

A minute later he was chuckling real quiet.

"What?"

"He find out it's real hard to pick up teeth when ya got broken fingers."

"*Muchas gracias,* pard."

"De nada."

CHAPTER THIRTY-TWO

At breakfast I told Gina that Marta's problem wasn't bothering her no more. Still had to get her outta there. Maybe Marta could burn the grub and get herself fired, or do what she done when she was put out with me and my too many beers with the boys. She musta put a pound of salt in my *guisado de puerco*. Worst pork stew I ever had.

"She too good of cook to do that," said Gina.

Don't know which was worse, the stew or the habaneros she chopped up in my rice pudding.

More "manual of the piece" all morning. That was getting boring, and we had a bellyful of training and sleeping in the warehouse. Cutter could see that. He told the battery that we'd clean the guns before dinner and then do some rifle shooting.

They liked that.

Steady.

I sighted on his head. Too many weeds. No clear shot.

"Ain't no way," whispered Cutter.

He moved another step. *Come on. A little more.*

A ghost of dust barely drifted to the left. *Not enough wind to matter.*

He took another step.

Got you now. My front sight's blade fit neatly in the rear sight's notch, which I'd stepped up to two hundred yards. I eased the muzzle down a tad, it being, I think, just shy of two hundred.

Take a breath, let a little out, take up the trigger slack, shift a smite left, he'd taken another step, squeeze like pinching a woman's nipple. A crack and thump in the shoulder.

"Damn!" shouted Cutter. "That's near two hundred yards. I'm trading in my carbine for a rifle. I'd never thought a four-inch longer barrel would make much difference."

"Told ya," Sanchez said.

Cutter sent one of the Mexes to fetch the Tom turkey.

"Will you sup with us tonight, Lieutenant?" I asked Cutter. "To celebrate your promotion?"

"Much obliged. Celebrating your promotion too. I'll bring the beer."

We headed back in from the rifle range. Most of the boys had done good at fifty paces. We'd hung newspaper sheets on bushes. They'd wanted to shoot beer bottles, but we'd had to turn them over to the supply staff. They were going to be used as canteens for the army. I kept thinking I was turning these boys into good shots and they might end up shooting at me. If it came to that, maybe they could finish me quick and not just wing me a bunch of times.

Tomorrow they wanted to do some pistol shooting. Only eight or nine of them even had revolvers. I was having second thoughts about teaching them to maybe shoot at me.

We were outside the warehouse cleaning rifles when a big ruckus started up at the *hacienda*. A mob of riders was coming in with a lot of arm and gun waving—one was waving a saddlebag, some joy shots, and whooping it up. They were all wearing orange sashes and roaring into the compound like a thunderstorm. Couldn't tell how many cause a bunch of the guards were riding with them.

Later a guard rode by and Sanchez asked, "*¿Qué pasa?*"

"*¡Los ladrones de bancos han regresado y tienen mucho dinero!*"

I caught enough get the gist. The robbers of banks had come back with a lot of money.

Sanchez looked at me, and I grinned. First thing that come to me was them sumbitches Brownie Jaeger and Charlie Kern finally come back. Good thing they didn't know me, I hoped.

The guard went on to tell Sanchez that they'd not only robbed the Del Rio bank, but banks in Eagle Pass and Carrizo Springs, a Western Union office someplace, and a couple of stagecoaches. I hoped it wasn't Ol' Debs Freemont. A stagecoach driver could get fired for allowing his stage to be robbed. Ol' Debs had eight kids from his Mex wife. I guess they's married.

The second thing that come to me was my money was there now. The third thing was that there was a whole bunch more money.

Everyone was lining up for supper after remaindering that we weren't to say nothing about the guns. Me, Sanchez, and Cutter were going to get dobs of beans and rice to have with the turkey we were roasting. Gina said they were feeding two hundred-seventy-six now. She got out of Marta there were thirty-two in the *hacienda*, not counting workers.

The one hundred *zapadores* ate apart, getting pretty poor grub, mostly rice and beans, which they cooked themselves, and stale tortillas. She said they weren't being paid, just fed and promised loot. Came to my mind that somebody like that might be swayed to throw in with you for just a little cash or better chuck. I'd keep that in mind.

We were going to groom the horses and mules when a messenger boy showed up. He saluted Cutter and gave him a note.

"Fellas, we have to report to the American Troop right away. Fall in and we'll march on over there."

We'd practiced on the guns a bunch, but marching like soldiers, not so much. When we got to the tents, the little American Troop had fallen in too with Mitchel standing out front. The general's adjutant, Major Francisco Ignacio Elizondo, was there too. He looked the part of a Mex cavalryman, stern, tough, and proud.

The adjutant said for all the Mexican troops to fall out and assemble over to the side. I was sudden like having a bad feeling. Remember Goliad? I wished I'd left that pistol hidden in the tent. There weren't any loaded guns closer. I still had my knife. Sanchez cut his eyes to me and stepped away with the Mexes.

Right in front of us, a tent's flap flew open and out stepped Brownie Jaeger, his eyes flashing round at us all. Then out came Charlie Kern, gripping Marta by the arm.

What the hell? That rattled my chains. He shore don't know nothing about her, or he'd know by her eyes that a wildcat was about to cut loose on him.

"Any y'alls know dis gal?" shouted Jaeger, still talking funny.

Marta didn't even glance my way. She was playing it good. She didn't look scared, just real pissed. This might not go well for Jaeger and Kern.

Atwood looked at me quick like, and then looked away.

"Dis here gal's named Martha or thumthin' and's from Del Rio."

How'd he know her name, even if it's the American way of saying it, and know where's she's from?

"She belong to a cowpunch named Bud Eugen, 'posed to be some kinda outlaw hunter."

Mitchel looked at me, but turned his eyes looking over the bunch of us. But now he knew. I could see it in his eyes in just that fast look he gave me. He knew who I was. Had to be that damn newspaper story. That's probably what clued in Jaeger too. But how'd that give Marta away? I knew, her name was in that story, and it had said, "a young comely dumb Mexican girl..."

I didn't particularly like them saying that about her.

Everybody was looking round, so I wasn't worried about being given away like that. Atwood looked at me again. This was his chance to give me up if he was thinking on it. He turned away and shrugged.

Cutter looked all confused.

Mitchel stepped up and looked at the adjutant. "Major Ignacio, what's he playin' at and who the hell is this man?" pointing at Jaeger.

The adjutant spoke good American. "He see this *niña*, she serve food. He try talk to her and she *muda*, no talk. He say she woman of man who chases *El Xiuhcoatl* to Mexico. He say she kills *El Xiuhcoatl*. I do not believe."

"Ya seen this gal 'fore?" asked Mitchel "What's your name anyway?"

"Thargeant Brownie Jaeger...jus' promoted."

"Sincerest congratulations. You seen her before, Sergeant Jaeger?"

"I ain't."

"So's why you think she's the same gal?"

Jaeger bristled up. "The newthpaper. There was this thory. How many dummy Mex gals are there?"

"I don't likely know. How many dumbass Texicans are there?"

"Who ya callin' a dumbass? You callin' me a liar?"

"Jus' questionin' your judgment. I'm an officer, and that's what officers do."

"I do not understand this," said the adjutant.

"Me neither," said Mitchel. "So ya got a Mex gal what can't talk, and you say her name's Martha. She tell you that?"

"No. Course not, t'he's a dummy."

"So how'd ya..."

"I axed 'nother cook girl. T'he thay tho."

"So how'd she tell this other cook who she is? She write it? Ya know many Mex gals that can write?"

"I don't know..."

"And this tiny little horsefly of a gal's a notorious bandito killer and belongs to this fella Bud-whoever, and you think this fella's here?"

"I do."

"Well, if he is, what of it?"

"He'th a bandit killer hith own thelf," Jaeger whined.

"If he's here, so what? Looks like we've drawn a bunch of riffraff here." Most of the Texicans laughed. "I'd say that he's here for the same reasons me and you are. If he's here."

He turned to Marta. *"Niña, conoces un hombre llamado Bud?"*

Marta shook her head and looked confused, her eyes crossing. She was sure good at play-acting. Even drooled down her chin.

"Major," Mitchel said. "You see any more reason to be wasting our time?"

"I do not. Everyone to go back to duties." He looked at Jaeger. "I will not mention this to the general." To Marta he said, *"Mis disculpas, señorita. Te puedes ir."* He'd apologized and she could leave.

She turned, kicked Jaeger in the knee, and took off for the *hacienda.* Everyone was laughing excepting Jaeger, even Kern.

She never looked at me once. Mitchel gave me a wink. He knew who I was for sure.

The artillery battery marched back to the warehouse in its own way—not very well.

Sanchez puffed his cheeks, blew his breath out.

"Yeah, that was too close."

He nodded. "Who is that asshole, Jaeger?"

"He's the one that shot the banker dead in Del Rio."

"He's going to have to be kilt too."

I nodded. "As dead as can be."

"What the hell was that all about?" asked Cutter, walking up.

"I ain't got no idea," I said. "You ready for some of that Tom turkey?"

"Yes I am. That little no-talking gal was supposed to have killed that *Xiuhcoatl?* Wasn't he supposed to be some exemplarly, mean murdering bastard?"

"Worse than that from what I heard," I said. "But you know how

them stories are."
"Yep, just stories."

CHAPTER THIRTY-THREE

Cutter had it in mind to do some more shooting. We'd leave again in the early morning, but take only one .45-caliber Gatling and the 1-incher — what the Mexes called the *Gatling poco* and *Gatling grande*. Guns would stay back with the Hotchkiss for crew drill. They couldn't shot off any more ammunition. The boys didn't mind, even if the chow wasn't as good, so to speak. They didn't have to put up with all the army stuff, formations and marching round.

In my bedroll, I did my best thinking there, I tried to ponder out what we could do to knock out the guns, get the money, and get outta here with the girls. That was all a tall order. It was over a hundred beeline miles back to Texas.

The biggest snag was the money. It was in a safe and under guard in the hacienda, a fort inside a fort. It wasn't a real big safe like the one in Del Rio, but it looked pretty stout. Might as well be in a bank in damn New York, or on the moon. Maybe I'd have to settle for blowing up the guns and forgetting the money. I'd at least get the thousand from the army. That didn't sit well with me. I wanted my, our, money. I had to get the girls out too. Another thing, it could turn into an ever harder ride back than before with a whole army chasing us, seeing they were heading in the same direction. It was all real thorny.

I wasn't any good at planning stuff. Whatever happened, we had to blow up those guns. All the Texas Rangers, army, and militia could be waiting on them at the border, but those guns gave the Guerreroistas an edge. So, what was the best way to blow them up? Could we do it right there, Sanchez and me? First get some dynamite sticks from Zach. Everyone sleeping, we'd sneak round, put two or three sticks between the barrels, light the fuses, and get outta the building. Our horses would be saddled outside.

That just weren't no good. We'd have to saddle the horses first. There were guards at the corrals and outside the warehouse. Sneaking round lifting the traps, putting in the dynamite, and then going back round to light the fuses, all with the boys sleeping all over the place. Then we'd have to ride out of the base through the horse guards after the warehouse was blowed to hell and back. Something else. I made a point of not getting to know these boys in the battery, Texicans or Mexes. But you can't help it. Most of them were down and out. Peons never having a chance to own land or anything, outta work cow punches, other fellas who had no luck. What kinda man would I be to light off twelve sticks of dynamite amongst sleeping men? I wasn't that way. I didn't think Sanchez was like that, either.

What else could I do? The next day, we were taking the guns out, but just two of them. Blowing up two was better than none. Shoulda thought of this the day we had them all in the valley. The valley was a few miles off. No one else round. No, wouldn't work. We were not staying out for the night. When would we be able to put in the dynamite? When could we even get the dynamite from Zach?

The way things felt, we were going to be moving soon, going north. We'd be on the trail for days. We'd be camping out for no telling how many nights, and everyone would be bunked by the guns. There would be guards, pickets they call them. Same deal as in the valley. Too easy to be catched.

Where were the girls going to be? Were they taking cooks with us? Most likely. Made sense they'd take Marta and Gina, being the goodest cooks, and bring their own horses. But maybe they'd leave them back. I'd just have to see. We'd do what we have to do to blow up the guns and maybe even get the money. The girls could slip away and make their own way home. They got down here on their own, didn't they?

That plan was not worth a damn. Even if I made it back, I'd be worried sick about them on their own and no way to help them. Leaving Marta behind to fend for her own self, I knew she could do it, but I wasn't letting my daylight fade away. I was bringing her out with me one way or the other. Gina too, since I got her into this.

And the money. What about the money? They had to be taking it with them. How? In that safe on a freight wagon? Small safes on different wagons? Hidden in saddlebags? They were sure going to keep it quiet where it was, and anyone asking about it...well, not a good idea to let on that I even knew about the money. That safe, that was a problem. But we had dynamite. But they'd have guards. Mitchel said something about the American Troop doing escort duty. Maybe he could help and come up with an idea. If we could get to it, how much money could we carry? No matter, I only wanted my two-thousand and eight hundred fifty dollars, and if I had a little pocket space left, well.

My head was hurting. I needed to go with Sanchez to visit Gerónima, I mean Zach, my own self and talk this out. No time for secret letters.

We woke up earlier than intended. Outside were a whole bunch of ox carts and freight wagons lining up. Cutter said to get our mules hitched up to the guns we were taking and to saddle horses. We were to stay out of the way of the convoy forming up. I sent Sanchez over anyway to find out what was going on. He walked over like he belonged there and talked to some farriers.

Coming back, he said most were loaded with fodder and feed. All the wagons full of scaling ladders we'd helped make when we came here were also loaded with picks, shovels, and axes. They were headed for Sabinas and said they were starting a couple of days early before the rest of the army cause they were slower.

We headed back to the canyon and spent the day shooting the Gatlings, rifles, and revolvers. One of the boys bagged a whitetail. Made for a finer supper. We cleaned the guns before dark and took our time heading back in. When we got there, most of the *zapadores* were all lined up with what little they had rolled in a serape and carrying a shovel or pick. They had water-filled beer bottles with cording tied round them for carrying slings. Some of them carried old .50-70 Remington rolling-block rifles. While we were unhitching the mules, they marched off singing some song.

I said to Sanchez, "It looks like we going to be moving out. It's going to happen fast. We need to see Zach tonight, face to face."

"When we going? They might say no one can leave."

"Soon as we can slip out."

I wasn't able to see Gina during the whole day, so I had no idea what had happened with Marta and wasn't able to tell Gina what was going on. She'd probably heard every rumor anyway, so I needed to see her in the morning.

Cutter had left while we were grooming the mules and horses. Just about when we were through and ready to go for our visit to town, he came back.

"Been talking to the adjutant. Orders. We're going to be moving out before first light. We've got everything pretty much ready. We need to load all the feed sacks we can and some fodder bails too."

It came to me that since we had work to do that Sanchez and me might not be able to visit Gerónima. I needed an excuse.

I went to Cutter. "Lieutenant. I'm sorry. Something I been putting off. The trace hook on number two's limber's busted. We can do with a cord loop, but if we're going into business, we best have everything in order. Cord might break. I'll take the busted one over to the blacksmith and have him turn out another. Shouldn't take long."

"Take care of it, Spud."

The warehouse was mostly empty with the boys tending the horses and mules. Taking a pry bar from the limber's tool chest, I snapped the trace hook and unscrewed it from its bracket. A shame, seeing it was brand new.

I took Sanchez with me to see the smith cause his helper didn't speak American. We had to have a new one tonight. He'd take care of it. Would take less than a couple of hours. Sanchez stayed with it, and I rode out, putting on my orange sash like the guards. Took my time riding over to the southwest side like I was patrolling. No one stopped me in the dark.

I followed the tree-lined arroyo to the woods as it curved to the right. It had been sometime since I'd come this way and only once. I couldn't remember distances. It all looked different in the dark too. Just followed the stream and kept my eyes and ears open. I knew I'd find that rock outcropping, and the camp was maybe a half-mile or so beyond as best I could recollect. Sure enough, there was the outcropping and there were two stones on the flagstone. I got off Clipper and picked up the secret letter to take to Sanchez.

I rode, on making small noises passing through the brush. Didn't want to sound like someone sneaking up. Let them hear me. Hard to tell how far I'd gone, and I was worrying that I might have gone too far. They'll have no fire after dark. I smelled horse shit. Fresh too. Then I remembered the fallen juniper tree, and there it was on the arroyo bank. I got off Clipper again and headed into the trees quiet-like, banging two sticks together and saying every few steps in a low voice, "Friend coming in."

Right in front of me two sticks thumped. "God's own truth, Bud. Ya liked to scare the shit out of us," whispered Musty.

"What, you don't get many visitors?"

"Not even a hoot owl."

We shook hands hard. It was good to hear his voice. He held his Whitney Kennedy carbine crooked in his arm.

His dark shape led me to the hidden camp. I could hear the horses stirring nearby. "Hows you keeping with the lieutenant?"

"I's bored as can be. The horses and mules gettin' tired on me caring for them so much, never been so well groomed. Zach's no trouble. He reads a lot and tolt me all 'bout some fellas named Homer and Ulysses and a lady named Penelope. I knew a sweet gal up in Victoria named Penelope, excepting she weren't as faithful as that Greek gal."

Zach came up, shook my hand. "Good to see you, Mr. Eugen. Is there a problem?" He sounded a tad nervous with me showing up like this.

"That's Sergeant Watkins, and no problems, just things are starting to happen. We're moving out in the morning."

"Sergeant? Congratulations." He seriously shook my hand again. I thought it queer that he'd congratulate me for making sergeant in the enemy army, but then I thought it meant I'd gotten in good with them.

"I gotta hurry and get on back. The way this sits..." I told him everything I knew, which wasn't much. The battery was pulling out before light. I didn't know if it was just us, everyone, or just part of the army. When I'd left the base, there wasn't much going on. Told him about the feed and fodder carts and scaling ladder wagons going and then the *zapadores* just now. I told all about the battery and that maybe I did too good a job helping train them.

He asked me a lot about Guerrero and other people like that adjutant and Cutter. I told him that I was pretty sure Mitchel was on our side and why I thought that. I told him of Atwood too.

"You must use extreme caution in dealing with either of them. Do not tell any more than they absolutely need to know."

I had to tell Zach that I didn't have an inkling of Guerrero's plans. I only knew we were going to Sabinas, and maybe Allende was where he was heading. Seemed like everyone was going meet in Sabinas, what Zach called a "rendezvous."

"Wishing there's a way we could do away with Guerrero. This whole shindig could come to a stop without letting a bunch of men get dead."

"*Honi soit qui mal y pense*," said Zach. "That means 'Evil be to him who evil thinks.'"

"That ain't Mex," said Musty. "What is it?"

"Latin."

"Latin. Ain't never heard of that injun tribe. They way up north?"

"More eastward," said Zach.

I told Zach what the problems were about trying to dynamite the guns. Just too many people round and no way to make good our escape. He understood, but we had to find a way. "This is critical beyond all things."

"We'll have to go with however we can pull it off. There's always a time someone slips up. We just need to be ready for it and not slip up our own selves."

I didn't say nothing about trying to bring the girls out. I knew he'd say they weren't important, or getting my money back. I did tell him about the bank robbers coming in with more loot.

"I foresee another major problem to overcome," said Zach. "I cannot fathom how we will be able to remain in communication once you reach Sabinas and then as Guerrero advances north. All we can do is follow the column on one flank while remaining unseen."

"Keep on one side or the other then," I said. "That way if we have to run for it, we'll head in your direction if we can. That sound good?"

"Indeed." He checked his map. "It appears that the most favorable terrain for us would be to the east of the road to Allende."

"They had wanted to use Sanchez and me for scouts. The battery can get along without us when on the road. I'll see if we can work as scouts. That way we can maybe patrol out to the east. You'll see, and maybe we can even hook up and tell you any news."

"That is an excellent plan, Sergeant. We'll make a soldier out of you yet!"

Musty laughed.

I hope not.

"Maybe when we get to Allende, we'll meet you on that road they tried to bushwhack us on. Maybe you can watch it at night for if one of use can get away."

"Good plan. Destroying the guns though, that will be paramount," Zach said, real serious.

"It is."

"Do you think you can covertly convey a small number of dynamite cartridges without being discovered?"

"They ain't checked no one's saddlebags or warbags. I think I can."

"I will give you eight cartridges and eight thirty-inch Brickford fuses with detonators. Do remember to cut off the first four to six inches because of moisture buildup. A twenty-four-inch fuse burns for approximately one-minute. Remember, they do not always burn consistently."

"I got it."

"You and Corporal Sanchez…"

"He's only a trooper in our army," I said, real serious like.

Musty cackled. Zach didn't.

"…should each carry four cartridges. Carry the fuses separately, as far from the dynamite as possible. One cartridge will destroy a gun if inserted between the barrels or in the firing mechanism."

"What about the cannon?" I asked.

"Good question. One dynamite cartridge slipped into the muzzle or breech will inflect irreparable damage. Two would be even better, or load the gun and drop a stick into the muzzle. For the Gatling, two cartridges would be better too. For either weapon, you only need to light one fuse. It will detonate both cartridges, but if possible, light both in the event that one may flash off."

I rolled the dynamite up in my poncho tied behind the cantle and hid the fuses in both saddlebags.

"We do have another consideration," said Zach. "When we start shadowing the army once it commences moving, we will have to release the spare and the pack mules. I see no way in which the two of us could covertly follow with three unridden animals."

I hadn't thought about that and didn't cotton to not having a spare, but I could see his reasoning. I talked him into keeping the spare unless it became troublesome.

Zach got all the more serious than he was already. "Mr. Eugen, or should I say Sergeant? Your country is counting on you to aid in defeating this threat to our freedom and way of life. I know myself and your country can count on you and Corporal Sanchez. Godspeed to both of you."

We shook hands.

I ain't never heard anyone say something like that before, except the general that one time, and I didn't buy that spiel. Zach was dead serious about it. I meant it when I said, "I'll do my best."

Musty walked me back to the arroyo. He looked at me in the moonlight. "Bud, you best take care yourself. Your woman's counting on you coming back, and I'm counting on you for a job. And if anyone tries to kill you, you best kill 'em right back."

"You'll have that job, but I got a feeling Clay DeWitt ain't going to like letting you go."

"Hell, I'll have to work for both of you."

I stopped walking. "Speaking of my woman, she's here."

"What! Marta's here? How'd she...?"

"She showed up with Gina. They followed us. They're cooking for the army."

"I be damned if that don't beat all. It figures they be cookin'."

"I'm going to have to figure out how to get them outta this too."

"Damn."

"Don't tell Zach."

"My lips is sewn shut with rawhide."

I remembered Musty telling me he'd seen that done to some deserving loudmouth once.

I didn't know when or even if I'd be seeing Marta and Gina again before we left. I just wanted them to go on their own. Safest thing I could think of. But what if Gina couldn't get the word to her? I'm going to do nothing but worry.

I got back to the base in time to collect up Sanchez and the trace hook, and we got it fixed to the limber.

Laying in my bedroll. *How we going to do all this stuff? Damn.*

CHAPTER THIRTY-FOUR

They had breakfast for us long before sunrise.

"How's Marta?" I asked Gina. She looked tired.

"I no see last night. I no see joo."

"We got back in from training after supper, and I couldn't get to the tree. You haven't heard nothing from her?"

"No. I no worry. I see maybe tonight."

"Ain't you heard? We're moving out. We're going north."

"Joo mean joo not going to dee training? That what they tell us, joo go to train."

She was confusing me. "No, we're not going to train. I don't know when I'll see either of you. Have they said anything about cooks going?"

"They say we go sometime. Not when. I do not know. They say we go to train."

"You're going to train?"

"They say."

"Look, Gina, both y'all need to get horses tonight, any horses, and get outta here. Go to the Dew. Don't worry about me. Stay away from Sabinas and *los Cinco Manantiales* and just get on home anyways you can."

"Marta say she no go without joo."

"She has to go. Tell her I said so. Bad things are going to happen here, and we'll be leaving soon. I can't be worrying 'bout you two. You gotta go."

"Joo leave us? Why joo go?"

"I ain't got no choice. We have to go. There's a reason for us being here."

"I try and tell Marta," she said. "We go if joo wish." She was really sad sounding.

"I wish it."

We hitched mules to the guns and battery wagons. Everything we needed was loaded. Everyone got their horses and rigged bedrolls. Cutter said, "We won't be coming back. Keep the orange sashes put away."

I said to Sanchez, "We're jus' about on our own, pard. It's going to be pretty much on us to blow them guns to bits."

Sanchez looked at me. "Nothing new. Been on our lonesome this whole time."

"True 'nough."

"Zach and Musty are going to follow us out to the east. If we've got to run for it, head east and maybe we'll find them. I told him too about us volunteering to scout and we'd try and do it to the east. If that don't happen before we get to Allende, we can meet them on that road outside Allende where those peons tried bushwhacking us."

I passed him his four dynamite sticks and fuses.

We moved out, and it really hit me that we weren't coming back, and we were leaving behind Marta and Gina. I had no idea what was going to happen or where we were finally going. We were told to move fast, not stop for anything, not talk to anyone as we passed through Sabinas, and not let any of the guns or wagons fall behind. Sanchez and I had the job of making sure everyone kept up.

One of the farriers flicked a bullwhip toward Sanchez, not liking that he told him to speed up. Sanchez' hand went to his revolver, but I shook my head, and he went on. I knew he'd not use it rashly. I sidled up to the farrier, an American named Collerick, kind of lazy. "You pop a whip at anyone again, I'll let them use it on you. Understood?"

"Yes, sir." The bullwhip demonstration we'd seen was enough for him.

"Just shut up and keep up." I rode on.

We'd barely got going and were passing the hacienda when a courier with his white armband ran up to Cutter's horse. Cutter turned and rode down to me. "How about coming with me, Watkins? The general wants an update before we head out."

Cutter put Guns in charge, telling him we'd catch up directly, and we trotted through the hacienda's guarded gate. Inside we found Sergeant Kraig hurrying round. Major Ignacio was in a hurry too. He was carrying a stack of papers that would last the Dew's outhouse for a season. Two guards stood at the general's door.

The major said, "The general will see you."

"Ah, Lieutenant Cutter and Sergeant Watkins, thank you for taking time off from your urgent duties. Is your battery and all the guns ready for action?"

"It is, sir. The men are ready, and we have everything we need, sir."

"Very good, very good indeed."

The safe was still there. The big green rug was rolled up behind the general's desk. There was a two-foot wide track like used for coal mine dump cars laid on the floor from the safe's corner leading out the door in the other corner. There was a back door down the hall. The safe sat on the tracks, and a couple of really thick ropes were tied round it. Packing crates and valises were stacked beside the corner door.

I smiled to myself. The safe was going to follow us.

"Sergeant," said the general, "we are taking everything of use on the campaign. Tell the cooks to provide you with a case of beer to cut the trail dust."

Cooks? "Yes, sir. Thank you, sir."

I went down the hall to the kitchen at the other end of the building. Two women were putting airtights in crates. No Marta.

"*El General dice den cerveza.*" I got it close enough for them to understand. "*¿Dónde está Marta?*" I was taking a chance doing this.

They tittered and pointed to the storeroom. The door swung open, and there was Marta, her eyes bigger than I'd ever seen them. She 'bout jumped on me, hugging me hard, holding on, and crying. Right then, if there was any way I could of gotten another horse, I would've just rode out of there, leaving behind Musty, Sanchez, Gina, Zach, the money, the guns, and give up trying to stop this stupid war.

She grabbed me by the arm and dragged me to the outside kitchen. It was partly covered by a tin roof, putting us in dark shadow.

It's the first I'd seen her in daylight where we were alone since we'd left the Dew. She laid her head against my chest and just held me. I didn't wanta let go any more than she did.

"We're going to get out of here. It's all going to be over soon." I didn't know how or if that was even true, but I was going to try. Why the hell did I ever get into this? Oh, yeah, it was because of her, sorta.

As best I could, I tried to tell her to get a horse, find Gina, and go back to the Dew. I'd get there somehow. She was shaking her head the whole time.

From behind me came, "Well, if dish don't beat it all to hell, Bud Eugen and his Mex dummy." Brownie Jaeger's Colt was pointed at my middle, and he was coming toward us with a sneer. "The bandit killer that ain't 'posed to be here."

I raised my hands, trying to push Marta away. He took my holstered guns. The Schofield was still in the back of my belt. I'd use it, but it crossed my mind that I'd have a hard time explaining why I shot him. "He complained about the cooking?" No matter, he was as good as dead, or else what we were trying do was going to fall apart.

There was a soggy *whack*, and Jeager, kinda cockeyed-looking, staggered into me, knocking me against the wall and making Marta take a fall. She was up before I was with her Colt Lightning in her hand.

Ormsby Mitchel was standing there with a foot-long iron double-end pot-hanging hook. "Looks like Jaeger was right, this is your woman from that newspaper story."

It took me some seconds before I could start talking. "Where'd you come from?"

"I saw ya head back here and was goin' to talk to ya, but then I saw Jaeger follows ya in." He was kneeling beside the facedown Jaeger. "Well, I do believe he's as dead as a cow pie."

"You killed him?"

"I had to defend myself," he said, all put out.

Marta dropped the Colt into her skirt pocket before Mitchel saw it.

"Damn, what we going to do with him?" I asked.

"Same thin' I always do, hide the body," the Ranger mumbled.

We dragged Jaeger to the other side of the kitchen where Marta was pointing at a wooden bin. Sacks of cob corn were stacked beside it, I guessed pulled out to load on wagons. We dumped him in a bin.

Marta picked up his Colt and threw it in and handed me my guns.

"Look, Watkins," said Mitchel, "we both have to get outta here. They're bringin' the cooks tomorrow, so don't be worryin' 'bout your woman here. Y'all be able to meet up soon 'nough."

I nodded and tried the best I could to get Marta to understand. She weren't happy about it, but she stayed there anyway.

"I figured ya're workin' for the army all 'long. Ya done good gettin' in with Gatlings. Is that your job, to take them out?"

"And I know you're a Ranger." That surprised him. "We're supposed to blow them up or steal them back, but we're trying to stop this shindig any way we can."

Mitchel nodded. Looking at Marta wet-mopping Jaeger's blood and brains off the flagstone floor. "That little gal really kilt *El Xiuhcoatl?*"

"Twice over."

"I bet. Get goin' then," ordered Mitchel. "I'll be 'long. Helpin' escort the general's safe."

And my money. I gave Marta a kiss and a hug, grabbed the case of beer, a last look into her eyes, and I took off. This was working out just dandy. I tried to tell myself that.

Cutter was waiting outside. "What took ya?" We caught up with the battery, and I set the beer case in Hobbs's wagon. I found Sanchez and told him what had happened to Jaeger—he laughed—that Mitchel had done him in and was with us. Then I told him about the safe being readied to load on a wagon and Mitchel was escorting it. "Like setting a fox to guard the chicken coop," said Sanchez. "I don't trust no Ranger."

Everyone stayed quiet when we got to Sabinas. Couldn't help but make some noise. A few folks poked their heads out, but soon as they saw us, they got scarce. We were on the road alongside the Rio Sabinas, the same road we'd first gone through the town with Zach and Musty. Sanchez and me was bringing up the rear, and we made out the iron bridge ahead. The battery was crossing the tracks and turning left. There was a freight train on the siding, not a coal train like was there when we first come through. The battery pulled round the far side of that big ol' warehouse. A couple of dozen *zapadores* were laid out in the building's shade.

An old man was selling them *pulque*, passing around his single cup filled from a little two-wheel cart. The keg was filled with the milky liquor made from fermented maguey plants. It'd get a man drunk, and we didn't need that. I chased him off.

Cutter rode up. "Get everyone dismounted and wait here. I'm supposed to get orders. No one leaves. If anyone asks what's going on, tell them it's a militia exercise to protect against injuns up on the border."

"Yes, sir," said Sanchez.

"What in tarnation is that smell?" asked Cutter.

"Smell like someone ain't dig some graves deep enough," said Sanchez, trying to keep a straight face. I tried to keep from laughing.

"Well, y'all stay here and keep an eye on things."

Cutter rode off. I said, "There anything we can use in that warehouse? You still got the keys?"

"I do," said Sanchez. "Maybe we can use some of those picks and shovels in case we gotta dig-in these guns sometime."

"We really wantta help them out by letting them dig the guns in?"

"Yeah, just my soldier head talking to me," he muttered.

"There's that 12-gauge coach gun in there. Might come in handy."

Sanchez nodded. "When I get the chance."

I rode past Atwood, sitting on the lead Gatling's limber with a Mex farrier.

"You doing good, Matt?" I wanted to sound hospitable like. Needed to keep an eye on him all the more now.

"What's going on…Sergeant Watkins?"

"I don't know much. Cutter will be back. He's getting orders."

Atwood kinda smirked at that too. He didn't take all the army stuff real serious, either.

Cutter returned and called together the four gunners, Hobbs in charge of the battery wagons, and me. Cutter looked befuddled like.

"Well, boys, change of plan. We aren't marching to Allende."

"They change their mind about having this war?" I asked, just hoping.

"We're going by train." Slapping the side of the boxcar we were standing beside, he said, "This one here."

A bunch of thoughts ran though my head. We could be in action today. Allende was only a few hours away by train. There were a fair number of cars. I hadn't counted them yet. It sure wasn't enough to carry the whole cotton-picking army, though. I hoped Zach and Musty had followed us. I looked to the east, but mesquite blocked the view, not that I'd expect to see them. If they're out there, they couldn't tell what was going on here. I wondered if they discovered

Jaeger yet. What about the girls? What were they doing? Hell, what were *we* going to be doing?

Cutter said, "We're going to be loading all the guns and wagons on this train, but only taking two mules for each. The others will come along later. Can't haul the guns much distance, but we can move them around once we get to where we're going. Now here's what we have to do. The guns will be loaded on certain cars behind sandbags so we can shoot them from the train. Looks like we're going to be rolling straight into Allende and take it over before anybody's got an idea of what's going on."

"Where we gettin' all them sandbags?" asked Guns Dollenberg.

"They got those zapador fellas over at a quarry filling bags since yesterday, and the first wagon loads should be showing up before long. We got some zapadors here to lend us a hand."

"Which cars the guns going on?" I asked.

"There's a flatcar hitched up ahead of the engine. The cannon and the 1-incher go on it. Behind the coal tender are two boxcars. The other two guns go in them. In the first boxcar, the gun's going in the right door and the left door on the second car. We're going to build up three-foot sandbag walls in the doors. All the doors in case we have to shift a gun to the other side. Walls need to be two sandbags thick. The limbers will go in the cars with their guns."

"What about the horses and mules we're taking and the wagons?" asked Hobbs.

"The wagons go on the two flatcars, and we got two boxcars for the animals. Not just ours, but some others."

"Dang," said one of the Americans. "We ain't gotta clean those cars out, do we?"

That got a laugh.

CHAPTER THIRTY-FIVE

We set to work because we had to load the guns and limbers before stacking sandbags. The station had a couple of plank ramps for loading. It was a lot of work getting the limbers and wagons aboard. We had to put the fodder and cans of water in the horse boxcars. All our gear and dry rations went in the boxcars with the guns.

I told Cutter I thought Atwood's gun should go in the forward boxcar. I'd be in that one too, so to keep an eye on him. Cutter said he would be in the front gondola with the 1-incher and Hotchkiss. Sanchez would be in the second boxcar.

In my head I was trying to work out what to do next. With the guns on the train in three different cars, it was going to be a hard chore to blow them all up. Couldn't see any way to do that with the crews aboard and ready for a fight. Only had a few hours to do whatever it was we were going to do. We'd be rolling into Allende ready to shoot the place up. And how were we going to get away from a moving train? I was remembering how fast that thing went. Our horses would be in a boxcar to top it off.

It was a hard biscuit to chew, realizing I'd lost my chance days ago when we took the guns out shooting.

Sanchez walked up and handed me the coach gun from the warehouse, a nice Colt Model 1878.

"Good going, pard." I broke it open. It was loaded with No. 1 buckshot, .30-caliber I recalled. "Where's the rest of the shells?"

He gave a long frown and walked back to the warehouse, digging out the key.

The short-barreled shotgun had a woven rawhide cord, so I slung it muzzle-down, deciding to keep it with me.

I took a walk down the length of the train. Maybe I could get some ideas. For once I was wishing Zach was there. I was going to fret myself to death over Marta and Gina. I needed to see what all was hooked up to the train and see what we were dealing with. Besides the artillery battery, who else was going with us?

I thought about how all the guns were being set up to shoot up a storm. Was there anyone waiting for us in Allende? When we started off on this, the major told us that most of the Mexican Army round these parts had been sent to Chihuahua and Sonora to chase injuns. Maybe the general was just being careful. Allende was his objective. I guess it was there that he'd make his headquarters and recruit soldiers from the villages of the Five Springs. Then he'd do whatever it was he was planning next. Going for Piedras Negras on the river and then Eagle Pass, maybe because he was looking at taking part of Texas too. Slim chance, no matter what I did or didn't do.

Ahead of the engine puffing steam was a flatcar, what they told me was really a low-sided gondola. It had only a two-foot high plank wall round the sides and ends. The cannon, 1-incher, and their limbers were loaded and waiting for sandbags. After the tender, there were the two boxcars with the Gatlings. Lots of room inside, even with the limber. Behind them was a passenger car, but it didn't have as many windows as most and had big doors on both sides. Then there were two flatcars for the wagons. Hobbs was arguing with Cutter about taking four more mules for the 1-inch Gatling and one of the battery wagons with a heavier load. Hobbs got his way. The horses and mules were going to be loaded into two more boxcars.

"The animals will be loaded last thing," said Cutter. "No sense cooping them up till we have to."

"When we heading out?" I asked.

"Don't know," was all he said, giving me look to mind my own business. "Just get everything loaded."

Behind the animal boxcars was another boxcar. Its doors were open. Nothing inside. Behind it was a kinda short flatcar, but the back half of it was like a boxcar with doors on both ends and windows. The last car was a low-sided gondola like at the front. Some *zapadores* were stacking feedbags like sandbags round the sides of the gondola and on the strange looking car. All told, there were eleven dark-green painted cars. I walked back to the front of the train. I wanted to see how they were going to set up the cannon and 1-incher on the gondola. Not an idea one popped into my head. I was stumped. I'd talk to Sanchez.

Cutter had some of the boys herd all the mules and horses down to the Rio Sabinas for watering. I could tell who the vaqueros were. They knew what they were doing and had no trouble running that much livestock. Sanchez had gone to look after them. Two wagons pulled up full of sandbags. Cutter had them park beside the front-end car. They got a bucket brigade going, passing sandbags and stacking them in the gondola's front right corner for the cannon and then a little less than halfway back on the left side for the 1-incher. They took the wheels off the 1-incher and mounted its axle tree atop a sandbag platform. The gun could be traversed in any direction and not blocked by the high wheels. I saw what they were doing. The Gatling could fire straight ahead and to the left and the right if they had to.

I helped them roll the Hotchkiss gun in behind the sandbags, and we blocked the wheels with more sandbags. The cannon and Gatlings were kept covered and guards posted at each. The *zapadores* were sure curious about them. There weren't any townspeople or even the coal-collecting kids hanging round. I noticed that the town seemed real quiet, even though it was late morning.

Waiting for more sandbag wagons, everybody was taking a break, and I walked over to the engine. I'd never been this close to one. It was surely big and kind of scary with steam hissing, water dribbling from pipes, and making alarming noises inside. It sure didn't know how to hush up. The engine and tender were all black but for its front end where the boiler thing was green.

I walked up to the cab, and a big, tubby fella was sitting on a step lighting up a clay pipe. He was an American wearing bib-and-brace overalls. Surprised me.

"Howdy, Mr. Engineer."

"Howdy yourself, young fella." He had a hot bit of coal held in a pliers and lit his pipe.

"I didn't expect to see an American running a train down here."

"Most of the engineers down here are 'mericans," he said. "I'll tell ya 'nother thing. All the railroads, most of 'em anyways, are built and owned by 'mericans. This one by Collis Huntington and the

Southern Pacific Railroad."

"I did not know that."

"Yep. This here line, Mexican International, runs all the way down to Monclova and up to Eagle Pass. From there it's run by Slow Poke, what we call Southern Pacific, and goes to San Antonio, Houston, and Galveston. It's going to connect up to Torrecon further south and the Mexican Central line before long."

"That's pretty amazing."

"It is. Modern times. Name's MacFadden. You?" He teeth-pulled his glove off and shook my hand.

"I'm Watkins. Tell me about your engine here, Mr. MacFadden."

"It's called a locomotive. Not an engine."

"There's a difference?"

"The steam engine's just part of the locomotive and provides the motive power to the locomotive."

"Sounds like an engineer's gotta be smart. Where you learn to run one of these?"

"I learned on New Orleans-Memphis run long time ago. This one was built by Baldwin Locomotive Works in Philadelphia."

"Came all the way here from Philadelphia?" I could hardly say that word. "It any good, being damn Yankee-made?"

"Sure 'nough. She's a gooder. Made like a watch, only lots bigger. She's what we call a two-eight-oh."

"Two-eight-oh?" The number on the front and the tender said "103." Had *Internacional Mexicano* painted on the side of the cab.

"Yep, step back and take a look at her. See, there's two little leading wheels on one axle in the front, eight big driver wheels, four on each side, and no little trailing wheels under the cab."

"I see." I guess that was important. Lost on me. "You lose the trailing wheels?"

The engineer looked at me, puffing his hairy cheeks like there was steam building up. He didn't say nothing. Guess he thought I was funning him.

"How fast will it go?"

"She can reach better 'an fifty mile an hour, but on this line, it's usually twenty-five, thirty mile per cause of all the stops. Too hard to brake if we're going faster."

"Fifty miles an hour. Truly amazing." I'd heard say some horses could get going to forty miles an hour. Not often anyone went more than twenty, and a horse could hold that only a short time.

"Vaqueros sometimes race me," he said after a few pipe puffs. "I always leave 'em behind, but they give their best."

"They always do," I agreed.

Two Mexes were on top of the coal tender.

"What they doing?" I asked.

"That's my ash-cat, my apprentice fireman, Juan. He's going to be running this locomotive someday. His son there's the brakeman, Marco. They're checking how much water's in the tender."

"There's water in there?"

"Coal and water. Needs water to make steam."

"What's the brakeman do?"

"Oh, the pin-puller rides on the tender and sets the brake to help slow down."

"Brakes, pins?"

"Yep, each car has a brake wheel." He nodded at the small steel wheel up on top of the tender and then pointed to one on the following boxcar. There was a ladder climbing up to it. "Ya see, a locomotive doesn't have any brakes like a horse-drawn wagon, what we call a barefoot. We stop by reversing the engine and setting the rolling stocks' brakes. He's called a pin-puller because he also sets the coupling pins. He'll likely lose some fingers before he finishes his apprenticeship," he said, shaking his head.

I noticed Juan was shy of a trigger finger. I told MacFadden, "I knew a fella in Austin, had no fingers on his right hand, losing them to a self-dump hay rake. His hand looked queer, and nobody'd shake it."

The big-bellied engineer laughed real hardy like.

"Sounds like its hard running one of these things."

"It is," he said. "But I ain't in charge. The conductor runs the train."

"The conductor, he's up there in the cab with you?"

"Oh no, he rides in the last car, the caboose. Only right now we don't have one, but using that maintenance-of-way car. Anyway, they've got that gondola coupled at the end. He makes sure we're on schedule, that the cargo and cars are picked up and dropped off, helps with the coupling and uncoupling, collects the ticket fares, and does all the paperwork."

Sounds like a majordomo at a ranch, I thought. "He back there now? I didn't see him."

"No, Milkcan's got himself a little Mex gal in Sabinas here. He's got one at just about every whistle stop," he said, winking at me.

"Milkcan?"

"Nickname, handle's Chat Millican."

The morning train from Piedras Negras came in. We could hear its whistle and see its black smoke from way off. It rolled in with whistle screaming, steam spewing out all over, and wheels squealing as they braked. I saw what the engineer meant about stopping. The locomotive's big wheels were spinning backward, and it came to a stop with a lot of clanging and banging from the cars.

I was surprised the engineers didn't wave or shout at one another. It was like they were making a point of not looking at the other. Maybe they had a feud going.

The Piedras Negras train was only there for a few minutes. A couple of folks came off and no one got on. As it started up, its engineer gave MacFadden a quick look with a fast head shake. *Something's going on here*, I thought. He gave the whistle three short blasts, a long, and another short, and then the train rolled out stirring up coal dust.

The engineer looked up at those whistle blasts, and he and the fireman stared at each other.

"What was that about?" I asked.

He said, "That string of whistle blasts, it means there's danger on the track behind him."

"I noticed you and the other engineer were ignoring each other."

"They told us not to be talking to one another because of this secret thing y'all doing."

"It's just militia exercise," I said.

"I'll ask ya what ya asked me. What's 'merican's doing with it?"

I had to think fast. "We just ex-soldiers they hired on the help out. But why the whistle warnings?" I asked, changing the way this was going.

"I don't rightly know. We'll have to keep an eye out when we start up."

"You know when that's going to be?"

"I was going to ask ya the same. They just said to be ready at any time."

"That's what they told us," I said.

"Lotta strange goings on, though. Hope I'm doing the right thing," he said, glancing sideways at me.

I looked straight at him. "Me too."

"Maybe we shouldn't be talking about this," he said.

"You're right. Good taking to you. We'll just see what happens."

And I walked on.

Passing by the couplings between two boxcars, I heard gravel crunch.

A hoarse whisper said, "Hoist 'em hands up, ya' sumbitch!"

CHAPTER THIRTY-SIX

"Dammit Musty! You about scared the pee outta me!"

He was cackling like an old lady.

"What the hell you doing here? And take off that orange sash. We ain't supposed to be wearing them."

"Trying to see what's going on. Zach's all fit to be tied not knowing."

"Where y'all hiding out?"

"Over by the river, 'bout two hundred yards below the bridge. There's a dam there, and we good hid in a stand of oak. He won't let us set a fire, and I'm gettin' tired of jerky and eatin' from cold airtights."

"You need to get out of here, pronto."

"Hell, I been walkin' round like I own the place, and nary a frown from no one."

"Yeah, but if the American Troop shows up, which I expect soon, you'll see more than a frown." I was worried Cutter might show up and get suspicious on seeing him. "I'll fill you in, and you need to make tracks." We ducked between two boxcars so we'd be on the train's side away from the station where most of the eyes were.

"Any idea when this shindig's bustin' loose? That's the first thing Zach wants to know."

"It could be today, late, but I think more likely tomorrow, maybe leaving outta here at daylight."

I told him what little I knew and all about how we were setting up the guns. We walked down the train's length so he could see. I was wanting him out of there. Nobody was paying him any mind though, just another gringo. Told him I didn't know where the girls were. I was hoping they'd gone on.

"There'll be a bunch of whistle blowing when this thing starts up. You and Zach be ready to go. You won't be able to keep up with the train. If we're able to blow up the guns, I don't know how we're going to get away or meet up with you." Then an idea barged in. "If nothing else, just look for us at the Fitch Hotel in Eagle Pass."

We looked round, and no one was nearby. We shook hands, and he stepped into the mesquite. I felt a little better that they were near, at least for now.

A loaded coal train came through heading north to Texas. Wish I could just get on it, but not without Marta. It slowed down, and some *zapadores* run up, climbed into one of the hopper cars, and when they reached the north end of the yard past our train, started tossing chunks of coal off to the kids who came out of the mesquite with their bags. The *zapadores* jumped off before the train was going too fast. I wondered if that little hard bargain-driving *niña* was there fighting for a few lumps of coal. I walked up there but didn't see her in the swirling coal dust. I hoped nothing happened to her.

They came back from watering the mules and horses and run them into a holding corral near the station. Sanchez walked up and handed me a Katz coffee tin filled with a couple of dozen shotshells.

There was a commotion down the track with some riders coming it. I headed that way and saw Mitchel. With him were almost a dozen men including Charlie Kern, the expired Jaeger's pard. I guess Mitchel was keeping an eye on him by keeping him close. Good that he got him away from the hacienda.

"Watkins," Mitchel shouted, "ya seen Sergeant Jaeger, that fella ya had the squabble with?"

"You mean here? Last I saw him was this morning outside the hacienda heading to one of the corrals."

"Ya seen him leave?"

"I did not."

"Ya see him, tell him he's in hot water with me for duckin' out." Mitchel checked out the passenger car. Dismounting, he climbed up on the loading platform and opened one of the big doors on the car's side.

He waved me over. "You know what this is?" he asked, waving

his arm about the car.

"Some kind of passenger car, but no seats." There was like a counter and cabinets and shelves at the car's other end, but most of it was empty.

"It's a baggage car. They carry mail in it too."

"We're carrying mail?"

"Nope, something better. A one-ton safe."

I nodded. This was getting better.

"Watkins, we're loading the general's safe. You can stick round if you want."

"Sure, I'll help guard."

"I figured you'd volunteer," he said and grinned tight.

It wasn't long the big freight wagon with six horses rolled in, the safe covered by a tarp. They backed the wagon up to the platform and lowered the tailgate. Four other guards spread out round the wagon, and four more stayed with the wagon.

The safe was on rails in the wagon bed, and they laid out three more sections crossing the platform and into the car. With men tugging on the ropes and the rest of us, including Mitchel and me pushing, once we got it going, we rolled it through the door and had trouble stopping it before crashing through the other door. They tied it down real good with the ropes.

"That damn thing weighs two thousand pound," said Mitchel. "Stop too fast, and it'll go right through the end of the car."

Let's see, I thought. *We've got eight sticks of dynamite. I wonder how many it'll take to bust those doors open? All of them?* It came to me that the general would be riding there. So I said to Mitchel, "I guess the general his own self will stick close to his safe."

"You can bet on that," he said without looking at me. "The whole army's meetin' up here today. Some of them'll be comin' in tonight and maybe some in the mornin' too. This train'll probably be leavin' 'fore everyone gets here. Major Ignacio let it slip that there's some men already in the villages on the way to Allende."

"Any idea what he's planning after that?"

"No idea. Probably usin' Allende as a base, and he'll recruit more men there and the other towns in the Five Springs. After that, it's anyone's guess, but I don't expect him to dally round. Keep your eyes and ears open."

Another freight wagon showed up, and they loaded cases, valises, and boxes into the baggage car. Guards stood at its doors, and others walked round the car.

Troops raising clouds of dust came in all day long and set up bivouacs along the tracks north of the station and warehouse. Guards chased off the coal kids, and everyone was told to stay in the camp. They chased off vendors selling *pulque* and beer. Food sellers could sell what they had. Late in the afternoon, they pulled the train up and onto another siding. It proved to be a lot of work herding mules and horses down to the river. Little coal fires were built to heat beans and frijoles. Lots of rumors were stampeding all over.

I stood back looking at the train. Everything was loaded except the horses and mules and troops. Everybody was milling round, squatting, sitting, or lying about on the shady side of the warehouse and train. I'd found out most what we needed to know. I knew where the Gatlings were. I knew where the money was. I knew where Guerrero would be. I knew Zach and Musty were close-by. I was sure as I could be that Mitchell was on our side and Atwood too so long as he could get his share of the money. After that, he'd be on nobody's side. That engineer, MacFadden, seemed a reasonable and cautious fella. I didn't think it would be hard for him to see things our way.

What was twisting me up was I didn't know where the girls were. Riding home, I hoped. Most likely. I think Gina could of talked Marta into that. I still didn't know when this shindig was going to kick off. Could be anytime, but soon for sure.

We still had the same jobs. Blowup or steal back the Gatling guns and cannon, get the money back—that part was my plan, and if we could, spoil Guerrero's plans like fouling a water well by pouring in quicklime and axle grease.

Simple. I could do all that in one move. I'd just steal the train.

CHAPTER THIRTY-SEVEN

"Ya shitin' me, right?" said Mitchel with a look like he'd seen a sheep and a wolf sharing supper.

"Not even a little," I said.

"Guess I shouldn't be surprised, ya bein' the fool that went after *El Xiuhcoatl* all by his lonesome. Nothing like bein' audacious."

I didn't know if that was good or bad.

"Let me think 'bout it," said the Ranger.

"Don't take all day because most of the army's going to be here before long."

"Don't ya get pushy on me! I'm a Ranger, remember that."

"You're just another gringo down here."

His brown face just about turned red. Texas Rangers hold themselves in high regard. "Hey, I saved your scrawny butt. Remember that too!"

"I woulda taken care of Jaeger my own self. I still had a pistol on me, and so did Marta."

"She did?"

"She did," I repeated.

"I best mind my manners round her."

"That would be the smart thing."

"So, how's you propose to abscond with a whole train?"

"Unset the brakes, toot the whistle, and run like hell for the Rio Grande?"

"Audacious, like I said."

Audacious must be a good thing. "Look, we've got everything we need on the train, the three Gatling guns, the cannon, the safe with all the treasure, and ourselves." Excepting Marta and Gina, but they were supposed to be on their way home.

"Can you drive the engine?"

"It's a locomotive. The engineer's an American. He's suspicious like on what's going on and a smite nervous. He may go along with us..." I looked him in the eye, "especially if you were keeping him company in the cab."

He looked full of doubt, rubbing his chin.

"There ain't nothing ahead that'll stop us."

Down the tracks another troop of men rode in with a cloud of dust.

"There's going to be lots more here directly," I said.

"Let us depart with speed," he said. "How ya want to do this, seein' it's your smart idea?"

"Well, I ain't give it a lot of thought seein' I just came up with it."

"Then ya better think up somethin' fast."

"Right then. The engineer knows me. You and me'll go up a talk to him. One way or the other, he'll go along. I'll get the two guards out of the Gatling gun cars and put Atwood in the first car."

"Can we trust him?

"He's all we got. I think he's in because about five thousands of them bucks in the safe belong to him, four thousand two hundred and seventy-three to Clay DeWitt, and two thousand eight hundred and fifty is mine."

Mitchel's mouth about dropped open. "Is that what all this is 'bout, you come down here to get some money back?"

"It is." I scuffed my boot in the corral dust.

"Are ya shittin' me about that money? Ya just sayin' it's yours. Where'd ya get that kind of money?"

"From *El Xiuhcoatl* and the gun trade."

"That money's gotta be sorted out, belongs to banks and other people. That's the state's responsibility."

"Relax, we ain't taking it all, just what belongs to us. I ain't seen no one else giving us a helping hand."

"And I thought ya was workin' for the army."

"We are, to blow up or steal the Gatlings back."

"The army payin' ya?"

"They are."

"Ya stand to make a good haul."

"If we live through it."

"True," the Ranger said, looking round.

Mitchel was a head taller than me. I stretched up, looking him in the eye, and told him, "Don't get between me and my money."

He turned his gaze to me. "I won't, Bud Eugen."

"Then I'll go back find Sanchez and Atwood and get the guards outta the boxcars. Then we go and convince the engineer. When we got him cooperating, I'll get the guards off the front car. We get the train going and get outta here as fast as we can."

"What about the guards in the baggage car?"

"How many?" I asked.

"Four."

"We'll worry about them later," I said. "What they going to do back there, you think?"

"Keep guardin' the safe, I expect."

"One other thing, there's an army lieutenant and one of my boys out there shadowing us. They see the train leaving, they'll follow."

"That's good to know." Then it came to him. "Those two wit' ya when we met up."

"That's the ones."

"They been hidin' out here all 'long."

"Sure have."

"So what are ya and Sanchez goin' to be doin?"

"We're going to be in the second boxcar, and we'll clean out the baggage car. Can maybe you get one or two of the guards outta there?"

"Nope. The inside guards belong to the adjutant, and they're to stay with the safe no matter what. I've got four more men on the outside. I'll just tell them we're goin' to pull the train up a bit so's they don't get suspicious."

"Good idea."

I waved Sanchez over to me. Walking up to us, I said to him, "¿Listos?"

"Sí. ¿Qué pasa?"

"We're going to steal the train."

"All right. Now?"

"Yep."

"What do I need to do?"

"Let the boxcar guards go for chow. Tell them we'll guard the cars. We're going to talk to the engineer, convince him to go along with us. We'll cut loose the guard on the front car when we're ready to go. Get our horses loaded too."

"What are you and me doing once we get going?"

"We're getting in the second boxcar and will clean out the guards in the baggage car." I looked at him. "Where the safe is."

"Now?" said Mitchel.

I nodded. Then things kinda happened fast.

Atwood came walking up. "Cutter says for me to talk to you."

"Yeah, get your gear pronto and throw it in the first boxcar. We may be pulling out directly."

Sanchez let the boxcar guards go and fetched our horses, putting them in the boxcar behind the flatcars. He brought our carbines and extra ammunition and put them in the second boxcar.

I introduced Mitchel to MacFadden, and the Ranger got straight to the point. "I'm a Texas Ranger, and what's going on here iffin ya ain't figured it out, is that this fella Guerrero's goin' to try and carve out a piece of Texas and Mexico for his own self. We ain't lettin' that happen."

"I figure something sneaky was going on." Turning to me, he said, "You a Ranger too?"

"Nah, I'm working for the army. Look, you a decent hardworking American. You don't want to be part of this. You throwing in with us?"

"No question there. What'll you want me to do?"

"Fire this thing up and take us to Eagle Pass."

"Now?"

"Now," Mitchel said with a nod.

Then there was a commotion, and soldiers were coming to their feet, waving, saluting, shouting ¡Viva el General! ¡Viva la República del Río Bravo! A coach rolled up to the baggage car on the side away from the station. Major Ignacio, the adjutant, climbed out and then the general. The general turned back to the coach and held out his hand to help down Esmerelda. All three were in gray uniforms. The girl had on a skirt. The general looked our way, and we both quick saluted. He gave us a nod. Esmerelda glanced up, glaring straight at me. I couldn't read anything on her face. They climbed into the baggage car, and the coach wheeled and left.

"Looks like we got some passengers," I said.

"Damn, I was hopin' to get outta here 'fore he showed up," said

Mitchel.

"There going to be a bounty on him?" I asked.

"Probably so," said Mitchel.

"Then let's get going!" said MacFadden.

MacFadden called in his fireman and brakeman and told them to get ready to leave. I got down and told the front car guards to get chow, and they hopped off the gondola. Mitchel had Sanchez tell the baggage car guards that the train was moving up some.

I heard the general tell Mitchel not to move it too far because some more of his staff was joining him.

Atwood came a running and climbed into the first boxcar. "Where's the guard?"

"I let them go for supper."

The young brakeman trotted up the track and threw the siding switch onto the mainline.

Mitchel came running fast. "You two get in that boxcar. There's another train comin'!"

"Another train, what train?"

A whistle blew down the track behind us.

CHAPTER THIRTY-EIGHT

"You know about this?" Mitchel shouted at MacFadden. "I don't know nothing about it! It ain't scheduled that I know of."

"Get this engine movin' then!"

"It's called a locomotive."

"Come on!" I yelled at Atwood as I ran by the first boxcar. "Get in the second boxcar with us. We'll be needing your help."

Sanchez was already in the boxcar leaning over the sandbag wall as the train started to creep forward. I grabbed his arm, and he hoisted me up to scramble over the sandbags, followed by Atwood, all confused looking. I could hear shouting in the baggage car.

I looked ahead, and the brakeman jumped onto the locomotive cab's steps as it went past.

"Just what the hell's going on here?" Atwood shouted.

I turned to him. "We're going to be getting your money back for one thing."

"How you doing that?"

"It's in the baggage car with the general, and we taking them both to Eagle Pass."

He grinned big, I think more happy to be going home than anything else.

Heck, now what?

The train was slowly picking up speed. Too slow. I hanged out the door to see what was going on. A Mex in a gray uniform jumped off the baggage car, I guess a guard deciding this wasn't the ride he wanted to take. Farther back there were some riders galloping after us. The whistle screamed. The riders weren't gaining, but they weren't falling back, either.

I grabbed my rifle, laid over the sandbags, hanging farther out than I liked. I cracked off six shots as fast as I could. Saw some dust pops near the riders. Didn't hit anyone, but they slowed down. I pulled myself in real fast, realizing I was flapping like laundry in a West Texas windstorm.

I could see a cloud of black smoke from the other train. Who'd of thought we'd leave right before a freight train come through. Better being ahead of it than behind it and trying to get away. It would be stopping at stations along the way.

There was a clatter behind us. The brakeman, Marco, crawled through a small sideways sliding door high in the end wall and dropped into the car. He looked to be fifteen or sixteen. He said something to Sanchez.

"He say the big Ranger tell us to not let them uncouple the rest of the train from us, or we'll lose the safe."

Crap, I hadn't thought of that. There was a door on the end of the baggage car with a porch thing. They could step onto the porch and uncouple the car. Couldn't let that happen. A man could jump up to the sliding door in the car's end, but that was nothing to stand on so he could shoot down at the porch.

"We need some tools, something to bust a hole in this here wall. Ask the boy if they got anything," I told Sanchez.

The boy nodded, and Sanchez boosted him up through the door.

Heck, I can make a loophole. I unslung the coach gun. Two loads of No. 1 buckshot with sixteen balls apiece should do it. "Stand back," I shouted and let go with one barrel and then the other. A lotta smoke and splinters. The hole was only 'bout five inches across.

I picked up my rifle and peeked through the hole. I was looking straight down the baggage car through a shattered window in its end door. Some of the buckshot had hit it. I didn't see anyone.

Splinters flew off the wall, jabbing some of us. I didn't hear the shots with the train's noise. Everyone hit the floor. I came up on a knee and emptied the last nine .44-40 rounds into the baggage car. Crossed my mind Esmerelda was in there, I hope hugging the floor.

Sanchez threw a sandbag against the wall, and we built up a pile in a couple of minutes. I reloaded. Looking through our loophole, the shot-up door was only about four feet away. I fired at the hinges with the scattergun, and it fell through the gap between the cars with a crunch. Several bullets smacked into the sandbags as I ducked. With the door gone, no one could hunker behind it to make a try for the coupling pin.

Marco dropped back into the car after tossing in a crowbar and cross-peen hammer. I fired another barrel to reminder them to stay down, grabbed the bar, and hammered it into the loop hole. A second shot took the bar out of my hands. Sanchez started shooting through the wall with his carbine.

"You hit?" he shouted, seeing me fall back with the bar flying.

"I'm good." Hands stung like hell.

Marco decided he had more important things to do on the tender and scrambled through the forward door without anyone needing to boost him.

I'd took a fast peek through the loophole and could see the safe.

"Sanchez, take the left door and Atwood the right. Shoot anyone you see trying to get off, excepting the girl they got with them."

"What girl?" said Atwood.

"The general's woman. She's wearing gray."

"Oh."

I was trying to think. Too much happening too fast. The general was going to stay with the safe and do anything he could to keep it. All we had to do was keep him from cutting loose from the train. We were right on top of the coupling. So, when we got to the Rio Grande, he was not going to stay with us. He'd cut loose the cars behind the baggage car instead of rolling into Eagle Pass.

There was a thump on the roof. Bullets starting punching holes in the ceiling and cracking into the floor. We scrambled round and fired back, making a lot more holes in the ceiling. A body dropped between the cars, making a sickening sound hitting the rails. Dammmn. I hope he was already real dead.

I figured there were two guards left and the general, the adjutant, and the girl, not that I was worried about her shooting at me.

Mitchel dropped into the boxcar.

"You good with leaving MacFadden alone?" I asked.

"He's good. Marco said there's a lot of shootin' going on here."

He crouched down when he saw the bullet-riddled wall. I jerked my head toward the ceiling.

"I hope they don't try the underside." He laughed, and we all looked at the floor.

I told him what I figured the general would do when we got close to the Eagle Pass.

"Well, Peyotes is comin' up. Nothin' much there, but the word I got is that there's Guerrero's men posted at all the stations."

"Atwood, you and me, let's get in the first car and man that gun. Sanchez, get on this gun in case they got someone on that side of the tracks. Mitchel, cover the baggage car here." I left the scattergun and the coffee tin of shells.

Me and Atwood crawled through the high doors between the cars. I cranked the gun, swiveled it about, and stuck in the magazine feed. Atwood brought over a dozen cartons of cartridges and racked the first ones into the feed.

Once in a while they'd fire a shot or two from the baggage car, I guess thinking they were giving us a bad time. They didn't know we'd piled sandbags.

I gave the crank a couple of turns, cracking off four shots per turn.

The whistle blew, and we seemed to be slowing. "What's he doing?"

I leaned out and saw the small station building coming up. There were a half-dozen men on the platform with rifles and orange sashes.

I heard rifle cracks behind me. Someone was shooting at the Guerreroistas from the baggage car. They scattered like a flock of quail. "What the hell?" Then I saw what was happening. The general had the guards shoot at them so they'd fire back at us. Their rifles were coming up, and they started cracking shots at us. I swung the Gatling toward them and ran the crack as fast as I could. The adobe station front, platform, roof posts, and men splintered and shattered in a storm of lead. As we roared past, in those seconds I saw sights I'll never get away from.

Mitchel fired several rounds through the loophole, and more bullets thudded into the wall and sandbags. I leaned out, looking back at the station falling behind. There wasn't a man standing on the platform. A few were in the back mounting horses. I ran to the other door, and there were two riders coming in hard. I raised my rifle. Hell, it was Musty and Zach. I leaned out and yelled my head off to slow the train, but my voice got lost to the wind and the *clickety-clack*.

Finally Sanchez leaned out and waved at me. Musty and Zach fell behind but didn't slow. After a couple of minutes, we started slowing, and they came in. No one was shooting at them. I guess the general thought they were his men with Musty's orange sash flapping.

"What the hell we slowin' for?" Mitchel yelled.

"My two men are getting on." They caught up, flung themselves off their horses, and scrambled aboard the first boxcar with rifles and saddlebags. "Cover the side so no one gets off."

I fired at a head that stuck out of the baggage car's side door, and there was a sudden barrage of bullets hitting the wall. Bullets and splinters spewed through the car, and something stung my right leg. Mitchel and me flattened on the floor.

There was a sudden jerk as the train picked up speed then a second jolt threw me on the floor. Bullets peppered the wall again. Our speed picked up. I hands-and-kneed across the floor and peered through the splintered loophole and watched the baggage car and the rest of train rolling away from us. One of the general's men had pulled the coupling pin. I emptied my rifle at the baggage car for no good reason.

We started slowing again and came to a complete stop. I could hear and feel the locomotive wheels spinning. Then we were moving again. We were moving backward! I looked through the loophole, and we were coming up on the baggage car. It had been rolling slowly after us but had now stopped. Bullets from the baggage car started hitting us again.

"Cover me!" I yelled at Mitchel as I tumbled over the sandbags in the door, leaving my rifle. I knew Sanchez, Musty, and Zach wouldn't let anyone out the baggage car on the right side. I stayed low, running beside the moving boxcar. We slammed into the stopped baggage car and kept rolling backward, not stopping altogether like I'd expected. It finally slowed and stopped, and I expected I better get in there fast and stick in that coupling pin. I could hear the locomotive drive wheels spinning to start forward again. I crawled between the two cars and jammed in the pin hanging by a chain. It only went in partway and stuck. The cars jerked, and I just about got knocked down on the rails. I pushed the pin again and it set. They were shooting like mad into the boxcar, but I was down on the ground, and they couldn't see me.

A horse leaped out of the second boxcar behind the flatcars with the battery wagons. The general was on it. Hatless, he lashed the horse and took off at a gallop. I raised my pistol, but a man came out of the side door, dropping to the ground to fire at me. Something hit my left leg and hand. Mitchel hit him twice before I got off two shots.

The gunman fell back, and the baggage car's wheel went through his arm like it wasn't there. Mitchel sent some shots after the general. The train was rolling forward again, and I barely caught up for Mitchel to help hoist me in. I saw for the first time his face was all bloody from bullet fragments and splinters.

"You doing good, pard?" I asked.

"I've had better, but a lot worser. How many ya reckon still in there?" he said, waving his Colt toward the baggage car.

"Just the major and a guard and the girl."

"That scoundrel upped and left his woman? They don't come no lower," he said with disgust.

"It don't surprise me, but I'd never expected him to leave that safe."

"Maybe he's going for help."

"No way he can head back there and then catch up with us. We just gotta look out for men at the stations." I patted the Gatling. "This should take care of them."

"They'll try and uncouple again. We need some help here."

"Cover the loophole," I said.

I pulled myself up to the end door and shouted into the first car. "We need a couple of hands in here, pronto!"

Musty climbed through first with Atwood following.

"Lordy all mighty," said Musty. "Never seen a place with so much vent-lation."

"Good seeing you again, pard," I told him as we shook hands. Mitchel shook his hand too.

"You know I lost a good horse comin' onto help ya. Zach ain't happy 'bout losin' his fine Morgan."

"He can bill the army."

"Can I bill the army?" Musty asked.

"Atwood, take the Gatling. Musty, cover the loophole. They'll try and uncouple again. They don't like us much as traveling companions. Stay low. They start shooting from time to time."

We started slowing down.

"What's going on?" I shouted through the door.

CHAPTER THIRTY-NINE

S anchez yelled back, "The lieutenant's going to cut the telegraph line so the general can't warn his men at the stations up ahead."

"All right, cover both sides and the coupling. They may try and run for it."

Atwood took the left side with the Gatling and Mitchel the right. I climbed out, feeling some pain in my leg. Figured it was some bullet fragments.

Marco, the brakeman's son, shimmied up the telephone pole near the tender. With side-cutting pliers, he cut the line and dropped it. He scrambled down the pole when a rifle slug from the baggage car nicked it. Mitchel cracked some shots back. The boy passed the wire up to Zach on the tender. He tied the thin wire to a steel ladder rung and waved to the engineer. The whistle blew—them engineers just gotta do that—and we started to slow-roll forward. More rifle shots cracked from the baggage car and were answered by Mitchel and Musty. The poles down the line were shaking as the wire was yanked off the glass things they were wrapped round, and we must have been dragging a mile of wire behind us. Zach, I guess, untied it later.

As the second boxcar rolled past, I yelled, "Coming up," and Atwood dragged me in.

"I don't guess you weren't banking on this when you threw in with us?"

"Only thing I'm banking on is getting my money back and burying it. No more banks for me."

"I know what you mean," I muttered. "Something don't feel right."

Mitchel was leaning way out of the door. "Looks like they just lightened our load.

I poked my head out, and we were leaving behind four or five cars after the boxcars for the horses and mules.

"They sure pulled a fast one on us," said Mitchel and spit a stream of tobacco juice.

"We going to try and hitch them back up?" I asked.

A bunch of shots came from the baggage car.

"This is gettin' plum annoyin'," said Mitchel. "No we ain't goin' back now. Who the hell woulda done that?"

It came to me, there's one person would do that. "The girl. She's saving her own skin," I said. Then something came to me. The safe combination was her birthday. Dynamite it was going to have to be.

More bullets punched through the wall. The loophole was getting bigger.

"We gotta put a stop to this nonsense," said Mitchel.

"Musty, you up to going in with us to clean them varmints out?"

"Ya bet, pard."

"You going too, Mitchel, for the honor of the Rangers?" I tried to joke.

"Guess I ain't got much choice, ya puttin' it to me that way." He looked at the Gatling. "There's a way we can make this an easier chore."

Mitchel starting dragging away the sandbags blocking the Gatling's wheels. We swung it around to the rear of the car and blocked the wheels again.

"All right, y'all, make sure all's ya pistols are loaded and your rifles too. Atwood, ya stack all the rifles beside the gun and cover us. Make sure ya don't shoot none of us when we come back in."

I checked my shotgun too and was going in with it. Then I got behind the Gatling, and Atwood racked in all the rounds it held. He ripped the tops off about two dozen cartons and was ready to feed them into the magazine as I fired. I shouted, "I ain't stop firing until we run through about two hundred rounds. When I stop, go. I'll be right behind you." Mitchel had a Colt in both hands, and Musty held his two pistols.

"I'm going to make a hole. Get behind me cause of flying splinters and cover all y'all's ears."

I set the gun for free-traverse as the manual called it and aimed to the left of the loophole. I nodded at Atwood, and he held a 20-round carton of .45-70 rounds ready to load. Taking a breath, I cranked the gun, tracking it up, to the right, and then down, and then sweeping it back and forth without stopping. Felt like nails hammered into my ears. Splinters and chunks of wood flew, the top sandbags came apart throwing sand and dust all over. The doorframe and parts of the baggage car's end wall came apart. Between the black powder smoke and sand dust, I was blind.

I was still turning the crank with the emptied gun going *clack-clack*. My ears hurt terrible. Steam came off the barrels, and there was kind of a crackling sound.

Mitchel yelled, "Follow me!" and went through the dust-filled opening, firing one of his pistols blind. Musty and I followed. There was so much splintered and busted wood all about that I stumbled and just about knocked Musty down. Mitchel went down. I thought he was hit. Musty rose up and emptied a pistol over Mitchel's head and dropped down, and I let go both scattergun barrels.

Mitchel had tripped over the valises and cases. He was reloading and came back up shooting and jerked back to fall over the valises. I noticed they were filled with more holes than a screen door. The safe's side was marked all over with lead strikes.

We were all reloading, and someone was banging shots at us that wanged off the safe. Musty upped and emptied a pistol, and then I fired both shotgun barrels. I saw a body on the floor the other side of the safe. I was pretty sure it was the last guard, but he had so many holes and so much blood that I couldn't tell for sure.

Mitchel was hit in the right arm. May of even broke a bone. A lot of blood. Musty helped him tie on a couple of bandanas. I told him to get back to the boxcar. He was in a lot of pain and white-faced, but he crawled back. Atwood helped drag him through the hole.

Taking a fast peek round the safe, I saw that even the back part of the car was wrecked above the level of the safe. The shelves and desks back there were all shot to pieces. Even the back end wall was full of holes. I couldn't see anybody. Behind the car were two flat-cars, each with two battery wagons. With the piled wagon shafts, single- and doubletrees, yokes, traces, and other tack, it was hard to see anything behind the wagons. The wagon loads of gear and cases were covered by tarps. I could tell now that there was only one of the boxcars for horses behind the flatcars. I was trying to remember, I thought two boxcars, the queer maintenance car, and gondola had been uncoupled by the general and left behind and Esmeralda with them. I bet she wasn't happy being cut off from the safe. And neither was the general, but he was only trying to save his butt now. I knew someone was back there and suspected who. We still had the two boxcars with the Gatlings, the baggage car, the two flatcars with the battery wagons, and one box car with horses.

"Major Ignacio?" I shouted.

Nothing.

I squirmed round the safe, staying low, shotgun ready.

The man on the floor, dust settling over the blood spatters and the puddles on the floor, wasn't the major. The guard had taken a lot of hits in the head and body. None in the legs having been behind the safe. I never seen no one so shot full of holes.

There was a pile of wooden cases behind the man. I threw a chunk of wood over it. Nothing.

"What's going on, Bud?" said Musty.

"I think the major's someplace here, Guerrero's adjutant," I added seeing Musty didn't know who I was talking about.

I crawled up to the cases, dragging myself through the blood and stuff on the rocking floor. "Major Ignacio?"

Nothing. I could tell he wasn't behind the car's end wall because of all the holes. The door swung back and forth, and the glass was shot out. The wagons then. There was all this gear, feed sacks, boxes, and stuff stacked all over. Some it all jumbled because it hadn't been tied down.

"Major Ignacio? I know you're back there."

I could barely hear it over all the train noise. "Who are you?"

"Sergeant Watkins, sir."

"Watkins?" There was a pause. "You don't have to call me sir under the circumstances, and I hereby revoke your sergeantcy."

"Well dang. Do you want me to come back to give you that green armband?"

"Certainly."

"Look, Major Ignacio. I thought you were a pretty decent fella, honorable. I know you didn't like that flogging the general gave Sergeant Montero any more than I did."

"He no longer a sergeant, either."

"Well, yeah. I get that, him being dumped in a three-foot-by-three hole."

No answer.

"I gotta lot of men with me. We're going to root you out one way or the other. Nobody else has to get kilt."

No answer.

"We'll slow down, and you can get off the train, with your guns. Whatta you say?" I couldn't figure why the major was being so loyal. He'd been left behind.

"I tell the general that I will protect his safe and return it back to him."

"It's over, Major. We're heading into Eagle Pass. Then you'll be at the mercy of the Texas Rangers, and you know how that always turns out."

Six shots cracked into the car. Ducking down, I'd seen some smoke, but with the wind of the moving train, I couldn't tell where he was.

"He say 'Hell no,'" Musty said from behind me.

He's stalling, I thought. For what?

"Damn, I gotta do him in. Can't just leave him back there shooting at us. Musty, bring up three rifles and make sure they're all loaded."

I spent the time trying to talk sense into Ignacio. Besides maybe getting myself kilt or Musty as part of the deal, I really didn't want to have to kill him. He kept on shooting and didn't want to discuss it no more.

Musty brought up the rifles, giving one to Atwood and me.

"I can't tell where he is. Somewhere behind the first wagon maybe. I'm going to tell him one more time to give it up, but he always shoots when I say that. Soon as he fires, all three of us will up and empty the rifles. Then I'm going in with the scattergun. You two cover me with your pistols and be ready to shoot him if I flush him out. Try not to shoot into the boxcar because our horses are in there."

"Maybe yours, but mine ain't," complained Musty. "You jus' be damn careful. I'm counting on you for a job."

One last try. "Major, your general left you to protect his safe. You know he ain't coming back. Likely he's got another stash of money to get a new…" Two shots cracked. "Now!" I yelled, and we came up emptying the rifles. I dropped mine, grabbed the scattergun, and jumped cross the gap between the cars, trying to keep low. Had a hard time seeing through the smoke. Wait, smoke? Something was burning!

The tarp on the wagon on the first flatcar was burning. I knew there were cases of ammunition in the wagons. I got up and tripped on a trace chain. I went on hands and knees and shots cracked. The smoke was thicker and pouring back over the second wagon. I saw something move under the wheels and fired one barrel. Ignacio fell and disappeared in the smoke. Cartridges started popping. No worry cause when they burned, they just split open with a bang, and the bullets didn't go no place.

I moved to the back of the second wagon and could barely breathe and saw nothing. With cartridges popping, I couldn't tell if the major was shooting. I worried too that Musty and Atwood might start shooting with all the popping and hit me. Smoke was getting into the horse boxcar, and they were pitching a fuss.

Ignacio slammed into me, knocking the shotgun outta my hands. I grabbed his jacket and fell backward with him landing on top of me. Like to knock the breath outta me, but I tugged him close with him thrashing to get away. I felt warm wet on me, and he was bleeding. I worked my pistol out, jammed it into his side, and he saw what was coming. His face was an ugly mad and snarling.

"The general's grand plan would have…"

I pushed him off the flatcar. He made kind of a little noise. I don't know what it was.

The first wagon blew up, sending wood, unburned cartridges, and metal fittings flying all over. I just about fell off the car my own self. The blast went up and out, and I was mostly behind piled gear. I was swatting at burning stuff that landed on me. Musty and Atwood were pushing burning parts of the wagon off the car. There wasn't much smoke now.

"You good, pard?" Musty shouted.

"What?" My ears was ringing. I made out Atwood saying something about me standing, so I must be good.

"What blew up?" I spit some blood out.

"Most likely all the cartridge boxes packed together. They start burnin', and they all go off at once." Mitchel was standing on the baggage car porch. He sure looked white.

"You making it?" I asked.

"Me? You the one got blowed up."

"Well, I know one thing, I ain't no sergeant no more, got demoted."

The horses were kicking the boxcar walls. We would have to get them settled down.

The train jerked and started slowing to a stop. Now what?

CHAPTER FORTY

Clouds were drifting over, and the breeze picked up. Nice day, not too hot.

We all collected at the engine, all of us soot-covered and limping and wrapping bullet nicks. Mitchel sat on the cab steps. First thing Zach wanted to know was what all happened back there, and I told it. "Why'd we stop?" I wasn't happy about that.

"MacFadden needs to oil everything. He would have done that at the normal Peyotes stop. I need to tell everyone what we're doing next."

The locomotive crew was crawling all over, oiling and checking the wheels and stuff.

"The next stop is Leons. There's nothing much there, maybe not any *Guerreristas*."

"There were two there the day we came down here," said Musty.

"Let us hope there are no more than that today. We need to stop there."

"Stop again! Why for?" I said. "We've already stopped one too many times."

"The station's not manned, but MacFadden tells me there's a locked cabinet with a telegraph key."

"So?"

"I can send a message to Eagle Pass and alert Fort Duncan. They'll be waiting on us."

"You know how to use a telegraph?" asked Atwood.

"Of course."

"Do you think we'll need their help?" I asked. "We're doing tolerable well."

"One never knows."

"It ain't over until it's over," said Musty. "And I'm hungry."

He was right. "All right then. We need to be ready for more than a couple of *pistoleros* hanging out at Leons. Let's get the Gatlings checked and make sure your rifle and pistols are loaded."

"How about the 1-incher?" said Atwood.

"Let's not," said Zach. "Not here. Please do use caution when firing the Gatlings, and avoid hitting the telegraph cabinet. We also need to cut the telegraph line after I send the message."

"Or just take the telegraph thingamajig," said Musty.

"We'll do both," said Zach.

After oiling, Musty, Sanchez, the fireman, and brakeman went down to the horse boxcar, got some water cans, and pitched them on the smoldering flatcar. Bullets had stopped popping off.

Me and Atwood checked the guns and oiled them. "I'd surely like to see what that 1-incher can do," said Atwood.

I hope we don't have to, I thought. "What's the next station after Leons?" I asked MacFadden.

"Allende."

"That's what I think was Guerrero's, what'd you call it?" I asked Zach.

"Objective. It is possible, highly likely, that there will be *Guerreristas* present. Perhaps a not inconsiderable number."

"We'll have to use that 1-incher after all," I said.

Atwood grinned.

"And possibly the Hotchkiss," said Zach. "Does anyone know how to fire it besides myself?"

"Sanchez and I do," I said. "We've both fired it a few times along with the 1-incher."

"Very good. We are indeed understrength for this endeavor, but with perseverance, we shall prevail."

I think he meant I might be able to collect my thousand bucks. That safe was on my mind too, just about as much as Marta was.

"Zach, how much dynamite did you bring?"

"Do you still have the eight cartridges I gave you and Sanchez?"

"Yes."

"I brought all the rest, seventeen cartridges."

"I'm hungry," said Musty. "Tired of jerky."

"I'll buy you a beefsteak supper at the Fitch Hotel," I said.

"Y'all getting paid by the army, right?" said Atwood.

"Yep."

"Well, I ain't. That's not fair."

Mitchel stood up, kinda shaky. "Raise your right hand, repeat after me, 'I, state your name, do solemnly swear…'"

Atwood said, "I, state of Texas, Mathew P…."

"Ya nitwit, jus' your name, not your state!"

"Well, you said…"

"Jus' your name!"

"I, Mathew P. Atwood, do solemnly swear that I will bear true faith and allegiance to the State of Texas, that I will serve honestly and faithfully against all their enemies whomsoever, and that I will obey the orders of the governor of Texas and the orders of the officers appointed over me, according to the laws, rules, and articles for the government of the State of Texas. So help me God."

"Congratulations…Ranger."

Atwood grinned. "How much I get paid?"

"Dollar a day, and your commission will likely be revoked by tonight."

"So I'm getting a dollar?"

"Ya want an advance?"

"Sure."

Mitchel held out a First State Bank of Austin banknote and snatched it away when Atwood reached for it.

"Hey!"

"I forgot, ya gotta pay a one dollar fee to the Texas Secretary of State for the expense of issuin' a commission."

"I'm still hungry," said Musty.

"We must be on our way," said Zach.

I said, "Let's get the second boxcar's gun to the left side." Mitchel staggered into the cab. Zach, me, and Atwood got in the first car after helping Sanchez and Musty move the second car's gun.

"I'm still hungry," said Musty.

"If I give you an airtight of apricots, will you shut up?"

"I'd be obliged."

Just as we were starting up, we heard a whistle blast a long ways off. There wasn't a one of us that didn't have a mouth hanging open. We knew what was coming and hadn't given it a thought before.

Zach grabbed his field glasses, ran back to the last boxcar, and climbed on top. "They're pushing the cars that were uncoupled from us. They're loaded with troops, and they're riding atop the rest of the boxcars too. I need three dynamite cartridges and two fuses. Quick! And two sandbags."

Zach was standing on the track behind the last car. I handed him the sticks. The rail was like an "I", and he laid the three sticks against the inside and put a rock against them to hold them. He took the two fuses and slid them between the sticks.

"Better to make a hole in the cartridge for the cap, but this will do. Start the train rolling," he shouted, and Mitchel waved back. Of course, the engineer tooted the whistle.

Musty and Atwood carried up the sandbags, and Zach laid them over the sticks. Zach lit the fuses with his flint lighter and said, "And a fire was kindled in their company; the flame burned up the wicked." Something from the Bible I guess.

We piled onto the moving train.

It started raining. The smoldering wagon wreckage on the flatcar steamed.

The dynamite went off, a really loud boom, adding gravel to the rain.

A half-mile behind us the other train stopped at the cut track and was tooting its whistle with MacFadden tooting back. I suspect they were saying something to each other.

Zach and I were on top of the boxcar. Zach handed me his field glasses. "What do you think, what are they doing?"

"It a far piece and the rain, but looks like they're backing up."

"I agree with your observation. They're going back to Peyotes to pick up rails and tools. I saw line maintenance equipment back there. Obviously the general's aboard that train. That delay will give us some breathing room."

Taking the glasses back, he looked forward. "Leons coming up. Let's man the guns."

We didn't have to do any shooting. The four Guerreroistas were under the shed, just a pole barn sorta thing, out of the rain and waving greetings. They may of not known what a Gatling gun was, but they figured out real fast that they best do nothing stupid with two guns pointing at them.

Sanchez told them the revolution had failed and they best save themselves by riding on home. I don't know where they went, but they sure left fast. One forgot his saddlebags. Musty rooted through them and found a half-full bottle of Cuban sugarcane brandy. "I wonder who he stole this from? Going to go down neat with them apricots."

Sanchez tore the telegraph cabinet open with the crowbar. Mac-Fadden walked up and said, "I have a key."

Zach was writing out the message. "I'm not so proficient that I can transmit it straight out of my head." There was a little book with Morse code addresses, and he found Eagle Pass. He tapped some test codes and got back some clicks. "The line's clear," he said. He began tapping, kinda slow. He read it out:

OFFICER COMMANDING FT DUNCAN TEX=

URGENT IMMEDIATE=

AM PRESENTLY AT LEONS MEX ABOARD COMMANDEERED TRAIN BOUND FOR EAGLE PASS STOP I AM PURSUED BY REB-EL FORCE ABOARD 2ND TRAIN STOP WILL ARRIVE EAGLE PASS 2 HOURS STOP REQUEST SUPPORT DETACHMENT TO PROVIDE COVER=

1ST LIEUT ZACHARIAH K RUNNELS TRP A 8 CAV CAMP DEL RIO TEX=

"You think we can make it in two hours?" I asked. The rain had stopped.

"I'd rather have them bide their time than be late for our glorious arrival. Let us depart. I'm not waiting for confirmation." We ran to the train with Zach carrying the telegraph key. The locomotive crew was doing their oiling chores. Atwood was trying to talk Musty into sharing the brandy. He didn't.

Marco had already climbed a pole when Zach gave the cut-throat signal, and the line was cut and dragged down as we chugged off. Zach was looking out the right door and noticed two boxcars with a flatcar between them piled with cross ties on the single siding.

"I have a crafty plan!" he said and jumped the sandbags, hit the ground running, and caught up with the locomotive. We began slowing, wheels spun, and we started backing. Marco ran past us, and leaning out the door, I saw him throw the siding switch as we backed onto it. He coupled the three cars to us and ran forward. We were still for a spell and wondering what was going on. Zach and Marco were walking back carrying a square metal can.

"What's that?" I asked.

"It's the kerosene reservoir for the headlight," said Zach. "Excellent for igniting fires."

They set it in the last boxcar just coupled to us. Zach got on the locomotive with Marco, and we started off again picking up speed.

Before long, we started slowing. "I wonder what his crafty plan is?" I said.

"I'm wishing Musty would share that brandy," said Atwood.

We stopped on a couple of hundred-foot-long timber trestles crossing an arroyo maybe ten, twelve feet deep. Zach collected us all up, except Mitchel stayed on the locomotive. Marco uncoupled the old worn-out boxcar from the flatcar. I guess they was using it for a work car. It had kegs of spikes and bolts, fish plates for linking rails, some short pieces of rail, and hand tools. He had us throw some out before he started dousing the boxcar with coal oil. He soaked a rag, threw it in, and tossed a Lucifer on it. There was a pop, and the inside of the car went up in flames.

Marco climbed atop and set the break while we tossed creosote ties off the uncoupled flatcar's end under the boxcar's end. Zach doused coal oil on the ties and set them afire.

"With any luck the trestle will burn too," said Zach. "Take the tools. Let us go." We threw them in the other old boxcar, painted on the side: *vagón de dormir*. It had some bunk beds nailed to the sides for line crews.

We collected at the locomotive's cab. Zach said, "There's no telling what's going to be waiting for us in Allende. We need to bring to bear all the firepower we can. I'm going to put Watkins and Sanchez in the front gondola with the cannon and 1-inch Gatling. Musty and I will be in the first Gatling boxcar, and Atwood in the second."

"Can you handle the Gatling?" I asked Zach.

"I've been familiarized with it. Have at least one fused dynamite cartridge with you so we can destroy the guns if necessary. Mitchel will stay in the locomotive. Are you doing well, Ranger?"

Mitchel nodded. "I'm making it. Been worse bit than this little hole."

"Very well. That spreads us thin. Make sure you have your rifles and a canteen apiece." Sounding like he was talking to himself, "I wish we had time to sandbag the cab."

"Me too," said MacFadden. "We'll manage."

"Do you want a firearm, Mr. MacFadden?" asked Zach.

The engineer held up an old army Colt conversion.

"In that case, Mr. MacFadden, let us depart and make haste to

Eagle Pass and deliverance. God speed to each of you." We all shook hands and began rolling, with the damn whistle tooting, as we climbed into our cars.

Zach stepped out from his boxcar with a Colt in one hand and shouted for all to hear, "Be bold, be brave, be brave! Whatever happens, we have got the Gatling guns, and they have not."

The boxcar behind us was burning like a hay barn with lots of black smoke.

It started to rain.

In no time we were rolling fast, the light rain stinging our faces. Kinda wished I was back in a boxcar.

Sanchez pulled the tarp off the Hotchkiss enough to load a cartridge, primed the firing lanyard, and then pulled the tarp back. He laid several cartridges out under the tarp.

"I figure if we see any assembly of troops when we come into Allende, I'll send a couple shells down the track, and then I'll load canister."

I racked ten rounds of 1-inch ball into the magazine and topped it off with canister rounds. Twenty-one lead balls in each. Crossed my mind that a lot of horses might have a bad day. I looked back down the line and could still see a black cloud. At least the rain hadn't doused the boxcar fire. I hoped that trestle was burning merrily. We were rolling into who knew what in Allende, and I didn't like having an army riding right up my butt.

We'd cut the telegraph wire, so they hadn't wired ahead and told them that some renegades was barreling at them. And we were going to surprise them with the Gatlings. Let 'em taste this storm of lead, and they wouldn't hang round for seconds. Maybe it'd be just a few men, like at the other stations. No need to worry. We'd just wave when we ran through the town.

CHAPTER FORTY-ONE

Up ahead we could see Allende's roofs and cooking smoke. The rain had stopped. Sanchez tied his orange sash onto the brake wheel on the car's front. Good idea. I swung the big gun to the left and banged off two loud shots and turned it forward. I remindered myself what Zach said, "We have got the Gatling guns, and they have not."

I leaned over the side and looked back down the train and could see the other two Gatlings poking out the doors. We were rounding a gradual curve. Something occurred to me. I swung the big Gatling round. On an inside curve like this, I could sight on our own cars about five cars back. As the line straightened, I saw a cloud of black smoke far off, but something was wrong. It wasn't far enough to be the burning boxcar. There was a train behind us, and it was catching up. I went to the other side of the car and yelled at MacFadden with his elbow crocked and leaning out the cab's right side. He just waved. I could make my way back there on the catwalk and handrail on the boiler's sides, but we were about to reach Allende. I couldn't leave the gun. I told Sanchez about the chase train.

"Not everything's downhill or downwind," he said with a frown.

MacFadden was slowing, just a little. I saw a couple of men with rifles atop an adobe. That wasn't good. The mesquite came up close to the track. We were on a slight curve, and then it straightened. Ahead was the adobe station on the left, a few boxcars on a siding to the right, and more men on top of them. I didn't like this...and then I made out a pile of crossties stacked on the track. MacFadden blew the whistle in one long blast and reversed the wheels. I wasn't expecting this.

Sanchez set off what was happening next by yanking the cannon's lanyard. A sharp loud crack with the gun jumping, and the round hit the barricade, doing nothing but throwing chunks of wood. I aimed at the tops of the boxcars and started cranking with the roofs and sides splintering, sending men falling and flying and jumping off. The Gatlings behind started rattling at anyone moving, and bursts were fired into the station. The cannon's second round hit the station front. There was so much dust I could barely see the blurred shapes running about. I kept cranking, and the big gun made thudding sounds, and then the canister rounds fed into the barrels. They made a sound like a buzzing scream. Such a racket was raised, I couldn't tell if anyone was shooting at us. They had to be. Then a bullet hit a sandbag and a couple of more followed. I racked in more canister rounds and pointed the gun at wherever seemed likely to hide Guerreroistas. Sanchez had one leg up on the sandbag wall, levering his carbine as fast as he could. He jerked and went down, was up and firing, then reloading and was firing again. I reloaded, kept firing. It felt like a shaving cut stung my face. We were nosed up to the barricade. Sanchez jumped off the gondola's side. More thumps were hitting the sandbags. So much dust and smoke and noise.

Musty shouted, "Give me your dynamite!"

I was afraid to leave the Gatling, to let it idle with the whole world shooting at me. I pulled the four sticks out of the saddle bags and tossed them toward Musty. I'd forgotten the fuses…I scrambled to Sanchez' saddlebags and threw his sticks over the side. The fuses were in the other bag. I tossed them too. I saw Musty's and Sanchez' heads over the car's front end. Sanchez was firing his rifle again, emptying it. I yelled and pitched him mine. The barrel bumped his head. He went down and was up again.

A burn streaked across my back. I racked in more canister cartridges, swung the gun to the left at what I figured was about ground level, and started firing, swinging it round to the front and then worked it back. Musty was yelling again, and the car jerked with more bullets hitting the sandbags. We were backing up. Sanchez climbed in, blood on his face and arm.

He was yelling as he went flat on the floor. "Fire in the hole!"

I hit the floor and felt more than heard the *ka-boom*, with pieces of crossties raining down worse than any hailstorm I'd ever been caught in. We jerked again stopping, and then with another jerk were moving forward, the whistle telling us so.

"Come on!" screamed Sanchez.

I cranked off more rounds and then went over the car's end. We pulled a couple of busted ties and chunks off the track as the car eased forward. I picked up my rifle, reloaded, and shot in any direction I felt like. I climbed back aboard, reloaded the 1-incher, and blasted into the station as we click-clacked past. As we wheeled past, the air was clearer. One of the boxcars on the siding was burning. I turned the gun toward the station's back as the angle of fire changed. I could make out moving shapes, and I cranked like a madman. Some were horses, I thought. I only fired short bursts now. We stopped again. There was less dust and smoke. There were still men moving round, closing in on us, running crouched low, and taking cover wherever they could. There were still shots and shouts, but now it seemed quiet in a way.

Then I heard Zach as clear and strong as a church bell on a spring morning. It was a military command, I'd never heard it before, but something inside me knew what it meant. It was an order to finish this and to give no quarter, "Clear the field!" Everything had to die. I cranked it one or two turns, four or eight shots, aiming at even the littlest flutter of movement, anything that gave a man cover and salvation…crates, a water trough, hay bales, barrels, anything. The inch-diameter bullets tore through and shredded whatever they hit. I saw an arm fly out from behind a splintered crate.

"Cease fire, cease fire!" I've never been so glad for anything. The whistle screamed, like I wanted to. We rolled forward. *Where's Sanchez?* I scampered to the gondola's right side and looked back. He was on the ground, on his hands and knees. I went over the side and dragged him to his feet. He was shaking, and his legs couldn't hold him up. I yelled for help as the first boxcar rumbled past, and Zach and Musty hauled him in. Musty was only using his right arm. I was breathing so hard and felt so light-headed that I couldn't get myself up in time. Shots cracked now and then. I grabbed onto the sandbags as the second boxcar passed, and Atwood dragged me in. He didn't look like he had got a scratch on him. The floor was covered with .45-70 cases. The Gatling was smoking like a pipe.

"You making it, Spud? You look beat to pieces." He handed me his canteen.

"I'll let you know later. I gotta get back to the gondola." I took a slug of water. "Now I wish Musty would share that bottle."

"You sure you wantta get back up there?"

"No choice. This most likely ain't over."

"We lose anybody?" he asked.

"No one I know."

The whistle started blowing, one short toot after another.

"What the hell?"

Our speed picked up. I leaned out the left door, and the other train was not far behind, but falling back. Maybe because it had a lot more cars than us.

The track made a gradual curve to the right, so I couldn't use the 1-incher. I remembered from the map that the line curved right all the way to Eagle Pass.

"We've gotta shift the gun to the other door so we can fire at the other train."

It only took a few minutes to move it and sandbag the wheels. I told Atwood how to fire at the train when the angle was right. I was getting like Guns Dollenberg. I wondered what had happened to him. Was he on that train? If he was, I was glad he didn't have a cannon.

I climbed into the first boxcar. Musty was binding up Sanchez' arm and leg. "Just grazes," he said with a shrug. We moved their Gatling to the car's right side.

Marco dropped into the car and talked real excited-like to Sanchez.

Sanchez said, "He say he'll go back to last flatcar, and we'll try and run it into the other train." He told us what we needed to do. Musty, me, and the boy made our way back to the flatcar. We went through the shot up baggage car. Yep, the safe hadn't gone nowhere. We crossed the flatcars with the wagons and then the horses' boxcar, crossing over on the catwalk — scary as hell up there. They were excited, but we didn't have time to settle them. I could tell Clipper weren't liking this place even a little bit.

On the flatcar Musty and me started one-two-threeing cross ties off the back. They wouldn't stop the train, but it would slow them, and they'd have to manhandle them off the tracks. We threw six, and four bounced right off the tracks. We were going too fast.

There were some thumps in the stacked ties. They were shooting at us from a long ways off and doing no good. We'd fix that soon enough. We started slowing. Hard for me to get used to, slowing when being chased, but we had to sometimes to do whatever we were going to do. I poured the rest of the coal oil on the stacked ties. I lit a rag with my Erie cap lighter and tossed it on the ties. Musty and me jumped on the old boxcar's ladder and took to the roof's catwalk.

We came to a stop and started to back up right away. Damn if we weren't running back to the chase train. Marco pulled the flatcar's pin, scrambled up the boxcar's ladder, and waved a red flag off the right side. We jerked and were slowing, came to a stop, and started forward again. The flatcar with a heavy load of burning ties was rolling fast toward the train. It had sure gained on us. I hoped this was worth it.

I sent Marco and Musty up front to get ready to fire at the train if they got close enough. I wanted to watch and see what happened when the flatcar hit.

When they saw what was coming, I could hear their whistle screaming, and they were slowing fast. It hit about when they came to a full stop. They didn't blow up and sure weren't knocked off the track. I saw some men jump off. Maybe they were checking the loco-motive out, and they'd have to put out the fire. Anyway, it bought us some time.

If we could get far enough ahead, we might have a free run into Eagle Pass. The track's curve hid the train as we speeded on. I made it back to the second boxcar and checked its Gatling. I told Atwood we'd slowed the chase train.

"What's next?" he asked.

"I hope a fast run to Eagle Pass, parceling out the money, and a beefsteak supper." If we could get that safe open. I didn't say that out loud.

For the first time since the shooting started, I thought of Marta. That made me feel bad, but that was a lot calling for my attention. If things had gone right—not like I was expecting them to—she and Gina would show up at the Finch Hotel before long or maybe the Dew.

"How many more stations are there?"

Trying to remember the map, I said, "I think four. Nava's next. Should be getting there anytime."

We started to slow, and the whistle began short fast toots again. Danger.

"Stay here." I jumped out the door and ran to the next car.

"Somethings blocking the track!" shouted Zach.

Again? "Let's take a look." There were no shots. Nobody was round. I realized my rifle was in the front gondola. I pulled both pistols. Zach and Musty followed.

A few yards from the gondola was a hopper car full of coal with a blue flag stuck between the ties in front of it.

MacFadden came hobbling up as I holstered my pistols and grabbed my rifle. Still no one to be seen.

"We may be in trouble, boys. That flag means there's a derailer there. That hopper car's been detailed, and we ain't moving it, being full of thirty tons coal."

"What's a derailer?"

"It's a device they lock onto the track and forces the wheels off the rail. The trucks'll dig into the roadbed and cut ties." He lowered himself with some trouble to look under the hopper car. Laughing, he said, "Never you mind. It ain't worked. They pushed the car by hand and couldn't get enough speed to derail it. They musta stuck that derailer flag there to trick us. I can just push it on up to that siding, and we'll be on our merry way."

"Make it so," said Zach. He stopped after turning to run back to his boxcar. "Wait, can we push that hopper car onto the siding, then run up the mainline till we're past the siding, back down the siding, and push the hopper onto the derail, and then, as you say, be on our merry way?"

"We can." He threw the flag to the side, and Marco dragged the heavy iron contraption out from under the hopper car and to the side.

"What do they use that thing for, anyway?" I asked.

"They set it on a rail before a section of track they're repairing so some fool engineer don't run a train through the line crew."

It took longer than I liked, to run the hopper car onto the siding, backing off, Marco throwing the switch, running the train up the mainline, the fireman throwing another switch while Marco set the clunky derailer on the mainline, backing down the siding, and running the car over the derailer to knock the truck off the tracks with a crunching, splintering sound. And we were on our merry way.

It didn't work that way.

I'd gotten back in the gondola and was checking the Gatling. I saw there were hundreds of cartridge cases covering the floor. We were barely moving and rifles cracked. I looked back down the side of the train. A dozen riders were charging hard alongside the train. The other two Gatlings were on the wrong side. I didn't have time to turn the 1-incher rearward, and they were too close to the train's left side and outside my angle of fire. I got one with my rifle, then another. Atwood got one as he hung out his boxcar's left door. The rider went under a following horse's roofs, which tripped hard and threw its rider. More were coming up, farther out from the train. I swung the Gatling round and cranked off the half dozen ball rounds, just about gutting a horse as it crashed onto the ground, and shot off the rider's foot. I racked in a couple of handfuls of canister rounds. Hell was going to rain on them.

We were passing Nava's loading platform. Two horsemen, I mean real horsemen, leaped onto the platform and bounded down it. One man threw himself onto the burnt wagon flatcar followed by the next before I could shoot. I nailed him, and he tumbled off the car. Someone got the first man.

Others were coming in fast, and the train weren't going any faster than a cowpoke fast-walking to a saloon. Some were far enough out to be inside my angle of fire. They didn't know Dr. Gatling well enough yet. I gripped the crank handle to wipeout living men like the grim reaper.

My hand froze. "Oh-my-God! No!"

CHAPTER FORTY-TWO

A nother rider leaped onto the platform, swung over the right side of the saddle, and dropped onto the flatcar. Scared to death of what I saw, I let go of the Gatling's crank. Two more horses crashed onto the platform. I wasn't expecting Marta hanging on the saddle and scatter-gunning the man who had already arrived on the flatcar. She tossed the gun onto the car, bounded on the platform from the horse's right side, and crashed onto the flatcar, scrambling for the shotgun. Gina made a horrible dismount and tumbled onto the second car.

My head was running in circles. *How the hell and all that's merciful, what are they doing here? How'd they get here?* I heard shots from the flatcars. I couldn't see anything. I was scared to hell and back. I cranked the gun and "cleared the field," chopping down two more racing riders. The handful of riders left on their saddles reined back and fell behind as the train picked up speed. Other riders, though, were galloping after the last boxcar. I couldn't tell if any had gotten on. We needed to see for sure.

I picked up my rifle and slung my shotgun after making sure they were loaded. I'd forgotten where I'd left the shotgun. I had to get a grip. Now everything I wanted was aboard this train, like it or not. We were nearing Eagle Pass, and the chase train was stopped just about for certain. There could be some Guerreroistas aboard the last cars. It couldn't be that many. Maybe we could even cut loose some cars along with them.

But now I had to worry about those two. And keep from yelling at them for doing something so stupid. How the hell did they pull that off anyway? They had to have been on that other train. Where'd they get horses?

If some *Guerreristas* got on, we had a problem because they would be working their way forward. Couldn't let them cut the baggage car loose. We had to keep the Gatlings manned because we still had to go through Rosa, Fuente, and Piedras Negras, and cross that bridge over the Rio. For all I knew, Guerreroistas could be waiting at every station. I remindered myself that the Rangers and army was supposed to be waiting for us in Eagle Pass.

I made my way down the locomotive's catwalk to the cab. Mitchel didn't look so good, bloody sleeve and pale white face. MacFadden was sitting on the floor too with his pants leg ripped open and a bullet hole in his calf he was binding with a red handkerchief. The cab was iron plates, but the side windows were all shot out. The fireman was running the train and Marco shoveling coal. I told Mitchel what was going on and that I had to get back to the first boxcar.

"You takin' any prisoners, Eugen?" he shouted. No sense in using *nom de guerres* no more.

"Not if I can help it."

"There's a place for ya in the Rangers."

Zach, Musty, and Sanchez were in the first boxcar. They'd already moved the gun back to the left door. After telling them what all had happened, I said, "We gotta keep them out of the baggage car, and I need to find the girls."

Zach was pretty put out with the girls, seeing they was complicating our job.

Musty and Zach loaded up, and I climbed into the second boxcar. Atwood just about shot me when I poked my head in. He was as rattled as a dry pea in the tin can.

"Settle down, Atwood."

"What the hell's going on? Atwood asked. "There's a lotta shooting going on back there, and you all's are up here, so who's doing the shooting?"

"We picked up a couple of passengers, my woman and that other girl you saw me with in Del Rio."

"Well, hell. How'd they...?"

"You stay on this gun and cover the right side," said Zach. "We moved the other gun back to the left door, but you keep an eye out this left door too. We got three more stations to go through. And watch who you shoot at coming out of the baggage car. Might be one of us."

"I hear you," Zach said.

I changed to my shotgun, laying down the rifle, and kneeled by the blasted opening leading into the baggage car. "Gina. Gina, can you hear me?"

"Bud? I here."

"I'm coming in with two friends."

"You come. ¡Ándale!"

I picked up my rifle and crossed over the bouncing gap between the cars with Musty following. Marta and Gina were hunkered down behind the safe, Marta with her sawed-off shotgun and Gina with Marta's Colt Lightning. They were dirty and scared, and Gina had bloodied her nose from her landing. I could see why they was rattled. They didn't have no idea what was going on and were wondering where we were.

Marta's eyes were all excited, and she gave me a big smile worth the world. She scrambled into my arms, but the swaying train brought me to my senses, and I pushed her to arm's length. I held up my hands, stopping her. " ¡Alto! There ain't no time for that, not now!" I said, and Gina said something to Marta. She backed off, frowning.

"You know how many Guerreroistas there are?"

"The other mans? I do not know. Marta shoot one come though door." She settled her glasses, which kept slipping down her nose.

I peeked over the safe, and there was a body in the door without much of a head.

"Another man, he come and someone shoot him."

"Shot him? From where?" None of us were doing any shooting, couldn't even take a bead on anyone on the burnt wagon flatcar.

"I do not know. I no see. He falls off train."

Zach yelled, "Spud!" He was still calling me that. No need to anymore, but then I was still calling him Zach. "Rosa station's coming up."

I scrambled through the door onto the porch thing and leaned out the left side, hoping I didn't catch a bullet from behind. Rosa was just another pole barn shed with a few crates on the loading platform. Not a soul to be seen. I pulled back in. We were in luck.

I pulled back into the car, and Zach came across the gap. It was crowded behind the safe and all the wreckage with five of us. They were all looking at me for some grand plan. *Well, here goes.*

"Zach, hang back and cover me and Musty. We're going through and clear the two flatcars."

Marta squeezed my hand, a scared look on her face.

"Te amo, chica." We were just about to tie this deal up, so I don't need to get myself shot.

One of Marta's feet were sticking out from under her filthy black skirt. Blood was seeping out the seams of her laced brown leather boot.

"You're hit!" I said.

Gina gasped and asked her if it was bad. "It not bad, you go."

All I could do was shake my head and give her a quick hug. I went through the torn up door, jumped onto the flatcar, and went down behind the biggest piece of the first burned wagon left, the front part of the wagon box and seat. Not a shot one was fired.

Staying on hands and knees, I worked toward the second wagon, trying to watch it, the next car, and the high end door of the boxcar the horses were in.

"Zach, watch the boxcar end door real good." One less thing I had to watch.

I looked under the second wagon and the piled gear. Nothing. Soot and ash were blowing all round. I waved Musty up behind the end of the wagon, and then Zach got onto the flatcar, hiding behind the burned up wagon like I had. I crawled over to the second flatcar. The swaying gap was scary to cross. I got over to the left side of the wagon, giving me a bit more cover from the boxcar's end door. I wanted to get as close up under the door as I could. Anyone trying to shoot down on me would have to lean out the opening, making himself a prime target.

I was near the high end door, dropped to a knee, and kept the shotgun on the door. Our horses were in there, and I was hoping they'd be spared bullets when the lead started flying as it must. I didn't know what to do next. If I climbed that ladder, they'd hear me and would shoot through the end wall, or wait until I stuck my face through the door. I wasn't planning on suiciding my own self today. I couldn't blast a loophole through the wall because of the horses. I could uncouple, but I didn't want to lose the animals. *Might have to, though.*

I was trying to decide what to do when there was a click behind me from under the wagon — bushwhacked at about as close range as possible. I didn't have no choice. I let the shotgun down. By all rights, I should be dead. With me kneeling, Musty and Zach couldn't see much of me. They maybe didn't know what was going on. I turned slow, still easing the gun down.

"Esmeralda?"

"Mera. My friends call me Mera," she said in a whisper. I almost couldn't hear her with the wind and train noise. She held her little S&W .32 in both hands.

"What the hell! What are you...how'd you get here? I thought you were on the uncoupled part of the train."

"I never left, Mr. Watkins Del Rio."

Then I saw her clothes, face, and hair were covered with soot, her hair a windblown mess. One sleeve had scorch marks on it.

"Why in thunder did you stay? You itching to get yourself kilt?"

"I want the money." For such a beautiful face, it held an ugly but confused look.

"That's crazy talk. You'll get yourself kilt for money?"

She glared at me. "What are you doing here?"

I didn't say nothing, but stood up slow with my hands up. She kept the gun on me and picked up my shotgun. Now Musty and Zach could see something was wrong.

"Bud, whatta ya' doin'?" The question came from Musty.

"Ran into an old friend."

"Shit, what's goin' on here, Bud?"

She was lucky Sanchez wasn't there. *He might just shoot her to be sure nothing else goes stupid wrong.*

"Mera, we're going to get shot out here. We need to get back in the baggage car." I figured she'd go for that since that was where the money was. This might work out. She knew the combination. We'd let her open it, and we'd take it from there. There were five of us and only her scared lonesome.

She nodded and slowly stood, but she was scared all right, looking all round trying to watch everywhere at once. She knew she was in the open. The Guerreroistas in the boxcar must be holding their fire, watching to see what she'd do. I turned and headed to the baggage car, expecting to feel a bullet in the back from her or those hombres in the boxcar. We made it to the first flatcar and then the baggage car. Stepping cross the gap, I grabbed her arm and pulled her into the car. She kinda went pale with all the guns pointed at her. Zach and Musty followed us back in.

"Give up the guns," I told her. She handed them over and plopped down on the floor, all give out. I didn't say anything about her knowing the combination. I didn't expect her to give it up, and we had other chores first. Marta was watching me and Esmeralda. It might not be the best time, but I gave the little S&W to Marta.

With all the train noises, I hadn't noticed another sound, a thumping. There were all kinds of knocks, clanks, and bangs covering it. The end of the boxcar with the horses splintered, and a cross tie busted a hole out. All of a sudden, a bunch of rifle shots cracked through the baggage car with everyone scrambling for cover. Musty and me shot back and more bullets hit. The cross tie punched out a bigger hole and then more shots. Musty fired again. I couldn't make myself fire because of the horses. It'd probably end up that we'd have to. The hole was big enough for a man now.

Something came flying out the busted hole and hit the first flatcar. A couple more followed. Brown bottles, busting as they hit both flatcars. "What the hell?" From the high up sliding end door came a burning piece of wood. Zach yelled, "Take cover!" It hit the second wagon, and flames busted out. I figured those hombres had coal oil and beer bottles they'd found in the bunk car. Rifles fired and wood chips flew when they hit what was left of our car's end wall and door. We gave it back to them, raising a lot of noise. I made out a man coming through the boxcar hole. He went down, no telling who hit him. Other gunmen followed him, but with the smoke and fire, I couldn't tell how many.

We started slowing, the jerking knocking us all down. *Now what?* MacFadden must be going crazy as popcorn on a hot stove seeing all the smoke and fire back there. We didn't quite come to a stop, and then our speed picked up a little.

A man jumped off, and none other than General Guerrero came out of the gray smoke and shot the running man in the back. I shot, and I thought I winged him. He was down yelling, maybe a warning to his men that he'd shoot them too if they ran. Shooting his own men? Not even that evil *El Xiuhcoatl* done that.

Bullets were cracking back and forth. Nobody could see anything with the coal oil setting both flatcars afire. Gina had enough and was crawling the floor to the front end of the baggage car. Smart gal. I was wishing Marta would get the same idea, but she was sticking with me. She blew hair out of her eyes and gave me that smile that, well, there was nothing like it.

The train were still only creeping along and not picking up speed. I heard this queer sound, a rushing noise I couldn't place. *Water, it's like a waterfall!* I seen one on the Pedernales River. The sound got louder, and it was running off the roof with water spurting through the bullet holes in the ceiling. The water poured onto the burning flatcars right when ammunition started popping off in the second wagon. MacFadden had started the water tower flooding water onto the train as we rolled under the spout. Ash, steam, and smoke spewed. Another man jumped off and ran for it. This time the general's shots didn't catch him.

In all the smoke and the jolting train, I lost sight of Marta. Then I saw her behind some crates near the back door.

We were going faster now. With all the commotion and smoke and steam, no one could see much. I started for her, but I don't even know what all happened. Two men came through the door firing pistols, and Zach and Musty went down; something stung my left side. The two charging through the doors went down. Pointblank range shot, wood splinters, and bits of lead sprayed all over. Another man came through the car's door, and a shot knocked him back out. Mitchel had fired from the door. When did he get there?

I heard a familiar voice yelling, "Stop! Stop shooting!" All I could remember was that I was standing and so was the general, but he had Marta by the hair and was digging a Colt .45 muzzle into her neck, having yanked her from behind the crates. Her face was desperate. Esmeralda was standing beside me as wild-eyed as could be, pointing a Colt at me. I was pointing my Remington at the general. The sorry sumbitch was using Marta as a shield. He knew that as close as we were, just separated by the safe, that Marta made a pretty puny shield. Mitchel was steadying himself against the shot up doorframe, aiming his blood-slippery Colt. Musty and Zach were aiming at the general from the floor.

The general hoarsely said, "I will let her go and both of you too. All I ask is for you to put down your pistols and step off the train."

From the floor, Zach said, "You're under arrest, General Guerrero."

The general turned to Zach, but kept his pistol on Marta. Esmeralda kept hers pointed at me. I could have busted him, but with that gun on Marta, I couldn't take the chance.

"Aww hell," said Mitchel. "Lieutenant, you ain't got no jurisdictional authority to arrest him. We're still in Mexico. Anyways, anyone doin' any arrestin' will be me when we roll into Texas."

"Who are you anyway?" said the general. "I trusted you, I trusted you all." He sounded pretty dismal.

"That'll learn ya to trust no gringos," muttered Musty. His gun hand stretched out at the general.

"Lieutenant Nathaniel Bunt, Texas Rangers, at you service, sir."

The wide side door was open. Someone musta slid it open to let out smoke.

"I think this is Fuente," said Mitchel. A small adobe station building went past. Didn't see a soul and didn't hear a shot.

"My offer still stands," said the general. "No one else has to die today." He twisted the pistol's muzzle into Marta's neck. "But I promise you that someone will die if you do not follow my orders."

He had me convinced. Something clawed at my belly.

"Ya hiding behind a woman's dress, ya worm?" said the Ranger with a growl.

"This is hopeless, Estevan," said Esmeralda. "Can't you see that?"

"I will not surrender to these traitors!"

"What about me, Estevan?" asked Esmeralda, looking at Guerrero but still pointing her Peacemaker at me.

"I will deal with you later, woman," the general snarled. *"Me has traicionado dos veces"* — something about betraying him.

That was his undoing. She knew what he did to traitors.

She shot him right through the throat. Blood and stuff spattered on Marta. He dropped into a heap, and Marta kicked him she was so put out. He lay there gasping, his mouth looking like a fish outta water. Blood puddled on the floor with all the paper laying round. He finally stopped his mouthing.

Esmeralda backed away, swinging the six-gun from side to side. She was as pale as a daisy. "That's for Amado Montero, you *pendejo*," she yelled at the departed Guerrero. Gripping her pistol tighter, she said to us all, "I'll shoot."

Nobody argued with that.

She bent down, graceful like. "I'll just take this bag, and when I step off the train, I'll tell you the safe's combination."

"Just because I'm the curious sort, what's in the bag?" said the Ranger.

It was a hand-tooled satchel, fancy looking. Still holding the pistol, she worked open the clasp and pulled it open. Inside were four flat, shiny gold bars. They was stamped 1 KILO/999.9 FINE.

The train was slowing again and rolling through Piedras Negras. The train was moving at a walk. We could have stopped her. No need to even shoot her. I don't know why we let her go. Maybe her being a true beauty, her way about her, feeling sorry for what she'd been through, or maybe just glad she took away the trouble of dealing with the general. She'd saved Marta. She stepped onto the station platform, dropped the Colt into her skirt pocket, and said, "Five, seven, sixty-two."

She was gone.

The sound of the rails changed. The whistle tooted, long, long, short. We were rolling across the International Bridge into Eagle Pass, Texas.

CHAPTER FORTY-THREE

The train had stopped partway onto the bridge. We were still in Mexico. We could see soldier boys at the far end behind a big barricade of cotton bales.

The combination didn't work when Nathaniel Bunt set the safe's dial. Of course. He sure had some ugly words for that fine-looking girl.

"I can't believe you let her go before getting the safe open," shouted Atwood.

Zach had dumped out a valise with bound leather books and was page-turning through them fast.

"What ya doin'?" asked Nathaniel Bunt, glaring at the stubborn safe.

"Looking through Guerrero's journals for information of intelligence value." After flipping through a couple of the books, he said, "And this. Birthday's *cumpleaños* in Spanish, right?"

"Yes," said Gina.

"It's a reminder note to himself for that lady's birthday. August the twelfth, but there's no year."

I thought "lady" was stretching it. While Gina was working off Marta's boot, I asked, "If someone's twenty-one year old, what year were they borned?"

She squinted her eyes. "Eighteen sixty-six."

Smart girl. "Try eight-twelve-sixty-six."

That didn't work, either. Bunt looked like he was ready to chew through the safe. "Where's the rest of the dynamite?"

"Try it backward," said Zach.

Bunt worked the dial and gripped the handle. It turned as smooth as an oily gin glass. "Easy peasy."

We was all a mess. That was for sure. Bunt's arm had taken a bad hit and Sanchez too, still up in the first boxcar. Marta had a bad bullet cut on the side of her foot. She stood anyway, leaning against me. Zach, Musty, and me had taken grazes, and everyone was hit by bullet bits and splinters. Gina and Atwood were pretty much come out clean. I mean, they was as dirty as any of us, but hadn't been hit or grazed. Gina may have busted her nose, which was already a little crooked.

Everyone managed to make it to their feet and bunched round the safe. Seeing it was on its backside and the double doors about half as heavy as the locomotive, it took most of us to lift up the doors.

Inside were leather and canvas satchels. Some of the gray canvas ones said U.S. MAIL.

"Damn, that's gotta be more money than found in Heaven," whispered Musty.

"No one touch anything," ordered Bunt.

We were all looking at him. "I know some of y'all came in on this deal to get your money back, money stolen by Guerrero…"

"And we aim to get it without it being tied up to the end of eternity by the state of Texas," I said. I looked him in the eye. "We earned it, earned the right to get it back now."

Bunt looked right back at me. "I won't argue that point. I jus' wantta make shore all y'alls understand we ain't dividin' this trove up amongst us. There's three of y'alls got money comin' out of this. That understood?"

Everyone nodded without saying a word.

"Not good enough. Let me hear ya say it."

Everyone said, "Yes," excepting Marta. She nodded again.

"Good enough," said Bunt. "There's probably some unclaimed cash here, pesos, gold coins, and so on. I'm recommendin' to the state attorney general that a gratuity be paid to everyone as a sign of appreciation by the state for y'all's sacrifices and the like."

That appeared to make everyone happy.

"MacFadden too," I said.

"Agreed."

Bunt pulled out a leather satchel and opened it. "This'll do. Payday boys. Bud?"

"What?"

"How much, son?"

"Two thousand eight hundred fifty, sir."

He counted it out with everyone counting along with him.

He handed it to me, but Marta, with her funny laugh, took the money and counted it again. She squeezed my hand.

"And to Clay DeWitt?"

"Four thousand two hundred and seventy-three."

"I trust you'll deliver it to him."

"You can bank on it." I thought that was the right thing to say.

"Mr. Atwood?"

I popped in. "You told me five thousand, Matt. Needs to be dead on, or we'll have to wait and check with Roach-McLymont's."

"Yeah. Four thousand six hundred and forty-two American dollars."

Bunt found a receipt book in Mex and had us all fill out receipts. Gina wrote it for me and for Clay, her being my majordomo.

"My first official thing I do," she said.

Marta threw her arms round me. That made it all worth it.

Musty said, "I'm still powerful hungry."

Me and Marta limped up to the first boxcar and climbed in. Sanchez was hit in the arm and leg but was all right. Marta wrapped it up better.

"It's all done, pard," I told him. "The general's dead, just about everyone been bullet cut, but none serious. You're the worse off. We're heading in, and we'll get you taken care of."

"What happened to that girl Esmeralda?"

"You ain't going to believe this, pard. She the one shoot the general, right through the throat, and she got off at the last stop."

Sanchez laughed hard at that, so much it hurt him.

Bunt and Zach went up to the locomotive and had MacFadden take her across.

We rolled across the bridge into Eagle Pass, Texas, with a whole lot of rifles pointing at us. Bunt had a white flag waving out both sides of the cab.

We stopped at the cross tie barricade at the bridge's end, and Lieutenant Zachariah Runnels presented himself to an army captain. They knew each other. Bunt came out and introduced himself to the captain. After a short talk, soldiers started pulling down the cotton bales and ties so the train could run in and stop on a siding.

Watching the cars roll by, it sure looked the mess. Bullet holes all over, the beat up baggage car, and the two burnt flatcars.

Guards were set on the Gatling guns and cannon and the baggage car with the safe, which Bunt had locked up.

Major Vincent Knott soon showed up, all beaming with joy. He congratulated us and invited us all to Fort Duncan on the east side of Del Rio for supper.

We had to get our horses out of the boxcar. One was dead and another had to be put down. Clipper was all right, but so put out with his own hard ride in that boxcar, he nipped at me a few times.

At Fort Duncan, we were all treated by the surgeon. Corporal Samson Long Shadow Sanchez was promoted to sergeant of scouts on the spot by the recommendation of Lieutenant Runnels. They kept him in the infirmary. They had to work on Bunt's arm too.

Major Knott put on a good spread, a much needed stew supper. At least it finally shut up Musty. Of course we had to tell the whole story. We made it short because everyone was pretty tuckered out. Runnels and Bunt stayed over at the fort. They had to write full reports the next day. The major had passed Musty and me envelops with War Department cheques padded with small bonuses.

The rest of us made our way to the Fitch Hotel. The last time Marta and me had seen it was last November when we left for the De-Witt Ranch and a new life. Mrs. Moran and Yolanda Ruiz greeted us like long lost family. Even though it was late, we all got much needed baths. Truly a great thing. Mrs. Moran even called in a doctor to mind our wounds and rebind them.

It was near midnight that Marta and me and Gina were sitting on the front porch drinking coffee with Mrs. Moran. I weren't in no mood to tell the story of either hard ride to Mrs. Moran tonight. Instead, Mrs. Moran told us a story, about the time an out of work cowpoke stringing along a feisty Mexican girl showed up at her backdoor looking cold, hungry, and grubby as any saddle tramps she'd ever seen.

"Why Lordy," laughed Mrs. Moran. "I knew I had two wild ones on my hands with Marta having trouble using a knife and fork and Bud thinking the white table napkins were bandanas."

That cowpoke seemed a stranger to me. Gina translated Mrs. Moran's tale for Marta, and during the whole blasted telling of it, both those girls was crying. I'll never figure girls out. All that smoke on the train was still stinging my eyes.

We didn't do squat the next day. Mrs. Moran laid on a prime breakfast spread. We bought fresh sets of clothes at the Cazneau Mercantile. It was the first time Marta had worn an American-style dress. The lady at the mercantile said bustles were popular up North and the East, but not down here because of the heat. I was too embarrassed to ask what a bustle was. Marta looked grand in the bottle green dress with all the pleats and drapes. She was so small that it was a girl's size dress.

At the railroad yard we watched the Gatlings being taken off along with the limbers, battery wagons, even the pieces of the burnt ones. Half of Fort Duncan guarded the train and half of Eagle Pass come to watch when the great safe was taken off and hauled to the fort. They had to hire a heavy freighter for that chore. I stayed away from the reporters. No more newspaper stories. After everything the army wanted was taken off, some Mex railroad officials and a couple of Mex army officers showed up. After much back and forth talking with Major Knott and some South Pacific railroad suits, the train was given back. MacFadden and his crew got it fired up, and we thanked and fare-welled them as they backed cross the bridge. The horns and drums of a Mex band on the other side could be heard.

We visited Sanchez at the infirmary twice. Brought him things he needed the second visit. I told him, "If you want a job change after you're back on your feet and your army contract's up, you got a job at my ranch, pard."

"Thanks," he said. "I thought about going to Oklahoma, but maybe not."

Runnels and Bunt were still working on their report, and they asked me some questions. I still called him Zach, and he called me Spud.

Mrs. Moran put on a great supper party for all of us that night. The only one not there was Sanchez. She'd bought high-grade beef-steaks, green peas, cotton-smooth mashed potatoes, and cornbread that Marta had baked in her usual grand style. We had hot apple pie coming.

When we all sat, I heard a giggle like church chimes and in came Major Vincent Knott. Hanging on his arm was about as good a looker as you can ask with long blonde and copper hair down the back of her fire-red dress, a narrow straight nose, high cheeks, and a strong chin. Her glowing copper eyes were wide open, staring straight into me.

I could feel everyone at the table stiffen, but no one said a word.

"Ladies and gentlemen," said the major — I think he was feeling something was off kilter — "it is my distinct pleasure to present Miss Ruby von Schlossenberg."

Us men stood and shaked her hand, introducing ourselves. "Bud Eugen, Del Rio," I said.

Marta shook her hand with a look, well, I couldn't read it. Maybe just as well.

Ruby said to her, *"Te ves magnífica de verde esmeralda."*

"Marta does look beautiful in emerald green," Bunt said with a laugh.

Marta ground her teeth like she was chewing marbles.

"Miss von Schlossenberg is pursuing a business venture and only arrived yesterday. I have offered her my services to escort her until she has settled in."

"Very kind of you, Major," said Bunt, "aidin' a cultured lady unfamiliar with the customs of the land. If I may ask, what line of commerce are ya in, Miss von Schlossenberg?"

"I am looking to possibly purchase or invest in a coal mine in Mexico."

"There's a coal mine down in Las Esperanza," said the Ranger. "I heard the owner suddenly and tragically passed away."

"Tragically? Indeed, Mr. Mitchel, I mean Mr. Bunt. So I have heard."

Zach asked, "Where do you hail from, Miss von Schlossenberg?"

"My friends call me Mera," she said softly.

"Let me guess," I butted in, "Schulenburg?"

"Why, Mr. Bud Eugen Del Rio, you are sooo perceptive," she said, flicking her red fan with Japaneseman letters at me.

"I feel like I know you..."

Marta kicked me under the table.

Two days and a morning's ride and we were back at the Dew. We were home and ready to start our own. It was Good Friday.

Epilogue

I wasn't putting things off no more. We got that money wired to the Fairfax Land & Cattle Company. A month later an agent representing Fairfax Land & Cattle brought the papers to the Dew for me to sign. Clay DeWitt and Early Thursday was the witnesses. Witnesses had to be land owners.

Marta and I rode all over the 12,000 acres. Gina went with us most of the time. We planned out what all we needed to do to the ranch house and the other buildings, and where the best grazing was. With a little help from some of the Dew and Thursday boys, we hazed the cattle I'd collected onto our spread. Marta named it *Rancho el Consuelo*. I thought she was naming it after someone, but Gina said *consuelo* means "comfortable." We were to live in a comfortable place. Sounded good to me. We came up with a brand one night, drawing ideas in the dirt by firelight. We settled on a "C" for *Consuelo* and an "E" for our family name.

Marta and me were married at Our Lady of Refuge Catholic Church in Eagle Pass. Musty was my best man — and I was his — and Gina was the bridesmaid. Clay gave away the bride, who never lost the smile off her face. The reception was at Fitch Hotel. It was some party. Not many fistfights and only two broken windows. Someone, I think Matt Atwood, just for fun stampeded all the horses tied up at the Fitch. He wasn't half as put out about my buying part of his grandpa's ranch as I'd thought. He was getting the rest, and I don't think he wanted to deal with that big of a ranch.

Musty married Jiggles, I mean Callie, and worked for me and Clay until he bad broke his leg. He took an easier job working for our son in San Antonio. Samson Long Shadow Sanchez was head wrangler, but after a few years, he went back to Oklahoma. Heard later my pard got himself married up there. Gina's still our majordomo and an aunt to the kids. She set up and runs a school for ranch kids. The Dew, us, and the Thursday spread threw in together and built the adobe schoolhouse on the Eagle Pass-Del Rio Road. Thanks to Gina, Marta and me learned to read and write tolerably well, and I got passable good speaking Mex, I mean Spanish.

Lieutenant Runnels made captain a couple of months after our train ride. He and Sanchez got the Medal of Honor. Zach's was presented by Brigadier General David Stanley commanding the Department of Texas. Sanchez' medal came in the mail and was tossed on his bunk. The army moved Zach round, but he stayed in touch, mainly with Doris, of course. He was out at Fort D. A. Russell at Marfa in the Big Bend a few years later and almost died from a bullet through the lung delivered by a Mex smuggler. He was invalided out of the army with a collapsed lung and half pension. As a guest at the Dew, Doris nursed him back to health, and he worked for a freighting company up in San Antonio. I didn't know army officers made good account managers. Clay decided one day to take life easy, like that was possible on a ranch. He turned the ranch's running over to Doris and Gabby. Doris and Zach soon married. I was best man and Marta the bridesmaid. Agnes, Doris's little sister, she never got over her bedevilments and nightmares. Clay had sent her to school in Austin with Doris. Agnes married a shipping manager and lived in St. Louis. She never set foot on the Dew again. Nathaniel Bunt came through for a visit once or twice a year. Done with the Rangers, he was marshal in a couple of Hill Country towns and ended up living outside Schulenburg. He married into an inheritance, fifth largest cotton farm in Fayette County, and had an interest in a coal mine down in Las Esperanza. His bride was Amber von Schwarzburg, quite a looker.

We had good years and bad years. Seemed like I was a bird flying backward sometimes. But it was all really good one way or the other. The best of the good were our kids. Thiago was born in 1890. A man couldn't ask for a more strapping, honest, hard-working son. He went to school in San Antonio and then straight into business, everything from a feed salesman, stockyard manager, cattle agent, wagon salesman, and then switched over to dealing in those new motorcar things. He married a beautiful girl from New Braunfels and gave us three grandkids. One of the sad things was when Patricia was stillborn to us. Marta had wanted a girl so badly. It was a tough time for us. Ricardo — Richard — arrived in 1893. After school, he was off to Houston and got into the timber industry living all over East Texas and Louisiana managing sawmills, timberline railroads, turpentine plants, and lumber sales. He married a Lufkin girl and had four kids.

Arsenia Renée Eugen was given to us in 1895. We had wished for a girl. We were granted a smart, pious, outgoing, self-confident girl with an irregular sense of right and wrong and what's fair. She was educated at St. Joseph's Academy in Eagle Pass as well as on the ranch by the vaqueros. Early on she'd become known as "Marta's Daughter." I guess it's strange to be tagged with a nickname like that, but it told folks who she was, where she'd come from, and explained her ways. In 1912, the second year of the Mexican Revolution, a series of peculiar events happened. Arsenia got pulled into the Revolution, and she became a legend, a notorious legend. There were things we weren't proud of in the path she took, but then in the long run, it's said she did a lot of good.

She did take time to give us two granddaughters, one being a stray she'd picked up.

In the end, our stories were those of ordinarily good men and women in a hard land willing to ride hard and do whatever was needed to make things right.

EL FINAL

Attribution:
The quote, "Whatever happens, we have got the Gatling guns, and they have not," was borrowed from a remark attributed to a fictional Major Blood in the narrative verse satire, *The Modern Traveller* — 1898 — by Joseph Hilaire Pierre René Belloc, in that instance referring to the "Maxim gun."

AN EXCERPT FROM GORDON L. ROTTMAN'S
NEXT BOOK: MARTA'S RIDE

CHAPTER ONE

The morning my *familia* was killed began as a very fine day.

Mama nudged me awake. I was always the first up, at least in the winter. My job was to entice the fire back to life. No one would crawl from the blankets and serapes until they see its glow.

We slept warm, almost, bundled up with Tlayolot, my brother, between myself and Mama with Malinalli, my little sister, between Mama and Papa. We huddled under a piece of old canvas wagon cover in a clump of trees. We camped away from the road so no one would trouble us.

Cold. Frost covered my serape, the ground, the mesquite leaves, the dead weeds, and my hair where the wool shawl slipped.

My fog-breath and the ash-dust mingled as I blew embers back to life. I enjoyed sharing with the fire my breath as it shared its warmth. I liked to watch it spring to dancing life. I liked to feel its generous warmth. I liked to watch it burn itself to sleep as my eyes closed for my own dreams. Did fire dream in its sleep? Did it remember me when I woke it?

Mockingbirds teased other awakening birds and scolded each other.

Splinters and dry leaves. I slept with the tinder to keep it dry. The awakened embers ignite the tinder. The tiny flame grew. Twigs and sticks. There was enough flame now to add bigger sticks. No logs. There was nothing for coals to cook this morning. When my *familia* emerged, I would add cow chips and boil the coffee. Mama would toast tortillas and warm the frijoles refritos—refried beans. I set the iron skillet on the fire to heat.

The fire, awake and growing, would let me leave to squat in the weeds to pee and brush my hair. The brush pulled and hurt. I hoped when we reached Uvalde that I could wash my tangled hair. It had gone too long without a soaping.

I always watched the Father Sun rise, a yellow or orange disc, the giver of life. It was the Sun of the Fifth Cycle, the Sun of Movement. It passed over the One World, *Cem-á-nahuac*, which has existed for millenniums. The Suns of the previous four cycles were controlled by Water, Earth, Fire, and Wind. Their cycles ended in catastrophes. The Fifth Sun watched over us, and it was not expected to end in devastation. Mama told us these legends were passed from the Aztecs a long time ago, before even Papa's own papa was born.

I kneeled beside Mama and we said the Rosary, touching our beads.

The wet-looking clouds were low, and the rising sun soon passed into them.

How far to Uvalde? I had not seen the place for so long. Papa said there would be work there. The cotton had been harvested. Men would chop up the stalks with machetes. Next, they would grub-hoe the stalks and roots into the ground for the February plowing and planting. It was November. It took many men to work all the farms. He said there were never enough *braceros*—laborers—for such work in South Texas. He would work ten hours a day, chopping and hacking the muddy ground in the chilling wind and rain for pennies. He never complained.

I would work too, keeping a fire going under the thatched-roof lean-to for the men to warm themselves. It was always hard to find enough dry wood. I ground coffee beans, boiled coffee, and heated their dinner frijoles. There was no pay for those chores except they let me eat a little. Being able to stay beside a fire sheltered from the rain was payment enough.

And the church. I wanted to sit in the quiet calm of a church to pray and think and listen. I had listened to priests and brothers read from the Bible and said their prayers and listened to other readings. It helped me learn many words. I only wished I could speak them to others.

We had left Leakey three days before. It had no church.

We had good work in Leakey. Papa sawed down cypress and cedar trees growing right on the edge of the rocky Rio Frio. He and other men sawed the big logs into pieces as long as my arm from elbow to fingertips. They squared the short logs and split them into shingles. The scraps became firewood. When the men driving the ox carts returned, they loaded the shingles. The carts left for the Rio Grande Valley where there were no trees useful for shingles.

When I showed I wanted to split shingles, there was much argument about allowing me to work.

"A girl does not do that kind of man's work, Jaimenacho," the *gerente* told Papa. "She is so small, and she will exhaust herself and hurt herself, even her delicate womanly parts." He said that with great embarrassment.

Papa convinced him to let me try. I would work for a week without pay. "She will show you. She has more heart than any other girl."

"But she cannot speak," said the *gerente*. "How can she learn?"

"She is mute, not stupid," said Papa.

I laughed in my peculiar way, which upset some people.

Papa did not always stand up to *gerentes* and *jefes*, but he did that day, for me.

I did not do well the first two days. I used a cutter called a froe and a heavy log club. My hands were not guided by skill or God.

Papa said, "We are in need of thick and thin shingles too."

I said the Prayer to Saint Joseph for Success in Work in my head, *"Glorious Saint Joseph, model of all those who are devoted to labor, obtain for me the grace to work conscientiously, putting the call of duty above my many sins; to work with thankfulness and joy…"*

By the end of the week I was making shingles as good as any man, straight and all the same thickness. Maybe not as many. In the second week, no one complained of my work. I would start splitting shingles while the men were still sawing down logs. We passed our quota for shingles this way. I was blessed. They even paid me half of a man's wages!

Every night my hands, arms, and shoulders hurt. I would not complain, even to Mama. She plucked splinters from my fingers and massaged them, whispering that I should not work so hard. But the pennies I made helped feed the *familia*.

It was so much better than sitting cross-legged beside saloon doors with my eating bowl — *my* eating bowl — for gringos to toss pennies into and ask me how much I charged for my body — *"¿Cuánto, chica?"* or "How much for a bang, *niña*?" I understood those *Americano* words.

I looked up at them, and nodding like a simpleton, I laughed abnormally, showing my grinning white teeth and empty black eyes. They left me alone. It was degrading, but we ate.

Now my feet and legs hurt. So much walking from dawn to dusk. So slow with the little ones. Most of the time Papa carried little Malinalli. Tlayolot was too proud to ask to be carried ever since he was five. He stayed right beside Papa, no matter how muddy or rocky the road. Sometimes the little ones rode on a wagon or cart driven by Mexicans going our way. But not that day.

No one built houses in the winter, so there was no need for shingles. We were turned out of the cedar plank *jacalito* — shack — we had built. "Come back in March," the *gerente* told Papa. Nodding at me, "Bring your shingle-cutter."

It did not take long to eat, pack up what little we had, and roll up the wagon cover, blankets, and serapes. Everyone except Malinalli carried something. My big wool shoulder bag held my one set of extra clothes, two blankets and a serape, the full frijoles pot, little bags of cooking spices, tortillas wrapped in newspaper, water gourde, my clay drinking and eating bowls, wooden spoon, boning knife, and my bag of menstrual rags.

We walked.

We lived on the road. We were *nómadas*. We worked as hard as we could. We lived as best we could. Papa said it was a better life than slaving for a dominating, cheating *hacendado*.

Our home was where Papa chose to camp, always away from the road. When we worked on a rancho or *granja* — farm — we built a *jacalito* with our wagon cover and whatever we could find: old boards, hay thickets barrowed from haystacks, tree limbs, cornstalks, or carrizo cane cut from river banks.

We walked up the road. It began to rain lightly.

When we crossed streams and rivers, we filled the water gourds. We camped near streams when we could for water and washing. Papa always said to cross a stream before camping in case the water rose during the night. It also kept us from suffering wet feet all morning.

When we started off, I ran ahead with my bag bouncing on my hip. For two years, since I was fourteen, my job was to walk ahead of the *familia*. I watched and listened. When I heard the snort of a horse, the jingle of wagon chains, a cough, or any sound made by men, it was the sound of danger. I would run back to my *familia*, waving my arm, and they hid in the bush. I usually could not reach them and had to hide alone. I was good at hiding. I was quiet and still. And small.

We would watch in silence as they passed: cowboys, drifters, freight wagons, ox carts, stagecoaches, soldiers, *indios*, tradesmen in their wagons, whoever. Sometimes it might be Mexicans — *vaqueros*, *peóns*, *nómadas* like ourselves — we would greet them. We would talk about the road behind ourselves and their selves, any dangers, and news and maybe trade for food.

One time I heard someone coming and warned the *familia*. We hid for the longest time. Papa became impatient and asked if I was sure I had heard someone. I nodded hard. Papa sent me to investigate, and I found a *nómada familia* hiding because they had heard us. We all laughed and traded food and clothes. I traded a rope I had braided from horse tail hair for a beautiful brown *rebozo*, a cape reaching to my waist front and back with a square center head-hole and embroidered with red, orange, and tan.

It was dangerous to meet gringos. Papa has been beaten once. We have been robbed, or they only took a few things because they could. Fortunately nothing bad had happened to Mama and me, something I feared. Papa now carried a short 12-gauge shotgun under his serape. If gringos found him with that, they would take it.

I walked on the road's edge, always looking at the hoof prints and wheel ruts. I could tell which way a wagon was going by how mud splatter and dirt grains were thrown from the ruts. I mostly listened, though.

And then I heard it.

The shrill war-whoop *behind* me.

I will never forget it. I have never stopped hearing it.

It went on and on.

Gunshots! Papa's shotgun banged. It fired four times.

I heard the screams. *That was Mama! That was Malinalli!*

Many gunshots.

I ran to my *familia*.

The screaming, the screaming. It would not stop.

I could see them, the *indios*, though the mesquite.

Two where holding someone on the ground. Another was on hand and knees hatchet-hacking.

Gunshots. Screams. Blood-tinged whoops. Sounds I could not believe.

My thin boning knife was in my hand, shaking. There were at least six *indios*. My soul, my heart told me to go at them. My mind, my wisdom — did I have any? — held me back. My hands shook until I dropped the knife and pressed them over my ears.

I hid, shaking. I cried. What was happening to my *familia*? I hid until the screams stopped. Then I crawled, shamefully, deeper into the mesquite where I huddled in a ball.

I waited, cried, prayed, and cried even more. Even though the screams and other terrible noises had stopped, I held my hands over my ears, because for me the sounds did not stop. They never have, and I think they never will. Ever.

I lay in the mesquite for what seemed like hours, or was it days? I heard the wind flowing across the campo, rustling in the mesquite. I heard birds undertaking everyday bird doings as if nothing terrible had happened. Over the screaming I still heard, I said the Rosary in my head, finding my beads in my deep skirt pocket. Rosary beads in one hand, my knife in the other. One for life, one for death. For a time I wanted death, but the Virgin told me that I should live to remember and honor my *familia*. Finally, after so long, I rose to my feet. At first I pushed through the mesquite, but my mind told me to slow down. To move silently and listen with each step. Were the *indios* gone? I crouched for a long time, only listening. My mind was numb. There was pain I knew I should have felt, but instead I was numb. I feared what I would find. I knew what I would find. I did not want to, but I had to. I walked forward, slowly, listening.

They all died in the worst ways.

They were destroyed, gutted, scalped, their faces caved in. Blood, blood, blood. Things that I could not even imagine. The smell....

I vomited until my insides, even my mind, were empty.

I did not cry. They did not want to see me cry.

I dragged each of them to lie in a line, as we did when we slept. Except I did not now lie beside Tlayolot. "Heart of the earth" was what his name meant. Ten years old. Mama — Asalia — the name I thought so beautiful and she so strong, and Papa — Jaimenacho — our guide in life. Malinalli — "little plant" — four years...what they did to her....

I had no way to bury them. No shovel for the hard ground, no rocks to pile.

I prayed over them, every prayer I knew. It rained, my tears spilling over the whole world.

The *indios* had headed southwest. Blood drippings followed one set of moccasin tracks. Another left bloody footprints and splotches of bubbly blood. I followed, to make sure they were gone. More blood spilled in one place. I found one. Smelly in greasy buckskins. His friends had taken his moccasins. Dead, hit by Papa's shotgun in the side. He had bled out. *Good.*

They left nothing except clothes they did not want, which they tore up and peed on. The *indios* had stolen everything, including stealing my *familia* from me. I had only what was in my bag and my skirt pockets. I had no money.

Where could I go? There was no one to go to. There were relatives in Durango, far, far away, who I had never met.

Uvalde. I would go to Uvalde. I would work in the cotton fields. I would show them that I could do the work, even when they said I could not. I had no other choices.

I walked to the road. I stood. I stood for a long time. I turned and walked south in the direction of Uvalde. My *familia* would stay behind to rest. Maybe a Mexican *familia* would take me in. Why should they? Another mouth to feed. I would have to be careful. I could not weaken. I could not feel sorry for myself. I did not have time to morn my *familia*. Later. For now I must look and listen. There was still danger on the road. From any *indio*, *gringo*, or Mexican. Especially if they were alone as I was alone. Mama had told me many times what happens to girls alone on the road. Men only wanted to use my body to feel themselves. I used to think she told me that to keep me from running away when I was angry. She always said I was too warm-blooded for my own good. I knew I was in danger, alone.

I must stay alive.

I was alone, had nothing, and I wanted only one thing. I prayed for that one thing. *Yo quería un protector.*

CHAPTER TWO

I wanted a protector.

Crossing a small arroyo washing over the road, I heard a horse nicker ahead. The *indios* did not have horses unless they had hobbled them some way off. My first thought was to run back as I always did to warn my *familia*. The pain was sharp when I remembered they were no longer following.

I ran into the mesquite to the right. My heart pounded, my hands shook, and fear tore through me.

I was too sacred to look, but made myself. I have never been quieter or stiller. I wanted to be smaller. I was not the *bruja* I liked to pretend I was, an invisible witch.

It was only an old gringo cowboy. He was talking to his horse, a *ruano*. I wondered what they were talking about. He rode on north. What would he think, what would he do when he found my resting *familia*? Would he and the horse talk about what they saw, what they thought had happened? I wished they would not see them. A *gringo*, he may not even notice them.

I waited, longer than I would have before for just a passing *gringo*. I tried to pretend my *familia* was still behind me but only resting. Finally, I found the courage to move on…without them. I stayed off the road for a time, but the brush was too wet. My foot wraps were soaked. I made for the road. It was not too muddy except for a few short stretches.

Two times I had to sit on the wet grass and scrape clay mud off my sandals. The rain had stopped. The sun made the clouds glow. It was still cold. I had been walking for over an hour since seeing the cowboy, but I did not care about the time. I never knew what time it was anyway. Clock-time was of no matter to us. Up at sunrise, work all morning, maybe eat dinner, work until almost dark even on long summer days, eat supper, talk around the fire, and sleep.

Behind me, a horse snorted quietly, and a voice muttered. I would not have heard it without being warned by the nicker. Someone was close behind me. The road curved a little, and they could not see me. I ran to the right. There was a small clump of trees and brush not too far away. The indios, were they looking for me? Had the cowboy come back? Why would he?

Whoever it is was very quiet. I would not have heard them except for a horse's snort.

Water dripped from the bushes as I peeked out. I was scared, breathing hard. I should not be breathing so hard for such a short run.

It was a cowboy. I was relieved to see it was not the same one. He was on a *bayo* with a mangy burro strung behind him. Strange. Not something one often sees, a cowboy with a burro. There was a bedroll and bags on the burro. Strange. *Gringos*.

But he had stopped and was looking at the ground. What was he doing? He raised his head. He looked straight at me.

It was like he knew I was there. Like he could see my trail through the brush and weeds leading to the trees. I was no *bruja* now. In no hurry, he looped the burro's lead rope around a limb. He was trotting toward me, still looking at the ground. Yes, he could see my tracks on the wet ground and where I had brushed water off the bushes. He knew that made the leaves look different. The clump of trees I was in had limbs high enough for him to ride beneath.

He was coming for me.

Not far away was another bigger clump of trees, lots of thick brush. He could not ride into that. If he dismounted, I was sure I could scramble through the brush faster than he. I was so small, barely five feet. And fast.

I ran.

My bag bounced hard on my side, throwing me off balance. The ground was slick clay under a layer of gooey mud.

I heard the pounding horse behind me coming fast. I did not dare look back. I ran and ran. It was a mistake. The bouncing bag, the slick muddy clay, the tangling weeds and vines. I slipped and stumbled into the ground, sliding facedown.

I desperately rolled over, sitting up, and the big horse was sliding with its hind legs hard in the mud, the *gringo* pulling back on the reins. I got to my feet as fast as I could. I needed to be on my feet if he came at me, which I was certain he would. The horse stopped, and the cowboy swung off his saddle, his boots shot out from under him, a clumsy silly sight, and he slid into me, knocking me back down. I kicked, expecting him to grab at me. No *gringo* would have his way with me. I would fight. Seeing him raise to his feet, his anger, I felt so small and weak.

I did not pull my boning knife out. Not yet. Papa, who had knife scars, said to wait and surprise them at the last moment. I was breathing hard and getting more frightened.

He grabbed my arm, and I tried to pull away, and then kicked at him again, missing. I even growled. He shouted something, and all I understood was *"girl!"* and *"stop!"* He dragged me to his horse, which just looked at me like I was a distraction. Instead of kicking again, which he managed to sidestep both times, I swung at him. He ducked that too, and held me with a firm grip. He pulled his canteen off the saddle, handed it to me, and said, *"Girl. Wash."*

The way he said it, him just using some Spanish made it feel like he was not a danger. Not yet, anyway. I let him know I was angry and did not take my eyes off him. I took the canteen and washed my face and hands. I had to let go of my knife I gripped with my hand inside my bag. He was looking me over, probably wondering why a Mexican girl was out there all alone. Had he seen my *familia* resting? I hoped not. He did not do anything else, only stood there looking at me. He did not look menacing, just curious. Well, he was going to have to stay curious because I could not tell him anything even if I wanted to, even if I could speak, even if we could understand each other.

I handed the canteen back and nodded thanks. He said something like he was asking a question. The longer he looked at me, the more it seemed that he just did not want to be bothered by a Mexican girl. Maybe he would simply get on his half-asleep horse and ride away. I could take care of myself. I sure did not need some cowboy trying to figure me out. Nobody else ever had.

And that was exactly what he did. He hung his canteen and climbed on to his horse. He said, "Goodbye, girl." He rode back to the road after picking up his burro, muttering to himself, or maybe to his horse, and was on his way in no hurry.

I tried to clean some of the mud off my skirt with handfuls of dead grass. It did not do much good. I would have to wait until I came to a wet arroyo. Giving up on the mud, I walked to the road and started down it. It was a long straight piece. Far up ahead I could see the cowboy. One time he looked back. That made me nervous again. I hoped he was not having second thoughts. Mama's warnings of what could, would, happen to a girl by herself came back to me. I truly wanted a protector now. But I knew that without my family, that would be impossible. I would be alone for the rest of my days. It came to me that the rest of my days could be short in number. I thought again of what happened to my family. I remembered also the story about Maria Sanchez. She was fourteen and had gone by herself to visit another family's camp only a few minutes' walk away. Her parents had let her go in the dark. The campfires of the two camps could be seen from the other. After two hours, Maria's father and brother went to the other camp to bring her home. She had never reached it. In the morning they found her a half a league away on a muddy stream bank, stripped, beaten, raped, and strangled by more than one man. Many of the *nómadas* thought the killers were gringo bullwhackers who had come through that day and had camped near the river. They had left very, very early. The *gringo* sheriff said he had questioned them, and they knew nothing of it. He said we should talk to other Mexican workers or the Negros who worked the cotton press. Mama reminded me of the story many times. It was serving its purpose now, scaring me.

I came out of my day-nightmare and the memory of Maria's body, bruised, face bloodied, and bites on her...I tried to think of something else.

But I could not and the cowboy ahead had stopped. That scared me, and I started to run into the bush. But then I felt steel. I told myself I was not afraid. I would ignore him and go on my way. Something too told me he was not dangerous. Was I just fooling myself? Telling myself that I was hard and fearless?

I knew I was not.

I came upon him and walked past like he was not there.

I was so proud. I had shown no fear, even if I was fearful.

I sensed he was surprised, or at least baffled.

He said *"Girl, burro?"*

Was he offering me a ride on his burro? I kept walking.

His horse was moving, and he passed me, riding ahead a short ways and stopping. The fear built again, but I would keep walking like he and his horse and burro were not there. He dismounted, and I was feeling true dread. I would not show my rising fear. I could run faster than he on foot.

I felt for the knife in my bag, found it, and slipped it into my loose right sleeve. He suddenly grabbed my shoulder strap. I have never moved faster. Fear could do much. I twisted out of the shoulder strap and jumped away from him. I was terrified, even with the hidden knife. At least I had not cut myself when this happened. I backed away a few steps. *Show strength*, I demanded. *Do not show fear!* I crossed my arms and gave him the meanest glare I could summon.

I stretched out my arm for the bag. He did not move. I stamped my foot and pointed with my finger. It looked like he was waiting for me to say something. Little did he know.

Instead of giving me the bag or throwing it at me and then jumping on me, he smiled, turned, and hung it on the burro. "*Let's go, girl,*" he said, as he patted the burro's behind.

He was offering me a ride of all things. I stared at him a long time, watching his eyes. He stared into mine, but he was a *gringo*, not like a Mexican who could just about read your mind through your eyes. What could he tell of me? What could I tell of him? But I saw something in his eyes, like an amusement or a curiosity. I did not see danger.

I nodded, stepped over to the burro, bent over, cupped my hands so he could see I needed a boost up, and then stood up.

He looked real surprised. I almost laughed, but I did not even allow a smile to show. He blah blah'ed something, looking a little put out. I guess he was not in the habit of boosting Mexican girls onto burros. I could have gotten on by myself, but demanding his help might show me if he really was trustworthy.

He bent over and boosted me upon to a big bedroll. I had to move around to get comfortable. The burro did not seem happy with the extra weight. Without looking at him, I made a show of slipping the knife out of my sleeve and dropping it in my bag.

I looked the cowboy in the eye. There was a certain kindness in there. They were blue like the sky. His hair was the color of sand or winter-dried grass. Then I recognized the shade, the light tan of a coyote. I would think of him as *Güero*. I nodded to him…we could go now.

We rode on south with me trailing behind him. *¿Qué pasará luego?*

ABOUT THE AUTHOR

Gordon Rottman lives outside of Houston, Texas, served in the Army for 26 years in a number of "exciting" units, and wrote war games for Green Berets for 11 years. He's written over 130 military history books, but his interests have turned to adventurous young adult novels—influenced by a bunch of audacious kids, Westerns owing to his experiences on his wife's family's ranch in Mexico, and historical fiction focusing on how people really lived and thought—history does not need to be boring.

http://www.amazon.com/Gordon-L.-Rottman/e/B00MEGAK3K

Hartwood Publishing delights in introducing authors and stories that open eyes, encourage thought, and resonate in the hearts of our readers. If you enjoyed this book, please spread the word.

THE HARTWOOD PUBLISHING GROUP
"Stories that echo in your heart long after the book is closed."

CPSIA information can be obtained
at www.ICGtesting.com
Printed in the USA
BVOW08s0722130418

513211BV00002B/100/P